GIFT OF GRIFFINS

DAW is proud to present
V. M. Escalada's novels of
The Faraman Prophecy

HALLS OF LAW (Book One)
GIFT OF GRIFFINS (Book Two)

V. M. ESCALADA

GIFT OF GRIFFINS

BOOK TWO OF
THE FARAMAN PROPHECY

DAW BOOKS, INC.
DONALD A. WOLLHEIM, FOUNDER
375 Hudson Street, New York, NY 10014

ELIZABETH R. WOLLHEIM
SHEILA E. GILBERT
PUBLISHERS
www.dawbooks.com

First printing, August 2018
1 2 3 4 5 6 7 8 9

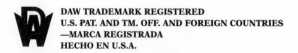

For Paul

Acknowledgments

My first thanks go as always to my agent, Joshua Bilmes, and my editor and publisher, Sheila Gilbert, who as of this writing has been nominated once again for the Hugo Award, Best Editor, Long Form. I hope you get this second one, Sheila. If there was a Hugo for Best Agent, I would nominate mine, and I'd vote for him, too.

I'd also like to thank my cousins, who, despite the fact that it's very difficult for them to read English novels, have always supported and encouraged me: Francisco Javier Hellin Escalada, Antonia Hellin Escalada, Mercedes Hellin Escalada, Ester Lopez Escalada, and Eliseo Rascón Escalada. Also, for their constant love and support, my friends David Edwards, Barb Wilson-Orange, and Patti Groome.

The Faraman Prophecy

Let all the people of the land awake and listen
For the day of joining comes
It comes near

Watch horses of the sea come clothed in thunder
Longships bring nets of blood and fire
Blood of the earth
Chorus: The First Sign

Hear the runner in the darkness, eyes of color and light
Speaks to the wings of the sky
Speaks to griffins
Chorus: The Second Sign

See the bones of the earth touch blood and fire
Net the souls of the living
Bones of the griffin
Chorus: The Third Sign

See the child eyes of color and light
Holds the blood and the wings and the bone
Child of the griffin
Chorus: the Fourth Sign

The child rides the horses of the sea
Bears the blood and wields the bones of the earth
Brings freedom and light
Chorus: Freedom and light are near; the day of joining comes

KERIDA Nast dried her hands on the front of her trousers and tried to roll the stiffness out of her shoulders. "I don't know how much longer I can keep this up." She tilted her head back and squinted, examining the ceiling of the tiny cavern, covered with stalactites, glinting red and gold and frosty white in the light she and Peklin Svann had with them. She could Flash the red jewel in the rock, thick veins closer to the surface here than anywhere else in the Mines and Tunnels. She reached both hands up toward the longest stalactite and concentrated.

"It isn't working," she said finally, lowering her hands. "The jewel's there, but it's not responding to me. What am I doing wrong?"

"I cannot know." Svann's accented voice came from behind her. "In Halia, we Shekayrin inherit our soul stones from those who have died without apprentices. Harvesting the raw stone"—Ker could Flash him shrugging—"I have only read of it, and the documents are very old, copies of items older still, and—"

"And mistakes might have been made." Ker turned around, not troubling to hide her exasperation.

"You push yourself too hard," he told her. "There is time—"

"No!" Ker ran her hands through her hair. "Sorry, but there *isn't* time. Just think what I might be able to do with a jewel."

"You have done much already. In tandem with Mind-healers, you have cleared the mist from many who have been touched by a soul stone."

"What about people who've been completely changed, not just misted? People like Jak Gulder? I haven't done much to help him."

"You were able to return Tel Cursar to his normal self."

"Yes, but I had *your* jewel, the jewel you'd used on him. To fix everyone else, I'd have to chase down every Shekayrin in the Polity and take away their jewels. But with my own . . . it's worth a chance."

Svann stood up, neatly folding the old stool he'd been sitting on and leaning it against the rock wall of the small cavern. "Come, let me help you. Perhaps if you were actually touching the rock." He pulled his jewel out of a pocket on his sleeve and gestured. Ker felt her feet leave the floor and told herself to relax. This wasn't the first time she'd been lifted by someone's Gift.

The cavern wasn't much more than a wide place in a seldom-used tunnel with a rough, uneven floor; nothing was remarkable about it except the stalactites. And the fact that it was the place the Talent High Inquisitor Luca Pa'narion had found the dormant jewel that no one, not even Ker or Svann, could activate. She hoped that finding one for herself would be different.

She drew up her legs and crossed them under her. Somehow hanging in the middle of the air was easier if her body felt like it was sitting down. Ker rubbed her palms together to warm them and reached up again. Now that she was so close, the red glints in the stalactites looked, in a way, as if the stone was bleeding. Though she couldn't be sure that wasn't an effect of her own aura, swirling around her in a sphere of movement. All human beings had auras, but only Talents like Ker had an extra stripe of turquoise. Weimerk the griffin had given her others, primarily the one that let her see the auras in the first place. But after she found she was able to use Svann's jewel, she'd found a thin line of red in herself which had started them all wondering if she could use a jewel of her own.

Focus, she told herself, but the rock stayed rock, and she'd already been Flashing it for hours without finding any loose pieces she could access and tune to herself, the way Svann's was tuned to him. Even touching the stalactite directly told her nothing new. She signaled to Svann to let her down.

Once on the ground Ker shook her head, shoving her cold fingers into her armpits to warm. "I don't know what else to try."

"Perhaps you should try doing nothing." Svann still looked up at the useless rocks.

Ker bit back the sharp answer that sprang to her lips. "Meaning?"

Svann rested his chin in his hand. "If doing something accomplishes nothing, perhaps doing nothing will accomplish something."

This time Ker snorted.

"Come," he said glancing at her. "You believe our magic, our Gifts, came from the griffins. Well, is this not the kind of logic Weimerk the griffin would find amusing?"

Ker opened her mouth and shut it again without speaking. In a crazy way, that made sense. It even sounded familiar. When her Talent had been discovered and she'd gone to Questin Hall to be trained, she'd been told over and over that Flashing worked best if guided but not pushed, not forced. The information to be Flashed was always there, she'd been told. It wants to come to you. Just let it.

She pointed upward. "Let's try this again." It took her a few moments to feel balanced, but finally she placed her palms against the large stalactite. *Just Flash*, she told herself. *Go back to basics.* What *can the stone tell me*? When *did the red veins form*? Who *were*—griffins, and bone, and blood and—Ker pulled back her hands, feeling suddenly dizzy.

"*Sun* fall." Svann cursed softly.

Ker opened her eyes. Right above her hung a smooth red lump where there'd been nothing but rough rock a moment before.

"Take it. It is yours."

"Right." At her touch the jewel slipped into her hand.

"It is as the old lore told us." Svann stared at the raw jewel on her palm, his voice heavy with awe. "The bones of griffins are here in plenty." The awe was tinted now with something Ker had no trouble Flashing as envy, with a little of greed, and an unexpected dash of hope.

Ker glanced up again. "Not bones, exactly, and not so plentiful as all that."

"Nevertheless." Something about Svann's aura made her think of an excited puppy. If it wasn't so exhausting, Ker would Flash everyone, all the time. "If you only knew the numbers of us in Halia who are turned away, netted or 'dampened' as you call it, because the supply of soul stones is so limited that they are kept for the very few, carefully chosen ones."

"Seeing the use you've put them to, that strikes me as a good idea." Ker looked from the jewel in her hand to the Shekayrin and back again.

"We are the tools of the Sky Emperor," he said. "Just as you Talents are the tools of the Luqs. We are none of us free to do as we like."

"That's not—" Kerida's protest died away. There was more truth in what Svann said than she wanted to admit. She'd had her own conflicts with the Halls of Law, before the invasion of the Faraman Polity by the Halians. Life in the Polity hadn't been all spiced nuts and wine by any means. But it had been better. "Talents maintain the Rule of Law," she said. "And the

Law rules even the Luqs." An old saying, but she'd always believed it was true.

"That is what Luca Pa'narion tells me. But he also noted that Feelers have not always experienced the evenness of the Rule of Law."

Ker drew in a breath. She didn't want to debate Polity history with Svann today. Or ever. "Right now, right here, all of us in the Mines and Tunnels are trying to make things right."

"And I with you."

Also true. Since meeting the griffin, Svann had been irrevocably on their side. But, like all Sunflower Shekayrin, he was a scholar, and that meant he didn't stop asking questions, no matter how unwelcome they might be.

"Do you think you have delayed long enough? Are you now ready to do what you know you must do?"

Ker looked down at the jewel, her mouth twisted to one side. She knew what to do all right. She just wasn't so sure she wanted to, after all. This would be her last chance for second thoughts. She'd seen how the facets on Svann's jewel reflected a pattern that appeared in his aura, sometimes as an inner framework, sometimes as an enclosing web—and *that's* what made her nervous. She looked at the smooth rock lying in her palm. What formed the facets? And what would it do to her? *And what does that matter?* She still needed the jewel. She couldn't let fear stop her.

"Come. You are not afraid."

"That's right." Ker almost smiled. "I'm not afraid." Before she could talk herself out of it, she raised the stone to her mouth and swallowed. She'd expected it to stick in her throat, but it passed smoothly as though it was no more than the egg it resembled. *Hope it's just as easy coming back up.*

Ker was concentrating so much on getting the jewel down that she didn't immediately notice the change in her aura. The red thread had thickened, become wider and more pronounced, yet softer at the same time, its edges less defined.

Unlike her other colors, which hung in curtains of light around her, the red circled, moving back and forth, crossing over itself, like the ribbons used by rhythm dancers at harvest festivals.

Except here the movement stuttered, threatening to tangle. Ker coughed and shook herself. She reached out, stroking the air, and the ribbon of color relaxed, as if following the motions of her hand. She smiled, watching it respond to her.

"What do you see?" Svann's voice made her aura shiver, and the red ribbon seemed to tighten as if startled before it relaxed again.

"You've never seen this, have you?" she said aloud. "Mother and Daughter, you mages have guts." Since Shekayrin couldn't see the auras, they had to swallow their jewels and take the effects on trust, without knowing what was happening.

But she *could* see. She could shape the jewel herself.

Moving both hands, Ker sketched patterns with the red ribbon in her aura, at first consciously trying to create something that resembled the facets on a cut stone, then relaxing her wrists, letting the patterns emerge as they would. She expected one would feel truer—a better fit—than the others, but pattern followed pattern, and each felt right in its own way. Ker sighed. It might have been easier for Svann after all. He hadn't had to choose.

"Why choose?" Svann said when she'd explained her dilemma. "Why not keep them all? After all, you are not a mage to be bound to one pattern. You are the Griffin Girl."

The Feelers had called her "Griffin Girl" ever since she'd awakened the newly hatched Weimerk. "Griffin Class" was what particularly powerful Talents were called. But Ker's title meant far more. Some Feelers thought she was part griffin herself, associated with the great beasts in a way that would only become clear with the fulfillment of the Prophecy that guided their lives.

"All right," she said. "I don't choose, I accept all patterns."

As if the words were a signal, Ker felt the jewel rising in her throat.

"It comes up harder than it goes down." Svann held her shoulders steady.

"I wonder what School you will be," Svann said from behind her, his voice flattened by the narrowness of the tunnel they now followed, the rock floor worn smooth by the passage of generations of feet. "So much depends on the extent and precise nature of your magic."

"Maybe a Sunflower, like you."

"I do not believe so." She'd heard that tone before. Svann wasn't sure how his next words would be received. "It is not spoken of, but I believe there were Schools of female Shekayrin in the past."

Before they were outlawed as witches, Ker thought.

"In the old texts, which only Sunflowers now read, there are Schools which use the feminine case. The Thistle, the Marigold, and I think the Crocus. Perhaps others."

"But you don't know what kind of mages they might have been." Sunflowers were usually scholars, and Svann had told her that Poppies were most often soldiers, while Daisies were usually advocates or administrators. There were Roses, but she'd forgotten what they were best at. All Shekayrin had the same skills, but the strength of the individual skills varied from School to School. Ker patted the jewel in her pocket. She knew the jewel was there, but she needed the reassurance anyway.

They had almost reached the more occupied section of the Mines and Tunnels, when the sharp light of an approaching glow stone made them slow down, blinking.

"Tel?" Many military had glow stones, but only Tel Cursar would come here looking for her.

"Finished for the day?" Tel spoke to her but looked over her shoulder at Svann.

"Finished for always. Look." Tel flinched as she held up the jewel, only glancing at it before looking back at Svann. Ker pressed her lips together. More than anyone else, Tel found it difficult to accept the Halian Shekayrin's presence. It wasn't just that Svann was a mage and had been part of the invasion of Farama. Before meeting the griffin had changed him, Svann had held them all prisoners, using his jewel to manipulate Tel's mind. He'd tried to kill Ker, and *had* killed their Feeler companion, Sala Far-thinker. Under the influence of the jewel, Tel had said and done things he still couldn't forgive himself for, nor Svann either.

Truth was, Ker found it easy to forgive their one-time enemy only because she could Flash him. "Did you think we'd get lost?" she said as lightly as she could.

"Are you all right?" he asked her.

"Perfectly." She nodded. "Does your commander know you're checking on me?" Tel was third officer, Black Company, Emerald Cohort, of the Bear Wing. "Didn't you tell me this morning that you were patrolling in the pass today?"

Technically, Tel slept with the rest of his company in the block of caves and caverns set aside for the Bear Wing's use, but he spent as many nights as duty would allow with Kerida in the far more comfortable rooms the Feelers had given her.

"I was." From their stronghold in the mines, the Battle Wing of Bears held the passes of the Serpents Teeth against the spread of Halians occupying the Faraman Peninsula. "A party of Halians tried to use the pass only this morning. They had some of our people among them, and my Faro wants you to have a look at them."

Ker stopped, letting her shoulders sag. "I am so tired of Flashing people to find out whether some Shekayrin used a jewel on them." All too often the answer was yes, though it might be only the mild compulsion of a mist, and not a complete change. She sighed and looked at Tel out of the corner of her eye.

"Where's Luca? Why isn't he doing this?"

"With all due respect to the High Inquisitor, when it comes to jeweling, I trust your judgment over his."

Svann winced. "We know, we know," she said before he could speak. "'Jewel isn't a verb.'" She gestured, and they started walking again. "So, what couldn't wait until I got back?"

Tel shot Svann another look, as if he didn't want to speak in front of the other man. Ker rolled her eyes.

"Errinn was the Mind-healer with us today," Tel said. "As she was putting them to sleep, one of them claimed to be a Talent."

Ker almost stopped again, but instead lengthened her stride to match Tel's much longer one. Another Talent, even one who couldn't see auras, would help to relieve the burden. "They had a woman with them?"

"It's a man—"

Ker's heart sank. "Oh, Tel, anyone would know that claiming to be a Talent would make us take them in."

"Which is why they were put to sleep before we came anywhere near a mine entrance. We know our jobs, thank you very much."

Svann cleared his throat. "If it is a young man, they may not have killed him immediately. Or perhaps he was able to shield himself from investigation, as Luca Pa'narion himself once did. Or . . ."

Svann went on lecturing, but Ker stopped listening. A young enough Talent might mean someone from Questin Hall, someone who'd been a Candidate like herself. Someone she knew. She might not be the only one to escape alive. Ker hadn't thought she could move faster, but for a step or two she outdistanced the men.

They were nearing the central core of the occupied Mines and Tunnels when Tel led them aside to an isolated grouping of rooms and alcoves in the western section of the mines. They'd learned very early that outsiders— whether refugees, those captured attempting the pass, or the military recruits trickling into the Serpents Teeth guided by hope and rumors—needed to be thoroughly checked and examined by a Talent before they would be allowed to join the community. Anything less would have endangered all of them.

Out-and-out traitors were dealt with harshly, but those who had been jeweled were a larger problem. Ker had been able to completely restore Tel because she'd been able to use Svann's own jewel. With those jeweled by other Shekayrin, she and the Feelers helping her had had limited success. Once or twice, when the person hadn't been jeweled very long, they'd been able to free them from the direct influence of the jewel, but they were like faded versions of themselves, tiring easily and having to be reminded of orders.

Both the Faro of Bears and the Feelers Council were beginning to fear that they were a drain on the limited resources of the Feelers. Before today, Ker hadn't told anyone, not even Tel, that she was hoping she could fix even these people with a jewel of her own. Maybe even people who'd been jeweled years before and turned into traitors by the Halians.

Finally, Tel pocketed his glow stone and all three paused to allow their eyes to adjust to the much dimmer light emitted by the luminous vines they wore around their wrists and foreheads. Out of deference to the light-sensitive eyes of people who had lived for years underground, soldiers who had glow stones tended to use them only when away from the main occupied areas.

The storage room Tel led them to had lately been transformed, with the addition of a proper wooden door and two well-armed soldiers, into a holding cell. Today's guard was made up of a square-built young woman with a shaved head, and a slimmer, older man with a pockmarked face. Errinn, the junior Mind-healer who'd been on patrol with Tel, greeted them with a grin from where she stood to one side of the door, close at hand yet out of the soldiers' way. Like the soldiers she now worked with, Errinn wore her black hair cut short. Of all the Feelers in the Mines and Tunnels, the Mind-healers had adjusted to the presence of outsiders most easily.

"Have you eaten?" she asked. Not all Feelers reacted physically to using their Gifts, but Mind-healers were notorious for needing to eat when they'd been healing, and they'd extended that concern to Kerida.

"I'm fine, thanks." Ker rubbed her hands, her fingers suddenly cold.

After touching her crest to Tel, the younger soldier pulled the door open to let Ker pass through. Four cots had been placed in the room, though only three were filled. Ker wondered what had happened to the rest of the Halian party attempting the pass and shook the thought away. She could always ask Tel if it became important.

"Kerida." Tel stood watching from the door. "Anytime today."

Ker waved him off with a lifted hand and approached the first sleeper. With only three men she *could* Flash them all from the doorway, but actually touching them was more certain. She fingered the jewel, tempted for a moment to try its magic instead of the Talent, but she wasn't ready for that, and she knew it. She blew on her fingers, spoke her trigger word under her breath—*Paraste*—and touched the first sleeper on the forehead. Instantly, the man's aura was laid out crisp and separate from the other auras in the room, and Ker was relieved to see the strong blue, green, and yellow of a healthy UnGifted person, with no overlay of red, just the dust of silver that marked the Mind-healer's sleep magic.

"This one's untouched," she said. "He's an Eagle. A courier from Blue Company, Jade Cohort."

"Name?" Tel turned from the doorway where he'd been passing the information to the older guard who was taking notes on a wax tablet under the interested eye of his younger partner.

"Ostik Seawater," she said, as she moved to the next cot. She glanced up at Tel, her fingertips still on the second man's forehead. "This one's a Bear," she said. "Penn Ferris, Second Officer, Red Company, Onyx Cohort."

Tel shrugged one shoulder, shaking his head. "Don't know him."

"A lucky thing, maybe," Ker said. "He's misted." Not fully changed by the jewel, but his spirit subdued and made obedient. Fairly easy to remove, if she only had the time. "Errinn?" She waited until the Mind-healer stood in the doorway, the strong silver stripe in her aura glowing. "Are there many waiting to have their mists removed?"

"Well, only three just now," Errinn said. "But we can't do anything without either you or the griffin, and you've been so busy. . . ." She shrugged.

Ker squeezed her eyes shut and tried not to sigh. "Well, I'm sorry to tell you this one's to join those others." More chores waited for her everywhere she looked. Honestly, sometimes she almost missed the days when all she had to do was run from the Halians. She massaged the muscles around her eyes and turned to the final prisoner, curled away from her on the bed farthest from the door. He was much browner than the first two, and thin enough that she doubted he was a soldier. She put her hand on his shoulder as she allowed the colors of his aura to spread around her.

"Barid." She snatched her hand back, unable to believe what her Flashing had shown her, even though the turquoise band of color in the young man's aura was unmistakable. And, even better, clear of any red mist or web. She had last seen Senior Candidate Barid Poniara on the morning the Halians had come to Questin Hall. She'd assumed him beheaded and burned along with everyone else. To find him here, under her hand and dozing, was almost more than she could take in.

"What is it?" Tel had taken a step toward her, his hand on the hilt of his short sword.

"I know this man; he was at Questin, a Candidate like me. I thought he died with all the others."

Tel nodded, his lips in a thin line. "The question is, then, how is he here? And in this company?"

"There's no red in his aura, neither web nor mist," she said. "He hasn't been jeweled," she added, as Tel's hard expression didn't soften. "He has the same blocks I do, the same ones Luca has. In fact, Luca's the one who taught them to Barid, and it's Barid who taught me."

"Then he might have tricked them into believing he wasn't a Talent, is what you're saying."

Ker nodded. "I'd still like Luca to examine him."

"Your Talent is stronger than his." Tel was nothing if not fiercely partisan.

"It is," she agreed. "But this isn't about strength. Luca's been examining people for forty years or more, longer than both of us together have been alive. He knows tricks I don't know."

"Like this block thing?"

"Like this block thing."

Frowning, Ker studied Barid's face. He'd grown a beard, and there were lines and shadows she'd never seen before. On impulse, Ker used her own aura to brush the dusting of silver sleep away from him. She stood back as her friend rolled to a sitting position, rubbing his face with his hands. She would never have known him with the beard, she thought. He lowered his hands and looked up, blinking in the light of Tel's glow stone. His lips parted, and his brow furrowed.

"Kerida?" He rose to his feet, his arms reaching out for her, but Tel's quick movement put a sword between them. Barid looked at Tel and back at Ker, licking his lips.

"You're safe," she said. "It's all right. This is my friend, Tel Cursar, of the Bear Wing. We're in a safe place."

"Safe." Barid sank down on the sleeping bench as though his legs wouldn't hold him up.

"Why weren't you killed with the others at Questin?" Tel's

tone was too sharp for Ker's liking, but the question had to be asked.

Barid licked his lips, stiff defiance in his face. Ker had seen the same look on the faces of children about to cry. "I'm not proud of myself." He focused on Kerida. "I know I should have done something to stop them, to help, but I couldn't think . . . I was up in the north tower, checking on the stored onions, when I saw the Halians approaching from the west. I knew right away—they couldn't be anyone else. We'd been in the gardens digging, we weren't—I, I wasn't in uniform like the rest of you. I snuck out the gate at the foot of the tower and ran. I thought I'd get help—" Barid looked down, licking his lips. "They found me on the road at nightfall. I played stupid. How did you. . . ?"

"I ran, too," Ker said. "I was in the kitchen cellars when the Halians came, and—I took a horse and ran." She took a deep breath. "I'm not proud of myself either," she said. "At least you were trying to get help." Though she had no intention of saying it aloud, she still had moments when she woke shaking in the night, her dreams full of flame and the bright blade of a falling ax. "But the truth is that neither of us could have helped anyone. By doing what we did, we're both alive now to help others."

Barid nodded again, lower lip in his teeth. "You're right. I know you are. That's what I've been telling myself."

"Never mind that." Tel was crisp. "How did you happen to be with the Halians in the pass?"

"There was a Shekayrin—"

"What School?" Tel interrupted.

"You know about the Schools? He's a Rose. Anyway, when he examined me with his jewel, I managed to keep him from seeing I was a witch." He looked at them, eyebrows raised, and they nodded. They knew the Halians called Talents witches. "Not that they believe men can be Talents. I told them I'd been a clerk in the Forsten's Holding, and this Shekayrin, Hantor

Kvent, thought he might use me that way." Barid grunted. "He needed someone who could read and write Faraman."

"So, you're a Shekayrin's clerk?" Tel's voice was hard, and who could blame him?

"Why? What would you have done?" Barid's voice was as hard as Tel's or harder.

The two men glared at each other. Then the thin line of Tel Cursar's mouth softened. "The same as you, I hope," he said. "Stayed alive to fight another day." The tension left the room. "But there wasn't a Shekayrin in the pass with you."

"I hope you kept a lookout, because he's less than a day behind me. Although . . ." Barid grew thoughtful. "It might be better to let him through, if he doesn't know we've been captured—"

"We are holding the pass against the Halians," Tel said. He turned to the door. "Anton? Let the Faro know we expect a Shekayrin coming through the pass. She should send a set of Feelers." The younger guard saluted and took off at a run. It took a at least three Feelers to counteract a single Halian mage. Though their magic came from different sources—at least according to their auras—mages and Feelers had similar Gifts. The problem was, mages had all of them, while for Feelers it was "one Feeler, one Gift."

Ker pressed her lips tight. Though everything in her told her they could trust Barid, not everyone found it easy to accept that Feelers did exist, that they weren't just bogeymen from children's stories. As it was, not even everyone in the Bear Wing knew who their new Auxiliaries were. But that hadn't been the part of Tel's instructions that caught Barid's ear.

"I'm sorry, did you say, 'the Faro'?"

"Juria Sweetwater, Faro of Bears," Tel said.

"There's a *Faro* in here?" For a moment Barid looked like he was going to giggle. "And with the Luqs dead, who gave Faro of Bears permission to enter the Serpents Teeth?"

"Ruarel the Third is dead, but her cousin Jerek Brightwing is Luqs of Farama, Prince of Ma'lakai, and Faro of Eagles."

"But Barid's a Talent; he's needed. He could cut my work in half." Leaving Tel behind to deal with the prisoners, Ker had gone directly to the small council chamber. Council members took it in turns to make themselves available to the community; today Ker found Ganni Lifter and Dersay Far-thinker sharing a quiet cup of mint tea. When they waved her to one of the empty seats, she took the stool that belonged to Hitterol Mind-healer and accepted her own cup of tea.

"You won't find that argument so very persuasive to many of us, my girl. It's Talents that cast us off in the first place, made being a Feeler a death sentence." Ganni was Ker's oldest friend among the Feelers, oldest in both senses of the word.

"We've been hearing stories of evil Talents our whole lives." Dersay was one of those who, until very recently, had never been outside of the mines. Even now she was edging closer to Ganni, though she'd known Ker for months.

"But *I'm* a Talent, Luca Pa'narion's a Talent. And Barid's my friend." She hadn't meant to say that, but if it would help . . .

Ganni exchanged a look with Dersay that made Ker squeeze her eyes shut in exasperation.

"You're not just a Talent to us," Dersay pointed out. "You're Kerida Griffin Girl, part of the Prophecy." She began to recite, and Ganni joined her on the last line. "'Hear the runner in the darkness, eyes of color and light, speaks to the wings of the sky. Speaks to griffins.'"

"You're the runner, you know that, girl." Ganni spread his hands.

Ker blew out a breath. "And Luca? You can't tell me he's part of any Prophecy."

"But he'd be one of the Guardians, wouldn't he, then?"

Ganni pointed out. "One of them as stood against the laws of the Talents."

"Part of the old stories." Dersay nodded. "The brave rebel Talents who rescued the Feelers of old and helped us hide away."

"But Barid *is* a Guardian." Ker leaned forward, set down her empty cup. "At least, he would have been. Luca chose him for that while Barid was still in Questin Hall."

Ganni paused, frowning, as though weighing his next words before he spoke. Finally, he sighed and shook his head. "Kerry, my girl, there's no point in making a rule and then breaking it the first chance that comes."

Ker closed her mouth. Ganni was right, and she knew it. There were procedures in place to manage all those "rescued" from the pass, to introduce them gradually into the general population of the Mines and Tunnels, exposed to the presence of Feelers slowly, and watched for signs of trouble. Feelers had been persecuted for too long to be comfortable with anything less.

Ker stopped drumming her fingers on the tabletop and stood up. "I'll let him know."

Tel and Barid were waiting in the corridor just outside of the room where she'd examined him. As soon as he saw her, Tel straightened up from where he'd been leaning, his arms folded across his chest. Barid stopped paying far too much attention to what was a very common section of the rock wall of the tunnel. It was obvious they hadn't been speaking. She looked from one to the other. They weren't at all similar—Tel so much taller, and thinner, with his pale eyes and sun-bleached hair, Barid bearded and dark—but right now they had the identical expressions on their faces.

"Didn't go well," she said. Tel rolled his eyes and Barid looked away.

"I can't say I blame them, but it goes hard for me." Barid

paused before continuing in another tone of voice. "What about going to the Faro of Bears?"

Ker shook her head. "She's more adamant about the rule than the Feelers are." Ker looked around as if she could see a different answer on the walls. "She won't—maybe can't—waive the rules for me, but there might be someone who would."

"I can't believe you're going to ask Jerek after the Feelers have said no." Tel sat on the edge of the table in Ker's tiny anteroom. It always looked smaller when he was in it.

"He's the Luqs." Ker pulled on her right boot and stamped it into position. "First, he'll listen to me. Second, no one's told a Luqs of Farama he couldn't do something since Jurianol united the Peninsula with the Eagle Wing behind her."

Tel crossed his arms and shook his head. "That's just it. Jerek was acclaimed as Luqs by the Bear Wing. He's more likely to do what Faro Sweetwater wants than what you want."

"Look, I need this." She curled her fingers into the front of his tunic, shifted as he opened his arms and put his hands on her waist. "We're the ones who got them Jerek, and with a proper Luqs to rally behind, the Battle Wings haven't fallen out among themselves. But what's happened since then? Talents are still murdered; the Halls of Law are still destroyed— Halians are still in control of the Peninsula for that matter." Ker fell silent, suddenly aware that she'd almost been shouting.

"We have a safe place here." Tel loosened her fingers from his tunic, raised them to his lips. "We've found Feelers and griffins—well, one griffin anyway. We're together. That's a lot."

"I know it is. It's everything. I'm sorry."

"Believe me, I understand. We don't seem any closer to pushing the Halians into the sea and freeing the Peninsula."

All of which might be easier, Ker thought a few hours later, than reaching Jerek today. Even with Tel beside her, Ker was stopped twice by duty guards at several turns and junctions in the tunnels leading to Jerek's new quarters.

"An appointment," she said when they finally reached the orderly of the day.

"Unless you're sent for, Talent Nast, yes." The woman who had the duty today was a Bear unknown to Kerida. If it had been Nate Primo, or one of the other Bears she knew well, she might have had a chance. As it was, she let Tel lead her away.

"Quarantine's only a month," he reminded her.

"I don't know if I've got another month in me," she said. "I'm exhausted. There's too much work for only two Talents."

"Can't Luca do more?"

Ker moved her shoulders, trying to relax the muscles in her neck. "He can't see the auras," she said. "And even if he could, he's preparing to go to the other Feeler strongholds. They know him; they don't know me. We need them, Tel, just as much as we need Talents. When he goes, my work doubles, and I'll have no time do my own researches."

"Like you were doing this morning?"

"I have a jewel now, Tel. Don't you see what that means?"

"No, I don't, since you ask me."

She stopped and took a firm grip on the front of his harness. She tugged, and he leaned down and kissed her. "You're not afraid I'll use it on you?" she said as soon as her lips were free for speech.

"No, I'm not," he said, and she knew he told the truth. "But I know you, I trust you."

"With a jewel of my own, I can restore more people," she said. "People who would have stayed loyal, if they hadn't been jeweled. I'll start here, with the people we know, like Jak Gulder, and then out there"—she waved one arm in the air—"out in the Peninsula."

"You'd be able to do that?"

"I won't know if I don't get a chance to experiment."

"Shhh." Tel turned away, his hand on his short sword.

"It's just me, O tall one." Wynn Martan followed her voice out of the dimness, her bright red hair, once again braided, looking subdued, here where there was so little light. "Heard you were turned away at the Luqs' anteroom," she added more quietly when she reached them, holding up a finger when Ker opened her mouth to reply. She exchanged a soldier's wrist grip with each of them. "Come along with me."

"Technically, I'm on duty at the next watch," Tel said.

Wynn made a brushing-away motion with her hands. "Then, technically, you should be on your way to your post."

Ker squeezed his forearm and gave him a little push. He hadn't gone far before the light changed, and she knew he'd taken out the glow stone.

"I can't help thinking life was a bit easier before we completed our assignment and returned to the Wings." Wynn stuck her thumbs in the belt of her own military harness. Though officially an archer with the Eagle Wing, she was under the day-to-day orders of the Faro of Bears, until enough Eagles were found to recreate the Wing.

"It does stick a bit in my throat to be told I can't see Jerek when they wouldn't even have a Luqs if it hadn't been for us."

"Well, thanks to you, there's a lot more to 'us' than the Faro of Bears and all her little cubs." Wynn tilted her head in the direction from which she'd come, and Ker fell into step beside her.

"You're going to invoke your right to speak to your own Faro?" The Luqs of Farama herself, or in this case, himself, was the official Faro of Eagles.

"Not a bad idea, but I've got a better one. Ennick?"

It was amazing that the big man could move so quietly in what was nothing but a small, dark space.

"Hello, Griffin Girl." Ker could hear the smile in his voice.

"Hello, Ennick. I haven't seen you for a while."

"I've been showing the Bears where they can eat, and sleep and—"

"We know what else they need to do, Ennick, thank you. That's very good of you, to help them like that."

"Jerek the Luqs wants me to help them," the large man pointed out. "Like he wants me to help you now."

"You know a back way into his chambers, is that it?"

"'Course I do. Tunnel four, secret track twelve, thirteen turns, and a tight squeeze. I know all the ways."

Ker didn't know exactly what had happened to Ennick to make him simple. His aura was clean and clear. It hadn't been dampened, though it lacked the extra colors that would make him a Gifted Feeler. Still, his uncanny memory for all the twists and turns of the mines and tunnels certainly felt like a gift to her.

"Thank you, Ennick," she said now. "I don't know what we'd do without your help."

"Welcome." He nodded at her. "Jerek the Luqs wants it, so it's easy for me."

"You'd do anything Jerek asked you to do?" Wynn asked as they set off following him.

"First Jerek the Luqs, then Ker Griffin Girl, then Weimerk the griffin. After that, no one unless I like them."

"I see, and who gave you those instructions?"

The big man furrowed up his brow until Ker was sorry she'd asked. She hadn't meant to worry or confuse him. He spoke, however, just as she was about to change the subject.

"The griffin, I think. And then Jerek. He's the Luqs, you know. People have to do what he says. And I like him." He smiled around at Ker. "I like you, too, Griffin Girl, and you, little Wynn Martan."

"I'm not little!" Wynn said in mock outrage.

"Maybe." Surely there was a chuckle hiding in Ennick's tone. "Maybe everyone looks little to me." He looked around again and blinked both his eyes, the only way he knew how to wink.

"Be so very careful in this part, please," he said, sounding like Ganni. "There's no lights, see."

Ker could tell from the way the sound of their footsteps had changed that they'd entered a much larger space. But Ennick was right. The soft glow of their wristlets and headbands wasn't enough to show them just how big the cavern was. Single file, she and Wynn followed Ennick along a track only he could see. Finally, he stopped them in front of an unremarkable section of rock wall, indistinguishable from any other part of any common tunnel.

"Tight squeeze," he said, and disappeared.

"Crap." Ker stepped forward, reaching out into the spot she'd seen Ennick disappear. *Paraste*, she murmured, and at once she could see Ennick's aura radiating out of a cleft in the rock face, hidden by its own narrowness as well as the lack of light.

"That's cheating." Now Ennick was definitely chuckling.

"How do you know I'm Flashing," she said as she stepped through, tugging Wynn after her.

"It itches," Ennick said. "It's all right, though, Griffin Girl. The lights don't hurt my eyes."

"Does he mean what I think he means?"

"If I ever find out, I'll let you know." Was it possible? Could Ennick see the auras, despite being UnGifted? He started to look worried, so Ker smiled at him and patted him on his immense forearm. He grinned again and, beckoning with his fingers, led them around several more turns, past a jakes, and finally into a small space furnished as a dressing room. Here, the big man patted the air in front of them with his hands, just as if he was signaling to a dog. Wynn waved Ker to the only chair, taking a small stool for herself.

When he saw them seated, Ennick touched where his crest would be if he were a soldier and disappeared without a sound, back the way they'd come.

"How are we going to get out of here?" Wynn said.

"No idea," Ker admitted. "I suppose I could manage it, but I don't like the idea of crossing that big cavern in the dark without Ennick, even Flashing."

As she spoke, the curtains on the far side of the room moved, and Jerek slipped into the chamber just as quietly as Ennick had left it.

The Luqs of the Faraman Polity was much changed from the boy with dirt on his face and straw in his hair whom they'd delivered to the Feelers and the Bear Wing at the end of Ice-month. He wasn't wearing the velvets, silks, and soft leathers he'd have been expected to wear at court in Farama the Capital, but something approximating court dress had been found or made for him—surprising, really, when there couldn't have been many people here who had ever seen court dress.

"The Inquisitor," Jerek said, as though she'd voiced her thoughts aloud. She kept forgetting he could do that. "Luca's been at court lots of times and spoken with the Luqs herself."

There might have been a time that Jerek Brightwing would have said that last bit with awe in his voice, even more so, per-haps, after finding out the late Luqs was his very own cousin. But Jerek himself was Luqs now, and the last month had worn some of the gloss off the whole adventure.

"Not all honey and cakes, is it?" Ker said, answering Jerek's tone rather than his words.

"You had to sneak in to see me, didn't you?" the boy pointed out, sitting with a thud on the edge of his bed. "And I only managed that much because I'm supposed to be having a nap. There are probably others who'd like to speak to me who don't know anyone to sneak them in." There were signs of weariness on the boy's face. "Every time I question something or want to do something, they either tell me that it's not the way things are done, or that I'm the Luqs and too valuable to risk."

The brave boy who'd risked everything, including his own life, to come with them, to help the Battle Wings and the Feel-ers, seemed far away.

"Jerek, look at me." Ker waited until he'd raised his head and met her eyes. Then she waited again, until his face relaxed, and his shoulders lowered, and he was really listening.

"You *are* the Luqs of Farama," she said. She spoke in an ordinary voice, stating the simple facts. "Nothing is as it was six months ago. Nothing. This isn't the Griffin Palace, or even Farama the Capital. Six months ago, none of us even knew that Feelers existed. Now you've given them citizenship. Nothing about our lives is the same as it was." Her hand went down to the jewel in her pocket. "Nothing has to be the way it was before if you want to change it. Do you hear me?"

He nodded, and the corners of his mouth began to twitch.

"Do you understand what I'm saying?"

"I do," he said. "You mean, 'don't be stupid, but don't let them push me around.'"

"Right. Think about things, take counsel, and make your own decision. You don't have to do something just because Luca Pa'narion or the Council of Mines and Tunnels or even the Faro of Bears thinks you should."

"Or even you." Jerek smiled, but his eyes were serious.

"Or even me," she agreed, half laughing. *I should have seen that coming.*

"You didn't come to give me a show of support," Jerek said, exhaustion returning to his voice.

"No." Ker wasn't going to beat around the bush. "One of the people Tel's company brought in this morning is a Talent, someone I knew at the training Hall. Barid Poniara. I'd like him to skip the quarantine."

"You want me to intervene." Jerek nodded, his brow furrowed. The nod didn't mean that he agreed with her, only that he understood. "The quarantine exists for the protection of the Feelers," he said. "They welcomed us here. If it wasn't for them, we wouldn't have this stronghold—it's better than a fortress. It's only right that we do whatever we can to keep the Feelers happy with their decision."

"But Barid's a Talent," Ker said. And how many times had she said this already? "We need more Talents, as many as we can get. Luca and I are being run off our feet examining the captured and the refugees. We don't have time or energy to do anything else—" She subsided when Jerek raised his hand.

"With the exception of Luca Pa'narion, the Feelers are actually more comfortable with the UnGifted newcomers than they are with Talents. It's Talents they regard as their traditional enemy, more than . . ."

"More than normal people. Yes, I know." Ker took a deep breath. "But Barid is one of the Talents Luca chose to be a Guardian, people who knew about and helped the Feelers. I was going to be one of those, too, remember."

Jerek nodded again. "I'm sorry," he said. "But it's a good rule, and I can't—I won't—rescind it because you're tired. Have him checked by Luca, who knows him best. Let Ganni meet him, and Hitterol as well. If they support your request, then I can reconsider." As he finished speaking, his face crumpled, and for a moment he looked as though he might cry.

Ker went to her knees and took his hand. "I'm sorry, I know you're tired, too," she said. "But I had to try."

"No, that's not it." He sat back and scrubbed at his eyes with his sleeve. "Or not all of it anyway. Ker, I'm afraid." In that moment he seemed younger than his thirteen years.

Ker sat next to him and put her arm around his shoulders. "What frightens you?"

"Something is coming. It'll be in the Peninsula soon."

A sudden chill made the hairs on Ker's arms stand up. "Did Larin tell you this?" Larin, though only six years old, was one of the rare Time-seers. Among the things she'd seen already was Ker's own arrival in the Mines and Tunnels months before.

"No," Jerek said. "I don't know how I know, I just do." He grabbed her hand. "Ker, I'm only thirteen. I'm due to be examined again in Grassmonth. What if . . ." His voice died away, too fearful to express the disaster aloud.

"What if you're a Talent?" Ker said. Though seeing something coming was the Time-seeing Gift, not the Talent.

"Mother, Daughter, and Son, save and protect us," Wynn said, even more quietly.

"'Talents do not live in the world,'" Jerek quoted, voicing their fears.

Ker nodded. No one knew better than she did what this meant. The Talent normally appeared between the ages of ten and fifteen. If it did, the person went immediately to the Halls of Law to be trained. Left family and the world behind, to become an impartial tool of the Law. No one was accepted in any profession, or any official apprenticeship, until after they were fifteen, and the Talent would no longer manifest. Jerek was Luqs by right of blood and acclamation, but only the extraordinary circumstances allowed him to rule.

That and the fact that the Feelers would not support a Regent.

"If I can't be Luqs anymore . . ."

It was Ker's turn to nod her understanding. "Who's going to lead us against the enemy?"

THE horrified expression gradually left Wynn's face, replaced by narrowed eyes and lips twisted to one side. "Wait a minute," she said to Ker. "Why aren't you more worried?"

Kerida looked from one white face to the other. "Jerek's not a Talent." She drummed her fingers on her knee. "But I'm not sure what he is."

"Explain."

"You're not UnGifted. Your aura has the purple and orange of a Gifted person, as well as the blue, green, and yellow everyone has, but–"

"How long have you known this?" Wynn asked.

"Since I first Flashed him." Ker kept her eyes on Jerek's face. "I could see right away you were Gifted, but I'm still not certain what your colors mean. You don't have the turquoise that Talents have, so at least that's one less worry."

"Is everyone else going to see it that way?" From the look on

Wynn's face, she already knew the answer. "Don't tell them," she added before Ker could speak. "No one can see the auras but you, so if we keep our mouths shut—"

"It's not that." Ker held up a hand. "His Gift will manifest eventually, and what do we do then?"

"They will make my father Luqs." Jerek's voice was rough. It had been weeks now, Ker realized, since she'd heard the boy's voice break.

"It's very unlikely the Wings would accept a man who went over to the enemy at the first opportunity, no matter what his bloodline." Ker kept her voice as tactful as she could. "It's far more likely they'll waste time choosing someone from among themselves, 'for the good of the Polity.' Either that or they move the capital permanently to Juristand and abandon the Peninsula entirely. The very things our finding you prevented in the first place."

"It's more than the Battle Wings." Jerek spoke so quietly Ker had to lean in to hear him. "The Feelers have given me their support, and I've given them my promise. They're citizens now." He waved at the walls around them. "We live here on their sufferance. They tolerate the presence of the Bear Wing in their tunnels *because* I'm accepted as Luqs. *Me*, not someone else."

Wynn nodded. "He's got a point. We may outnumber them, but this is their home, and they *are* Feelers, after all. If they wanted it that way, none of us would get out of here alive."

"You're missing the point that—" Ker broke off. The knuckles of Jerek's clasped hands showed white.

"*I* have to know," he said, with a slight tremor in his voice. He pushed his hair back from his face. It had grown long enough to touch his shoulders. Despite his being clean, well fed, and well dressed, it seemed that no one here in the Mines and Tunnels was looking after the finer details of the boy's personal appearance.

Ker massaged her temples. Even her facial muscles felt

tired. Still, she knew exactly how the boy felt. She'd been in the same position once herself, wondering whether the Talent would manifest when she didn't want it to. "Jerek, I've never examined anyone before. We should get Luca Pa'narion."

The boy rubbed his hands on his trousers. "I don't think so," he said. "He's a High Inquisitor. What if he feels he has to tell?"

Ker would have thought Jerek paranoid, if he hadn't been through what he'd been through. When your own father abandons you, claiming you aren't even his son, just to make his own hold on the throne surer, you can't be blamed for suspecting comparative strangers won't have your best interests at heart. "Then we won't take the chance."

Jerek sighed, relaxing. *How long has he been holding onto this fear?* Ker wondered. That because of him all their careful planning would fall into dust? How many nights had *he* gone sleepless, afraid to know, afraid not to know?

Ker knelt in front of him and took his hands. His fingers felt cold, but his grip was steady and strong. She took three deep slow breaths and murmured her trigger word. *Paraste.* Jerek's aura immediately sprang up around them, the colors spiky and surging like waves in a rough sea. Ker frowned, and glanced over at Wynn's aura: blue, green, and yellow, as compact and tidy as Wynn herself. Concentrating, Ker muted both Wynn's and her own aura to allow Jerek's to shine alone.

"Definitely no turquoise," she said, hearing the relief in her voice. "You're not a Talent." She passed her hands through the boy's colors, stroking the waves and smoothing them out. Jerek's shoulders dropped at least an inch.

And that's when Ker saw them clearly. Delicate threads, little more than hairs, so fine she'd almost missed them. Black, silver, gold, indigo, and pink. Feeler's colors, with the Far-thinker black line thickest.

"Wynn, you remember when we first saw Jerek? Me and Tel, you and Sala Far-thinker?"

"Of course. Sala saw him first, watching us from high up in that strange tower."

"Right. And Sala somehow knew it was a boy up there. And Jerek sometimes knows what I'm thinking." Ker sat back on her heels. "Let me try something."

<<Weimerk, can you hear Jerek?>>

<<He is with you.>> The griffin's thoughts brought with them a sensation of space and cold. Ker shivered.

<<I don't need you to find him. I meant can you hear him, the way you hear Cuarel or Dersay?>>

<<Or you? Let me see. >>

"What is it, Ker? What are you doing?"

"Give me a minute, Wynn. I'm talking to Weimerk."

<<I can feel him the way I feel you, but I do not hear him yet.>>

<<*Yet*? Will you be able to hear him?>>

<<When he is a little further from the egg, yes. What worries you?>>

<<I see a black thread in his aura, and black means Farthinkers, but there seem to be other Feeler threads as well, only much fainter.>>

<<And why should this worry you?>>

<<Ganni said one Feeler, one Gift. What do extra colors mean?>>

<<You have more than one extra color. What does that mean for you?>>

What did it mean? A couple of pieces fell into place. <<The Prophecy.>> She'd long suspected that Jerek might be the one the Prophecy foretold.

Ker turned to Wynn. "Is there any law about Feelers being apart from the world?"

"How can there be?" Wynn said. "We're the only ones who know they even exist. If there ever was such a rule—"

"Luca Pa'narion might know," Ker finished the other girl's thought. "But since we're not going to tell him . . ." She shrugged.

"I'm a Feeler?" Jerek whistled softly, but he had a new light in his eyes. "What kind? I'd love to be a Lifter like Ganni."

"Far-thinker, for certain . . ." She sorted through the threads again. "But it looks like you'll have more than one Gift, when you're a little further from the egg."

"What do you think it means?" Tel had already stretched out on the sleeping ledge in the inner room, and spoke to her through the doorway, where the curtain had been pushed to one side. The ledge was only just long enough for him, and Ker suspected that Ganni or one of the other Lifters had moved the rock to make it so.

She had finally returned to her own small set of rooms, after helping Errinn Mind-healer remove the mist from the more recently captured soldiers. She'd had the spark of an idea while they were working together, that she might be able to train the Mind-healers to remove the red mist by themselves. If they could calm people without seeing the auras . . . but it needed more thought, and more trial, something she was too tired to even think about right now.

"If Jerek has more than one Gift, you mean?" She paused with her right boot in her hands, too weary even to set it down. "I think it means he's the one the Prophecy is about, the one who is going to unite us all again. A Luqs who's a Feeler—doesn't that make sense to you?"

"You just don't want it to be you." Tel yawned, stretching out one arm.

Ker pulled her left boot off and set it down next to the right. She wriggled her toes, remembering the fleece-lined slippers she'd worn in Questin Hall. That life had never felt so far away. "I never thought it was me, you know that."

"I know you *hoped* it wasn't."

"Disappointed?" She pulled her tunic off over her head and laid it carefully over the back of the outer room's only chair.

Early military training in neatness had only been enhanced by similar training in the Halls of Law.

"No. This way it's far more likely that, when this is all over, we can get back to having a normal life together." He turned onto his side, back against the mossy wall behind the sleeping ledge, and shifted over to give her room.

Ker paused, sitting still on the edge of the bed. One of them had to say it. "Tel, I'm a Talent. I'm not allowed to have that kind of normal life."

Tel propped himself up on one elbow, rubbing her back with his free hand. "Let's not borrow trouble," he said. "The whole world is changing, Farama may never be the same. There'll be room for us somewhere." He chuckled. "Maybe in the Fog Islands."

Ker lay down and rested her head against his chest. Listened to the steady beat of his heart. Her eyes closed. Maybe he was right. Maybe there would be room for them somewhere in the new world, if they ever reached it.

Ker amplified the pattern she had chosen until it spread across the floor like a rug. "I wonder what will happen if . . ." Laughing, she stepped out onto the lines, pacing along the outer edge until a crossing line led her closer into the center.

"May I know what it is you do?" Svann's voice sounded far away, though he stood no more than a span or so from her. His face looked exactly like a child who'd been told he couldn't join in the game. Ker let the pattern loose.

"I'm so sorry, Svann, I got carried away. I was walking the pattern."

"No, no. It is quite all right. Curiosity is natural to a student, after all. Though I fear I do not make a good teacher."

"Don't say that." Ker linked her arm through his. "You've already shown me how to move things, and to lift myself." She wouldn't tell him that all she'd done was use the jewel pattern that felt right to her.

"Let me try something." She relaxed, allowing the colors of her aura to reach out and touch Svann's pattern. Maybe if she could get his to expand like hers had, he might gain—

"Stop! I beg of you."

Ker stopped immediately, catching hold of Svann by his arms. The Shekayrin's face was ashy, and his breath uneven.

"What . . . what did you do?"

Watching him carefully, Ker took a step back. "I tried to expand your web. Don't worry, I won't try again."

"Thank you. I felt as though you were pulling my bones out through my skin. Interesting, but I would not need a repetition." He allowed Ker to lead him over to where he could sit on a natural ledge in the rock wall. "Shall we go on to the next practice module?"

"Tomorrow," she said. "Tel's coming to meet me here, and I don't want to be in the middle of a test."

"True." Svann agreed. "He does not enjoy watching you use the soul stone."

Ker said nothing. Tel didn't mind that she could use the jewel—he agreed that it was important—but Svann was right. He didn't like watching her do it.

"Your progress is impressive." The tremor was gone from Svann's voice. His smile looked stiff, as if he was out of practice. "If I were not a confident fellow—indeed, a friend to griffins—I might be annoyed that you have accomplished seemingly effortlessly and in days magics that took me years of study and discipline to master."

"I can't imagine how you managed to do anything without the auras to guide you." Ker sat down next to him. Regardless of what Svann might say, working with the jewel tired her.

"Weimerk speaks of all magics as if they were the same." Svann's breathing had now returned to normal. "As if there was no difference between what moves in my blood and what moves in yours."

"He says it's like birdsong." Kerida searched the Shekayrin's face. His color was returning, but now he had the faraway look he got every time he thought about the griffin. "Birds all sound different, but it's all singing." She sighed. "Why can't he just tell us the things we need to know?"

"He is a teacher," Svann said. "If he merely told us the answers, we would never learn anything." He paused. "He answers the questions we know to ask."

Ker's head felt heavy. "There's a war on. We haven't time for all this mystery and scholarship."

"That is the only way we can get answers." Svann turned to Ker. "Consider this, you can use the jewel, Kerida. No one else here, none of the Feelers can. Neither I nor the Feelers can see the auras you and the griffin see, not even with your help."

"I think Larin can see them," Ker said.

"She is a Time-seer, perhaps she only sees some moment in time in which the auras exist."

Ker blinked. "I hadn't thought of that."

"Come, tell me, what does the jewel do?"

Ker rolled her eyes and sighed. Weimerk wasn't the only teacher in the Mines. "I'm not a Lifter or a Far-seer or a Mind-healer or a Far-thinker. By myself, I don't have any of the Feeler's Gifts. But—with the jewel—I do." She looked up at him. "With practice, I might have all of them. The jewel makes people into Feelers."

"So it would appear. However, not just the jewel, and not just any person." Svann had his approving-instructor look. "People must be marked with the magic of the world to be taught to use the jewel. And even those who have the mage mark are not *all* capable of being instructed. As I said, mastery of the jewel requires years of dedicated study, and for many—for most—the discipline required is simply too much."

Discipline again. What Matriarch had lectured Ker about

back in Questin Hall. "Thank Mother and Daughter I don't have that problem. Every minute I'm here practicing is time out of some poor jeweled person's life."

Svann grimaced. "A pity there are no studies of female mages for me to consult. I have seen no document which suggests they had your skills. We have always been taught that women have only the magic of the body, what you call the Talent."

"But you know now that's not true," Ker said. "You know that men have Talent as well, right?"

"You have said so, and Weimerk the griffin has said so, and I have seen persuasive evidence with my own eyes, in the person of the High Inquisitor, Luca Pa'narion," Svann agreed. "I would like to study the phenomenon more closely with a view to preparing a monograph on the subject when I have more time to devote to the study. I would like, for example, for you to explain—"

"Time is exactly what we don't have," Ker interrupted. Svann could lose himself for hours following blind scholarly alleys. "While the Halians control the Peninsula . . ." Her voice died away as an entirely new idea came to her. "We're looking at this the wrong way. The Halians aren't our first worry." She took hold of Svann's wrist. "They're not the ones who defeated us. It was you, the Shekayrin. You've been—they have, I mean, they've been jeweling key people in Farama for years. That's how the Peninsula was taken with so little force. Until the Shekayrin are stopped and their work undone"—Ker held up her jewel—"the Battle Wings won't be able to save us." Ker shivered. "Come on, we've got to see the Faro of Bears." She slid off the rock ledge and was helping Svann to his feet when Barid Poniara came out of the darkness.

The other Talent's face lit up when he saw her. "Did it work? Can you use the soul stone?" It was odd to hear the Halian expression from Barid's mouth, but good to see him bright and enthusiastic. Waiting was beginning to wear on him.

"Has your quarantine been lifted?" she said. When his face fell, she wished she hadn't asked.

"Not really." Barid shrugged. "Errinn said it was all right for me to come get you, since you aren't anywhere near the living spaces." He glanced around the small alcove. "It's not like I had anything else to do."

"How did you find us?" Svann asked.

"I *am* a Talent." Barid spread his hands. "I can Flash things like the right way to go." He took a step closer, holding out his hand. "Can I try it?"

Ker felt a powerful reluctance to give him her jewel. She squared her shoulders. She could do as she liked; the jewel wasn't in charge of her. "Here," she said. "Let's see what happens." Out of the corner of her eye she saw Svann reaching out to stop her, but the jewel was already lying in Barid's palm.

He drew his brows down in a vee. "I don't feel anything," he said. "What should I do?"

Svann relaxed. Ker glanced at him and then back to Barid. Svann's jewel had reacted to her when she'd first touched it. "Let me see," she said, triggering her Talent. Immediately, his aura sprang up around him. "I'm sorry, Barid, but you don't have any red in your aura."

Some of the light left Barid's face, and Ker felt as though she'd kicked a puppy. But how she felt didn't change a person's aura.

"Maybe there's a way to bring out some red," Barid said.

Ker swallowed, but before she could say anything Svann stepped in. "I am sorry also," he said. "But a mage cannot be created, any more than a Talent can. Without the proper Gift—the magic of the world—the soul stone will not respond to you."

Kerida held out her hand, waiting until Barid replaced the jewel on her outstretched palm. She closed her fist around it, and forced herself to put it away slowly, when what she felt was a frantic need to hide it.

"Couldn't the griffin give me the Gift? I mean, I'm Griffin Class as well as you," he said to Ker. "Maybe if I could see the auras . . ."

<<No. I will not.>>

"What does the griffin say?" Svann smiled.

<<This boy is not part of the Prophecy.>>

There really wasn't any good way to say it. "He says Barid isn't part of the Prophecy."

"He can't do it?" Barid frowned.

Ker shook her head. "I'm afraid it's more that he won't do it. He doesn't see any reason to, and we can't make him do anything he doesn't want to do."

<<That is definitely true.>>

Disappointment showed in the sag of Barid's shoulders, but he nodded. "Well, it was worth asking." His smile was weak, but at least he was smiling.

"What brings you here, young man? You did not come to try the stone," Svann said.

"No. No, of course not." Barid scrubbed at his face with his hands. "I came to fetch you. Faro of Bears wants to speak to you."

Ker took a deep breath. "That's lucky, because we want to speak to her."

The full council, made up of some thirty or forty people selected from both Gifted and UnGifted, met in the only space large enough to hold them, the cavernous main hall of the Mines and Tunnels. Shaped like a theater, its raised tiers were only dimly lit by baskets of the luminous vine. It would hold the entire Clan, some two hundred people, but now the upper levels were dark and empty. The small council, a representative from each of the Gifts, plus an UnGifted, were in their usual mismatched seats on the dais. Jerek had refused to take the finely carved chair that was the usual seat of the Time-seers, so they'd left Larin in her large chair and had found him another, very plain but sturdy.

Like Jerek himself. Ker, with Tel and Luca Pa'narion, stood at Jerek's right. Juria Sweetwater, Faro of Bears, stood at his left, and her second in command, the Laxtor Surm Barlot, stood at her shoulder. The Leaders of the Pearl, Sapphire, Jade, and Opal cohorts sat in the audience. Svann, alone, stood in the center of the circle, where he could easily be seen and heard.

Ganni stood. "I am Ganni of the Serpents Teeth, Speaker for the Mines and Tunnels. We welcome our Luqs, Jerek Brightwing, and his Battle Bears. If we may, lad—I mean my lord Luqs—we'd like to start by reciting the Prophecy. . . ." The old man hesitated.

"By all means, Speaker, proceed." Jerek inclined his head.

Norwil UnGifted cleared his throat and rose to his feet. "Let all the people of the land awake and listen. For the day of joining comes. It comes near."

"It comes near." Ker lifted her brows when Juria Sweetwater, her Laxtor, and Jerek also joined in giving the response.

Ganni stood as Norwil sat down. "Watch horses of the sea come clothed in thunder. Longships bring nets of blood and fire. Blood of the earth."

"The First Sign." The words reverberated as everyone in the hall repeated them.

Ganni sat down and Hitterol stood. The Mind-healer looked every bit as tired as Ker felt.

"Hear the runner in the darkness, eyes of color and light. Speaks to the wings of the sky. Speaks to griffins."

"The Second Sign," everyone chorused. Many of the people in the audience bowed in Ker's direction.

Midon Far-seer was next, his deep voice always a surprise. "See the bones of the earth touch blood and fire. Net the souls of the living. Bones of the griffin."

"The Third Sign."

Dersay Far-thinker stood, clearing her throat. "See the child eyes of color and light. Holds the blood and the wings and the bone. Child of the griffin."

"The Fourth Sign." As she spoke the words, Ker glanced at Jerek. His eyes were blue.

Finally, Larin slipped down out of her chair, and recited her lines clearly and with great seriousness. "The child rides the horses of the sea. Bears the blood and wields the bones of the earth. Brings freedom and light."

"Freedom and light are near; the day of joining comes."

Larin climbed back into her carved seat. At Ganni's signal, Svann stepped forward.

Ganni cleared his throat. "The Speaker of the Mines and Tunnels yields to the Faro of Bears, for a question of military strategy."

"Thank you, Speaker." Juria Sweetwater was nowhere near as old as Ganni, but she had gray in her fair hair, and the scar around her right eye aged her. She inclined her head to the older man before turning to address Svann. "Kerida Griffin Girl tells me that we cannot defeat the Halians in the Peninsula. As the only Halian present, can you elaborate on this?" The Faro managed to look as though she stood in a formal audience chamber and not in a cavern cut out of rock illuminated by glowing wisps of green vegetation.

Svann glanced at Ker and waited until she nodded. They'd decided between them that Svann should be the one to speak. "Faro of Bears, how long would it take you to move a full Battle Wing to Farama the Capital?"

The Faro's eyes narrowed, the scar pulling her right lid down. "Even using the nearest exit, it would take at least six days to march a Wing to the capital. Though if we cannot use the roads . . ." A raised eyebrow at Surm Barlot yielded a shake of the head. These kinds of logistics were his responsibility as Laxtor.

"And therein lies the difficulty." Svann hung his head, studied his clasped hands for a moment before continuing. "As you travel, you will receive no support from your countrymen. You may even find their hands raised against you, yet you cannot treat them or the countryside you pass through as though it were enemy territory." He paused again, looking around to judge the effect of his words. "Yours is not the first society we have overcome in this manner. If resistance is strong, the Emperor will simply send more troops."

"Blades of grass," Tel said under his breath.

"By sea? In this season?" Surm cut in.

"You forget that they will have Shekayrin with them. Rain, wind, or snow will trouble them no more than it would trouble travelers who had a Lifter and a Far-seer with them."

"Always we come back to the Shekayrin," Juria said, nodding. Clearly, she'd thought about this already. "If we can defeat the mages, we will have the greater part of two Battle Wings. We will regain not only the Bears trapped in the Peninsula, but all of the Eagles who survived the initial invasion."

Surm Barlot raised his hand and waited to be acknowledged. "I would like clarification of another point. Since there's no resistance in the Peninsula at present, why would the Emperor send more troops?"

Svann tilted his head to one side. "Because they have reached only one of the Sky Emperor's objectives."

Juria exchanged a neutral look with Surm, and he nodded as if Svann's words confirmed something for them. "People do not usually cross an ocean in force because they object to the rule of women in a foreign country, nor even to destroy what you call witches," she said.

"Many feel that motivation, of course." Svann's casual "of course" sent chills up Ker's spine as one of the witches in question. "But that is not why the Emperor sent them."

"Why, then?"

"To get them out of his court, to limit unrest and opposition."

Svann looked around at his audience. "We are made of two cultures. For generations the Horsemen of the Western Plains were a nomadic people, horse lords and herders, their armies sweeping across the continent of Gventha, absorbing societies as they rode until three generations ago they reached the eastern sea, the land of the Halians, and their chieftain sat for the first time on the Sky Emperor's Throne. Since then the culture has become more settled, but—"

"But what is he to do with his armies, and all those soldiers we've been told about?" Juria said. "What did you tell me they were called, Third Officer Cursar?"

"Blades of grass, my Faro," Tel said.

"Exactly. I would wager they did not all retire and become farmers when the wars of conquest were over."

"Precisely." Svann smiled at her as he would at a favorite pupil. "With such a tradition of warfare, with generations of men who boast of having been born in the saddle . . ." Svann spread his hands. "They will fight among themselves; they may even foment rebellion if they are not given someone else to fight. Luckily, the Shekayrin provided the emperor with just such a target."

"*You* did?"

Svann reached into his tunic pocket and pulled out his jewel. He no longer wore the uniform of the Shekayrin: the black cloak, the blue tunic with its pocket for the jewel formed by the crest on the sleeve. At first glance, he looked like one of the Feelers. As his fingers cleared the pocket, Tel leaned back. Ker wondered if he knew he was doing it.

"There are more people with the ability to become Shekayrin than there are soul stones to accommodate them," he said. "Our histories tell us that when we first spurned the magic of the witches and found our new lives, we brought our jewels with us, each Shekayrin with his own, plus many more unformed, ready for the Shekayrin who would be." He glanced at Kerida and smiled. "These unformed stones were stored in a great supply of dust made from the rock in which they are found, and which kept them alive and full of power."

"But not forever," Ker put in. "The power doesn't last forever."

"No, it does not. Eventually, a stone cannot be recharged, cannot be passed along to an apprentice." He surveyed the faces surrounding him. "Eventually, we needed a new supply, and our archives spoke of only one place such a supply was to be found."

"But this would have been a thing of legends for your people?" Juria said.

"To begin with, certainly. But in trading with the Fog Islanders, we established the whereabouts of Farama and the mountains known as the Serpents Teeth—and once we understood that no one here knew of the stones—"

"You couldn't have traded for them?" Ker felt shocked and angry in a way she hadn't been for months. Svann hadn't told her this part.

"How can you trade for something no one knows exists? And besides, once the crewmen and sailors with us understood that we were dealing with a place where there was rule of women, and carried this knowledge back to Halia, the Sky Emperor saw an opportunity to send away his discontented generals and their bored soldiers."

"Distracting them with a war as far from him as possible." Juria nodded. "As a strategy, it has brilliance. If it succeeds, his Shekayrin have a new supply of jewels. If it fails, he's siphoned off his malcontents."

"Precisely." Svann inclined his head in acknowledgment. "But you see that it is the Shekayrin and their desperate straits that fueled the invasion in the first instance. The emperor might still have organized an invasion somewhere—perhaps the Fog Islands—in order to occupy his military hotheads with their traditional methods of life, but Farama may not have been the target."

"So, we return to our point. We must rid ourselves of the Shekayrin." Juria's lips pressed together.

"I'm sorry, Faro, but we don't see our way so plain as to be agreeing to that." At Ganni's statement, Juria straightened, shooting him a hard glance. A murmur sounded from the Cohort Leaders in the audience, but the Feelers on the dais were all nodding. "If the mages are destroyed, how will the Prophecy be fulfilled? As Luca's been telling us, it's *all* the people who are to be united, not just us Feelers."

Larin giggled, swinging her feet, but didn't speak.

Juria Sweetwater's protest died away as Jerek cleared his throat and lifted his hand. His cheeks colored as everyone turned to look at him, but his mouth was firm. "Svann, would there be others like you? Who would come over to our side as you have?"

Ganni slapped his hands on his thighs and looked around with a wide smile.

Svann frowned. "Mine was an unprecedented set of circumstances," he began. "First, to have the opportunity to study Kerida Nast." Tel's hands closed into fists, his mouth so thin you could hardly see his lips. "To interact with her on the basic level of magic. Then, to be without my jewel for such a long period, having very little dust to sustain me. Then to meet Weimerk the griffin." His mouth snapped shut and his head shook. "To experience the Gifts of the Feelers. Without all this, would I have seen the truth of things? I cannot say."

"That means we can't count on others to see the light." Jerek nodded. "I remember the griffin symbol on the door of the town building in Gaena, all hacked to pieces. The Shekayrin can't all feel about griffins the way Svann does."

"That was done by some superstitious soldier," Svann said. "And, after all, a carved symbol is not a griffin."

"If I may, my lord. Svann has told us why the Halians came to Farama in the first place," Juria Sweetwater said. "But not why the Emperor would send more people."

Svann spread his hands. "He knows that we have not reached our first objective, to obtain more stones."

"And how does he know this?" Juria's voice was as cold as ice.

Svann bowed in Dersay Far-thinker's direction. "We have a type of far-thinking among us as well, where we speak stone to stone. The Daisy Shekayrin are particularly skilled at it, and can send messages even to the Court of the Sun itself."

The silence was so profound Ker could hear the blood moving in her ears.

"We need to free the Peninsula. Before more troops or more Shekayrin come." Something was coming, he'd said to her in his rooms. Something was coming soon. Jerek sat back, propped his elbow on the arm of his chair, and rested his chin on his fist. If it wasn't for his white knuckles, anyone would think he was relaxed. "You haven't been there, Faro of Bears. Not to see with your own eyes. It's not just the Talents they've killed, it's almost every female military officer. And it doesn't stop there. Women who are in business, or who own property, they've been dispossessed and stripped of other rights—or even their lives, if they object too loudly. We have to stop the Halians, we *have* to." Jerek took a deep breath. "And to do that, we need to defeat the Shekayrin—without destroying them all, if we can." He nodded at Ganni before returning to the Faro of Bears. "Is the signal at Oste Camp still functioning? Can we send for more troops?"

The look on the Faro's face was so bland that Ker's nervousness increased. No one took such care over their expressions unless they were hiding something. "I must confess that I have already sent messengers with such a request, my lord Luqs. Thus far, there has been no answer."

"I see." Jerek lowered his head slightly, his mouth twisted to one side. He looked up again and said, "In future, I would prefer to be kept informed, Faro of Bears."

Juria Sweetwater's cheeks reddened slightly as she touched

the crest on the left shoulder of her tunic. "It shall be done, my Luqs."

"If military help won't reach us soon," Jerek continued, as if nothing had happened, "what about the griffins?"

Ker stood straighter as it seemed everyone in the cavern turned to look at her. "My lord?"

"Isn't that part of the Prophecy?" Jerek looked from her to Larin. "Aren't they supposed to help us?"

Larin opened her eyes wide, shrugged her little shoulders, and started swinging her feet again. The Time-seer's chair was far too tall for a six-year-old child, but she always laughed at anyone who offered her a footstool. "Weimerk is helping us," she said finally.

"Could he bring us others?" Jerek said. "If one griffin alone had such a big impact on one Shekayrin, wouldn't many griffins be able to change more?"

"If Weimerk will go—" Svann began.

"No." Ker and Dersay smiled at each other; they'd both spoken at once. The Far-thinker deferred to Ker with a small bow.

"Does he not know the way?" Juria said.

"Oh, he knows the way," Ker said. "He may have hatched in the Mines and Tunnels only a few months ago, but he has all the knowledge of the griffins until the last Gathering, when they decided to withdraw, including where they should go."

"What is the problem, then?" That look Ker understood perfectly. That was the look of a senior officer losing her patience.

"If he'd seen a need to go, he'd have gone already," Ker said, not sure if she could make them understand. Not sure if she understood herself. Weimerk didn't think about things the way people did. What seemed obvious to him wasn't to anyone else.

"Maybe he hasn't seen a need because you haven't asked him," Tel said.

Could it be that simple? It was true that Weimerk volunteered nothing. "All right, I'll ask him," she said.

"He won't go so far without you," Dersay pointed out. "He's like a duckling and you're his mama."

"Then I'll have to go with him." Ker could feel a headache beginning behind her eyes.

"We need you here," Juria reminded her. "There are tasks only you can do."

There was no arguing with that tone.

"If Dersay says the griffin won't go without his Girl, then he won't," Ganni said. "He's not tame, Faro Sweetwater, not one of your couriers. You can't just order him to go."

"My lord," Juria said finally. "I recommend that we ask Talent Nast to remain here for five days to do what she can, and then have her take the griffin and go."

"A good plan." Jerek nodded. "Thank you, Faro of Bears."

Ker waited for the Faro to acknowledge Jerek's words before speaking herself. "It'll take us a while to walk that far"—*always supposing we can*—"but the griffins coming to help could simply fly back."

"We have another, similarly urgent need." Luca Pa'narion's dry voice should have been too quiet to hear. "At least one set of Feelers—a Lifter, a Far-seer, and a Far-thinker—go out with every patrol in case they encounter a Shekayrin. The Feelers of the Mines and Tunnels are doing everything they can, but they're being overused. If you mean to expand our campaign, we'll need more. Much as I would prefer not to leave you without Talents, I must go to the other Feelers and persuade them to come to our aid."

"It doesn't have to be you, lad, does it?" Only Ganni was old enough to call the Inquisitor "lad." "Wouldn't it be better if it's one of us that goes?"

"Nah, they'll see Luca as more neutral," Norwil UnGifted pointed out. "Especially the Springs and Pools Clan. He's helped as many of them as he has of us. They'd trust him sooner."

"I wouldn't be gone for more than ten days," Luca said. "I'd be back long before Kerida reaches the griffins, if they are where I think they are."

"You can always lift Barid's quarantine." Ker breathed slowly in an attempt to keep the impatience from showing in her voice. "At the least he can Flash the people trying to use the pass, like Luca and I do now."

"It would be useful to everyone if we could continue to get that information." Surm spoke directly to his Faro.

Svann leaned forward. "There is other information you might find useful. If I returned to Gaena, and again took up my position there, I could provide you with more recent intelligence of the Shekayrin's movements."

Ker heard Tel suck in his breath, and she tapped him on the ankle with the side of her foot.

"My lord, it would be good to have a spy in their ranks for once, instead of the other way around," Juria said to Jerek. "Those who have managed to reach us from the Peninsula are primarily from the ranks, and the information they bring is limited."

Jerek nodded, his dark brows drawn down. "I told you, most senior officers are jeweled—or dead. What Svann can find out might be valuable."

"Just a minute. You're not seriously thinking of setting this man free, never mind letting him go back to Gaena?" Tel looked around at everyone, particularly at the Feelers, where only Midon Far-seer looked troubled. Juria Sweetwater stared at him with her left eyebrow raised. Ker watched a slow blush spread up from Tel's collar. He might be admitted to this meeting as someone experienced in dealing with Halians and Shekayrin both, but he was still only a third officer, and for him to offer his opinion without being asked and in defiance of his own Faro was foolhardiness of the worst kind.

Surm answered him. "Thank you, Third Officer. The Faro will take your observation into consideration."

Really, Ker thought, it was more courtesy than Tel should

have expected. White spots had appeared on his cheekbones, and he touched his crest in obedience.

"If you would be willing to submit to examination, we could consider allowing you to leave," Juria said.

"With pleasure. I have already been examined by both Kerida Nast and the Inquisitor." Svann bowed toward each of them. "If I may, however . . . There *is* a way to guard against the stone's influence."

His comment was met with silence and stiff faces. Tel had put his hand to his sword. Jerek sat straight up. Only Juria hadn't moved, except for the slight tightening of her mouth.

"And your reason for not telling us this already?"

Svann spread his hands, a gesture he would never have used when Ker first knew him. "Primarily because it is something Shekayrin use to protect against each other, not to protect people from other Shekayrin. Here, I could not determine which was safer for me."

Ker clenched her teeth. She hadn't heard this cold dispassionate tone in weeks. Since the change in Svann, she'd managed to forget the series of experiments he'd conducted on her when he'd thought of her as just an interesting specimen.

"Explain yourself, Mage," Jerek said.

"Since I am the only Shekayrin here to guard against, how would you know I had actually protected you until it was too late?"

"I could have Flashed you and told them," Ker said quietly after it seemed that no one else would speak. "For that matter, I could Flash the people you jeweled. That's the kind of thing a Talent can Flash about a person."

Either the look of dismay on Svann's face was genuine, or he had a future as an actor at the Festival of the Son. "I did not realize, I am sorry. It is beyond my experience."

"With the Luqs' permission, you will perform the technique on as many people as possible, in order of priority," Juria said.

"Beginning with the Luqs." She waited until she had Jerek's nod before continuing. "Laxtor."

"Yes, my Faro." Surm Barlot stepped forward.

"You will assign priorities." Having given the order, Juria dropped it. "In the meantime, you, Talent Nast, will prepare to travel to the home of the griffins, and you, Talent High Inquisitor, to visit the other enclaves of Feelers. Once your assignment is complete, lord Mage, we will discuss whether you can be permitted to leave here. With your permission, my lord?"

"You have it," Jerek said.

"Does the Council of Mines and Tunnels agree?" Ganni collected nods from everyone on the dais. "Does anyone disagree with their representative?" There was shuffling in the audience, but no one spoke. "Then if we all have tasks to do, best we be about them." The old man rose to his feet. "With the permission of Lord Brightwing, Luqs of Farama and of the Mines and Tunnels, I say this meeting is adjourned."

A FTER almost two months in the Mines and Tunnels, where the temperature was constant and the light, for those without glow stones, dim, Ker found the outside world cold and bright.

"At least this brightness is mostly the sun on snow." Ker squinted upward. "And the sun will go down early." She shivered, trying to make her cloak cover more of her than it could. Tel, of course, couldn't understand what she complained about.

"I'll remind you," she said, pulling on her reins to keep her mule even with his, "that the last time I was on the northern side of the Serpents Teeth, let alone outside at all, was Wind-month."

They were out of the Peninsula now, in the province of Bascat, traveling on one of the roads built and maintained through the Polity by the Battle Wings for easy mobility and quick access to the borders. Snow covered this section, but the road was still clear enough that they could ride.

"And there was snow then, too, or don't you remember?" Tel smiled.

"Mostly I remember we were running for our lives, avoiding Halian patrols, and trying to reach the Bears in Oste Camp." Ker swung the right side of her cloak over her left shoulder for what felt like the hundredth time.

<<I would fly you to Griffinhome,>> Weimerk reminded her from somewhere high over their heads and far away. <<It would be as cold, or colder, but we would arrive more quickly.>>

<<Yes, but then no one else could arrive with us.>> They'd had this discussion before. <<Luca wants all of us to help him persuade the Feelers of the Springs and Pools.>> The "all" in this case included not only Kerida herself and Cuarel the Far-thinker to keep them in touch with the Mines, but Wilk Silvertrees, Ruby Cohort Leader of Bears, as the representative of the Luqs, and two more of his men. The Cohort Leader had wanted a larger party, but Luca had pointed out that more soldiers wouldn't convince the Springs and Pools to help them.

<<After that, perhaps, we will fly.>>

<<Perhaps.>> Weimerk had been trying to get her to fly with him since he'd grown big enough to carry her, and Ker kept finding ways to say no.

Tel looked sideways at her. "You've got that look on your face again. What does the griffin have to say for himself?"

Ker shook her head. Her relationship with Weimerk bothered Tel less than it had, but he still wasn't completely reconciled to the idea that she and the griffin could speak mind-to-mind. When she told him what they'd been talking about, however, Tel laughed.

"I'd go in a snap," he said. "Are you kidding? Fly instead of walking? Tell him I'll go if you won't."

"He keeps saying I'm the only one he'll carry," she said. "He did offer once to take Jerek, but the Faro said no."

"Will the kid be all right?" Tel lowered his voice; Luca rode only the length of a mule in front of them. "Considering what you Flashed?"

"I don't know," she said. "He puts on a good face, but you don't have to be a Talent to know that he's worried about it." It was some comfort that Wynn Martan had stayed behind, someone who'd been with Jerek from the beginning. "I don't know what problems his colors could cause, and I'm afraid to ask anyone who might." Anyone like Luca Pa'narion himself, for example. "This can't be the first time this has happened, even if we've never heard about it."

"Do you think they just dampened any royal who showed signs of the Talent?" Tel said. "Though, come to think of it, a Luqs who can know all about something—or someone—just by touching them? That would be brilliant."

Ker wasn't so sure. "If any royals had the Talent, they'd just go into the Halls of Law."

"But if they dampened them, then they could still rule."

"I don't think so." Her shiver had nothing to do with the cold. "Dampening doesn't just smother the Talent, it affects the whole personality. There was a gardener at Questin Hall, and a kid in the kitchen who was like Ennick with maps, except his thing was recipes. You couldn't be Luqs after you'd been dampened. Your brain just wouldn't work well enough."

"I know of a couple of Luqses whose brains didn't seem to work all that well."

Ker threw up her hands and her cloak slipped down again. "Daughter and Son save you." She reslung her cloak yet again. "Because I won't."

"You think Ennick was dampened?" Tel sounded more than curious. "You know, I tried to get him to draw me a map to North Falls Exit, but he just couldn't grasp the idea. Then I tried to draw one myself from his directions, and he only got more upset and confused."

"Ennick's not dampened," Ker said. "But remember, Jerek's

not a Talent at all. If anything, he's a Feeler." She shrugged. "And no one else in the Polity even believes they're real."

"Doesn't mean there isn't some law in some moldy old parchment somewhere."

"What moldy old law?" Luca must have heard something, but how much?

"Laws of chance," Tel said smoothly. "We were just wondering about the odds of the Talent showing up in the royal family," he added. "Neither of us remembers learning about such a case in school."

"An interesting question," Luca said, falling back to walk his mule next to theirs. "As you probably realize, neither the Talent nor the Feelers' Gifts are hereditary. If they were, we'd just breed the number of Talents we needed."

Ker's mouth dropped open.

"Oh, yes. Don't think it hasn't occurred to anyone to do just that. According to our records, only volunteers were used, but I've often wondered if that was true. In any case, the Talent appears in the offspring of Talents in the same percentage as that of the general population, which is to say, less than one percent. Though the experiment was never made, I'd guess that the percentage is similar with Feelers."

"What about the royal family, then?" Tel persisted. Ker appreciated his stepping in. Somehow the questions were less pointed coming from a soldier than they would have been coming from her. She tried to look only mildly interested.

"In a manner of speaking, the Polity can't afford to waste Talents in the royal family. Anyone can sit in the Luqs' Seat, but not just anyone is a Talent. Now, having said that, I'm sure you'll be surprised to learn that there has never been a recorded instance of a Talent in the royal family, let alone anyone directly in line for the Seat."

"So there never has been?" Tel looked from Ker to Luca and back again. "I suppose it's possible."

"That's not what he said." Ker watched the Inquisitor's look of bland innocence. "He said no such instance has ever been recorded."

On the seventh day they left the main road, turning into a track through what looked like otherwise wild forest. Ker wasn't sure, but she thought they might have walked their way out of the province of Bascat by now. The air continued to grow colder, but only a few drifts of snow remained in the most sheltered spots along the road. Four days later the track they'd been following disappeared and, after some consultation with the Cohort Leader, Luca led them into a small clearing where they stopped and made camp while the sun was still high in the sky.

"This is as far as we go," he said. "Here we wait for the people of the Springs and Pools."

The forest had thinned out, but the camp was tucked into the middle of a fair-sized grove of evergreens—cedars perhaps, interspersed with other trees that had lost their leaves. None of these others were birch, the only tree Ker could be sure of recognizing from its bark alone. She knew a good camp when she saw one, however. The trees here weren't tall, but they grew densely, and their branches, even those without leaves, were thick, giving a comfortable degree of cover. For the first time in days they were able to have a fire. Considering where they were going, they'd taken great care not to be seen.

Supper consisted of warm broth made from the bones of the two rabbits they'd killed the day before, and a share of travel cake. Even moistened with the broth, Ker had trouble chewing it and swallowing it down. It had never been one of her favorite meals, and now it just reminded her of how far from normal her life was.

Ker, Luca, and Cuarel were allowed to help set up camp, and took their turns at meal preparation with everyone else, but when it came time to set watches, only the four soldiers, including the Cohort Leader himself, took a turn as sentry. Ker suspected the old man enjoyed it. That night, he and the taller of his two aides drew the first watch and disappeared into the night.

"How long do we wait?" Tel took advantage of the Cohort Leader's absence to ask the Inquisitor questions.

"Until they come for us." Luca looked up from the fire. "Don't worry. It doesn't usually take very long. They have Far-seers, and they check this spot regularly."

Though they weren't allowed to be part of the military watch, Ker and Luca had formed the habit of splitting the night between them, Flashing for the presence or approach of strangers. They'd decided on the first day of travel that Luca should always take the first watch, and Ker the second, as the old Inquisitor seemed hardly to need any sleep at all, and Ker had the habit of waking up early from her training first in the military and later in the training Hall. As soon as supper was over, Luca settled himself cross-legged on one side of the fire, his eyes closed. Ker rolled herself in her cloak, and emptied her mind for sleep.

<<One comes.>>

Ker jolted awake, the griffin's voice echoing in her mind. Tel still slept beside her, so the watch hadn't changed. Where was Luca? <<Where are you?>>

<<Far, but I come.>>

Weimerk didn't stay close to them as they traveled. Not only would he attract far too much of the attention they were avoiding, but his dual nature demanded a great deal of food. He might have been half lion and half eagle, but he seemed to have the stomach of both.

<<I am still growing.>> Somehow his thoughts conveyed a clear feeling of offense.

<<Sorry.>>

<<You are not.>>

<<Let's argue later.>> Ker scanned her surroundings, but

the embers of the fire had burned so low there was no light to see by. The intruder likely wasn't close enough for anyone except the griffin to detect. *Paraste*

The first thing Ker Flashed were the six auras immediately around her, Tel's at her side, Luca's a few spans to the south where he now sat talking to Wilk Silvertrees, Cuarel just rousing on the other side of the fire next to the remaining Bear. Sitting up, Ker concentrated. At first, she Flashed no one else, but just as she was about to ask Weimerk for more detailed information, she caught a lone smudge of color far off to the west. A Feeler, a Lifter by the look of things. As she focused, the colors flared up, like a fire given fresh wood. Five auras, definitely five.

"What is it?" Tel's voice was pitched to reach her ears only.

"The Feelers are coming, get Luca and Wilk."

Tel rolled to his feet, tossing off cloak and blanket with one hand, picking up his sword with the other. He ran off into the darkness, heading directly toward where Ker could see the Inquisitor's aura, with its distinctive turquoise band.

Ker was on her feet, peering into the darkness, when Tel and Luca returned.

"He came almost to where the Cohort Leader stood watch and then he turned around," she said. "He's going away."

Luca squatted and put his hand to the ground, frowning for one long moment before he rose to his feet and trotted off in the direction the Feeler had gone. Luca couldn't see the other man's aura, but the Talent alone was enough to give him all the information he needed, once he knew where to look.

"Veriak!" they heard him call out. "Wait! It's Luca Pa'narion."

Cuarel sat up, and the sleeping soldier rolled to his feet as Wilk Silvertrees appeared in the firelight.

"A little louder." Tel's tone was sour. "Maybe there's a village nearby didn't hear you."

Ker cuffed him on the shoulder with the back of her hand. "There's no one else closer than a couple of hours' march." The military marched at a specific pace, so it was natural for them to measure distances in terms of time.

Luca rejoined them, panting slightly, but the other man, Veriak, stayed in the shadows on the edges of the clearing, eyes shifting constantly, alert for any movement he didn't like.

"Everyone, hold your position." The Cohort Leader pitched his voice to be heard by all. "This man is not a threat to us; let's not be a threat to him."

"You're not to bring people with you, Luca, you know that." The Feeler had a raspy voice, as if he'd strained it yelling.

"Where have I brought them, Veri? To a clearing far from the road? To shelter on a cold night?" The Inquisitor waved around the clearing. "This place is as open and public as a village square."

The man snorted, shaking his head. "You've not brought them here for shelter," he said. "You're here because of us, and don't deny it. The Far-thinker from the Mines I know, but what of the rest? These military? You're not telling me *they're* ours, are you?"

"Luca," Ker said. There were other auras now, closing fast. The man must have sent a message to his companions.

"I know, Kerida, I can Flash them, too."

"She one of *yours*, then? Well and good. But the soldiers?"

Ker glanced at Wilk Silvertrees. The Cohort Leader hadn't spoken since ordering his people to stand quiet, and it surprised Ker that he had the good sense to follow his own orders and let the Inquisitor handle things. She would have bet a day's pay—back in the days when she had a day's pay—that the Cohort Leader was too self-important to hold back.

"You'll have heard the Peninsula is taken by the Halians, invaders from over the sea. The Luqs is killed, and the Halls destroyed."

Veriak's eyes shut tight, and his mouth formed a thin line. "And the Talents?"

"Destroyed with their Halls. There are perhaps two hundred of us left, scattered and in hiding."

The cold crept up Ker's spine. She knew this. She'd seen the Halians at Questin, and found the ruins of Temlin Hall herself, but hearing the numbers left her numb. Out of some two thousand people, only a few hundred left?

"No Talents. Huh." Veriak looked from Ker to Luca and back. He didn't seem particularly upset. "Except for you, Luca, and your girl here?"

"There are others, as I've said. Many of whom are Guardians, friends to you and your people."

"And these military? They're friends now, too?"

Now Wilk Silvertrees stepped forward. "I can speak for the military," he said. Ker suddenly realized how smart Juria Sweetwater had been sending this gruff old man as her envoy, and as the Luqs' representative. Silvertrees was clearly not from the Peninsula himself, not an aristocrat, not one of the old Shield families. Orrin, his home province, wouldn't even have been part of the Polity at the time the Feelers were outlawed. The Cohort Leader was a gruff, plain old soldier with truth written on his face. Not that the Feeler seemed likely to take what he saw there for granted.

"I am Wilk Silvertrees, Ruby Cohort Leader of Bears. I bring you greetings from my Faro, Juria Sweetwater. But I also come on behalf of the Luqs of Farama."

Veriak looked sideways at Luca. "You said the Luqs was dead."

"Ruarel the Third died in Farama the Capital in Harvest-month, killed by the Halians. I speak for the new Luqs, Jerek Brightwing, grandson of Fokter the Fourth, acclaimed by the Bear Wing on the seventh of Snowmonth."

"And how does that make us allies?"

"Veriak, look at me." Cuarel was the only one still sitting down, her arms loosely circling her raised knees. Ker only knew three Far-thinkers at all well, and all of them were quiet types. When they did speak, it tended to be to the point. "You know me, Veriak Lifter, Cuarel Far-thinker. You know I came last year with Sala of Dez to help your Far-thinkers practice. What Luca says is true; we're allies now with the Bear Wing. We've taken them in, and they're barracked in the Mines and Tunnels, as is the Luqs himself. We have citizenship, Veriak, and the Cohort Leader is here to offer the same to you if you join with us."

"And if we don't join with you? What's he going to offer us then?"

Lips parted, Cuarel looked at Luca. No one in the Mines and Tunnels had expected an outright refusal. Ker's stomach dropped.

"This should at least go to your council, Veriak. If you would allow—"

"No." The man shook his head and took a step away, as if he expected one of them to suddenly leap the gap between them and seize him. "This is where I use my own judgment, and I say you're not coming any nearer to us, none of you." His glance slid sideways to Cuarel. "You must be insane if you think you can trust these people—to let them into your stronghold. . . ." He shook his head.

"But the Prophecy—"

"The Prophecy." The man spat. "That's all you can talk about, your precious Prophecy. You and your Time-seer have been holding that over our heads forever. 'The Prophecy says this, the Prophecy says that.' Much good it's ever done you, and much good it's doing you now."

Ker chewed the inside of her cheek, looking from Cuarel to Veriak and back again. This was the first she'd heard that the Prophecy wasn't embraced by all Feelers. Or for that matter, that there weren't other Time-seers besides little Larin.

"Veriak, listen to me." Cuarel got to her feet and took a step toward him, her hands spread, the scar on her face vivid in the moonlight. Veriak's eyes narrowed, but this time he didn't back away. "You know me. I've traveled outside in the world; you know I'm not a fool. Not everyone among us believed in the Prophecy either, but we have proof now. This girl, Kerida Nast, is the one who speaks to griffins. She found—"

"She's a *Talent*, Cuarel. How do you know she can be trusted?"

"Because I say she can be." Luca's voice cold and hard. "I vouch for her as Denah Qetrek once vouched for me. And Kerida is not the only one who has seen and spoken with the griffin. What we tell you does not rest on our words alone."

<<Where are you?>>

<<Coming.>>

<<Soon would be good.>>

"We waited in this clearing out of respect for your wishes. I haven't needed a guide to find your stronghold since you took me the first time, and Kerida here is a much stronger Talent than I am. She could find her way through the marshes and sands without anyone's help. But I've never presumed. I've always respected the rules your people have set."

Veriak focused on Luca's face as if he could read something there. Ker was only beginning to understand what it was like for people to live in a world without Talents. Talents could Flash when someone lied; good ones, strong ones, could tell even whether what someone sincerely believed was in fact untrue. When you didn't have Talents and the Rule of Law they made possible to guide you, did you live constantly in this fever of mistrust?

"You may come, then, Luca, to speak to the council. Cuarel Far-thinker and the Talent may come with you. But no one else."

Cuarel shook her head. "I'll stay here with the Cohort Leader. Kerida can tell the griffin what's going on, and he can tell me."

"Just a minute—"

Ker grabbed Tel's arm and held him back, shaking her head. "Don't," she said. "I'll be perfectly safe."

"And how do you know that?" His voice was stiff, but he looked at her, not the Feeler, and not around them into the darkness where she'd Flashed the others.

"Because Weimerk will be here soon."

Tel pulled his lips back, but she felt him relax. "Now *that* I'd like to see. It's not every day that something no one believes in drops by for a visit—emphasis on 'drops.'"

"Then you'll wait here?"

"I'll wait. I don't like it, but I'll wait."

"I tell you I'll be safe."

Tel showed his teeth again. "Safer than these guys, that's for certain."

"Veriak," Ker said, stepping to Cuarel's side. "Trust has to go both ways. We'll come with you, unarmed, but we have to know that we've left our friends in safety. There are four of your people watching us right now. Do we have your word that our friends will still be here when we come back?"

The Feeler lifted his chin. "You can't be so certain as that."

Ker closed her eyes and drew in a deep breath. "There's one three spans behind you to your left. He's a Far-seer. There's another fourteen spans over there." She pointed. "She's Un-Gifted but a good archer. Shall I point out the others? Shall I tell you their names? The names of their children?"

"I told you, man, she can Flash things I can't." Luca stuck his thumbs into his belt.

Gradually, the path Veriak Lifter led them along single file left behind even the thinning trees and entered a flatter landscape, swept bare of snow by a constant wind.

"Is it like this all the time?" she asked.

"In my experience, yes," Luca said from behind her. "I come usually in high summer, or in winter. Otherwise the ground is too wet to be safe."

Ker glanced back over her shoulder. "Wet?"

Luca swept his arm out in a gesture than included everything they could see. "All this moorland can turn into bog in the wet seasons. Sometimes it's so bad even the Springers stay put."

Ker nodded. Even now, it seemed, the path to the stronghold of Springs and Pools was treacherous. The land—some of it clearly mud—seemed uniformly frozen and solid, but Flashing told her a misstep could spell disaster. The safe way was narrow, and doubled back on itself, changing direction over and over, until Ker was completely disoriented. As Luca had said, she probably could have found the path by Flashing, but it wouldn't have been easy.

They had been walking for close to two hours, with only one break, when Kerida noticed the air growing warmer, and that the ground underfoot, while still solid, was no longer frozen. The sun was rising, but that alone wasn't enough to account for the warmer temperature. Ker pushed back her hood and allowed her cloak to swing open.

<<Hot springs.>>

Ker jumped and almost slid off the pathway. <<I wish you'd let me know when you're there.>>

<<I am always "here." I can be nowhere else. At the moment "here" is just above you.>>

Ker risked taking her eyes off the path long enough to look up. Nothing there but an empty, colorless winter sky. <<I can't see you.>>

<<But I am here, notwithstanding.>>

<<Can't you come down?>>

<<I would love to, if only to save you this trek, but there is no solid area large enough for me to land, and I fear to damage you should I merely pick you up as a hawk does its prey.>>

Ker snorted. <<Well, thank you for that.>>

After a while the air grew warm enough that Ker and Luca took off their cloaks entirely, and Veriak let them stop long enough to fold them into their packs.

"It's not much farther now," Luca said. The ground became gradually firmer, rockier, and finally the path widened to reveal a village that might have been anywhere in the Polity, except for the steam rising from scattered pools of water. The houses and buildings were more spread apart than usual, perhaps, but they were built of stone, or wattle and daub, or timber, just as might be found practically anywhere. The villagers—many of them Feelers, as Ker could Flash when she triggered her Talent—were dressed for warm weather, sleeveless tunics showing bare arms, and shirts with sleeves rolled up, depending on what task they were performing. The most wonderful thing for Ker was the smell of the air. Even the slightly sulfurous odor that drifted over from one of the steaming pools didn't cover the smells of green growth and warm soil that Ker hadn't experienced since helping with the harvest back at Questin Hall, before the Halians. Before winter.

Veriak brought them to a halt in the center of a cleared space too irregular to be called a square. People gathered from everywhere, hesitating when they saw Veriak wasn't alone. One skinny boy backed away so fast he fell over in the act of turning around to run. Cuarel had said there were Far-thinkers here, but there hadn't been one with Veriak.

No one could mistake the status of the white-haired woman who approached them now, the skinny boy who'd run away dancing at her elbow, her slow progress aided by a heavy wooden cane, darkened by time and use. Ker Flashed that a badly healed break had left one leg shorter than the other. Over the years the injury had affected the way the woman's muscles worked, and even displaced her pelvis, and the bottom of her spine.

"Something in my teeth?" The woman's voice was dry enough to crackle.

Ker blinked. While she'd been Flashing, the woman had finally reached them. "Sorry, I mean, I beg your pardon. I'm the Talent Kerida Nast." She'd been a Candidate so recently it still felt strange to announce herself that way. "If you have a Lifter who is willing to work with me, I might be able to fix your leg."

The silence was so profound Ker could hear the burbling of the nearest hot spring.

"Might you now," the woman said finally, her voice flat and hard. "I'm so used to it, it's hardly worth the effort. But how is it that you can do this?"

"The griffin showed me."

"The griffin showed you." The woman's tone softened and became kinder. Clearly, she thought Ker was mentally defective, simple, perhaps, like Ennick. "And what griffin would that be, my dear?"

Ker pointed upward. "This one."

She could hear Weimerk chuckling in her head as he landed, making people scatter to all sides. It wasn't that he took up so much room in himself, but his wingspan was easily as wide as the space they stood in, which he proved by flexing his wings with vigor.

"That. Is. Better." Weimerk shrugged his wings again, exactly like someone who wanted to loosen overworked muscles. "I am Weimerk of the Serpents Teeth," he said. "You. Are. Speaker. For. The Springs and Pools." The slight hesitation, almost a "click" between Weimerk's spoken words, that Ker had noticed when she first met him, had recently started fading away. Technically, of course, the griffin wasn't speaking words, but reproducing sounds.

The old woman visibly swallowed but gave no other reaction, and Ker gave her full marks for courage. The Miners had had months to get used to Weimerk. The Springers obviously hadn't taken his existence seriously.

"I'm Ylora, and I'm Speaker, all right." She bobbed her head. People began to edge closer again. Children peered around the legs of adults who kept them back.

"You. Seem. Surprised. To see me. Were. You. Not. Told?" Weimerk sat back on his haunches, front feet neatly together, the claws used in landing retracted.

"Us Far-thinkers don't get much practice." She tilted her head to the left and narrowed her eyes. "We got some garbled message, at least, we thought it garbled—your pardon, but what do I call you?"

"Weimerk."

"Thank you. Well, Weimerk, the people of the Mines and Tunnels are always going on about griffins and the Prophecy and such like. We don't listen so well. We here in the Springs have less time for such stuff."

Glancing around, Ker could see what the woman meant. The Springers may have been dressed for warmer weather, but they weren't *well* dressed. Their clothes, though definitely cleaner than Ker had seen lately, were homespun, and showed substantial wear. Children everywhere liked to be barefoot, but here, many of the adults were as well. In fact, except for the level of cleanliness, they looked like people from a poor village, one where the harvest had been bad for several years in a row. Light shone in some of the faces watching the griffin, especially if those faces belonged to children, but there were also faces showing no emotion at all, more such than Ker had seen among the Feelers of the Mines and Tunnels.

Somehow the griffin didn't bring these people hope the way he had to the others.

Ylora pushed her hair back with her left hand. "We're not going to talk about this here in the road," she said. "I call the council to meet. The rest of you, the day's well begun. There's chores won't do themselves, so get back to them."

Most people turned away quickly, pulling with them those who seemed disposed to linger. Four other people stepped forward, one after giving some instructions to a bony man who nodded, lips compressed, before jogging away.

"This way." Ylora turned, leading them to a building on the far side of the cleared area.

"Ylora," Luca said, his rough voice gentle. "Weimerk won't fit inside your council building."

The old woman turned around, compressing her lips a moment before speaking. "We don't have one bigger than this."

It surprised Ker that they had a building even this big. Lifters among the Feelers would have had no trouble with either the assembly or the positioning of any amount of rock or stone, but the building seemed large for the number of Feelers she'd seen. Had the group been bigger once?

"Weimerk can stay out here in the square," she suggested. "He doesn't need to be present to know what's going on. I can Far-think to him."

"*You* can Far-think?"

"To the griffin, I can." Weimerk had often said that Ker would one day be able to Far-think with others, but judging from the look on *this* Far-thinker's face, she thought she'd keep that to herself just now.

"No. Matter." Weimerk thrust his eagle's head between them. "I would like to See. And. Hear. For myself."

"We can leave the doors open." Ylora gestured without looking at Weimerk. In fact, Ker was sure the woman hadn't looked directly at him since he landed.

The floor inside the building was earth pounded hard by the pressure of many feet. In the center of the space was a circle of low, three-legged stools. The Feelers sat down, and two other stools were pulled forward for Kerida and Luca Pa'narion.

"I'm Ylora Far-thinker, Speaker for the Clan of Springs and Pools. There's Alubin Mind-healer, Fana Far-seer, Naishan Lifter and Volor, UnGifted. We've no Time-seer, as we've already told you. Now, who's going to speak for you?"

The silence dragged on long enough to become uncomfortable.

<<They are waiting for you to speak.>>

Ker cleared her throat. <<Why me?>>

<<You are Griffin Girl.>>

Ker cleared her throat again and began her story with the coming of the Halians to Questin Hall, the power and danger of the Shekayrin, the search for a new Luqs, and the finding of Jerek Brightwing. The story took long enough to tell that tea was brought for all of them. Though nothing to eat, as the rumbling of Ker's stomach reminded her.

"These Shekayrin, they're the real problem, aren't they?" Fana Far-seer frowned as though he could see the mages if only he concentrated enough. "Otherwise, it's just one bunch of soldiers against another. What all can they do?"

"They can move things in battle, like arrows or spears or rocks," Luca said.

"Like a Lifter," Naishan said.

"They can affect how people think, make them behave in different ways."

"Sounds like a form of Mind-healing," Alubin said, her nose wrinkling in distaste. "A bad one."

"Some of them can speak to each other over long distances," Ker added. "Like Far-thinkers. As long as they have their jewels, they can do many of the same things Feelers can. The difference is that the Gifts are divided among you, 'one Feeler, one Gift,' right?" She waited until she got some nods. "Every Shekayrin has all of the Gifts, though not all of them to the same strength."

The Feelers all looked at each other, every brow wrinkled except for one.

"So, they're more like Feelers than Talents, is what you're saying." It was Volor, the UnGifted woman, who finally spoke. "Are we sure we want to be against them, if they're more like us?" she said to the others.

"They will not ally with you," Weimerk said from the doorway. "Their. Magic. Differs. From. Yours. You are their ancient enemy. You. And. The. Talents. Both."

"What did *we* do?"

Ker understood Ylora's tone. When you're used to thinking of yourselves as victims, it could be hard to learn that others saw you as oppressors.

Weimerk rocked his head from side to side. "You outlawed them. You. And. The. Talents. Both. Their magic is alien to yours. Which. Arises. Out. Of. The. Natural. Body. Bursting forth, trained or untrained."

Ker had experienced that firsthand. It was impossible to hide the Talent when it came.

"The mages' magic also. Finds. Its. Root. In. The. Individual's. Body. And. Psyche. But. Without. Rigorous. Training. Using what they call soul stones. And. Determined. Focused. Discipline. Their. Magic. Is. Never. More. Than. A. Spark. Your. Forebears. All. Your. Forebears. Deemed. This. Magic. Unnatural. And. Had. Outlawry. As. Their. Price. For. Aiding. Jurianol. To. The. Luqs'. Seat. They will kill you if they can."

Ylora nodded slowly. "All right, then. If we do make common cause with you, what are your terms?"

Everyone looked at Luca, but he looked at her. "*We* can't make terms with you," she said. "The only one who can is Co-hort Leader Silvertrees, and he's back in the camp."

Volor leaned forward. "We're not walking some military man through the path, no matter what," she said. "Talent Guardians are one thing, and griffins." She bobbed her head at Weimerk, who blinked one eye at her. "But a soldier who's trained to re-member pathways? Ylora, no one would agree to this." From the look on the others' faces, Volor's "no one" included everyone on the council.

"She's right," Ylora said. "No one will."

"Then we'll have to go to him," Luca said, but Ylora was already shaking her head.

"I'm not up to walking that far," she pointed out.

Privately, Ker agreed. The thought of having to walk back through all those twists and turns was more than her leg mus-cles could bear. "Weimerk, would you carry her?"

"Don't matter if he will, I won't be carried." The blood had drained from the older woman's face.

Ker blew out a breath. "Well, then. Will you carry Wilk?"

"Even. If. I wished to, which I do not. He. Is. Too. Heavy."

Ker drummed her fingers on her knee and shifted on her stool. There was no way to get Weimerk to do what he didn't want to do. "You said once you'd carry Jerek."

Weimerk shrugged his wings. "I would. He. Is. Part. Of. The. Prophecy. As I am."

"Then you *could* carry his representative," she said as firmly as she could. Before Weimerk could respond, she added. "Would you carry Tel?"

Tel Cursar could afford to find the look on the Ruby Cohort Leader's face funny, since Wilk Silvertrees aimed the look at Cuarel. The other two soldiers developed a sudden interest in straightening firewood and examining the ground. The Cohort Leader's face wasn't the only thing making Tel smile. For him, the most important part of Cuarel's news was that Ker was safe and sound. Except for duty shifts, he hadn't been separated from her since she'd unjeweled him. Watching her walk off with the Feelers of the Springs and Pools had been almost more than he could take.

A chance to fly with the griffin—that was what really made him smile.

"I'm sorry, Cohort Leader," Cuarel was saying. "I'm only passing along what the griffin tells me. A speaker for the Luqs is needed, and it can't be you. Of the rest of us, Weimerk the griffin will only carry Tel Cursar."

Silvertrees squeezed his eyes shut and Tel took the chance to exchange a grin with the other soldiers. Nothing entertained the lower ranks more than a top officer being annoyed by someone else, though Tel kept that feeling off his face when the Cohort Leader turned to him. The older man frowned, fists on hips, and finally sighed. He opened the collar of his tunic and pulled out a gold plaque, careful to touch only the chain it hung on. He gestured Tel forward and transferred the plaque to Tel's neck, again carefully slipping it under Tel's tunic by the chain alone.

Jerek the Luqs had been the last person to touch the plaque, when he'd pressed his thumbprint into the warmed gold. Any Talent would know it was real and given freely as the Luqs' token.

"Tell the griffin he may come," Wilk said.

Cuarel didn't say anything, but Tel knew from the look on her face that Weimerk hadn't waited for permission.

"What people would you actually need?"

Tel took a deep breath and pushed his hair back out of his eyes. He'd lost the thin strip of leather he used to tie his hair somewhere over the last bit of moorland, and the braiding had been blown out by the griffin's speed. Ker could tell he didn't know he was still smiling.

"Well, Far-seers and Lifters would be the most useful, obviously," Tel said, dropping his hands and leaning forward, elbows on knees. He was too tall to stand comfortably in the meeting hall. "But Far-thinkers are also a real asset for communications."

"So, you'd take the most useful among us, leaving us without communications or protection for ourselves." Volor looked around and nodded at the others, as if to say: "I told you so." For some reason, the UnGifted was the most against them.

Ker frowned. Suspicion she could understand, all things considered. But could this be something more? She triggered her Talent again and allowed her awareness to float away from the council meeting. Just how many Springers were there? And how many of them were Feelers?

<<They are a much smaller Clan than that of the Mines and Tunnels.>>

Ker gritted her teeth. She liked to at least pretend her thoughts were her own.

<<There's a higher percentage of Feelers among them,

though.>> She sorted through the auras she could Flash from where she was.

<<That may be so.>>

Did that mean more Feelers had been brought here in the first place, or that they did something with—or to—the Un-Gifted who were born among them? They wouldn't be the first poor village or community who exposed children or their aged when they couldn't afford to feed them. It hadn't happened in the Polity for generations, but technically these people weren't part of the Polity.

Ker shivered. Did she want to know? They needed the help of any willing Feeler. Could they afford to look too closely into how those people lived?

"Enough." Ylora clapped her hands. "Or rather, it's not enough. Even if we agree the Prophecy's real, and I guess with the griffin breathing into our doorway we pretty much have to, how does that mean we should come out of hiding, let alone help the Battle Wings?"

"Citizenship—"

"Look, you seem like a nice boy, and I'm sure you believe what you're telling us—and maybe this new Luqs of yours does as well, but don't you see? We *had* citizenship. That didn't stop the Talents from turning against us and arranging to have us outlawed." She looked around. "No offense intended to present company."

Ker just stopped herself from rolling her eyes. According to what she'd been told by both the Feelers in the Mines and Luca Pa'narion himself, that accusation was, more or less, the truth.

Tel's lips were pressed together, his breath coming short through his nose. *Don't lose your temper,* she willed at him, praying to the Daughter that he somehow heard her. Weimerk's chuckling was like a tickle in her head. "What, then?" Tel asked. "Is there something else that might persuade you to help us?" Well, sarcasm wasn't *much* of an improvement over shouting, but Ker supposed it would do.

"The girl offered to heal me," Ylora said.

Speechless, Ker looked from Ylora to the others. "I said I would try."

"That's it?" Now Tel didn't care how much of his anger showed. "We heal you and you'll send us help?"

"Not me." Ylora spoke so quietly Ker almost missed it. She put her hand on Tel's arm, again willing him to be quiet. "I'm old, I'm used to my leg." Ylora shrugged. "The Mother knows I'd probably miss the limp if the girl actually fixed it. No, it's not me." She looked off into the middle distance, Far-thinking.

By the time she relaxed, two women had presented themselves at the open doorway, edging with much nodding and bowing around Weimerk's front paws. He retracted his claws again with an air of great politeness. They brought a small boy, maybe three or four, maybe older, who wriggled in his mother's arms, reaching for the griffin. Ker found it hard to tell whether his small size was due to age, or to the fact that he didn't look all that well fed. Judging from the similarities in their eyes and brow ridges, the woman carrying him was likely his mother by blood. The other followed with a small crutch, little more than a twisted bit of tree branch, in her hand. When the mother set him down, the boy balanced on his right leg and Ker saw that his left leg was too short to reach the ground. There was a knot the size of Ker's own fist in the boy's left thigh, the leg hanging crookedly from that point as if he had a second knee.

"First tell me, 'Griffin Girl,' whether this lad has a Gift." Ylora sat back, arms crossed.

Paraste. Ker scanned the child's aura and got the answer she expected. There was no telltale Feeler color, no matter how faint. Only the three colors shared by all human beings. <<Weimerk?>> she asked, hoping that the griffin could see more.

<<Nothing. I am sorry, Kerida Nast.>>

"This child isn't a Feeler," Ker said. "He's UnGifted."

"You can't tell yet," the second woman protested. "He's too young."

"The griffin can tell." Ker didn't bother to say she was sorry. Her sympathy wouldn't be welcome.

The mother spun around to the doorway. Weimerk tilted his head down and fixed his left eye on her. His wings hung low. Finally, the woman nodded and turned back, laying her hand with great gentleness on her son's head.

"Qela." Ylora's voice held all the sorrow and caring Ker couldn't express. "Even if we didn't trust the griffin, you know we'd have no choice. The boy's too young to have learned a useful skill. He can't walk or run, or even stand comfortably by himself for any length of time." The Speaker looked down at her own twisted leg. "He was injured too young," she said. "Even without the griffin," she repeated, "we couldn't afford to wait and see if he had a Gift. You know we'd have no choice."

The one mother nodded. The other, still holding the crutch, pressed her lips tight together but otherwise didn't move.

Ker swallowed, and forced herself not to look away. Her worst fears were confirmed, but she found she couldn't condemn these people—not completely. They had the survival of their whole group to think about.

"So, Qela, knowing what our options are, would you and Birroc be willing to let this Talent try something?"

"Something that would help the boy?" Birroc asked. Qela looked afraid to speak.

"It might not work," Ylora said before Ker could. "She can't promise anything. But seeing what the alternative is, I thought you might want to let her try."

"Yes, yes, of course. Please." Ker found herself in Birroc's arms, so startled she almost didn't feel the little crutch poking into her back. "Help him if you can, please. We'd do anything for you. Anything."

"Just wait, Birroc," Ylora said. "If she can do it, you won't be the only one in her debt." She turned to Ker. "What do you need, Talent?"

"Your best Lifter," she said. "And a few hours' rest."

Three hours later Ker was back in the meeting hall, being introduced to a Lifter almost as tall as Tel, though much thinner and much, much older. Older even than Ganni.

Lifters were so-called after the most obvious part of their Gift, the ability to lift and move things, or people, without touching them. They could lift items too heavy for normal strength, they could push or hold things out of the way. And if their Gift was strong, they could move the edges of wounds together and encourage them to heal. It was Mind-healers who could help anyone sick in spirit, sometimes even those who had severe flaws of character, but neither Feeler could heal a physical, interior wound. Lifters couldn't move or lift anything they couldn't see. And that included any interior sickness of the body.

Ker rubbed at an area under her left arm, where there *wasn't* a scar puckering the skin between two ribs. Lifters *could* heal what they couldn't see, if she could show it to them.

"Here." She beckoned to the old man with her left hand, laying her right on the child's thigh. "Put your hand here, where the injury is."

"Doesn't he have to be asleep or something?" the old man said as he came forward.

"I don't think so," Ker said. "It shouldn't make any difference." But the old man's attitude could make a difference. He seemed too withdrawn and cold to be able to work with her. She'd set bones any number of times with Lifters in the Mines, but they'd all been eager and enthusiastic.

Nevertheless, whether it was fear or disbelief, the man didn't let it stop him. He placed his left hand on the boy's thigh next to Ker's right, and allowed Ker to hold his right hand in her left.

"Ready?"

"As I'll ever be."

Paraste. The old man's aura was brighter and more robust than he was, and that gave Ker some hope. His six colors, though vibrant and glowing, were tightly contained, almost as if he held his breath.

"Can you relax?" she asked. "Do you need a Mind-healer?"

"Child, just get on with it." But the bands and waves of his colors did seem to loosen.

"Can you see anything?" she asked.

"Got my eyes closed, like you told me."

So that's a no. She nodded without speaking aloud. She took three deep breaths, letting each one out slowly. At first, the red pattern of her jewel distracted her, until she had to deliberately set it to one side. Then she allowed her own band of turquoise, the color that marked her as a Talent, to join the old man's aura, slipping around and through his colors and wrapping them loosely.

<<That is not what really happens.>> Weimerk sounded amused.

<<That's how I see it,>> she said. <<It helps me, if I imagine it that way. How did others do it?>>

<<There are no others.>>

Ker swallowed, and filed that away for later.

"I don't think this is working, Talent."

Ker couldn't understand; this was all she did when she worked with the Feelers in the Mines and Tunnels. Were they simply more open to working with her? Or was there something else? The Shekayrin certainly didn't seem to have any trouble influencing their victims. Wincing at the thought, Ker was still desperate enough to try it. She pulled her red thread closer and ran through its patterns until one felt right. She took the turquoise ribbon of her Talent and spun it thinner, looping and threading it through and over, augmenting the pattern of red almost as if she was making lace. Just as she closed the net around the old man's aura, he grunted.

"Wait a bit." His hand clamped down on hers and Ker gritted her teeth. "There's something. I see it. Don't move," he said, but Ker wasn't sure who he spoke to.

"You see where the healing went wrong?" she asked him.

"I do, I do. This is marvelous. Can you see this all the time?"

"When I'm Flashing, yes," she said.

"Well, Mother bless me, and Daughter slap my face. It's marvelous, that's all. Marvelous."

"Can you see how to fix the break?" she asked him. "You see here." She wasn't pointing—she had nothing to point with—and yet, somehow, she was. "Can you move that?"

The old man nodded. "I can. It's going to hurt the little bugger, but I can."

"Quickly."

Almost too fast for Ker to follow, the knot of misshapen bone cracked open. The boy cried out, but there were suddenly other hands, other auras, holding him still and giving what comfort they could. The boy's thigh bone suddenly straightened, chips of bone and bits of cartilage moving into place and fusing together.

"Get that bleeding," Ker said.

"I see it, I see it." The tiny spurt of blood stopped. "Anything else?"

"I don't think so," Ker said. "I think we're done." She gently disengaged her turquoise-and-red pattern. *Terestre*. She sagged back on her heels, found Tel supporting her shoulders. When she opened her eyes, the boy was asleep; there was a bad bruise on his thigh, but the leg was straight.

"*Might* be a bit shorter," the old man said, appraising the limb with his head to one side. "But not enough to make a real difference." There was a light in his eye, and a smile hovered around his lips that hadn't been there before. "There's others," he said. "Maybe not bad like the boy here, but others we can help."

Before Ker could answer Tel spoke up. "I believe you were about to make a decision."

Ylora rubbed her face, as if she'd been the one doing all the work. "What says the council?" She waited until she had nods from everyone. "So, then. We'll help you, in exchange for healing—and the citizenship," she added at a signal from one of the others. "But it must be volunteers, mind. I can't order anyone to go with you."

"That's all we want," Tel said.

Of course, it was, Ker thought. It had to be. The old man still grinned at her, eager and fresh. How many others would he want her to look at? And how long would it take? Even her eyelashes felt tired. She leaned her head back against Tel's arm. She'd just rest her eyes for a minute.

BAKURA Kar Luyn took deep, steady breaths, flexing the fingers of both hands. Breathing deeply to keep her hands from trembling, her face from twisting, tears from springing to her eyes. Her brother the Sky Emperor had said sending her away would keep her alive. She wondered if this would be so. She had foreseen nothing of her voyage, not the boat, nor the storm at sea the Shekayrin averted—nothing at all of her future, nor anything else since she had been netted.

"Honored One, we arrive."

Baku shook herself. The clouds that had fogged her brain *were* slowly fading, as were the tints of red she saw from the corners of her eyes. But she had little hope that her sightings of future events would return. "Speak in the language of Farama, Kvena. We must practice."

The girl nodded. "Yes, Honored One." But the corners of the maid's mouth turned down. With that attitude, her Faraman would never improve.

Baku stood to allow her maids to finish robing her. This would be the first time she wore the divided skirts since she had been a child in her father's summer herd camp. Imperial court ladies were not encouraged to ride. Baku kicked at the drape of cloth. She might have thought to practice walking in the skirts, had her head been clearer.

"This is a very clever design." Narl Koven, the Faraman woman who had been sent to Halia to serve her spoke with warm approval. "You look as though you're wearing an ordinary gown until you walk."

"I would ask for more such robes to be made." Baku did her best to mimic the woman's accent. "You will see to it."

"Of course, my lady. I mean, Honored One."

As the Sky Emperor's blood, as Daughter of the Moon, Baku had the largest of the rooms on the ship, but this was no river barge, no pleasure craft, but an oceangoing vessel. Even the largest rooms were smaller than her closets in the Imperial Palace. Larger cabins might have been built on a great troop carrier, but that was not the ship her brother had chosen to send. With the three women together, it was more than crowded. It was like living in a wooden box, tightly fitted and caulked, that creaked and groaned alarmingly as the ship was affected by currents of both air and sea.

Kvena twitched the last fold into place and stood back, her head bowed. Baku herself took the final thin veil, heavy with gold embroidery, from Narl's hands. Carefully, she placed it correctly over her elaborately coiled, pinned, and lacquered hair until it covered her to her knees. When Kvena stood back and folded her hands, Baku knew the veil was properly aligned.

"Stand away," she said. "I would view the imperial chest." Kvena scurried to one side, leaving Baku a clear path. Hidden behind the veil, Baku pressed her lips together. She'd given the woman no reason to be so skittish, but even after a month together at sea only "scurry" could accurately describe Kvena's movements. In contrast the Faraman woman moved to stand next to her fellow servant with a smooth, almost dancing, step.

The mesh of the veil was fine enough that it did not obscure Baku's vision; she was able to see the cedar wood chest, carved on every side with horses in full gallop, dragons in flight, and images of the sun. All symbols of the Sky Emperor. She knelt, careful of the veil, feeling the awkward movements of the heavy, unfamiliar skirts. She bowed, letting her forehead just touch the lid of the box. She had postponed investigating the chest and its contents, afraid to trust to her foggy brain. She could delay no longer.

"Father Sun, guide my hand." The words were spoken in the language of the Horsemen. Her brother had warned her that neither the foreign tongue nor even the Halian would work. Sure enough, when she put her hand to the box's fastening, it parted with ease, the lid popping upward the width of her little finger. With the tips of fingers and thumbs, Baku lifted the lid and let it fold back until the box was open, revealing its blue silk padding. She peeled back a layer of yellow silk from the bundle in the box, and then a layer of green, finally exposing the last layer, red as the lacquer she wore on her nails. She steeled herself and felt with her fingertips for an edge. She lifted her hands. Unlike the other layers, this cloth felt rough. She rubbed the tips of her fingers against her thumb. Dust, as fine as face powder. She sucked in her breath as the dust gathered itself together and dripped from her palms and fingers, as sand pours through an hourglass, back to the cloth. Her hands were left clean.

Too startled to speak, Baku acknowledged the cloth with a shallow bow. There was, indeed, power here. She reached out again, this time finding the edges of the cloth immediately. The red silk fell away, to reveal a mask carved from white jade. Her brother's face looked back at her, unmoving, the lips slightly parted, with almond-shaped holes where the eyes should be.

Narl Koven edged close enough to observe, and Baku forgave the maid her curiosity.

Lying next to the mask was a short ebony stick. Baku picked it up in her left hand and, once more concentrating on her breathing, fitted stick to mask, turning it until she heard a slight click. Lips pressed together, she held the mask up to her face, pressing against the veil. Her view was unexpectedly clear and full, not at all obscuring the sight of Kvena prone on the floor, trembling and moaning with her hands clasped over her head. Narl also knelt, but her face was impassive, and her hands were properly in her lap.

Baku lowered the mask. "Rise," she said again. "Kvena, go before me, make sure my passage is clear, and that rugs have been placed for my feet. Warn the captain that I come. Narl, you will attend behind me."

Kvena was in such a rush to leave the room that Narl had to reach quickly to prevent the door from swinging shut again. "It's raining, Honored One," she said.

"Bring the water shade." Baku paced herself to allow Narl to walk steadily behind her until they reached the deck. When she emerged, the crew nearest her were on their knees—not to her, but to the image of her brother the Sky Emperor created by the mask.

The captain approached and bowed low. "Honored One." Normally, the man would keep his eyes averted from the Princess Imperial, but while she wore the Emperor's image, it was allowed that men should look at her. Behind the captain were the chests and boxes that made up her possessions. And held the documents that formed her marriage contract.

"The Sky Emperor thanks you for your great care of his sister."

Baku shivered, knowing that no one would see it beneath the veil. For the voice that had issued from the mask was not hers, but her brother's. She knew the mask was magicked, and she knew that it was called "Voice of the Emperor," but she had always believed that to be a metaphor.

She began again. "The Sky Throne will not forget your service."

For a moment she thought the captain would join his crew on his knees. Even though he must have been warned what to expect, the sound of her brother's voice coming from the mouth opening of the mask was enough to make the man turn pale. Recovering, he inclined his head. Baku read his thoughts as though he had spoken. The captain depended on the Imperial memory to make his fortune. His would be always the ship which had carried the Princess Imperial to her new land. To bind the Faraman Polity to Halia with her marriage, and her children.

The mask lowered but still in her hands, Baku watched the pier come slowly closer as five smaller boats, each rowed by four men, pulled her ship into its anchorage. The wind came off the land, with nothing familiar in the smells it brought with it except wet stone. Baku shivered, though she was well-layered against the cold. They were close enough now that she could see the strange clothing and even the faces of the people standing on the quay. Many seemed to be going about the work inherent in the place, but a great crowd stood with banners aloft, flapping with the wind, very obviously here to welcome her.

Baku felt her heart beat faster. There were women there. Women dressed in much the same clothing and the same colors as the men. Women with faces uncovered. Women had ruled here. As little as six months ago, the Luqs had been a woman, the niece, it was said, of the man to whom that chest of documents married her. She found herself standing at the rail, her servants at her side. Was there magic in this land, that allowed it to be ruled by women for so long? Was it gone now that the witches were gone? Or might there remain some vestige to help her? For what was she, with her visions of the future, but a witch?

"Honored One, if you will pardon me, the men need access to this portion of the rail."

Startled, Baku stepped back. It had been so long since the ship had been in port that she had forgotten the location of the opening where the ramp would be affixed that would allow her to reach the dock. A bustle behind her made her turn, and she saw the great chair being lifted from its storage in the hold. She looked again at the men and women on the quay. She saw horses, but no chairs, neither open nor closed.

"I will not need the chair, Captain," she said.

"Honored One, if you please, the Emperor your brother left most precise instructions. He himself provided the chair."

"Captain, when I write my brother the Sky Emperor this evening, I will tell him of how I used his magnificent chair, and how it conveyed me in utmost comfort to the palace of my husband, the Luqs of Farama. I will give you this letter with instructions that it be given into my brother's own hand. He will be most pleased with you, I think, Captain." Baku raised the mask slightly closer to her face.

"It is a privilege to serve you, Honored One." The captain gestured to the men still swinging the chair to the deck. "The chair will be delivered to your palace with the remainder of your belongings." He turned back and studiously stared at where her feet would be if they were not hidden by her clothing. "If I may, Honored One. Since you do not use the chair, you will find your legs awkward when you step upon the land once again. I recommend using your servant, or a walking staff, to aid you."

"A staff, then." Was the man, after all, a fool? Surely her maid would have just as much trouble walking? Staff in hand, Baku stepped carefully onto the ramp. A rope railing had been affixed to one side, so evidently even the sailors suffered from this affliction. She tightened her grip on the mask. It would not do to drop it, though she had been assured it was not easily broken. Taking small steps, as steady as she could make them, she reached the pier having only twice felt unbalanced. Her alarmed squeak had been smothered by the veils. She hoped.

By the time Baku had walked at the same deliberate pace to the land end of the pier, however, her legs already felt less like cooked noodles, and more like something that would hold her upright. She hesitated as she reached the last of the wooden planks, looking around her.

Finally, the Daisy Shekayrin who had accompanied her from Halia, ostensibly to guide and protect her, made his belated appearance, standing just behind her left shoulder. Baku had early realized that the mage saw his work as more protection than guidance. He had been uncomfortable in her presence, finding excuses not to eat with her, and responding to her questions with the shortest possible answers. Which, as common sense should have told him, could only lead to more questions. Had she been in her own wing of the palace in Halia, she would have been amused, but on board the ship, with no real support, she feared it as a sign of things to come.

Narl Koven had been far more helpful than the mage. On the second day of their voyage Baku had been given a demonstration of the difference between Halian and Faraman women.

"Honored One," Narl Koven had said. Kvena dropped to her knees, horrified that a servant had spoken before being spoken to, and expecting the worst.

"The veils," Narl had continued, oblivious. "Do they have a religious significance?" She must have felt the silence because she glanced up from her sewing, looking from side to side not as would a trapped animal, but as an actor taking the temperature of the audience. After her own initial shock, Baku decided this was something she intended to enjoy.

"They do not," she said. "It is a Halian custom which my Horsemen ancestors were obliged to adopt. It is a way for a man to keep his possessions out of the public eye." Baku smiled.

"In Halia, it is also the custom that servants do not speak until spoken to." She held up her right hand as Narl began to apologize. "Here in Farama I will not require this in private. However, I suggest that you obey the custom when there are others in the room."

Narl had been more careful during the rest of the voyage, taking her cue more often from the behavior of Kvena.

Baku wished now she could ask her maid who these solemn-faced dignitaries were. Several bowed to her as she stepped off the ramp, though no one spoke. The Daisy Shekayrin beckoned, and her chair was brought forward. The mage held out his wrist for her to place her fingers on and made a wide gesture toward the chair. Baku pressed her lips together. She thought she had already made her wishes clear.

"For whom are the horses intended?" she asked.

"For myself and the elders of the city, Honored One," came the answer she expected.

"I will ride," she said.

After a noticeable pause, the Daisy Shekayrin spoke. "Honored One, there is no other horse."

She turned her head toward him, knowing that the veil obscured her features and her expression. "Then I will take yours, as it is undoubtedly the best."

It was gratifying to see how his body stiffened and his face grew darker. "Women do not ride," he said.

For answer, Baku raised the mask she carried in her left hand until it covered her face. Through the eyeholes she saw the Shekayrin flinch back from her. "The Princess Imperial is not a woman," her brother's voice said. "She is the Voice of the Emperor. She will ride." Baku smiled when she saw the crimping of muscles around the mage's mouth. Let him grit his teeth. In truth Baku had not been completely certain that the mask would be obeyed by Shekayrin. This small victory reassured her. Having her brother's voice might be more protection than she had thought.

Her stubbornness resulted in wet clothing, but Baku was still glad she had carried her point.

The rooms in the Luqs' palace were larger than she expected, though they might have seemed so only because she had been living in such close quarters aboard ship. The furniture was heavier than Baku was used to, the woods darker and the fabrics thicker.

"This weaving is excellently done," she said, dropping the edge of a curtain. "And the colors well-dyed, chosen with a good eye." She would have to accustom herself to the images of trees she did not recognize and of griffins where her people were more likely to embroider horses. There were no flowers in her rooms, but there were green plants in plenty; one or two even looked familiar.

She had arrived late enough in the day that no ceremonial appearances were expected of her. It was assumed that she would need to rest and refresh herself after her long journey. For Baku, refreshment could only come from walking about in the free air, under the open sky, on a surface that did not move. Pacing up and down her sitting room, as large as the place was, was not at all the same. In truth, she had the wish to walk alone, to be alone, though she could not recall ever having been alone in her life. Even in her brother's many-roomed palace, someone was always with her, even in her bedroom while she slept.

She turned before she reached the fireplace in the west wall of the sitting room and began walking back. At first, Kvena and Narl tried to walk with her, but that at least she could put a stop to. Kvena was happy enough to sit on her stool. The Faraman woman watched from a window seat. Baku could not decide whether the impassive face hid boredom or anxiety.

As she approached the fireplace at the east end of the sitting room, she slowed and veered toward the door to the left of the hearth.

"What is this wood?" she asked. She had never seen a wood so golden with such a wonderfully straight grain.

"It is oak, Honored One," Narl said from her seat.

"As these are the consort's rooms, the symbolism of the carving is perhaps a trifle heavy-handed." Baku tightened her lips into a line. She drew her finger along the edge of a plump wooden apple, largest of the fruits depicted in the wood. The carving in no way resembled that on the chest of the mask sitting on a wall table nearby.

"Narl."

The Faraman woman was immediately on her feet, making her way to where Baku stood. "Yes, Honored One."

"Does the Luqs sleep alone in his bedchamber?"

"Well, it's early." The woman sounded ever so faintly amused. "I imagine he's still at supper."

Smiling, Baku turned to face the woman. "I did not mean now," she said. "I meant when he goes to bed in his chambers, is he alone, or are there servants and guards in the room with him?"

"Oh, I'm sorry, Honored One." The woman inclined her head, but not in time to hide the quirk of her lips. "I thought you meant . . . I should say, the Luqs usually sleeps alone, my lady. Servants and guards sleep in the anterooms, and of course there is someone on the balcony outside of the Luqs' rooms." The woman looked down. "There's no rule for it, but the consort customarily goes to the Luqs, my lady."

"Does she? Well, that is good to know. And may I ask, how do you know this?"

Narl swallowed, all humor gone from her face. "I was aide to the late Luqs, my lady."

Frowning, Baku examined Narl more closely. She would have thought the woman too old to serve as a bed maid, but perhaps . . . "The Luqs uses women servants?"

Narl lowered her eyes. "The late Luqs *was* a woman, my lady."

Buzzing in Baku's ears. She had known that, of course. "Was every Luqs a woman?"

"No, my lady. Generally, the first child inherits—inherited—so sometimes it's a woman, and sometimes a man."

"I see." Baku took a deep breath. Time to get back to her real purpose. "As the Luqs sleeps alone in his bedchamber, I will sleep alone in mine." A gasp brought Kvena to her feet. Baku rested her hand on the mask box and fixed the woman with a steely eye, an expression of her brother's she had been practicing. Her body maid stopped in her tracks, lowering herself to her knees. Baku nodded sharply. Out of the corner of her eye, she thought she saw the Faraman woman smile again, but by the time Baku turned her head, Narl's face was once more impassive.

"I would walk in a garden," she said finally. Narl went to the door and spoke in a low tone to the inevitable guard. The woman then pushed the door completely open and bowed to Baku.

"When you are ready, Honored One."

A very few minutes later Baku stood in the doorway of a walled garden, surveying the neatness of the extended paths, the carefully trimmed hedges, fruit trees pollarded against the nearby southern wall. The ground before her was dry and hard, with none of the ice and snow she had expected.

But it was the *ground*. Even at the docks Baku had walked on carpets spread for her on the paving stones.

Would there be magic in this earth to help her? With no further delay Baku placed her right foot firmly on the land of Farama.

Nothing. No change. *What is there here to help me?*

Jerek Brightwing jolted awake, groping for the knife he kept under his pillow. "Wynn? Was that you?"

"Was what me?" Wynn sat up. She'd been sleeping on a mat

across his door. It made Jerek feel silly having someone do that, but he felt safe, as well. Especially when the someone was Wynn Martan.

"Did someone call?" he asked her. "Did someone ask for help?"

"I didn't hear anything," she said.

"But that doesn't mean there wasn't anything to hear," Jerek said, lowering his voice. "What if it's me?"

Wynn scrubbed at her face, then lowered her hands. "Far-thinking you mean? Who? Dersay or Cuarel?"

"Find out if there's news, can you? Without, you know . . ."

"Of course." Wynn got to her feet, moved her bedding out of the way, and opened the door a handspan. She spoke quietly to the guard on the other side of the door. Jerek only heard a few words, his title, and "can't sleep" and "put his mind at rest" before she shut the door again.

"There," she said, sitting down again. "They'll send and ask, and if there's any news, we'll know shortly."

He nodded his thanks and pulled the blankets closer around him. He wished that Kerida Nast was back, but he didn't want to say so out loud. He was sure of one thing. The something he'd been expecting had arrived.

"What is it now?" Ker hitched her pack a little higher on her shoulder and concentrated on putting one foot in front of the other.

"I'm not used to following you when we're out-of-doors," Tel said. "Usually, I'm the one with the good sense of direction. I've seen you get turned around in a hallway when you weren't Flashing."

"Very funny." Ker peered upward, but though she knew Weimerk flew above them, he was too high for her to see. "It's not really me you're following, and you know it."

"Sure. But I can't see him, can I? And Daughter knows, I can't *feel* him, or Flash him, or whatever it is you're doing."

"Still no excuse for you to be so grumpy."

Tel's pace, steady until now, skipped a step. Ker looked around at him. His brows were drawn down, but he wasn't frowning. "What is it?" she asked him in a totally different tone.

"I was just thinking how strange it is that I'm not grumpy at all, I'm not angry, or upset, or even much worried." He gave her a sidewise smile that brought an answering grin to her own lips. "I was just thinking that it's been a long time since it was just the two of us—I don't count him," he added as Ker opened her mouth to contradict him. "The griffin's not really here with us, even though he's here." Tel brushed her forehead with the tips of his fingers.

Ker looked away, but she nodded. She knew what he meant. It *had* been weeks since they'd been outside together alone.

The track they followed, once they'd left Luca with the Springs and Pools to decide which of them would go to the Mines, eventually met with a Polity road wide enough for five soldiers to march abreast. They were headed east, Tel had told her. East and a little north, and while snow dusted the road here and there, there wasn't as much as there had been when they'd first come out of the Mines. Their mules they'd left behind, where they'd be more useful to the Springers. Even mules didn't cover many more miles in a day than soldiers at a marching pace. And they couldn't be fed on snow.

"Do we take the road? It's going in the right direction." While in the Peninsula they'd avoided using roads whenever they could, for fear of running into Halian patrols. "In theory we should be safe. All the Halians are in the Peninsula."

"Not all," Tel reminded her. "Didn't my Faro tell us they'd landed in some other ports?"

"But that was to the west of here," she said. "This is the way the Panther Wing would have gone, either back to the far border of Polstef, or south and east to Juristand." Ker slowed again, and Tel slowed with her. "Tel, isn't there a Hall on this road?"

This time he frowned. "Yes," he said finally. "If I'm not completely turned around, and that's not likely, Descoria Hall should be about three days' march ahead of us." He looked sideways at her. "But you could check that, couldn't you?"

He meant she could Flash the road. Ker blew out her breath in a silent whistle. The last time she'd done that had been months ago, when they were on their way from their first encounter with the Feelers, she to Temlin Hall to join the Talents there and carry the news of the Halian invasion, Tel on his way to Oste, to rejoin the Bear Wing, and carry the same news.

Only the Halians had already found Temlin Hall, and burned it to the ground, killing everyone in it, Talent or not. That was how much they feared what they called "the magic of the body."

"I'm not saying you should do it," Tel said now.

"No," she said. When had she stopped walking? "You're right. I don't want to walk in on a bad surprise, and I certainly don't want to spend the next three days wondering what we're going to find. Better if we know now." Without giving herself a chance to change her mind, Ker pulled off her glove and placed her hand firmly on the roadbed, ignoring the chill of the frozen surface. *Paraste.*

Since the griffin gave her the ability to see auras, she could Flash people without touching them. But objects—and the Hall, and the road itself for that matter, weren't anything but big objects—she had to touch, just like any ordinary Talent.

<<What do you look for?>> Weimerk, as usual, had been alerted when she triggered her Talent.

<<I want to know if there's a Hall up ahead.>>

<<Ah.>>

Ker shook her head. Griffins had been the mythical tutors and mentors of advanced and powerful Talents, according to the stories. For centuries any such student was called "Griffin Class" and given early to the Inquisitors for special training. It puzzled her that Weimerk had always seemed bored by the idea of other Talents, showing no interest in finding or helping any of them.

<<I do not know them.>>

<<Would you *please* stop responding to my thoughts unless I'm actually speaking to you.>>

"Well? Is the Hall there?"

Cursing, Ker pulled her hand off the surface of the road and rubbed feeling back into it on the front of her tunic. "Yes, it is, as it happens. And the Panther Wing is there as well."

"That's good news, or isn't it?" Tel took her hand and began to rub it between his own. "Isn't your sister Faro of Panthers?"

"What? Yes, sorry. My oldest sister, Tonia." Except that Talents weren't supposed to have sisters. "It's just that Weimerk's always in my head, I've got no privacy." She shook her head. "You've no idea what it's like."

"Of course, I do. It's like being Flashed by a Talent, except all the time."

Ker blinked, lips parted. Did everyone feel that way about it? Tel grinned at her look and kissed her on the forehead. She pushed him off. She hated to be kissed on the forehead— which, of course, was why he did it.

It wasn't until they set up camp for the night, and the flickering light of the fire hid their faces that Ker felt comfortable enough to talk about it.

"I don't actually know what you're thinking," she said.

"I don't mind." Tel bumped her shoulder with his elbow.

"No, really, it's more like I know *you*, yourself. I know what you *would* think about something, not the thoughts themselves." *Necessarily.*

"That makes me feel *so* much better." He laughed and slipped his arm around her, hugging her close.

"I don't know how you can find it funny." But she relaxed into his embrace.

"After what Svann did to me, I find it wonderful." The laughter was gone, but he spoke calmly, easily. "You're not trying to change how I think or feel about anything or anyone. You just know *what* I think or feel. Really, it's almost comforting. And it's certainly easier than lying all the time, like the Halians do."

"What do you mean? How can they be lying all the time?"

"You know what I mean. Everyone tells certain kinds of lies. 'No, that tunic doesn't make you look fat,' or 'No one notices that you're losing your hair,' that kind of thing. But about important stuff, life-level important, there's never been any point in lying. Someone could always ask you to let a Talent check, so you might as well tell the truth to start with. I mean, most people wouldn't ask a Talent to find out if someone really did love them, but everyone knows that you could."

"That's funny. That occurred to me when we were with the Springers. How hard it must be to live never being sure what someone else really thought or meant. I never thought about how it made things different for us."

"Well, I think lots of people just never bothered with the big lies, you know, the 'I love you' lies." He rested his cheek on her hair. "You know how I feel, without my having to say it."

"Yes, well it can't come up that often," she pointed out. "'Talents do not live in the world,' remember?" She shivered, and Tel pulled her closer. She tried not to think about that. They were working to restore a world in which they couldn't be together. And now she had to meet with her sister—who she couldn't acknowledge. She pushed the thoughts away.

"But Talents must have fallen in love with Talents," Tel pointed out. "And if you think that no one in a Battle Wing ever fell in love with one of the Talents assigned to that Wing, then you don't know how the human heart works."

"Have it your way," she said. "Right now, this human heart wants to sleep."

But Ker found she couldn't fall asleep no matter what she'd told Tel. The presence of Weimerk above them meant they didn't have to keep watch, but she slid herself carefully out of the circle of Tel's arms and sat up, rubbing at her face, and particularly at the muscles around her eyes. She'd spent the whole day squinting at sunlight on the few patches of snow. Maybe it would be easier to travel at night. She reached out to Weimerk and was startled to find him asleep as well, drifting and floating on some updraft so far above them as to be almost in another world. She'd known that certain birds of prey could nap while floating on a thermal, but she'd never thought that applied to Weimerk even though he *was* half eagle. Though he slept, and didn't answer her, she felt his deep awareness of her. If she needed him, he would be awake, alert, and at her side almost before she could complete the thought.

She pulled out the small pouch she wore on a cord around her neck and let the jewel slide out onto her hand. The facets seemed as solid as the ground beneath her, but she knew that if she focused on them, she could make their pattern change. Her dream of helping jeweled people seemed farther away than ever. She wished she had more time to study, to practice. Svann had talked about the years of study it took to become a Shekayrin, study and discipline and practice—not unlike what Talents went through at Questin Hall.

Svann: Kerida Nast, is this you?

Ker dropped the jewel and had to fumble it out of the tangle of clothes in her lap before she heard the voice again.

Kerida: Svann?

Svann: This is extraordinary. It is the specialty of the Daisy Shekayrin to use the stone to communicate. I begin to think you must be the one the Prophecy speaks of.

Kerida: Never mind that. She turned the jewel over in her fingers, finally letting it lie flat on her palm, faceted side up. She spoke to it, and Svann's voice seemed to come from it, as if she heard it with her ears, and not with her mind. **How is this happening?**

Svann: I believe it may be due to your ability to mind-speak with the griffin. This may have opened those channels in your abilities which allow you to use the stone to

communicate. I could devise a series of tests which would clarify—

Kerida: Svann, maybe another time?

Svann: Of course, your pardon. But you must admit, it would be a fascinating study.

Kerida: How is everyone? Excited by the prospect of research, Svann would forget to tell her if the Mines were on fire.

Svann: Three new Talents, followers of Luca Pa'narion, have arrived. Otherwise, no losses since you left us. However, it now appears my former countrymen have finally realized that parties sent to the Pass do not return.

Kerida: Luca is on his way to you now with Feelers from the Springs and Pools. They should reach you soon.

Svann: So the Far-thinkers have told us. I hope the High Inquisitor will persuade the council to agree to my return to Gaena, before anyone should come looking for me. I have been gone more than a month, and while no one would expect me to communicate with the stone, neither have I sent any word to anyone. Indeed, my powers of communication are weak—this success must be to you alone, is it not fascinating? Barid may be sent with me.

Ker rolled her eyes. Typical of Svann to jump from topic to topic.

Kerida: Barid?

Svann: He has been restless since you refused him a soul stone. He asked the Time-seer to give him the stone Luca left in her keeping. I am afraid she laughed at him.

Kerida: She's just a child—at least when she's not seeing the future. Maybe Luca can sort this out. But is it even safe for you to go back?

Svann: Your concern is heartwarming, but do not fear for me. I am planning to tell them that I received information about a cache of jewels and went to investigate. In my excitement I neglected to send any messengers. I am a

Sunflower Shekayrin. We are known to become lost in our studies.

Kerida clapped her hand to her mouth before her laughter could wake Tel up.

Kerida: If you say so. You shouldn't go back alone.

Svann: No, no. That would seem very peculiar, would it not? As many as possible of the soldiers who accompanied me in the first instance should be with me, to lend verisimilitude to my story. They will all be blocked against other Shekayrin, of course.

Kerida: Run at the first sign of trouble.

Svann: That would be the plan. Was he laughing? **But it is possible that I would need to stay behind in captivity to give the others time to escape.** And he would do it, too. Ker saw that as clearly as if she were Flashing Svann directly. **Still, I believe Barid will be allowed to go with me, if only to ensure I do not go back to my old ways. Barid could Flash me whenever he feels the need.**

Kerida: I'm not sure how much help that will be. Barid would be more useful in the Mines. There's too much work for so few Talents, even if most of them are Griffin Class.

Svann: I feel sure all will be well.

Ker would feel better if it were Larin making that prediction.

Kerida: I'm afraid to let you go. What if we can't do this again?

Svann: Once is usually enough to establish the connection, though it will get stronger with use. I wish I were with you. I would see the Griffinhome.

Kerida: Maybe when all of this is over. Let me know when you reach Gaena.

Svann: As you wish.

Ker sat tapping the jewel to her lower lip for some time before finally putting it away. That was certainly interesting.

*   *   *

Ker related her conversation with Svann to Tel the next morning as they packed up their camp.

"Too bad you haven't learned how to use the jewel to push things away," Tel said as he watched large fat flakes drift steadily from the sky. "That would be a whole lot more useful right now than being able to tell Svann it's snowing here." He peered at her from behind snow-dusted lashes. "Do you think it might be worth a try?"

Ker sighed. "I didn't want to tell you, but I've already tried it." She also didn't want to tell him about the panic she'd felt when she'd dropped the jewel into the snow and couldn't find it until she Flashed for it. She'd been so shaken, she'd forgotten to use her Talent. "I couldn't keep it up for more than a few seconds at a time. We can't lose the road in any case," she added. "I can Flash that whenever we need to, and Weimerk can help us with directions if we need more than that."

"And where is he?"

"Above the storm."

Tel hefted his pack with a sigh. "Don't say it, I know. He can take you but not both of us.'"

The snow fell gently, and without wind, but it fell steadily, accumulating more quickly than Ker liked. Tel constantly stamped his feet, though they were snow-laden again in an instant.

Finally, Ker stopped, grabbing hold of Tel's sleeve when he didn't stop with her. "We can't keep this up," she said. "We may not get lost, but we'll wear ourselves out. Let's find a place to hole up and wait out the worst of it; at least we can take turns breaking trail for each other once the snow stops."

"If it ever stops," he said.

Ker triggered her Talent and focused on the sides of the road, searching for some copse of wood or a rock formation that might give them some shelter. She finally found what they were looking for several dozen spans farther along, where a shallow-rooted tree had fallen in some recent windstorm and now leaned, its branches intact, against an outcropping of rock.

"It's all rock here," she said, as they broke enough branches to allow them entry to the center of the tree, where it formed a canopy above them. "The tree couldn't put its roots down deep enough to survive the wind."

"We're lucky it's a pine tree." Tel grunted with the effort of weaving a branch into three others. "More coverage."

Ker nodded, not wasting any more breath. If she didn't sit down soon, she'd fall down. Mind-speaking to Svann during the night had exhausted her as much as a full day's worth of Flashing. And it would only get worse without proper training. Food would help, but all they had with them was the travel cake they'd brought from the Mines. The people of the Springs and Pools had offered them other food, but Ker would have been ashamed to take it from them.

It was a relief to sit quietly, feeling abused muscles relaxing as the wind picked up and the storm wailed around them. They were too well trained to fret over something they couldn't help. Both the Halls and the military taught a certain sense of fatalism, the patience to let go of the things they couldn't control.

"What about trying the jewel again?" Tel said.

Ker rolled her eyes. "Here I was thanking the Mother that neither of us was the type to get fidgety when we had nothing to do but wait."

"Just a suggestion." Tel grinned. "I could suggest other things, but I'm afraid you'll say it's too cold, or we're too tired."

"Well, *I'm* not too tired, and I should think we'd get warmer, wouldn't we?"

He smiled as he reached for her.

Sometime later, Ker wondered whether she should trigger her Talent, see if she could tell anything about the storm, but even as she thought of it, she fell asleep.

"Still snowing," Tel said, when Ker opened her eyes.

"It's so dark."

"I'd say the sun's gone down. The wind's picked up, and the temperature's dropping."

"That's good." Ker sat up. "If it gets cold enough, it should stop snowing all together."

"Sure, and we know how to keep warm."

Ker cuffed him with the back of her hand. "That's hard to do while we're taking turns breaking trail, which will also keep us warm. Give me a chance to see what I can Flash about the storm." *Paraste.*

At first, all Ker Flashed was the snow itself, where it turned from water to ice crystals at some unimaginable height. Weimerk's above that, she thought. He's higher than the storm.

<< If you require my assistance, I will come.>>

<<Nothing you can do here, unless you want to come and brush away snow from the road.>> A shudder was all she got in response. Chuckling to herself, imagining the griffin shaking snow off his great paws like any cat, Ker returned her attention to the world immediately around them.

Colors Flashed out at her from the direction of the road. "Tel! There are people out there, in the storm. They've wandered off the road."

Tel was up on his knees, uncovering the entrance to their shelter when he stopped and looked at her. "Halians?"

She shook her head. "They're Panthers, five of them. One of them is injured, not seriously, just a sprained ankle, but he's having trouble walking and is slowing the others down."

"They'll leave him behind," Tel said. "They'll have to."

Ker squeezed Tel's arm. He'd been injured and left behind himself once and might easily have died from his infected wound if Ker hadn't come along. He still didn't talk about it much, even though he didn't blame the soldiers who had left him. They had done the right thing.

She pulled on the cloak she'd been using as a blanket.

"They've lost the road," she told him. "If they don't find it again before the snow stops, none of them may live to find it." She felt Tel straighten, his muscles tense. "We have to go out for them," she said.

"Right." Tel pulled his own cloak out from under them. "You'll have to Flash us there and back again. It'll be crowded, but at least the Panthers will be safe."

Ker wriggled her way through the embrace of branches and out into the storm. She almost turned back as the full force of the wind-driven snow struck her in the face. She felt Tel take her hand and, shutting her eyes, she began to lead the way back to the road, using only her Talent, and the illumination her aura gave her. From the road, the Panthers would be easier to reach.

Ironically, it wasn't until they reached the road that Ker slipped and fell. Tel hauled her back to her feet and hugged her for a moment. She clung to the front of his cloak and realized that he was praying under his breath. "Listen to him, Mother, Daughter, and Son," she whispered herself. "Help us now." She patted him with both hands, then pushed him gently away. Taking his right hand once again in her left, she set off in the direction of the stranded Panthers.

"Start calling," she said over her shoulder as they got nearer. If there was one thing that the military did better than the Halls, it was voice training. Officers needed to be heard over distances, something rarely true for Talents. "Let them know we're close."

"Panthers!" What she knew to be Tel's best bellow seemed unlikely to penetrate the sounds made by the storm. "Panthers! Sing out!"

They kept moving, and Tel kept calling at intervals, and finally there came an answering shout.

"Stay where you are," Tel bellowed. "We'll come to you."

It was likely that only strict military discipline prevented the stranded Panthers from disobeying and coming through the snow on the run—and likely getting themselves into worse trouble. As it was, they were almost stepping on the soldiers before the Panthers even knew they were there.

"Save it," Tel said, as one of the Panthers started to identify herself. "We'll get you back to our shelter first."

Getting them back was far more trouble than finding them. Ker could still Flash the route clearly, but even in this short a time the wind had started to fill in their tracks, and they had almost to break the trail a second time. The injured soldier still had trouble, and it was so awkward for two of the others to give him a seat on their crossed hands that Tel finally picked the man up and slung him over his shoulder. With one hand to hold the man in place, he still had one to give Ker. The injured soldier himself reached out a hand to those following.

After what seemed an eternity they reached the fallen pine. Tel sank to his knees under the man he carried, unable to take another step. The injured man, easily the freshest of them all, eagerly helped enlarge the shelter enough for them all to squeeze in. Tel took out his glow stone and set it at his feet, muffled with a corner of his cloak.

"Thank you," a woman's voice came out of the dimness, once the panting and huffing and puffing had subsided. "How did you do that?"

"I'm a Talent," Ker said. "I could Flash the pathway."

"Huh. Well, thank you, Talent. I didn't know you people could do such things."

"It doesn't come up all that often," Tel said. "And not all Talents are as good at it as Kerida—Talent Nast, is."

"Nast? Then you must be—" The woman's voice stopped abruptly. The Faro of Panthers was Tonia Nast, Kerida's oldest half-sister. But as Talents did not live in the world, they no longer had any family outside the Halls of Law, and it was highly incorrect for anyone to suggest that they did.

"Thank you, Talent," the woman said again. "I'm Rascat Skyfeather, Barrack Leader, Red Company, Ruby Cohort of

Panthers, though I guess I don't need to tell *you* that. These others are part of my barrack. We were scouting to the west when the storm hit, and we thought we could keep ahead of it. We were wrong, and lucky that you people were here."

"I'm Tel Cursar," Tel said. "Third Officer, Black Company, Emerald Cohort of Bears." He hesitated, but he knew that he had to say something if he didn't want to raise even more questions. "We're on assignment from my Faro."

"If you've a ways to go yet," the Barrack Leader said. "You'll be able to rest a bit at the Hall. We've camped there, watching the road. Uh—" She cleared her throat. "You might be interested to hear that our Faro is with us."

Ker kept her face still and her breathing steady. Of course, her older sister would be with her Battle Wing. She might even have news of her other half-sister, Ester—or their parents. *If* Tonia agreed to see her. In any case, it might be best not to— She took a deep breath, and she felt Tel's long fingers wrap completely around her wrist.

"What we're interested in," she said, "is whether you have anything to eat besides travel cake."

With everyone taking it in turn to carry the injured man or break trail, it still took them three more days to reach the Hall.

Descoria Hall was much smaller than Questin, where Talents from all over the Polity and beyond had come to be trained, before the Halians burned it to the ground. It was smaller even than Temlin Hall, which Ker had seen only in ruins. This part of New Province was sparsely populated compared to the Peninsula and wouldn't warrant a permanently occupied Hall of Law. Descoria would be a place where traveling Talents—and others who had permission—would put up while using the road.

The two-story, timber-framed building had strong wooden shutters but no glass windows. The Halls of Law would have contracted with local farmers to keep Descoria supplied and in repair. There was a rough stable that would hold no more than five horses, but there'd be no gardens, no fruit trees, nothing that would require residential care.

Once or twice Tel had hinted to Rascat Skyfeather that he and Ker could be on their way much faster by themselves, but each time the Barrack Leader had countered his hint by pointing out that with more of them to break trail on the road they were making decent time, or that without the Talent, there was the possibility the Panthers would lose themselves again. Technically, Tel outranked Skyfeather, but the Panthers outnumbered them. Ker was just as happy that Tel didn't put his authority to the test, once it became obvious that the Barrack Leader wanted them to accompany her. The last thing she wanted was to be delivered to her sister as a captive.

<<Skyfeather is a good name. A good omen.>>

<<I'm glad you think so.>>

<<Do not fear, Kerida, my heart. I will come for you if the Panthers think to keep you.>>

<<What about Tel?>>

There was a longer pause than she was used to having in her mental conversations with the griffin. <<I could return for him once you were safe.>>

Ker took a deep breath. <<We'll keep that in mind.>>

From the look of the encampment around the Hall, at least three cohorts were here to support their Faro. They were welcomed with enthusiasm when they reached the perimeter guard. Medics were summoned to deal with the injured man, and Ker and Tel were passed along with an escort almost before Rascat Skyfeather could thank them again.

The camp was set up along the same lines as any permanent Wing camp or fort. A main track leading to the Hall building was surrounded by the tents of the soldiers. Snow had been removed or covered over with branches to improve the footing.

"I don't like the look you have on your face," Tel said out of the corner of his mouth "What are you thinking?"

Ker shrugged. "Easy in, but not so easily out. Griffin or no griffin."

"The Faro's quartered in the Hall building," their escort said, once they'd passed through most of the camp. "Faro's kept our Talents with us, so I'm not sure what room there is. Not to worry, though, Talent Nast. I'm sure some junior officer will get turfed out, so you'll get a bed."

Ker exchanged a look with Tel. Neither of them had expected to run into other Talents.

"Thank you, but I'd just as soon stay with my escort, if it's all the same," she said.

"I'm sure that could be arranged, if you don't mind sharing a tent." The Barrack Leader didn't sound convinced.

"Until not long ago, I shared a dormitory with twenty other Candidates," Ker said. "A tent with only a Barrack to share with will feel like luxury."

66 $\mathbf{H}$ONORED One, I am Horse Captain Inurek Star, chief
of your personal guard."

The man's use of the old-style title rather than the Halian
rank of Tekla, told Baku immediately that here was one of the
new traditionalists, those among her brother's people who re-
vered the old nomadic days before the Horsemen reached the
Halian Empire and made it their own. That and the smell.
Tradition had it that their nomadic forebears had only bathed
in the warmer months, so these new horsemen would be deliberately unwashed until the spring.

"Greetings, Horse Captain. I trust I do not take you from
your duties?"

"It is our privilege to guard and escort the sister of the Lord
of Horses." Inurek Star and the two men with him all bowed
in the direction of the chest that held the Voice of the Emperor.

That was unexpected. At home—in Halia—even the new
traditionalists referred to her brother as the Sky Emperor.

Why should they feel freer to pursue their eccentricity here? "You are here to escort me to the public audience room?"

"We are, Honored One."

"Very well. You may proceed."

Any other time Baku would have found the manner of her escort amusing. Her guard walked three before and three behind, and while alert and evidently ready to draw their weapons at any provocation, they walked like horsemen, swaggering, proud, defiant, and looking every man in the eye.

At the moment, however, while she welcomed the distraction they afforded her, they were not enough to make her forget what was ahead. She had formally met her husband, the Luqs of Farama, in the council room on the previous afternoon. The marriage documents had been read aloud there. She was hearing them for the first time and had been a little unnerved to hear herself referred to constantly as "the Princess Imperial" as if she had no name of her own. Even knowing it was the traditional form of such documents had not helped. Yesterday, every attendant in her entourage had witnessed the ceremony, but only Narl accompanied her today, walking immediately behind her left elbow. Inurek Star and his men led them into a room somewhat larger than the council chamber, but here there were no rugs, just a polished wood floor decorated by a pattern of inset tiles. Her escort walked her across to the consort's chair and arranged themselves behind and to the side.

"Am I ever going to see you without the veils?" Dern Firoxi's conversational tone surprised her. She had expected something more aloof.

Baku wore the informal silver-embroidered overveil, covering a new gown with divided skirts that Narl had had created for her overnight. "Of course, my lord Luqs, but in privacy." She mentally reviewed the number of veils she had brought with her. She would be more often in public now than she had been since childhood.

"Oh, yes, that's right. They told me." The man looked around him with one eyebrow raised. "Well, I don't know what it was like in the Emperor's court, my dear, but here you'd better watch your step."

Baku straightened. She couldn't tell from his dry tone, but was he threatening her? He might be Luqs, but as the Princess Imperial, she was more important to the Halians present than he. Inurek Star might not care about her as a person, but he would defend the sister of the Horse Lord to the death. She wished now that she had not listened to Narl's advice to leave the mask behind.

Then she saw Dern Firoxi stiffen, and she realized it was not he that should concern her.

The Shekayrin who strode into the audience room at this moment was not a tall man, but his manner made him seem so. Somehow, the mage's dark red hair looked bloodier than was natural, and his long blue tunic bluer, leeching what little color there was from the walls. As he came nearer, Baku made out the poppy on his tunic front, and tattooed around his eye. She had never seen him before. Until now, there had only been Rose and Daisy Shekayrin around her. It had been a Poppy Shekayrin who had examined her for her brother, who had netted her. Baku was glad that her veils covered her involuntary shiver, and her glance toward Inurek Star standing to her left, his arms crossed in front of him.

The Poppy came directly to them, speaking to Dern Firoxi first. "Most of the cases this morning are of no consequence. You may address them as you please. In the matter of the inheritance of Kennaru Holding, you should decide in favor of the uncle."

The instruction did not surprise Baku; after all, clerks and aides were employed precisely to free judges—including the Emperor—from having to research the cases and petitions themselves. But that it was a Poppy, and not a Daisy or a Rose, that *was* unusual. And his tone—no one, not even a

Shekayrin—would dare to use such a tone to the Sky Emperor. She clasped her hands together under the veils.

She had not thought she could sit up any straighter, but when the Poppy turned his eyes—incongruously, the pleasing color of dark chocolate—on her, she felt her spine stiffen. She wished she had not done it, but it seemed the mage took no notice. She expected him to introduce himself and was further taken aback when he addressed her with no courtesy at all.

"I've heard about the nonsense at the dock when you arrived. It's embarrassing that a Shekayrin should be so superstitious about some trifle of uncivilized barbarians. Don't expect a repetition."

Without turning her head, Baku glanced at the man who was Luqs. Dern Firoxi looked away, toward the door, as if he were absorbed in thought—but the tension in his jaw showed he pretended.

"You will address the sister of the Lord of Horses with more respect." Inurek Star spoke, smiling, and it was not a smile Baku would have liked aimed at her.

The Poppy inclined his head to the Horse Captain in a shallow bow, more than he had offered her or the Luqs. "As you say, Tekla."

Which was not in any way an apology, or an earnest of future improvement. He turned back to Dern Firoxi. "The first petitioner will be sent in, my lord Luqs." The mage turned on his heel and left as quickly as he had come.

Baku should have been frightened; she knew that was the Poppy's intention, but she felt nothing but anger, hot and furious.

"You did very well. It's best not to provoke him when you can avoid it."

"I see." She did not trouble to hide her scorn.

The Luqs turned and looked at her fully for the first time. His gaze was calculating, but not unfriendly. "How old are you?"

Baku could think of nothing more irrelevant, but she had no reason to refuse an answer. "I have almost fourteen years."

"Thirteen. Huh. Then I shouldn't have to tell you what Poppy Shekayrin are best at—and what they aren't best at. If Pollik Kvar decides you're not cooperating, he'll mind-bend you, or whatever it is you people call it. And it's the Sunflowers who are best at that, not the Poppies. With Poppies, it's like cutting meat with a hammer, instead of a knife. Do you understand me? It isn't just that you'll think and act however he wants you to, it's that his work is so clumsy it damages your mind, damage that might never be undone. You'd lose your real self forever."

He waited, but Baku had no idea how to respond. It had been a Poppy who netted her. Was that the explanation of the headache and fogginess? But they were fading now, weren't they?

"I know it probably goes against the grain to be polite to the man, but at the very least, if you can stay yourself, there's hope." His smile at these words was painful to see. "Who knows, Kvar might be reassigned."

"I thank you for your counsel," she said as loudly as her tight throat would allow. *Never leave the mask behind again*, she told herself. *Never.*

Whatever furniture had been in the room originally was gone. Three years away from her own military life, Ker still recognized the portable furniture packed and carried by a Battle Wing Faro from camp to camp, ready to be set up in any command tent in any field. Faro Tonia Nast's desk, chairs, and benches, while just as foldable as any Ker had ever seen, were more expensive, made up of a variety of woods, some of them a dark purple in color, with intricate inlays around the edges of the desk. Matching stools and benches were padded with both leather and silk cushions.

Tonia Nast, Faro of Panthers, sat behind her camp desk, leaning back in the only proper chair, studying a scroll she held unrolled in both hands. Her dark hair seemed more gray-streaked than Ker remembered, but then, she realized with a shock, she hadn't seen her oldest sister in more than five years. It had been from the tent of her other half-sister Ester, Ruby Cohort Leader of Eagles, that the Halls of Law had taken her when her Talent had been discovered.

"Third Officer, you are out of uniform."

"Yes, Faro." Tel didn't sound worried.

Was it possible? Was that a twitching in the corners of Tonia's lips? Her blue eyes still scanned the scroll in her hands, and Ker realized that Tonia used it as an excuse not to look up. Not to look at *her*. Suddenly, her chest felt tight, and Ker blinked. She couldn't even take Tel's hand to comfort herself.

"Please elaborate."

"For the first part of our assignment, we accompanied the Talent High Inquisitor Luca Pa'narion to some contacts of his. He decided we'd be better off wearing civilian clothing."

"In order not to frighten the 'contacts,' or because you weren't sure who had control of the lands you had to pass through?"

"A little of both, Faro."

"And you, Candidate?"

Tonia still didn't look up, but at least now she was speaking directly to her.

"Talent, Faro of Panthers. The Talent High Inquisitor Luca Pa'narion has passed me as a Full Talent."

At that, Tonia almost looked up. Instead, she frowned, narrowing her eyes to better focus on the scroll. "And you are also not in uniform. For the same reasons?"

"Yes, Faro. As well as the added danger of being captured by the Halians while dressed as a Talent."

"Understood." Tonia let the scroll roll shut but chose and opened another without looking up. Ker was developing an itch between her eyebrows, and another between her shoulder blades.

"I have received messengers from the Faro of Bears, telling me that Jerek Brightwing has been acclaimed Luqs, and also of the presence of certain"—her glance flicked up at Tel and back again—"allies, in the mines of the Serpents Teeth. Can either of you confirm this of your own knowledge?" Tonia kept her eyes firm on Tel, who licked his lips and glanced sideways at Ker.

"I confirm both statements," Ker said.

"Your witness as a Talent?"

"Yes, Faro." A Talent's witness held good in any part of the Polity, and in many of their allied or even enemy countries as well.

Now Tonia set down the second scroll and leaned forward until she could put both elbows on the edge of her camp desk. "And I take it that your present assignment involves more than bringing me this confirmation, or any other message from the Faro of Bears?"

"No, Faro. I mean, yes, Faro." Tel raised one hand and let it fall again without saying anything more.

Tonia waited and when Tel remained silent, she sighed, all the time careful not to look at Ker. "Please tell me what your assignment is."

"We've been sent to a valley in the Duralla mountain range," Tel said. "We expect to enlist other allies in an assault against the Halians' Shekayrin."

One of Tonia's aides leaned forward and murmured in her ear. She gave a short nod and waved him back. "I am reminded that there is no known valley in the Duralla range. Those mountains are inaccessible. Natives, such as there are, call them 'The Pillars of the World.'"

Tel shot Ker another glance from under his brows. *Your turn,* he seemed to be saying. And it was true; anything to do with griffins was more the territory of Talents or Feelers than military people.

"They are not inaccessible to griffins, Faro," Ker said.

"Griffins?" This time Tonia did look directly at her, if only for a split-second. "You are telling me there are griffins in the Duralla Mountains."

"That is what we have been told, yes."

"By some of your new allies?"

"Yes, Faro." Ker wasn't sure what made her keep Weimerk's existence to herself, but in the next few minutes she was glad she did, when a tap at the door revealed as it opened a young soldier, red-faced with annoyance.

"Pardon me, my Faro, but Talent Setasan insists on being admitted."

Tonia Nast shut her eyes and, without opening them, said, "Then have her enter, by all means."

The Talent must have been standing right behind the young soldier because she was in the room practically before Tonia finished speaking.

As soon as she saw her, Ker's heart sank. The Talent was a small woman, shorter than Ker herself, and considerably older; so old, in fact, that Ker would have assumed she'd retired to a permanent Hall long ago. The lines of her face were the kind that showed she scowled a lot and didn't smile much. Maybe no permanent Hall would accept her.

Ker made sure her flicker of amusement didn't show on her face.

"Faro Nast, I must protest." Sure enough, the old woman's tone revealed a touch of satisfaction that she was able to make a complaint. "Why was I not informed immediately that a Talent had arrived?"

"Evidently, you *were* informed." Ker knew her sister well enough to know that Tonia also fought to keep a smile off her face.

"That is not the point. As senior Talent to the Panthers, I should have been present from the start. If I have been correctly 'informed,'" she said, wrinkling her nose, "the Talent has come from the Peninsula, and therefore has important matters to report."

"Do you?" Tonia turned to Ker and raised her eyebrows.

"I don't know," Ker said. "I wasn't sent here to report to anyone. In fact, I wasn't sent here at all."

"Nonsense. You must tell me immediately what you know of the events following the Halian invasion. How do the Halls fare?"

This time Ker raised her eyebrows. "And you are?"

The old woman opened and shut her mouth several times. Ker hoped she hadn't given her a seizure.

"As you have no doubt heard, I am Talent Setasan." That the old woman introduced herself the old-fashioned way, by her surname only, told Ker all she needed to know.

"I am Talent Kerida," she said. Instinct told her not to let this woman know that she and Tonia were related. "Though I wasn't sent here to report to you, I will tell you as a courtesy that all the Halls in the Peninsula have been destroyed."

Ker couldn't tell if Setasan got any paler, but the jump of the tiny muscle near the woman's jaw showed that she'd clenched her teeth.

"All? Even Questin?"

"I saw Questin burning with my own eyes as I fled from the Halians." Ker swallowed. She'd let the Daughter turn her green before she'd go into details.

"You are a Candidate, then, not a Full Talent." If ever a tone said "I thought so" this one did.

"I am a Full Talent, examined and passed by the High Inquisitor Luca Fanon Pa'narion."

More lip pressing. "You saw Questin burning? But you did not see it burned? It may have been saved after you . . . fled."

Ker might have gone on being polite if it wasn't for that pause. "Listen, you old hen. Inquisitor Pa'narion saw the place in ruins, burned to the ground and the stones pulled apart. It's gone: all the teachers, all the books, all the artifacts. Gone."

The old woman put out her hand to save herself from falling, and Tel stepped forward, catching her by the forearm and elbow. He gave Ker a look that she acknowledged with the slightest of shrugs. She'd had months to come to terms with the loss of the training Hall; this woman had only just learned of it.

After a few minutes Setasan jerked her arm away from Tel without thanking him, and Ker felt less guilty. "Then there are only a few of us left," the old woman said, half to herself. "The travelers in the outer provinces, and the Talents with the Battle Wings." She drew herself up. "I shall certainly not allow you to go traipsing around the countryside like this. You are far too valuable to risk in such a way. You will stay with us. I don't know what Pa'narion was thinking."

Ker was speechless, but luckily the Faro of Panthers was not. "No doubt he was thinking that as a High Inquisitor, his decisions would be respected, and his orders would be carried out." Only the blandness of Tonia's tone kept the words from being a challenge.

"I'm not at all certain that this young Talent has given us an accurate account of Pa'narion's orders. She should be examined." As she turned toward Ker, Tel put himself between them. Ker put a calming hand on his shoulder.

This wasn't something that could worry her. She'd long ago been taught blocks that were impenetrable by any but the most powerful Talent, and if that wasn't enough, she thought she could use her aura or the jewel to protect her. But she wasn't going to allow this woman to bully her. Tel's instinct to protect her was right.

"Talent Setasan can't examine me without my consent," she said. "Only the Inquisition can compel other Talents."

"Nonsense!" Setasan said again. "I am senior to you, and I insist."

"You are *older* than I am," Ker said. "But since we're both Full Talents, you're not senior."

"This is an outrage." The old woman spoke through clenched teeth, but there was nothing she could do, and everyone knew it. "Then I shall examine the soldier."

Except for that.

"I'm afraid I couldn't allow that." Tonia seemed to be the only one still calm. "He's not one of my Panthers, and I'd have to answer to the Faro of Bears if I order her Third Officer to submit to examination. After all, what grounds could I give? There's no criminal case to resolve. There's nothing here but your curiosity."

"I see." The old woman looked them all in the face, as if expecting more defiance. "You will hear more about this, Faro of Panthers." And she pushed her way out as abruptly as she'd come in.

"I wonder who she thinks she's going to report me to?" Tonia said. "So," she added in a much brisker tone. "One Talent and one junior officer are all Juria Sweetwater could spare to find and recruit these . . . griffins?"

"The Bears are low on numbers, and we've been quite successful in previous assignments," Tel answered.

"Of course. It was you who found the Luqs, then?"

"Ker did, yes. That is, Talent Nast."

The Faro of Panthers nodded, leaning back again in her chair. "You've given me much to think about, Third Officer Cursar. I'm not at all convinced I shouldn't lend you half a Barrack or so to help you keep the Talent safe. In the meantime, see the camp commander for a billet. You will be given a room here, of course, Talent." Tonia avoided saying her name aloud. At one time, Ker had hoped to be one of the Talents assigned to the Battle Wings. This reminded her why that would never have happened. Between her sisters, some cousins, and two aunts, too many of her family were still in active service.

"If I may, Faro. Third Officer Cursar is my official escort. I would prefer to keep him with me." And what a Talent preferred was, generally speaking and under the Law, what a Talent got.

"I see. Then he will have to be billeted with you. Unker, see to these arrangements, will you?"

"At once, my Faro." The junior officer who had whispered in her ear left, closing the door gently behind him.

"That will be all, Third Officer. Talent, thank you for your report and assistance." This time Tonia looked Ker straight in the face and raised her right eyebrow, while winking with her left eye. She was the only one in the family who could do both simultaneously, and Ker used to beg her to do it whenever Tonia was home on leave, it gave such a comical cast to her sister's otherwise solemn face. For Tonia to do it now sent a rush of warmth right through Ker's body. Her sister had acknowledged her in the most discreet yet tender way. Ker felt just as she had as a child. That everything would be all right.

"How do you know she'll come?" Tel asked, from where he'd sprawled on the bed. They'd been given a simple cell, suitable for any traveling Talent carrying only a pack of clothing. A cot had already been added to the room, so they hadn't turfed out just one officer, but two.

"Because she's right outside the door." Ker got to her feet. Now for the real meeting.

The latch lifted, and Tonia Nast entered the room, barefoot despite the cold, and dressed in an old shirt and loose trousers— exactly the kind of thing Ker could remember her sister sleeping in at home. Tel was on his feet so fast Ker hadn't seen him move.

Tonia smiled at her; without knowing she meant to, Ker threw her arms around her and buried her face in her sister's neck. Tonia smelled of lavender, and the scent brought back enough memories that Ker had to blink back tears. Finally, she stepped away, though her sister kept her hands resting on Ker's shoulders.

"Well, little cat." Tonia cleared her throat, and this time Ker blinked faster. Her older sisters had called her "little cat" since she started walking. "Mother and Daughter both must be smiling on us."

"Is there any news?"

Tonia's face stiffened and relaxed so quickly Ker couldn't be sure she'd seen it. "The last I heard, our father and grandmother were well, and your mother was well and busy." Ker's mother was their father's second wife. "But that was months ago. And of Ester . . ." Tonia fell silent.

Ker nodded. There hadn't been any news of surviving Eagles since the Halians had overrun the Peninsula. "Do you have anything that belongs to them? A lock of hair or . . ." Ker's voice died away as Tonia shook her head.

"Could you Flash something from such a thing?" she asked. "Your Talent must be Griffin Class, then." Tonia smiled. "'Nasts are always in the first rank.'" Ker laughed. Tonia's imitation of their grandmother was perfect.

"You going to tell people you were sleepwalking?" Ker said, still smiling. "Where's your escort?"

Tonia sat on the bed, pulling Ker down next to her, and linking arms. "While it's true that a Faro is never— technically— alone, who can stop me wandering around my own camp if I feel like it? And which of the people who share my quarters would be surprised if I visit my sister the Talent, while she's in said camp, under my roof, and in the middle of the night when everyone can claim to be asleep?"

"The Talents would know." And that old woman would love to find her breaking the rules.

"My people are prepared to face that, but what Talent will ask them? After all, it's *you* who'll get into trouble with your superiors for talking to *me*." Tonia tilted her head to look sideways at Tel where he stood by the door. "And you vouch for this soldier."

It hadn't really been a question, but Ker answered it all the same. "I do."

Tonia looked from her to Tel and back again, eyebrows lifted. "So, there really are Feelers, and there really is a griffin." Tonia shook her head, half-grinning, clearly not expecting an answer. "We live in the age of myths, apparently." She looked sharply at Tel and then back to Ker. "I take it this is not general knowledge among Bears?"

"The full extent of the Feelers' Gifts isn't completely known, no," Ker said. "As far as the soldiers are concerned, we've been emphasizing the Gifts that have an obvious military application: Lifting, or Moving as some of us call it, and Far-seeing."

"And the ones you don't emphasize?"

"Far-thinking and Mind-healing. People are going to be afraid that their thoughts are being read without their consent, even when you explain that's not how it works. Some are made so nervous by the idea that even the sworn word of a Talent won't convince them. For that reason, we're being a lot quieter about those two Gifts."

"I can see how you'd have to be. I'm not sure I'm happy about it myself."

"But if I may, Faro," Tel put in. "Far-thinkers are such a valuable aid to long-distance communications that they're almost as important militarily as Lifters and Far-seers."

"Ah, I hadn't thought about that. Are there many of them? Could there be one with each Faro, for example, for communications between Battle Wings? Or, more useful perhaps, would be to have one with each Cohort within a Wing." Her gaze narrowed while she worked this out.

"I don't think there's enough of them," Ker said. "And besides, there's a limit to the distance their Gift will span. Right now, for example, we're using the griffin as a relay. There doesn't seem to be any limit on how far his Gifts will reach."

"'We?' You're not speaking just of the Bears and their allies. When you say 'we,' you are speaking directly of yourself. Are you telling me that *you* can Far-think?"

"Only with the griffin," Ker shrugged.

"Oh, of course, 'only with the griffin.' Should that reassure me? Does that mean my sister *isn't* turning into a Feeler, as well as being a Talent?"

"That's not what's happening at all. I can Far-think with Weimerk because of a special connection he and I have, not because I'm becoming a Feeler. That's not even possible."

"If you had asked me two months ago whether the existence of Feelers and griffins was possible, I'd have said it wasn't," Tonia pointed out. She leaned forward, elbows on knees, tapping her lips with her clasped hands. Then she sat up again. "Kerida, why am I here?"

"To speak to me?"

"No, not why am I here in this room." Tonia's smile brought out the laugh lines in her face. "Why am I here in Descoria Hall, with the better part of three Cohorts camped in tents around me? Why am I not in Juristand?"

Ker shook her head, then glanced at Tel with eyebrows raised. She hadn't thought on this level of military strategy in years. Juristand was the second city of the Polity, after Farama the Capital. It had started out as the farthest outpost to the east, a military camp, and then a fort, and then a town, and finally the center for day-to-day administration for what became the eastern provinces. With the loss of the Peninsula, it had become the gathering point for Battle Wing Faros.

"You're keeping options open," Tel said, his voice almost too quiet to be heard. "As long as you're not in Juristand, you don't have to decide whether you accept the Bears' acclamation of Jerek as Luqs. You don't have to commit yourself."

"I'm not committing anyone else either," Tonia said quietly. "With Juria Sweetwater in the Mines of the Serpents Teeth, me here, and Arrian Xent with his Wing in Ma'lakai, we can argue there is no quorum of Faros in Juristand. No official decision will be made to declare this boy as Luqs, but he can't be rejected either."

"You're going to wait and see what happens." Ker didn't trouble to hide her disappointment. "But, don't you see, your support could make all the difference. Once we stop the Shekayrin, you could easily retake the Peninsula with both the Bears and the Panthers."

"And when will that be? Do you see the position the rest of us are in? Most of the other Faros haven't had any direct contact with these mages—"

"That you know of," Tel broke in. "Feelers and Talents may not be able to manipulate people's thoughts, but Shekayrin can. They can change someone's loyalties or make them blindly loyal. Some are better at it than others, but most can do something. I've seen this with my own eyes."

Ker kept herself from looking at Tel. No point in making Tonia worried about him.

"And you're suggesting, Third Officer Cursar, that some of these changed minds are in Juristand right now?"

"The orders to abandon the Peninsula came very quickly, didn't they?"

"I may believe you, but others won't." She nodded and took a deep breath. "These allies you're going to now, they'll help you against the Shekayrin?"

"That's what we're hoping, yes. The Shekayrin also have a mythology about griffins, and it's possible that knowing the griffins are with us will be enough to make at least some of them withdraw from the conflict. Without the mages, the regular Halian army will be vulnerable to ordinary warfare. And, who knows, if we could at least establish some diplomatic channels, we might be able to do something besides kill people." Ker waited.

"It's too bad you weren't able to tell me all this before," Tonia said finally. "As things stand right now, I'll either have to stop you from going or send a large force with you. Either way, things won't work out the way you want them to."

"But, Tonia—"

"Relax, I'm not planning to do either. The trick is how to arrange for your escape from the middle of my camp. I should have insisted on your having a tent. You'd have had a better chance of sneaking away than you will from inside these walls."

"There is a way." Ker looked at Tel. "A daring daylight escape."

"Not for both of us," he said, understanding her right away. "Lucky you don't need me."

Oh, yes, I need you. From the look in his eye it was as if he'd heard her. "No, I guess not," she said aloud.

"Are you two going to tell me what you're talking about?"

"The griffin," they both said at once.

Larin laid the Luqs of Swords down on the Talent of Swords and sat back, wriggling on her stool and laughing.

"No one is this lucky." Jak Gulder tossed his cards down on the tabletop, chalking the new score on the slate next to his right hand.

Jerek grinned. He had his three tricks and so was safe. Larin had taken her last—and winning—trick from Jak Gulder. Jak was looking better, though according to other Bears, the former Kaltor still wasn't completely himself. He'd been jeweled by a Poppy Shekayrin and turned into an enemy, just like Tel, before Svann had brought them both to the Mines. Kerida Nast had been able to restore Tel completely, but Jak hadn't been so lucky. Errinn Mind-healer said that maybe he'd been turned too long to ever return fully to his former self, but Jerek still had hopes. If Jak couldn't be cured, what did that mean for all the others in the Peninsula who'd been jeweled much longer, some of them for years?

Jerek swept up the cards and squared them. "My turn to deal," he said as he shuffled.

"Do you think she's cheating by looking into the future, seeing what cards are coming?" Jak's smile didn't quite reach his eyes. He gripped the edge of the table abruptly, almost as if he was losing his balance. Then he relaxed.

"I don't see what else it could be. She's not old enough to be so good."

"It's rude to talk as if I'm not here." Larin's voice suddenly sounded like someone's old granny. Even her face took on a tougher, more angled look.

"Well, actually, Ara, you're not here."

The strange semblance of another, older woman faded away. Larin fell into a fit of giggles.

"Can you really hear her?" Jak looked from Jerek to Larin and back again. "The old Time-seer?"

"Most of the time, yes. I can't see her, not really, though Kerida says she can."

"That's 'cause you aren't the Griffin Girl." Larin made a dealing motion with her hands. "Jak Gulder, were you a better card player before the Shekayrin jeweled you?"

Jerek paused with only three cards dealt out. Everyone was used to Larin and her abrupt statements, but this cut a little close to the bone. At the same time, he was curious; what would Jak's answer be?

The older man frowned, his eyebrows drawing together. A look of uncertainty passed across his face. "I'm not sure. I think so, but . . ."

Larin hopped off her chair and ran around the table to pat Jak on the knee. "Don't worry, Jak Gulder. You'll have to be in a different time, but you'll be better again."

"Was it something you saw?"

Larin never answered that kind of question directly, but before Jerek could step in, the little girl unexpectedly spoke up. "It was, it is. But I won't play cards with you after that."

"I'll try to bear up under the disappointment." Jak smiled.

A woman wearing the colors of the Opal Cohort appeared in the doorway from the anteroom. "Your pardon, lord Luqs. Errinn Mind-healer's come for the Kaltor." Soldiers in the Bear Wing still gave Jak his rank, though he no longer had any duties, not even the administrative ones that Kaltors—usually from high noble families who wanted their offspring to get some military service—usually fulfilled.

Jak rose to his feet. "Coming, Commander. With your permission, my lord," he bowed to Jerek, "My lady," and to Larin.

Jerek watched him walk out of the room, trembling ever so slightly, like a much older man.

"Did you really see him back to his old self?"

"'Course I did. I thought *you* listened to me. I thought you weren't like the rest of them." Larin's lower lip popped out a little, but her eyes sparkled with mischief.

"Of course, I do. You know you can count on me." Jerek winked at her, and Larin winked back. What must it be like, he thought. Did she just see things, or did she occupy different times simultaneously, as Kerida thought? Only Ganni Lifter and Hitterol Mind-healer seemed completely comfortable in her presence. *And I thought I had it rough.*

"That's right, so that's why I'm giving you this." Larin was wearing a small pouch attached to the sash belting in her tunic, just like a grownup would. From it, she took out what was unmistakably an inactive jewel.

"Where did you get that?"

"From Luca." Larin gave him a look that plainly said: "You idiot." "Kerida needs it. You give it to Tel Cursar, and he'll give it to her. She'll know what to do."

Jerek accepted it, trying to hold it by the tips of his fingers. He knew it was inert, completely unfaceted, but that didn't make him feel any better. "Whatever you say, Larin." He knew there wasn't any point in reminding Larin that neither Tel nor Kerida were here.

The child stretched up to pat him on the head. "You're a good boy, my dear."

———

The second time Kerida caught herself drumming her fingers on her thighs, she crossed her arms. When she caught herself drumming on her upper left arm, she shoved her hands into her armpits, as if she was trying to warm them. She didn't want to look nervous. Soldiers, especially Company Commanders like those around her now, were trained to notice things like that. They'd wonder why she was fidgeting. As a Talent, they might not ask her, but they'd keep their eyes on her. And they might notice that she was trying hard not to look upward.

Company Commanders noticed things like that, too. Or so her sisters had always told her.

Had they been in an actual fort instead of a makeshift encampment, she might have been allowed to stay in the Talents' quarters, but under field conditions everyone not on duty, including Talents, had to show themselves for morning parade. And it gave her an excuse for being up, dressed, and outside as early as possible.

<<I knew I should have stayed near you.>>

<<We're lucky the storm didn't blow you farther away.>>

<<I was *not* blown away. I merely wished to avoid the worst of the snow. It weighs down one's wings.>>

"You've got that faraway look on your face again," Tel's voice in her ear interrupted her. "Try frowning or something. Talents usually frown."

He was right, now that she thought about it. Except for Serinam, one of her tutors at Questin Hall, and Luca Pa'narion himself, most Talents *did* frown. And, come to think of it, she could frown at how tight and uncomfortable her clothes felt. It had been quite a trick to choose the most necessary items from her pack and at the same time find spots to distribute them in, under, and around all the clothing she could wear without any unusual lumps showing. The job hadn't been made any easier by their complete lack of information as to what she could expect, either on the journey or at Griffinhome itself.

<<Weimerk, as soon as we can, Tel and I are moving around to the south side of the encampment, near the latrine ditches.>> That was the only place she could be sure of reasonable space along with some privacy. The privies were communal, but basic politeness would keep people as far from her as they could manage. Not that she planned to be actually squatting when the time came.

<<When you see that you have room enough, I want you to swoop down and scoop me up.>>

<<I have already said, my dear Kerida, that I fear I might damage you if I, as you put it, 'swoop down and scoop you up.' Should I land, it would be much safer.>>

Ker wondered if the griffin could hear her sighing. He seemed to hear so much else. <<But if you land, the soldiers will shoot at you and—>>

<<And they will not hit me.>>

<<Of course, but they'll try to stop me from going with you and—>>

<<And I will stop them from stopping you.>>

<<That's exactly what I'm afraid of.>> These soldiers weren't the enemy, they were her sisters' Panthers. <<I don't want you to hurt anyone.>>

There was a long pause. <<That certainly complicates matters.>> Another pause in which Ker had the sensation of wind in her face. <<Very well. I agree.>> Another pause. <<I cannot carry you both.>>

<<You won't have to. Tel will be staying behind.>>

A snort. <<He will not like that.>>

An understatement if she'd ever heard one. <<No, he doesn't. But there really isn't any other way.>> They'd spent a large part of the night before discussing that very thing. Even though Tel had been the first to suggest that he shouldn't go with them—never losing sight of the fact that Weimerk couldn't carry them both—he'd still gone over the plan from all angles to see if there wasn't another way.

<<He prefers that these people continue to hold you prisoner?>>

<<They're not holding us prisoner; they want to keep us safe. And, besides, my sister is the one helping us get away.>> Which Tonia was doing by creating extra assignments which reduced the number of people who were free to access the latrine area.

<<Tel's going to pretend to pull me down as you swoop at us, and I'll pretend to get away and run, as if I'm panicked. Can you pick me up while I'm running?>>

<<Indeed. It is, in fact, preferable. It will lessen the impact as I "scoop" you.>>

Ker had a feeling she'd come to regret teaching him that word. <<Any preferred direction?>>

<<Not at all. Merely begin to run, and I shall shift to your direction and "scoop.">>

Crap. She was already regretting it.

She heard the whistle that signaled the release of the ranks. Finally. The soldiers around them split off to attend to their orders, a few Barracks returning to their cook fires while the others trotted off under the watchful eyes of their Barrack Leaders and Company Commanders.

"Think you'll ever make it to Company Second Officer?" They were strolling leisurely to the latrines, and conversation along the way was more natural than silence. There were glances exchanged as they passed other soldiers, and from the number of people who whispered into the ears of their neighbors, they were passing along the news of who and what she was. But no one stopped them, the direction they were taking explanation enough for the curious.

"Promotion's always faster under battle conditions, you know that."

<<I am directly above you. Your aura indicates distress.>>

<<I'm fine.>>

<<You are frightened.>>

<<Of course, I'm frightened. I'm about to be scooped up—>>

Crap. Now he had her doing it.

<<You would prefer not to do this.>>

<<I'd prefer . . . >> Ker hesitated. She'd been about to say that she'd prefer to be sitting in a classroom in Questin Hall being examined on whether she could Flash all there was to know about some dusty old artifact no one else cared about. Everyone there would still be alive—but then she wouldn't have known Weimerk . . . and she wouldn't have Tel. Ker took a deep breath and straightened her shoulders. She was about to leave him, maybe forever, and she couldn't even kiss him goodbye because that would *certainly* be noticed—

<<Take his plaque with you, as you once did that of Nate Primo.>>

"Crap," she said under her breath. Why hadn't *she* thought of that? "Weimerk says I should take your plaque. Can you give it to me without anyone else seeing?" she added in answer to Tel's grunt.

Tel exhaled. "You'd know where I was, how I was." He touched the front of his tunic, just where his plaque would be hanging on its loop of braided leather. Soldiers got their plaques when they finished their training and wore them until they left the military, or died, whichever came first. The symbols stamped onto the metal identified each soldier and recorded any change in their status. There were some twenty-year veterans who had two plaques, and Ker had heard of someone with three, but she'd never seen it herself.

"You'd be in trouble for losing it," Ker said.

"I'll be in trouble anyway, for losing *you*. We'll just have to hope your sister can cover for me both ways." He'd loosened the ties of his tunic and the closure of his shirt as if he found the air too warm. He had the leather thong in his hand, but Ker knew he wouldn't be able to break it by yanking. Everything that could be done to make plaques hard to lose was done.

Suddenly, Tel started to cough. He put his hand on Ker's shoulder and bent far over, still coughing. Much more slowly he straightened up, his fist still at his mouth. "Sorry, spit went down the wrong way." As far as they knew, there was no one close enough to overhear them, but better to be safe.

"You all right now?" She put her hand over his and palmed the plaque from his free hand. It was warm from contact with his skin.

"Yeah, I think so."

<<This would be a splendid time.>>

"Now, he says."

They'd spent another large part of the night before practicing this maneuver. At Ker's signal, Tel pushed forward with his outstretched arms aiming for the small of her back. At the same time, he stepped backward with what had been his front foot, so that instead of actually pushing her, his palms merely grazed the small of her back. To any but the most experienced and careful of watchers, it would look as though he'd tried to push her down, or at least out of the way, but had been foiled by her starting to run.

At just the right moment, Weimerk scooped her up.

———

"Enough!" Jerek was so angry he wasn't surprised when everyone stopped talking. It felt like heat was being generated by his body. "I've seen children in the schoolyard behave better than this—and I've seen it *recently*," he added, rubbing at his forehead. Wynn, standing behind his chair, was the only one here not annoying him.

"Right," he said into the silence. "Only one of you speaks at a time. The next person who interrupts anyone leaves—and loses their vote. You don't speak unless I point at you, and when I point at someone else, the person speaking stops. Are we clear?"

A couple of people pressed their lips together, noses wrinkling, but everyone eventually nodded. Jerek pointed at Oraleth, the Springs Far-thinker, spokesperson for her group.

"It's very simple, lord Luqs." She spoke with a lilt, in a voice that sounded as though she didn't use it much. "We'd like to patrol together, as a group. We're used to each other, and we don't know anybody else."

Jerek held up his hand, palm out, to the person about to interrupt. "Don't try it." He turned back to Oraleth. "I understand being in a strange place, with people you don't know," he said. "But you must see you're not being reasonable. No patrol *needs* two Feelers with the same gift. From the eleven of you, we can make up at least seven new patrol groups—at the very least, that gives everyone a longer rest period."

Cheval Far-seer, who'd had horizon sickness on the way to the mines, tugged at Oraleth's sleeve. She folded her arms. "Those are our conditions."

Luca Pa'narion cleared his throat, and Jerek pointed at him. "I would remind you that when you agreed to come and help— indeed, you volunteered—no one asked for conditions. The People of the Springs and Pools agreed to fight the Halians with us in exchange for services and full citizenship in the Faraman Polity. The services you've already received, and the citizenship you have."

Oraleth shook off the Far-seer's hand, still on her sleeve. "We didn't know there would be so many people here," she said. "We don't have a voice in council, we're just lumped in with the Mines and Tunnels." Her nose wrinkled again. "And the soldiers look at us with suspicion. We fear for our safety if we're split up."

Jerek pressed his eyes shut. He wasn't sure which group

they objected to most, the soldiers or their fellow Feelers. "Very well, you may go."

"Lord Luqs?" Oraleth blinked rapidly. The other Springs behind her exchanged nervous glances.

"You may go." Jerek brushed the air between them with the back of his hand. "If you don't stand by your word, we can't use you."

Oraleth cleared her throat. "That leaves our Clan in your debt."

"I suppose it does. I can't ask you to return the service Kerida Griffin Girl gave you, and I wouldn't even if I could. You can have that as a gift."

"The citizenship—"

"No, I won't take that away either, at least not from the others. Your council agreed on behalf of all the Springs and Pools, not just the eleven of you. If you want to give up your citizenship, that's fine, but I can't let what you do change things for everyone else in your Clan."

The Springs group turned toward each other, to confer in what privacy they could create. The Mines and Tunnels Feelers waited off to one side, murmuring together. They didn't look very happy either, and Ganni was trying to talk them into something. Jerek could rub at his forehead in peace because at least no one was speaking to him.

"Got a headache?" Wynn muttered from behind him.

"I'm not sleeping," he said.

"I've noticed." Of course, she would notice; she still slept on the floor across his door. He understood exactly how the Springs and Pools felt. Since Tel and Kerida had gone, Wynn was the only person left in the whole of the Serpents Teeth who had known him before he became Luqs, the only one who still spoke to him, in private at least, like he was plain old Jerek Brightwing. The only one he felt *he* really knew. He straightened in his chair. The Springs seemed ready to speak.

"We won't go against what our council agreed to," Oraleth said in a tone that meant she'd been outvoted. "So we'll stay. But if we're to be split up, could we be sent out only with the Talents we know? The Guardians like Luca Pa'narion and the others? The rest . . ."

Jerek respected the Far-thinker's reluctance to spell out the reaction of the Talents who weren't part of Luca's Guardians group. Not many had made it to the Serpents Teeth. So far, they were thankful enough at being safe to set their prejudices aside and simply ignore the fact that four months ago they would have had to kill most of the people around them. But that might change.

"That seems reasonable," he said aloud. "Faro of Bears"—he pointed at Juria Sweetwater—"do we have enough Guardian Talents?"

The Faro conferred with her Laxtor, Surm Barlot, before answering. It was the job of the second in command to keep duty rosters in his head. "It appears so, my Luqs. Not every party requires a Talent, but all require Feelers. Undoubtedly, some reasonable schedule can be created."

Huro, one of the Springs' Mind-healers, raised her hand; Jerek pointed to her. "May we take some of our food—what's given to us and not eaten—and set it aside to be taken back with us?" Did all the Springs sound as though they hadn't spoken for months?

Jerek tapped his index finger on the arm of his chair. He'd been told about the conditions at the Springs and Pools. Luca had given him a full report, and Cuarel Far-thinker had filled in more detail. He knew that the place was poor compared to the Mines and Tunnels.

"We're all one people now," he said to Huro. "You're under my care, like any other citizens of the Polity, and your welfare is my responsibility. Ganni? I'd like to send a Barrack with some supplies. What can we spare?"

"We're fairly well-stocked right now, thanks to the griffin.

Dried meat and sausages is what we can spare most, I think. But there's others who know more than me."

"Thank you, I'll leave it in your hands." He turned back to the Springs. They looked more relaxed. "As for the council," he said. "Will you, Oraleth Far-thinker, be speaker for your group? Keep in mind that in this council, you'll be speaking for all the Springs and Pools, not just the eleven of you."

She hesitated, brows drawn down. "I can Far-think with Ylora back at the Springs, my lord. Therefore, I would be able to speak for us all."

Then why didn't you do it now? He didn't say it aloud. From the sound of her, the old woman who Spoke for the whole Clan wouldn't have had much patience with their complaints— which probably explained why they hadn't involved her. He rubbed at his upper lip to hide his grin.

"Very well," he said when he had his face under control. "If there aren't any other issues, can we call this meeting over?"

The Springs and Pools made the gesture, more than a nod but not quite a bow, that people used for the Luqs when in informal council. The full salutation, with kneeling and all, was reserved for something formal. Juria Sweetwater made the same gesture but stopped to talk to Luca Pa'narion on her way out. Jerek wasn't surprised when the Talent Inquisitor stayed behind.

"Have you gone to a Mind-healer about your sleeplessness, my lord?" Somehow Luca sounded like everyone's favorite uncle. Protocol told Jerek that Luca couldn't Flash him without his permission, but that didn't mean he *wouldn't*. Jerek never forgot that the man was a High Inquisitor allowed—and able—to do things that ordinary Talents were not.

"Of course, I have." Jerek allowed a bit of his annoyance to show. Really, did Luca think he was stupid? "It goes away for a few days and then comes back." There hadn't been a recurrence of that strange episode when he'd thought that someone was calling for help. But he *had* dreamed about it, and those dreams *were* disturbing his sleep.

The Inquisitor's mouth twisted in a wry smile. "Goes away for a bit and then comes back? That sounds like everything else we're going through, doesn't it?" He shook his head. "Don't hesitate to ask for help, my lord. Without you, everything will come apart."

"If that was supposed to make me feel better, Luca, it didn't work."

Without the heat from the griffin's body, Kerida would have frozen to death. As it was, she was far from comfortable. She couldn't see anything with her face buried in Weimerk's neck feathers, but if she lifted her head, the wind threatened to rip it right off.

<<Can we slow down?>>

<<Are you hungry? Must we hunt?>>

<<No, no thank you.>> Ker's stomach lurched at the very idea, and she was glad that it was empty. Otherwise, she'd be vomiting for sure. Especially on the downward swoops.

<<You are ill.>>

<<Apparently, I don't like flying,>> she said. <<But I'll be all right. We don't have to stop.>> She remembered the light in Tel Cursar's face after his flight on Weimerk and reminded herself to be annoyed with him when she saw him again. Strangely, that made her feel a little better. Still, why should *he* be the one who could enjoy flying with the griffin?

<<I can fly another two days without stopping to rest or feed,>> Weimerk said now. <<But I fear this is not true of you. If I fly slower, will you be able to eat as we go?>>

Ker's stomach lurched again. <<No! Uh, no, I'm afraid not. We'll have to land.>>

<<You *are* ill.>>

<<I'm trying not to be.>> She sighed. She'd have to tell him. <<I think flying makes me nauseated.>>

<<Ah! Is that all? That is easily fixed. Flash my aura and find the fire color.>>

The fire color. Great. At this point, Ker was willing to try anything. *Paraste.* She'd expected to see the colors of their auras streaming out behind them, like ribbons in a wind. Instead, they swirled around them just as if they were standing on the ground, unaffected in any way by their movement through the air. Ker immediately began to feel better.

<<Seeing the auras so still and normal seems to be settling my stomach,>> she said.

<<But you will not be able to Flash indefinitely, even with my help. No, I seek a more permanent solution. Do you see the color I speak of?>>

Concentrating, Ker began to sift through the colors swirling around her. Many looked familiar, though others she had no name for. She found one that made her think of glowing embers, and began to move toward it–

<<No, not that one.>>

Ker cleared her throat, swallowed uneasily, and set herself to look again. Finally, after considering and discarding several more colors, she saw one that looked like metal heating on a forge.

<<Yes, you have found it.>>

<<So now what do I do?>>

<<Have your colors dance with it.>>

Ker already knew there was no point in asking the griffin to clarify his instruction. Like everything else, this was both a lesson and a test. Swallowing, she took a tighter grip on the feathers under her hands. Weimerk's colors were so strong and vibrant that hers looked washed out and pale by comparison. Ker took as deep a breath as she could manage and concentrated again.

How am I supposed to get my colors to the metallic flame, let alone dance with it?

She spun her aura into a ribbon, sending it out toward Weimerk, just as she would do if she were working to help heal someone. Not that the griffin was like anyone else. But there she stuck. It was one thing to manipulate her own aura, or even that of other people, but how could she touch the griffin's? Still hesitating, Ker reached out for the flame color, but the other colors kept getting in the way.

"No," she murmured under her breath. "They aren't in the way. I don't have to make them dance, they're dancing already." They moved in patterns, like a group of people performing one of the elaborate harvest dances in honor of the Mother. Except that here there was no dance floor, there wasn't even a flat surface. The patterns moved all around her, above her, below, in front—every direction she could think of. All at once. Her head spinning, Ker took a deep breath and tried to concentrate. Rather than looking at the colors themselves, Ker focused on the spaces between, trying to keep her own "steps" heading toward the metallic fire she could see dancing along with the others.

Dodging, with more luck than grace, a color she couldn't name, Ker finally made her way through. Just as she wondered how to attract the attention of Weimerk's ribbon of metallic flame, she saw that she had it already. As it responded to the movements of her own multicolored ribbon, it separated into strands, one of which detached completely, and wove itself around and through Ker's aura. Almost immediately, Ker felt a rush of warmth across her back, and her shoulders, which had been hunched against the cold, began to relax. The new color strengthened and thickened as her aura accepted it, and her stomach settled back into something she could ignore until it told her she was hungry.

"All right, then, now to get back out." It took her just as long to step out of the dance as it had taken her to enter it. Other colors kept teasing her, trying to get into pace and pattern with hers, and she had to be very nimble to avoid them. Gently, she disengaged her aura from Weimerk's, half afraid that the nausea and the cold would come back when she did. She held her breath and cracked her eyes open, more than a little surprised to find them flying in darkness.

<<I'm feeling much better,>> she told the griffin after a moment. <<Warmer, and my stomach's settled.>>

<<Less cold and not nauseated, yes,>> Weimerk said. <<We have far to go.>>

<<How long will this last?>>

<<Why would it change?>>

Lids once more closed against the wind, Ker rolled her eyes. If something changes once, she might have answered, it can change again. But then Weimerk would simply had said something like "true," and she'd be back where she'd started.

She leaned forward again as her stomach growled, telling herself she wasn't hungry enough yet to break out the travel cake, and wishing she'd brought something else.

"We would never have been able to walk this far," she told Tel in her mind.

6

66 **T**HE Bear officer tried to push the Talent to the ground, my Faro. He tried to save her." They'd been lucky in their witness. Pariah Costa was a young man, practically a boy, in his first year with the Panthers, and in horrible awe of his Faro.

Tel Cursar stood at parade rest right in front of the Faro of Panthers' camp desk. The arrival and departure of the griffin seemed to have taken no time at all—in fact, there were many among the Panthers, including the Jade Cohort Leader standing at the Faro's elbow, who hadn't seen anything at all, and was more than a little skeptical of the story.

"And you were where, that you saw this so clearly?" Normal procedure would have had them questioned by Carmad Noria, Laxtor of Panthers, a tall woman with ebony skin and a white streak in her dark hair. But since the Laxtor was on her way back from Juristand, Tonia Nast interrogated the witnesses herself, as was her right. Tel Cursar tried to look cowed and not at all as though they'd fixed this up between them ahead of time.

"Well." Pariah shifted his feet. "I was at the latrines, my Faro. I was relieving myself." He blushed to the roots of his hair. When he'd been in the Wings for longer, he'd get over that sort of thing.

"Then how could you possibly see anything?"

"Uh, I was sitting down, my Faro." Poor kid looked like he needed to sit down right now. He also looked as though it was a good thing he was coming *from* the latrines, and not going *to* them. Tel stared at a mark discoloring the wall behind the Faro's camp desk and fought to keep his face straight.

"Continue." Tonia Nast leaned back in her chair, propping her chin on her right fist.

"It was enormous—and *fast*. It fell out of the sky like a hawk after prey and picked up the Talent as though she was no more than a mouse. A griffin, my Faro, for certain."

"How could you know this 'for certain'?" The Jade Cohort Leader used a tone meant to make the boy feel as small as a mouse himself.

The youngster flushed an even deeper red, his ears turning pink, but he held his ground. "The local holding lord nearest my village has stone griffins marking the road to his house. I've seen them lots of times. Body like a big cat, head and wings like an eagle. And that's what I saw today." He closed his mouth firmly, lips pressed in a thin line. No one was going to get him to change his story, Tel thought, and he wouldn't be paying for his beer until every Panther in the Wing had tired of hearing it.

"I'm satisfied, Cohort Leader." The Faro lifted her head, stopping any further commentary. "That was well reported, soldier. Go, and tell your Barrack Leader I said so."

The kid turned sharply on his heel, face still red though now for a different reason. The older woman with the scarred face and the steel-gray hair hovering just outside the door was probably the Barrack Leader in question.

As if the young soldier's departure had pulled a cork out of him, the Jade Cohort Leader erupted. "What have you to say for yourself, Cursar? By the Mother, man! You were right there; you should have prevented it!"

"And what do you suggest the young man should have done, Cohort Leader?"

Again, Tel fought to stifle a grin. You often heard a tone like that from a Company Commander speaking to those under her, occasionally from a Cohort Leader, rarely from a Faro. But rumor had it that the Nast family worked themselves up through the ranks. Impossible as it might seem, Tonia Nast, Faro of Panthers, had at one time *been* a Company Commander.

"My Faro, if he had called for archers while the beast was still in range—"

"They could have killed the Talent just as easily as the griffin which took her. This way, if what Third Officer Cursar tells me is true, we can at least know that she is safe." Under Tonia Nast's words ran the unspoken awareness that the Talent in question was the Faro's own sister. If *she* wasn't concerned, her tone said, no one else needed to be. The Faro looked back to him. "We do know this, Third Officer?"

"Yes, Faro." Since he was a Bear, not a Panther, he didn't call her "my Faro."

"Can you speculate as to where the griffin might be taking her?"

"I can't know for sure, Faro, but I'd imagine he's taking her on to the allies we told you of."

"In other words, completing your assignment."

It wasn't a question, so Tel didn't answer her.

"Very well, Third Officer. The officer of the day will assign you a billet until I receive an answer from Juristand. I will use you to convey that answer to your Faro."

"Excuse me, Faro? The Bear Wing is still severely under count. I'm needed there."

Tonia Nast examined him with a blank expression. "Very well," she said finally. "You are dismissed. You may return to your Faro with my compliments and good wishes as soon as I've written them down."

Tonia Nast stopped looking at him, and Tel was out of the room before she could change her mind. If he couldn't follow Kerida and the griffin, he could at least go back to the Mines and the Bear Wing, where he belonged.

Ker felt she'd always been on the griffin's back, the wind had always been blowing through her hair, and all her life before was just a dream. *We definitely couldn't have walked this far.* The few times they'd landed to allow Weimerk to hunt felt like something she'd read in a story. They'd always been flying, and she'd always been clinging to the griffin's back. At least she wasn't cold, and her nausea had disappeared, now that she had her own flame color. Ker gave her head a shake and rolled her shoulders as best she could, considering she couldn't let go of her grip on Weimerk. She'd been tightening and releasing all her muscles periodically, but she could already feel the stiffness that waited for her once they landed again.

If they landed again.

A change in the angle of their flight woke her from thoughts of Tel whistling while he was trudging along a road. She woke completely to find his plaque clutched tightly in her fist, Weimerk climbing and showing no signs of leveling off to fly through a pass, as he'd done so many times before. Slowly, the sound of the air rushing past them faded, and Ker's head felt somehow larger.

<<Swallow.>>

Obediently, Ker swallowed. With a barely felt pop! the sound of the rushing air returned, and her head felt normal. She kept swallowing as they climbed higher and higher still, until—what felt like hours later—Weimerk leveled off.

<<Look, Kerida. The peaks of Griffinhome. The Pillars of the World.>>

Ker raised her head and blinked into the wind. All around them were sky-piercing peaks: black, gray, white, blinding where sun hit snow. These mountains made the Serpents Teeth look like foothills, and they continued as far as the eye could see.

<<These mountains? This is it?>>

<<Look again, my Griffin Girl.>>

Shaking her head, Ker shut her eyes. She should have known Weimerk meant her to Flash. *Paraste*. Instantly, the sharp grays and whites and blacks of the mountains ahead of them were replaced by vibrant auroras of colors, hundreds of them, rising from the peaks in front of them, impossibly high, and rippling as though following patterns of air and the movement of winds she couldn't see. Her breath caught in her throat, and tears which had nothing to do with the wind sprang into her eyes.

Waves of color reached out to them as they flew nearer. Weimerk gave one of his great screams, forcing Ker to press her head tightly against his neck feathers as she tried to muffle the sound. Her ears rang until she couldn't hear the wind rushing by.

Then came other calls, and Weimerk abruptly rose higher still, like a kitten bouncing into the air, ecstatic that he was finally being answered by his own kind. But where were they? All Ker could see were the curtains of color they swam through, as though someone had emptied the contents of dye vats into tumbling river rapids.

Weimerk stopped moving forward. His wings folded and, quivering with excitement, he looked around alertly, like a bird watching for prey.

<<So many.>> Was there a note of fear in his voice?

Ker blinked and looked around. Still nothing but waves of color. What were they standing on? She shivered and took a deep steadying breath.

<<Can you not see them? Ah.>> The satisfied tone of some-one who has laid down the last card in a pattern of Solitary Seasons. <<You are not yet seeing like a griffin. Dismount, and you will see what you wish to see.>> He lowered his body until his front legs stretched out in front of him, like a cat in front of a fire.

Dismount onto what? Ker examined their surroundings more carefully. Weimerk did seem to be standing on a wave of color, but it moved and shifted enough to make her cross-eyed. What was holding him up? And would it hold her up as well? Weimerk certainly seemed to think so.

Before she could lose her nerve, Ker shifted her grip on Weimerk's feathers and slid carefully between his body and his right wing. Her toes touched something firm, and Weimerk shifted his wing to free her. Ker turned around, and the breath stopped in her throat. The auroras were gone, and in their place were the rocks and trees and greenery of a mountain valley, vaulted over with white fluffy clouds in an azure sky. There were ash trees and birches, with a few scattered pines. There were birds in the trees and bees circling the wildflowers growing out of the grass. All that was missing were goats, and maybe a goatherd.

<<Not what I expected,>> she said, looking around her. <<Not at all what I expected.>> Though she couldn't have said what she *had* expected. <<I thought we were too far up for a valley like this one.>> A cold breeze suddenly touched her cheek, and she shivered. The sun was bright enough to make her squint, glinting off rock faces and casting deep shadows into the groves of trees, but she didn't feel the warmth that should have come with it.

<<What you see is not truly there, in the sense that you use the word "truly.">> Weimerk tilted his head. <<Nor in the sense that you use "there." Like a griffin, your mind has imposed its will on the auroras, and created an image it finds acceptable.>>

<<Wonderful.>> Ker rolled her eyes. <<So nothing I see is real?>>

<<Everything you see is real. It is merely not here.>>

<<That's so helpful, thank you.>> If she didn't stop rolling her eyes, she'd get a headache. She thought she saw color and movement out of the corner of her eye, but when she turned her head, it was gone.

<<*She* is real, and surely you see her?>>

Looking in the direction Weimerk was pointing his beak, Ker clenched her hands to fists, and took a step back. What she'd taken for a huge boulder, she saw now as the statue of a crouching griffin—until she saw the tail whipping back and forth. *I hope she didn't see all the eye-rolling.* Ker lifted her chin and straightened her spine.

Weimerk had been a hatchling when they found him, and he'd grown quickly to the size he wanted to be, that is, large enough to carry Ker on his back. Ker now realized she'd assumed he'd reached his adult size. Apparently adult, fully grown griffins were much larger. Several times larger, if she was any judge. Too large, perhaps, to carry a human in comfort.

Size was almost the only difference between them, however. The griffin in front of them had the same gold fur, the same rainbow iridescence to her wings, and the feathers on her head. *And how do I know she's a she?* Her beak shone with the same shade of bright copper. With their eagle heads, griffins had little or no expression on their faces, but Ker had learned to read Weimerk's feelings from the tilt of his head, the movement of his wings, and whether he used one eye or both. Going by those cues, the griffin watching her showed disapproval, though the half-cocked set of her wings looked a bit like surprise.

Weimerk raised himself slightly, his tail lashing back and forth, like a kitten eager to play. The female watching them tilted her head to one side, and suddenly the valley rang with an immense sound as if a gong the size of the valley itself had been struck by an enormous hammer. It sounded just once, and while the ground stayed steady, the air shimmered, as if with the passage of the sound. All of a sudden, there were griffins everywhere. Some Ker could see clearly, their shapes and the hues of their wings detailed and clear. Those that were standing or sitting farther off, however, were blurry, as if she saw them through water.

Or through waves of color, she thought. Just because she no longer saw them didn't mean they weren't there. No longer Flashing, Ker couldn't see the auras, though she thought she could feel them in the space around her, as if they brushed against her. Tinkling sounds, like delicate silver wind chimes in the distance. Ker felt her spirits rise and knew that she was smiling. There wouldn't be any difficulty now, not with all these griffins to help them.

<<Weimerk. You are welcome.>>

Weimerk's answer was wordless, just a wave of joy and curiosity and fear and more joy.

"I am Deilih. I shall speak for all." Ker no longer heard the griffin's voice in her head, but through her ears. Deilih's voice had the same resonance and sense of space, but didn't sound like Weimerk's, either when he spoke aloud or mind to mind. Ker wasn't sure how she'd describe the difference. In fact, there was no way to tell that Deilih was the griffin in front of them. Any of the griffins she could see, or even one she couldn't, might be the one speaking.

"Talent, what brings you to Griffinhome?"

Of course, Weimerk didn't need a reason to come to what was, after all, his home, though he'd never seen it before. Ker squared her shoulders and coughed into her hand. Colors shot through the edge of her vision, and in that moment the ghostly images of griffins lined the hills around her. Every muscle ached from holding on to Weimerk; the skin on her face felt tight and dry. She wanted nothing more than to crawl into a bed and sleep on something that didn't move—and that she didn't have to cling to.

"I'm Kerida Nast, Talent of the Halls of Law. I'm here on behalf of the Feelers of the Mines and Tunnels, and the Springs and Pools, and the Luqs of Farama." Ker paused, but there was no acknowledgment. "We believe the time of the Prophecy has come," she continued. Still no reaction from the gathered griffins. "We've seen at least two of the Signs of the Prophecy. Farama has been invaded by the Halians, who are horsemen from across the sea, and we . . ." Here she hesitated. "We found Weimerk, and the Talents and Feelers are getting together. But we need help dealing with the Halian mages, the Shekayrin. We've seen how at least one of them reacted to Weimerk, and we think that with your help, we could persuade them to—" What was the military phrase? "Cease hostilities. They would listen to you, about the Prophecy I mean, and if you help us, well, then the Prophecy would, uh, come to pass. With your help." Ker could feel heat spreading over her face. This had all sounded so much better in her head.

"You are not the one the Prophecy calls for."

Ker blinked. "I never said I was. I'm part of the Second Sign, I'm the one who speaks to griffins," she told them. "I'm speaking to you now and asking for your help."

"You did not need our help to destroy the world that was."

That sounded a little petty to Ker. "But the Prophecy—"

"The Prophecy is not a book already written, but one that is writing itself even as we speak. You Gifted have the ending in your hands, to make or unmake the world that is so important to you. We griffins were driven from our place of blood and bone by the warring of the Gifted. We could no longer teach those who took our Gifts and used our lessons as permission to turn on one another."

Ker couldn't pretend that she didn't know what Deilih meant. She knew that Talents had once turned on Feelers, having them outlawed, and stamping out all official mention of them, making them into half-legendary bogeymen for children. And long before that event, she'd been told Talents and Feelers together had cast out the mages. "But there are so many UnGifted! What about them?"

"They are not our concern. Only those who received our Gifts are of importance to us. Until they once again use those Gifts as we intended, the Prophecy is not fulfilled, and we shall remain in Griffinhome."

The buzzing was back in Ker's head. She couldn't speak, the words choking her as they tried to get out of her mouth. Finally, she clenched her teeth; she couldn't let her disappointment rise up and overwhelm her. She took several deep breaths and looked carefully around her, doing the best she could to hold back her anger and shock. She'd thought she'd have to plead her case, and she didn't think they'd be her friends right away. But she certainly hadn't expected them to reject her request out of hand. She never thought they wouldn't care at all.

"Yes, well." She cleared her throat and swallowed. "I won't thank you for more than your time, since that's all you're giving me," she said. "If you don't mind, I'll take myself and my Gifts back to my friends and do what I can to keep them alive long enough for the Prophesied One to come."

"It is not yet determined that you will return."

Cold touched the back of her neck. Weimerk shook his head and partially opened his wings. The claws on all four feet were showing.

"You claim to be the Second Sign. What proof can you offer us?"

Proof? Surely the griffins could recognize their own Sign? "I'm speaking to you, aren't I? Isn't that what the Second Sign is all about? 'Hear the runner in the darkness, eyes of color and light; Speaks to the wings of the sky; Speaks to griffins,'" she recited. "That was me, the runner in the darkness, and this is me now."

"Did you speak to Weimerk, or did he speak to you? If he awakened your ability, then you are not the Second Sign."

"She awakened me," Weimerk said. "I was lost and crying. I was first out of the egg. But. I was alone. There. Was. No. Parent. To. Wake. My. Mind."

From the way he was mixing his intonations, Ker could tell he was upset. Griffins always laid three eggs, but the first one out always ate the other two. That's why Weimerk had been alone.

Deilih inclined her head in a slow nod, acknowledging Weimerk's implied criticism. "Your parents were lost to us. With them gone, there was no way for us to find the nest they had left. No way to find you until you hatched, and we could sense your presence."

Ker's eyebrows crawled upward as realization dawned. Each set of parent griffins must have laid their nests in a spot known only to them. If Weimerk's parents had disappeared, then knowledge of his location would have disappeared with them.

"You would not have been abandoned but for their loss."

"I hatched. When. Kerida. Entered. The. Serpents. Teeth."

"But—no, nothing." Ker had entered the mine less than a day before she and Tel were found by the Feelers. Weimerk had already hatched. Was he lying to these others? Or . . . technically, she and Tel *had* been in the mines longer. The entrance they'd used as a cave while Tel's wound got better, *that* was part of the mines.

"I. Wandered. Lost. And. Alone. Until Kerida found me and woke me. When I became myself, I knew immediately that together we were the Second. Sign." Weimerk seemed to be calming down.

Griffins had a kind of racial memory they could access only when they were awakened, usually by one of their parents. The memory consisted of everything that griffins knew up to the time of the last Great Gathering. In Weimerk's case, that included the creation of the Prophecy. There hadn't been a Great Gathering since then.

After a long period of silence, Deilih spoke. "We accept that the Talent awakened you. Has there been any other manifestation of her continuing importance to the Prophecy?"

Ker had to shut her eyes. What, for the Mother's sake, could they possibly want from her? She rubbed her face with her hands and groaned aloud.

"Can you at least tell me what kind of proof I need?" The griffin nearest them, whether it was really Deilih or not, didn't respond, other than the slow blinking of her enormous eyes. None of the other griffins were close enough for her to look directly at them. Ker turned to Weimerk, but at first got no more answer than the same slow blinking. Were they communicating among themselves?

Finally, Weimerk turned his eye toward her. "You know what you must do."

Pulling in a deep breath preparatory to speaking her mind as loudly as possible, in the last moment Ker did nothing more than let the breath out through her nose and thrust her hands into the wide sleeves of her overtunic, wrapping her arms around herself. The sun on her face was warm, but nevertheless Ker felt chilled inside. What would happen to her if she couldn't come up with the proof Weimerk said she had? Why wasn't being the Second Sign enough?

As she pushed her hands deeper into her sleeves, something shifted under her shirt. At first, she only remembered Tel's military plaque, and had to fight down an urge to Flash it, to touch at least part of him. She raised her hand but instead of the plaque, she felt a lump under the cloth. Her breath caught in her throat. The jewel. The soul stone. *Blood and bones of griffins.*

Hurriedly, she pulled out the little silk bag that held her jewel, emptying it out into her hand. It caught at the light, glinting and sending out sparkling flashes of color. Ker had never seen this effect before, and for a moment she smiled in delight. She looked up, but neither Deilih nor the other griffins showed any reaction. Ker triggered her Talent, and the jewel's pattern of facets leaped into prominence, forming a hemisphere over and around her. Focusing, she nudged the pattern to another configuration, changing the form of the jewel "at rest" to a lacier effect, and then to something more resembling a spider's web. For the first time, she saw the net charged with other colors, overpainting the jewel's natural red.

Finally, she closed her fist on the jewel and stopped Flashing. Breathing heavily, she looked around again. This time she saw what she recognized as delight in the way Weimerk stood, with wings slightly arched, and eyes half-closed. She could almost hear him purring.

"Well?" she asked. "Is that the proof you were looking for?"

"It is." There *could* have been a tone of satisfaction in Deilih's voice. "We are satisfied that you hold more than one Gift, and that you will play a continuing role in the Prophecy. You may rest here, and food will be provided. One of us will return you to your home when you are ready to leave."

"No. I. Will. Return. My. Kerida." Weimerk was upset again. "I. Must. Return. Also."

"You will remain here. You are the last hatchling from the eggs left in the Serpents Teeth. You are too valuable to us to return."

"I. Am. Awake. I. Hold. The. Same. Memories. And. Knowledge. As. Any. Griffin. Like any of you, I may do as I wish."

"You are a hatchling. You have the memories and the knowledge, but you lack the experience to use them. You will remain."

Weimerk's wings drooped lower than Ker had ever seen them. She didn't need to look at Deilih to know who had won. Ker clenched her fist over the jewel. It was bad enough to be separated from Weimerk, a close and loving friend, but to return to Farama with a strange griffin, who wouldn't even be staying? After all this, there were no griffins coming to help them, and she'd managed to lose them the one griffin they had.

"No." Weimerk trembled enough that the feathers on his wings seemed to vibrate. "Kerida is mine. I will not give her care to another."

"You are too valuable to us, hatchling. You must remain."

"No. I am part of the Prophecy. I am the griffin spoken of in the Second Sign. I must stay with Kerida." He was clearly still angry, but Weimerk seemed to have finally mastered his speech.

"The Second Sign concerns one who will speak to griffins, and here she stands. Your part in this has been played. We will send another to return the Talent to her place."

"Wait." Ker grabbed Weimerk's wing tip. He looked as if he was ready to launch himself, but whether into the air or at the larger griffin she couldn't tell. "Can we come to a compromise? Let Weimerk take me back to my friends. Then he'll come back to you."

"No," Weimerk said.

"Listen," she said, tugging on a feather that had been ruffled out of place. "There's nothing we can do." She glanced around. Griffins and more griffins as far as the eye could see. "We can't afford to alienate them, even if they're not going to help us. But please don't make me go back on some strange griffin." Weimerk shook his head, and Ker thought she could hear him growling. Finally, he nodded.

"Very well. We will allow it. Do not think to remain with the Second Sign, hatchling. Should you tarry, others will come to remove you."

Weimerk's tail lashed, but he bowed his head.

"Once the Second Sign is rested, you may go." Deilih turned her great head to look directly at Ker. "We shall meet again if the Prophecy is fulfilled." The colors rose up, and the valley with all its griffins faded away.

"Not if I get a vote," Ker muttered.

Bakura kept her eyes tight shut, unsure what had awakened her. Once she would have expected visions, but though she waited, nothing came. Nothing had come since her netting. Perhaps nothing would ever come again.

She pushed the thought away and opened her eyes to find her bedchamber in complete darkness. Surely, she had left a candle burning, a candle long enough to last through what little remained of the night once she had finally settled herself to sleep. Baku sat up and rubbed at her eyes. Where was her—oh, yes—she had asked to be alone in this room. That was one of the reasons it had taken her so long to fall asleep.

"Yes?" Just in time she remembered to speak in the new language. "Is someone there?"

Jerek: Is someone there? Can you hear me?

If it had just been the first sentence, she might have thought it an echo of her own question, but she certainly had not said the second part.

"Yes, I can hear you," she said. "What—who are you?"

Jerek: Not so loud. You can just think the words. I'm Jerek Brightwing. Who are you?

And who or what was a Jerek Brightwing? Baku pressed her lips together. She had heard of mages speaking to one another through the medium of their soul stones, but this seemed to be something of another order. Provided it was happening at all. Should she answer? She was sure her brother, and her brother's advisers, would counsel against it. She smiled.

Bakura: I am Bakura Kar Luyn, Princess Imperial of Halia.

Jerek: You're *what*? Where are you?

Bakura: Farama the Capital, where are you? If this was not a dream, could it be some kind of hoax? Perhaps one of the Shekayrin, who sought in some way to influence or even frighten her. She needed to find out.

Jerek sat up in bed. He glanced toward the door, but Wynn lay fast asleep, curled up like a cat on her mat. This Far-thinking was astonishing enough without having someone raising an alarm. He was sure Kerida would want him to keep this to himself. Still, it wouldn't be a great idea to let this Bakura know where he was.

Jerek: If you don't mind, I won't tell you where I am just now. He took a breath and decided to take a chance. **I wouldn't want my father to find me.**

Bakura: Who is your father?

Jerek: Dern Firoxi. This time the princess paused for so long that Jerek wondered if the connection had stopped as unexpectedly as it had begun.

Bakura: I do not know of any son. There was clear skepticism in her voice. Jerek could almost feel her frowning.

Jerek: He denied me. He told everyone I was only his stepson. He hoped she didn't hear any bitterness in his voice. He hoped he'd come to terms with his father's abandonment. **He wanted to be sure that nothing stood between him and the seat of the Luqs.**

Bakura: This is the man to whom I am married? Someone who would deny his own child?

Jerek: It's politics, he said, rubbing at his forehead. *Married?* He threw off his blankets.

Bakura: Of course, you are right. I know such things occur. My own brother, the Sky Emperor, has sent me here to save my life. Perhaps your father sought to do the same with you?

Jerek: I tell you what. Why don't you ask him? He rubbed at the bridge of his nose. **How does sending you here save your life?**

Another long pause, but this time Jerek knew to be patient.

Bakura: Ah, what harm can a voice in my head do me? You may as well be told. I have the taint. When this is discovered in the women of Halia, they are most often put to

death. **My brother sent me away, so that my magic should not be discovered. So that he would not have to kill me.**

Jerek: **Aren't you in danger here? What if the Shekayrin find out?**

Bakura: **I have been netted by a Shekayrin so that my magic is checked and does not reveal itself.**

Jerek: **You don't think what we're doing right now is pretty revealing?**

Bakura: **How is it that we do this at all? I have no soul stone, and this is not a magic that can be done without one.**

Jerek: **We call this Far-thinking, and Feelers do it here without jewels. Your magic—we call it a Gift—must be more like a Feeler's than a mage's.** And what was her—their—range? If the princess really was in Farama the Capital, that was farther away than any Far-thinker he'd ever heard of.

Bakura: **Much good may it do me.** Her tone was bitter now. **It will not help me in my present predicament.**

Jerek: **Which is what, exactly?** He sat up again. Could he help her in some way?

Bakura: **You mean in addition to marrying a strange man who is nothing more than a pawn of the Shekayrin? I am sorry to speak so of your father. You are silent; I have offended you.**

Jerek: **No, I was just wondering if there was any way I could help you?** Another long silence followed. Jerek thought he understood. She was angry, bitter, and frightened. He knew what that felt like. She probably didn't even know what she really wanted. **Are you still there?**

Baku: **No one has ever asked me this. I am given only help for which I did not ask.**

Jerek: **Aren't you a grown-up? I mean, you're married.**

Baku: **A "grown-up?" I have almost fourteen years. A female may be given in marriage with thirteen years in Halia.**

Jerek: Well, not here! You have to be seventeen at the very least. Jerek hoped he didn't sound as shocked as he felt.

Baku: Still, I am married. The documents have been signed by representatives of both sides. A contract between the Princess Imperial of Halia and the Luqs of Farama.

Jerek: Ah, well, actually, *I'm* the Luqs of Farama. The legal one, anyway. An invading enemy made my father Luqs, and that doesn't count. I was acclaimed by the Battle Wings. That makes me the real Luqs. Another long pause.

Baku: The contract contains no names, neither mine nor your father's. It is often done this way when there is a journey or time between the couple. Thus, the contract could apply even if the principals were changed.

Jerek: Then you could be married to me?

Baku: Yes.

Jerek: And if you were, would your people follow you?

Baku: The traditionalists in the army might very well. It is a question of blood. Among the Horsemen, bloodlines are of extreme importance. Even now, because of my bloodline, I would have importance for the children I will bear. In addition to this, they would follow the Voice of the Emperor.

Jerek? Which is who, exactly? Jerek listened to her explanation with growing astonishment. That was a piece of magic nobody here in Farama had ever heard of—except maybe Luca Pa'narion. The Inquisitor seemed to know everything. He realized with a start that Bakura had stopped talking. **I think I see a way we can help each other.**

"It has come to my attention that you have not yet visited your wife."

Dern Firoxi placed his fork neatly to the side of his plate before looking up. He'd noticed his clothes seemed looser, and while his appetite had decreased, he knew he still had to eat. "I thought I'd give her more time to get adjusted. She seems frightened."

Pollik Kvar raised an eyebrow. "Women are generally frightened by their marital duties. At least to begin with. I suggest you visit her this evening."

Dern smiled. "I suppose it can do no harm."

Bakura Kar Luyn rose from her chair and smoothed down her dress, and her overveil. She looked taller than she had in the audience room, but she was still shorter than a Faraman woman would be. Dern wondered if they fed their women differently, over in Halia.

Perhaps she just hadn't finished growing.

"You're taller than I expected," he said aloud. "I didn't really notice when we were in the audience chamber."

"You are darker than I expected, lord Luqs. But I am told that many races make up the Faraman Polity. To me, everyone's face seems very pointed."

Dern nodded and looked around. "Are your rooms comfortable?"

"Indeed. It was kind of you to visit me here. My ladies have prepared refreshment." She gestured to a low table, where a steaming jug of spiced wine sat keeping warm over a candle, waiting to be poured into the cups provided. There were bowls of dried flowers and herbs scenting the rooms with a subtle, calming aroma.

Dern nodded again, hooked his thumb in his belt, stared around the room. He'd never been here before. No need to, of course, the Luqs had his own rooms. The view from the window was interesting. An interior courtyard like his, but not the same one.

"My lord Luqs?" Her quiet accented voice made him recall where he was.

"I'm sorry. Did you speak?"

"Shall my ladies stay?"

"Stay?" By the Mother, these people had some odd customs. What were the ladies expected to do? "By no means. They may go." The older maid, clearly Halian from her dress, scuttled out of the room as if dogs were trying to bite her. The Faraman woman walked more sedately, but tight-lipped, shooting him a sharp glance as she passed him on her way out the door. He felt a flare of anger that died away as quickly as it came. She wasn't important enough to bother with.

He stood watching the door for several minutes after it had closed behind the ladies. Finally, he turned to the princess, clasped his hands behind his back, and smiled, lifting his eyebrows. The princess waited, but when he didn't approach her, she spoke.

"Would you help with my veil, my lord? It is difficult to remove by oneself. In fact, the overveil is not meant to be lifted off by the wearer at all."

"Who does it, then?" He took the lacy thing by its lower edge and folded it back over the princess' head,

She looked at him with lowered brows. "One's maid, usually."

"Or your husband, is that it? No one explained this to me."

"The Shekayrin would not trouble to, and the army officers would not think to." She folded the veil carefully and laid it over the back of a chair. "From now on, it is permitted that I go without the veil in your presence, even when my maids are in the room."

"This is the first time I've seen you without it," he said. He cleared his throat.

The princess lifted her chin. "I have seen you already, of course. Do you sing? Your voice shows signs of it."

"No, do *you*?"

"In Halia, women may play instruments, but we are not taught to sing. My women tell me that before the Shekayrin came to Farama, both men and women played and sang, equally."

"Before the Shekayrin came . . ." Dern realized that he had no idea how he was going to end that sentence. He looked around again. Nothing in the room had changed. "Do you think you'll be able to stop wearing the veils entirely?"

The princess drew in her brows. "I think that would depend on how many Halians there are about me. It will seem very strange, very wrong, to many of our people. To see your women with their faces uncovered is strange and unsettling. To see one of our women—that would surely be worse."

"Your Faraman is very good."

"The Shekayrin who traveled with me saw to it."

"Of course." He looked around again. "Here in Farama we usually don't sit down until our hostess asks us to."

"Ah, forgive me. This has been explained to me, but there are many customs, strange and foreign, for me to learn. In Halia, a man would not wait for a woman's permission to do anything." She waved at an armed chair halfway between where he stood and where she was. After giving her a short bow, he took the seat.

"It's not a man/woman issue here," he said. "It's more a guest/host issue. What's courteous for one is courteous for all."

"I see." Baku lowered herself into her own chair. "But I believe it may be like the veiling. Only time will tell whether we modify our ideas to yours, or you to ours."

His brows lifted again, as if he hadn't expected such words from her. "You're right, of course. Things that seem ridiculous at first can quickly grow familiar, and the reverse is also true."

She got to her feet. "I have not offered you any refreshment," she said.

"Listen." Firoxi cleared his throat and raised his eyes to her face. "Listen, I'm sorry, and with every respect to your customs, but I can't." He swallowed. "I can't have sex with you."

She lowered herself back into her seat. "You cannot seal the marriage?" Her voice was so faint he couldn't tell if she was offended or relieved.

"It's nothing personal, I assure you." Now that he'd made his position clear, he was finding it easier to speak. "But here in Farama, adults don't have sex with children, and to me you're still a child. We don't do such things."

She frowned again, then nodded. "I am the Princess Imperial. I have been given in marriage. Do you not do 'such things' in Farama?"

"Alliances, of course, but not formally until the participants are at least fifteen. And the marriage isn't expected to be sealed until they're both at least seventeen. We wait until we can be sure neither one has Talent."

"That neither is a witch." She swallowed.

"Yes. Here we believe men can be witches as well."

"So I have heard."

"And you see that to me you're still a child?" He cleared his throat again.

She nodded again, her eyes lowered. Had she ever looked him in the face? "I do see. It shall be as you wish, my lord. Only, what shall we tell the Poppy Shekayrin?" Her skin was so clear he couldn't tell if she'd turned paler.

"Is he likely to inquire?"

"It is better, perhaps, to be prepared for what he can do, rather than rely on whether he is likely to do it." She glanced at him so quickly he didn't even see the color of her eyes.

"That's very good thinking." He chewed on his upper lip, tapping his fingertips on the arm of his chair. "I suggest we lie."

"I agree." She tilted her head to one side. "I wonder if you have considered this, my lord? If we produce a child, there will be no further use for either of us. At least, from the Poppy's point of view."

Dern blew out his breath in a silent whistle. "Oh, that had occurred to me, all right, but I'm afraid I hadn't expected it to occur to you."

"We women may have no power in Halia, but we live close to power, and we can watch and learn. When I was a child, there were nine people between my brother and the throne of the Emperor, but there he sits." She paused, and a look of pain passed over her face. Dern wondered what she was thinking about. "But tell me, Dern Firoxi, if we are not to do what is expected of us, what shall we do? For it is certain you must remain here some time."

"Do you know how to play Seasons?"

TEL Cursar staggered to his feet as Juria Sweetwater, Faro of Bears, entered the portion of tunnel being used as her anteroom. It had taken him eleven days to walk back to the Serpents Teeth from Descoria Hall, and he felt every cold, dirty step of it. His effort to come to prompt attention was ruined by his head ramming against the roof of the tunnel.

"As you were, Third Officer, before you knock yourself out."

Tel wasn't sure whether he'd sat down because his Faro had given her permission, or because his legs had given out under him. Faro Sweetwater had already swept by into her office alcove. The Laxtor, Surm Barlot, jerked his head at the swinging curtain, and Tel scrambled to follow them into the room. The Faro, already seated behind her camp desk—much newer and less ornate than the Faro of Panthers' furniture—had tossed her bearskin cloak over a stool where it dragged on the floor until the Laxtor picked it up and hung it more carefully on hooks embedded in the room's rock wall.

"You have something for me, Cursar?" She nodded to his left.

Startled, Tel remembered the scroll under his left arm. It had ridden in his pouch all the way and was, therefore, only damp instead of damp and dirty. "Yes, my Faro. From the Faro of Panthers, with her greetings."

Faro Sweetwater broke the seal on the scroll and unrolled it, her eyes shifting from left to right as she read.

Tel had examined that seal a hundred times as he made his way back to the Serpents Teeth, pretending each time that he *wasn't* looking for a way to break it open without getting caught. Now that he stood in his Faro's presence he was very glad he'd failed. Her eyes lifted above the top of the scroll.

"So, you have misplaced the Talent, Cursar?"

"What?" Tel swallowed. "I mean—no, my Faro. What we did was—" He halted at Juria Sweetwater's raised hand.

"The Panther has explained it all very satisfactorily," she said, allowing the scroll to roll closed and handing it to her Laxtor, who immediately opened it and began reading. "So, the last you saw of Kerida Nast, she was disappearing into the sky on the back of the griffin?"

"I would have followed them, my Faro, but I had no way to know which way they'd go."

"You did not read this message yourself?" She tilted her head toward Surm Barlot, still reading.

Tel felt his face grow hot. Could she tell that he'd tried? "No, my Faro."

"No." She nodded, looking off into the distance. "And Tonia Nast did not tell you what it contained." It wasn't a question, so Tel didn't answer it. He wasn't sure that the Faro would have heard him if he had. She seemed to have stopped listening. In fact, she seemed to have forgotten about him. The Laxtor laid the scroll on her camp desk without disturbing her. Finally, Tel couldn't wait any longer.

"Your pardon, my Faro, but has anyone had news of Talent Nast?" The Faro brought her gaze back from the distance but didn't speak. Tel looked from her to the Laxtor and back again. "The Inquisitor, what's he been doing? Or the Far-thinkers—have they heard from the griffin?"

But the Faro only glanced at the scroll on her table.

"You're dismissed, Third Officer," the Laxtor said. "The Talent High Inquisitor has asked for you."

His lips pressed tightly together, Tel turned around as quickly as he dared and left the room. Outside, he ignored the duty officer's curious face and turned left, heading toward the quarters he shared with Kerida. Once there, he used a jug of tepid water to wash his face, changed into clean clothing, broke off a piece of the travel cake he detested, and ate on the run. The place to start looking for the Inquisitor was his assigned workroom. Once he reached it, Tel stopped in the doorway, mouth full of food.

The last time he'd seen it, Luca Pa'narion's workroom had been an empty space about the size of a village school. Now there were a half-dozen tables, and people working at them. People dressed in modified versions of Talents' clothing. No black tunics, Tel saw, so Luca remained the only Inquisitor. Two of the assembled Talents were Flashing objects, but some were examining people, hands on throats and foreheads, or holding hands across the tables. Tel hoped they were being as careful and as thorough as Kerida would have been.

Luca Pa'narion himself stood looking over the shoulder of a fair-haired Talent with dark brows, the two of them frowning at something Tel couldn't see on the woman's tabletop. Before Tel could step forward, Luca looked up and saw him, but the Inquisitor's smile never got any further than a twitch of the lips. The man excused himself to the other Talent and joined Tel in the doorway, taking him by the arm and turning him back into the tunnel outside the workroom.

"You're alone? Where's Kerida?"

Tel filled the older man in on what had happened after they'd parted at the Springs and Pools. "Hasn't anyone been in contact with them? What about the Far-thinkers? Have they spoken with the griffin?"

"We can ask, of course, but I hardly think they would have heard from their Griffin Girl and not informed me. From what I've been told, they can't speak to the griffin at all unless he speaks to them first."

"And since Kerida's with him, why should he give a thought to the rest of us?" Tel rubbed at his face. He glanced at the Inquisitor, but the man didn't contradict him. "What about Wynn Martan? She still with the Luqs?" If he could get to Jerek, he might get some answers, or at least permission to go looking for some.

But Luca shook his head. "Not for long, She's getting ready to go to Gaena with Svann."

"What? Why should *she* go? Who'll stay with Jerek?" Tel pulled the Inquisitor to one side even though there was no one else in the tunnel to overhear them.

"However it may look from your perspective, young man, you are not in command here, nor am I, and nor is Kerida Nast, if it comes to that," Luca pointed out. "We advise, but we don't decide."

"The Feelers will do what Kerida wants." Tel chewed on his upper lip.

"But she's not here to tell them what she wants."

"Then who *is* staying with Jerek?" The boy might be the Luqs, but he was still a boy, and with Wynn going, that left only Tel himself who'd known him before he left home.

"I am."

Tel jumped and whirled around, his hand on the hilt of his sword. "For the Mother's sake, Ennick, you almost scared me to death. How can you be so quiet?"

The large man looked stricken. "I'm sorry, Tel Cursar. I don't mean to scare you, but I can't tell what you hear and what you don't."

"It isn't just that we don't hear you coming, my boy." Luca patted Ennick on the arm. "It's that we don't see you either."

Frowning, Ennick looked from one to the other. "But I'm right here."

"Of course, you are." It was Tel's turn to reassure the large man. At least he could reach Ennick's shoulder without stretching. "The question is, however, *why* are you here? Did you need Luca or me?"

"I need you, Tel Cursar. Jerek the Luqs wants to see you and speak to you." The large man lowered his voice to a confidential murmur. "Sometimes, you know, he just wants to see people, not speak to them."

"Shall I come now, Ennick?"

"Yes, please." Now Ennick smiled. "I know a way where no one will see us."

Baku sat in the most comfortable of her chairs, Kvena and Narl on low stools at her feet. The two maids were sewing, hard at work on another of the riding costumes Baku was coming to prefer. She had cloth in her own lap, and she held a threaded needle in her hand, but unlike her maids, her thoughts were elsewhere. Specifically, on the strange man who was her husband. He had come several times to play cards with her, each time, she thought, at the direction of the Poppy Shekayrin. It would be better if the man came of his own volition. Surely it would look more natural?

At the sound of a tap at the door, Baku jumped, sticking herself with her needle. Finger in her mouth, she nodded at Narl who rose and went to the door. Dern Firoxi came only in the evening, and it was not the usual time for an audience, so Baku put aside her sewing and let her veil fall over her face. At the door, Narl bowed low and stepped out of the way as the Poppy Shekayrin entered. Baku shivered under her veil and hoped the mage did not see.

In Halia, she had dealt most with Rose or Daisy Shekayrin, who were given to administration and the law. Before Pollik Kvar, she had seen Poppy Shekayrin only in the company of the Emperor. Once the Poppies—best at moving objects—had been of lesser importance than the others, but since the coming of the horsemen and their armies, they had risen in status, accompanying the Emperor everywhere, especially into the field.

Kvar she had not seen since the first public audience, and his expression did not give her hope that this was a courtesy visit. Pray gods he had not come to ask her about the sealing of the marriage.

She stood. Today she had dressed in a Halian gown, with its narrowly confining skirts, and padded jacket. Her indoor veil attached to her headdress, easy to let fall over her face. She wished now she had worn one of her riding outfits, though both were soiled.

"Honored One, I am the Poppy Shekayrin Pollik Kvar, administrator of the Faraman Peninsula."

It seemed odd that today he *would* introduce himself, though the belated formality did not reassure her. More particularly since he had not said "the Sky Emperor's province of Farama."

"It is unusual for a Poppy Shekayrin to be given an administrative post, is it not?" Baku gestured the man to the chair prepared for guests, with its small table of refreshments to one side. She herself would stand until he had left the room. Women, even a Princess Imperial, did not sit in the presence of men unless given permission. The consort's throne was the only exception.

"This is still a province at war. The time for Rose Shekayrin has not yet come." He took a sip of the tea Kvena had poured out and replaced the cup on the table. He looked around the sitting room, his glance coming to rest at the window seat, where Narl bent over her sewing. "I believe I am actually getting accustomed to seeing women's faces." His smile made the skin on Baku's back crawl.

Kvar made a gesture with his hand that had Kvena scurrying to the other end of the sitting room. Narl went also, but more slowly. They could not actually leave her alone—though what use they would be if he menaced her Baku did not know. She wished she had had the foresight to fetch out her mask. To reach it now she would have to turn her back on him. As if he had read her thought, the man's gaze went past her, to where the mask's box sat in state on its thick silk pad.

"I have been busy, Honored One. Otherwise, I would have visited you before this."

"I thank you for your visit." Baku tried to clear her throat without making any noise. "It is, however, growing late, and I would not keep you from your duties." That was as close as she could come—or would come—to asking him to make his point.

"Then I shall be brief. I am here to take the Emperor's mask into my safe custody."

Baku felt her body turn to stone. For a moment, she could not even draw breath. Finally, she was able to relax enough to speak. "I thank you for your kindness, Shekayrin Kvar, but I have been instructed to keep the Voice of the Emperor always by me."

Pollik Kvar rose to his feet and took a slow deliberate step toward her. "What did I tell you about your nonsense?"

As if his words freed her, Baku spun around. If she could reach the mask, the man would be forced to acknowledge its magic, and she would be safe.

But she had forgotten the Halian gown. Only a quick grab at the back of a chair prevented her from falling over completely, and before she knew it, a sudden force like a vise closed on her arm, and she was held in place. Pollik Kvar smiled, his right hand slightly raised. She did not know what shocked her more—that he would defy the Emperor's orders, or that he would use his magic to touch her.

"You are too lively, Honored One." The last words were said with a sneer that made Baku clench her teeth. Kvar gestured with his finger, and the invisible grip on her arm shook her upright. The mage reached into the small pocket created by the poppy crest on his tunic and took out his soul stone. As chilled as she was, Baku felt a drop of sweat roll down her spine. She fought to loosen the magic's grip, but it drew her closer to him. She tried to keep her face turned away, but her veil, held tightly in place by the grip closed around her arm, worked against her, and Kvar was able to lift the stone and place it on her forehead.

He will see it. Her heart hammered in her ears. *He will see the taint and destroy me as a witch.* But no, it appeared that she was safe. She had heard that one mage's block was not always detectable by another, and apparently what she had heard was true. With what, then, was Pollik Kvar threatening her? Her sight dimmed, and her legs shook under her.

He released her, and she staggered and would have fallen but for the chair behind her. Clinging to its back, she took in a shuddering breath. Her legs—all her muscles, it seemed—trembled with shock and revulsion.

"This lethargy you feel will fade—for a time. But it will return, each time worse, until I remove it."

The smile that followed these words was something Baku wished never to see again. Behind him, she could see her women. Narl was on her feet, being held back by Kvena's grip on her elbow. "My brother—" she began.

"Your brother has done what I needed him to do. He has sent me here and given me an army."

What could he mean? Baku drew herself up, surreptitiously pulling at her skirt. If she could reach the mask, she would have a chance . . . but before she could take even one step, Kvar held up the stone, reaching forward with his other, empty, hand.

It was not empty long.

Before she could even turn to look, the box holding the mask jumped past her and landed in the Shekayrin's hands. Baku's hands flew to her mouth, to stifle any sounds she might make.

"I will take charge of this, Honored One, as I said." His voice was silk. "Consider your position here. Cease this useless defiance. That is, if you wish to permanently regain your strength."

"The Emperor—" Her voice was no more than a whisper.

"Is not here." Kvar spoke slowly and clearly, as if she was the foolish girl he thought her to be. "Lulled by my reports, the Horseman who disgraces the Imperial throne of Halia did not even send more troops with you. If the Halians and Shekayrin who met with your great-grandfather had not been fools and cowards, your brother would not be sitting there at all. We should have driven your people into the sea. Your brother may have some slight trace of the magic of the world, but he has no soul stone, and the supply of those will shortly be in my hands. As is Farama. Your brother will have to deal with me or lose the support of all the Halian Shekayrin."

Without saying more, Kvar turned and left the room, leaving the door to stand open until Kvena went to close it.

As soon as the door was securely shut, Narl ran to her, hands extended. "Honored One, my lady, please, sit down. You're shaking."

Fool! Fool! Fool! How did she not see that these Shekayrin were capable of rebelling against her brother? How did *he* not see the possibility of it? Though perhaps he had. Perhaps that was the real reason he had sent the mask with her. If so, it had no more occurred to him than it had to her that they might take away the Emperor's Voice along with the protection it gave her.

Before the netting, I would have foreseen this, and taken steps to avoid it. Though she had to wonder what those steps might have been. She was powerless now.

Slowly, her strength returned. But for how long? **"Jerek? Jerek Brightwing! Do you hear me? Are you there?"**

In a room in the opposite wing of the Griffin Palace, Pollik Kvar contemplated the carved box that held the Emperor's Voice. This mask, and others like it, had come to Halia with the Horsemen who believed that it somehow chose their leaders. Superstitious nonsense, like so many of their beliefs.

The box that held the artifact had been locked, on the other hand, by a Halian Shekayrin—a Daisy, and a powerful one—and it took Kvar a little time to ferret out the secret of opening it. It did not really need the voice of the Princess Imperial to unlock, of course, not if one had a soul stone and was able to see the mechanism and move the—ah, there. Open, and it only took him twenty minutes.

He frowned at the elaborate silk linings. Though there were some Sunflower Shekayrin who suggested that silk had a way of dampening the effects of magic, it had never been proven to Kvar's satisfaction. "Pure superstition," he said, as he had many times before. He twitched the layers of cloth aside and lifted out the mask, using the tips of his fingers. He had worked with the Emperor many times and recognized what an astonishing likeness this was. Magnificent. A true work of art. Further proof, if any were needed, that the mask was no ancient artifact. Otherwise, how could it have Guon Kar Lyn's face on it?

Kvar turned it over and found the inner side just as smooth, just as carefully polished. It would have to be, he reasoned, if one were to be able to wear it for any extended period. Finally, he lifted it to his face. At first, he found peering through the empty eye holes a trifle disconcerting, though his vision was only slightly obscured. It fit surprisingly well, considering the mask had not been made for him. Smiling, he began to speak. Nothing. He cleared his throat and tried again. Still nothing. It took several more tries until he would admit it would not work for him.

He went to lift it from his face, but it did not move. Between one breath and the next, the mask grew tighter and then tighter still, until he could not breathe at all. He tried to fit his fingertips under the edge of the mask, but there was no room, not even for a fingernail. Desperate, he grabbed his soul stone, and with it augmenting his strength, he *lifted* the mask from his face using magic. His face free, he staggered backward, drawing in huge gasps of air, his throat raw as if he'd been screaming. The mask had fallen neatly into its box. At this moment Kvar would not have been greatly surprised if the wrappings had enveloped the mask of their own accord.

He approached the box now with caution, his stone clutched in his hand. The white mask lay faceup, the wrappings only layers of cloth after all. He gritted his teeth and picked the mask up again with his free hand. Nothing. It did not try to bite or smother him.

He raised the thing over his head, ready to smash it against the stone mantel of the fireplace. But then he waited. If the mask would only work for the Princess Imperial, then he had only to control the girl. And he was already doing that.

Ker dipped her hands into the cold water of the pond and splashed her face. She shivered. She hadn't bathed or washed since leaving the Springs and Pools; she wasn't about to bathe in this frigid water, but a clean face felt good. She tied back her hair with a leather thong. This wasn't a time to be remembering the warm bathing pools of the Springs. "Are you going to be much longer?" she called to Weimerk, floating in the middle of the water, his wings spread out, his chin resting on the surface, his tail lazily swishing back and forth, holding him in place like a man treading water.

"It was you who wanted to stop." Weimerk's voice sounded completely adult now.

Ker reached over her head, clasped her hands, and stretched her torso first to one side, then the other, feeling the muscles in her back and sides loosen reluctantly. They had no reason to hurry—in fact, the contrary. Ker wasn't looking forward to bringing bad news to those waiting in the Serpents Teeth. And once she was safely back, Weimerk would have to return to Griffinhome. "I needed to feel real ground under me," she said, her hands now in the small of her back. "And I'm getting stiff. It's like I've been on horseback for days. I ache all over. Hey!"

Weimerk appeared beside her on the bank, shaking water off his fur and feathers like a wet dog, lifting each paw in turn and giving them a shake as well. "You do not use the soul stone to its full potential. It can be used to heal others. Why not yourself?"

Ker finished wiping water off her face and lowered her hands to her hips. "It can be used to heal? When were you going to tell me this?"

"I have just told you."

"But why didn't you tell me before? Never mind." She held out a hand, palm toward the griffin. "Because I never asked you. You should tell me things that I might find useful, even if I don't ask."

"That is not the way. Rather ask yourself why you have not asked this question earlier? You know that the jewels give Gifts that are similar to those of Feelers. Why have you not investigated this yourself?"

"Oh, right. In my copious free time." But that didn't mean Weimerk was wrong. She should have thought about how she could better use the jewel. As soon as she got back, she'd have Svann help her. "Wait, Feelers can't heal, at least not without me."

"But you have you."

Ker squeezed her eyes shut, reminding herself that Weimerk wasn't doing this on purpose.

"If I were rested and feeling better, would I be able to use the jewel to speak with the Far-thinkers? Or are we out of range?"

"That is immaterial. They have no soul stones."

Right. "But what if I needed to speak with someone at the Mines?"

"Are there no others with jewels?"

Ker felt like slapping herself on the forehead. She must be even more tired than she'd thought. She pulled the jewel out of the front of her tunic and held it in her hand.

Kerida: Svann?

Svann: Kerida Nast, I have been attempting to reach you, but it seems I am not strong enough to sustain the connection myself.

Ker rubbed at her upper lip. She'd been ignoring a warmth under her tunic for days. Like an idiot, she'd never connected it with the jewel.

Kerida: I'm afraid that might have been me. I didn't know what it felt like to receive a message.

Svann: I am pleased, nonetheless. Tel Cursar has returned safely.

Kerida: I knew, thank you. Ker touched the lump under her tunic that was Tel's plaque. She checked it every morning.

Svann: I have finally received permission to return to Gaena. I will be leaving in the morning after—

"Svann? Are you there? Svann?" Ker looked up at Weimerk. "What happened?"

"One or both of you lost concentration. Do you find it tiring?"

Ker tucked the jewel away again. "I know. More practice, more discipline." She'd been hearing that advice for years.

"That does not make it less true."

"Look, it's not like I'm cutting classes and going fishing, I'm doing the best I can with no time and not much help and—" Ker sucked in some air and shut her mouth. And she was tired, and alone, and frightened, now that she knew the griffins wouldn't come to help them, and Weimerk was all well and good, but he wasn't Tel, and soon he'd be gone as well. . . . She swallowed. "Sorry. I'm all right now," she said.

"I never doubted it."

Ker rubbed at her face with hands grown suddenly cold. "So, what about Far-thinking with Dersay, or Cuarel?"

"Think what you ask. You are a Talent, and with the jewel you are a mage. . . ."

"But I'm not actually a Feeler, so I don't have their Gifts, not exactly."

"Precisely."

"But what if I need to talk to someone at the Mines? Once Svann goes, there isn't anyone there I can reach."

"Certainly, there is. You have done it before. You and I together. Focus your attention on the one to whom you wish to speak."

Of course, the person she really wanted to speak to was Tel. It was good to know that he was safe, if tired and hungry, but it wasn't like speaking to him.

"It must be someone who can hear you."

"I know, sorry."

If only Sala were still alive. She was the Far-thinker Ker knew best. *Think of someone else. Think of someone else.* For all she knew this power of the griffins would allow her to contact even the dead.

"Now you are being silly."

Who then? Dersay, or Cuarel?

Jerek: Who is that? Baku?

Kerida: It's Kerida Nast. Jerek? Who's Baku?

Jerek: Thank the Mother. Are you all right? Luca came back without you, and Wynn's going away. . . . Even through this tenuous connection, Ker could hear worry in Jerek's "voice." **I heard that Tel is back, and I've sent Ennick for him. He should be here any minute.**

It had been so long since Ker had smiled that she felt her dry lips crack. Could she hold this connection long enough for Tel to reach Jerek's rooms? Would the giant Ennick take him around by the back way, or—

"It is I who maintains this connection, and you are wasting time."

Jerek: Kerida? Ker? Are you still there? What about the griffins? When will they arrive?

Ker's heart sank. She glanced at Weimerk, but he didn't look any happier than she was.

Kerida: They're not coming.

Jerek: What do you mean they're not coming?

Kerida: They say they won't come until the Prophecy has been fulfilled.

Jerek: But it's *their* Prophecy!

Kerida: They say they're through giving Gifts to us, that now we're on our own. Jerek, I'm so sorry—maybe if someone else had gone.

Jerek: No, you're the Griffin Girl. No one else could have reached them but you.

He was quiet long enough that Ker feared the connection was gone after all, though she could tell by how her head felt that it was still there.

Jerek: Fine, then. That means we don't need them. We have *you*. *You're* the one Larin saw, you're what we need. You're their last Gift.

"He is not wrong."

Ker blinked. Trying to listen to both of them at once was giving her a headache. Jerek sounded determined, but not as if he had any real hope. She didn't envy his having to tell everyone else that the help they were counting on wasn't coming after all.

Kerida: Jerek, there's more. Weimerk can't stay with us. He has to go back to Griffinhome.

Jerek: Mother help us. We were counting on him to hunt for us when we sent supplies to the Springs and Pools.

Kerida: Listen, Jerek, I don't think you quite—

Jerek: No, *you* listen. There's nothing we can do about the griffins, but there may be another way. A way to solve the problem of the Shekayrin and the Halians at once. I need you to go to Farama the Capital right away. I need you to help Baku escape.

Kerida: And what, for the Daughter's sake, is a Baku? And how was that going to make things better?

Jerek: She's the Princess Imperial and she's on our side and she planned to help us from the palace, but she's not safe there anymore, so she needs to escape. They say she's married to my father and . . .

Ker bit her lip. Could the girl be telling him the truth? Was it even her? What if this was some ploy to trap Jerek himself?

"Far-thinkers cannot lie to each other in that way," the griffin said. "She cannot disguise her identity, nor her purpose if it is truly felt."

Jerek: She may be the only one who can help us now, but no one here will listen to me. Now he really sounded desperate. **I'm going to send Tel.**

Kerida: Tell him to meet me at the Ram and Boar Inn. It's in the theater district.

Ker waited, but Jerek didn't answer. "Did he hear me?"

"He heard."

Ker could barely summon the energy to stand up. She leaned against Weimerk's flank. "Then it's off to Farama." Her voice sounded odd and she cleared her throat.

"I will take you there, but then I must return to Griffinhome."

Ker pushed herself upright. Knowing something was coming didn't make it any easier. "I wish you didn't have to go."

"My kin cannot be disobeyed in this, though I will never forgive them for parting us."

Ker felt exactly the same, but it wouldn't help Weimerk to let him know how angry she still was. "You're going to need them someday, even if it's only to mate."

"I know you are right, but I will not forgive them."

Ker scrubbed at her face with hands that felt grimy. "Well, I guess we'll have to fulfill the Prophecy without you."

"Not without all of me. We can still speak to one another; distance will not part us. And, through me, you can speak to others. There is other help I will give you now: griffin colors like the flame that warms you. Flash me."

Paraste. Weimerk had already helped her with her nausea and feeling cold. What else did he have for her?

"I wondered if you might like to be invisible?"

"She's all right? You spoke to her?" Tel could barely keep himself from grabbing his Luqs by the shoulders and shaking him until more information came out. "Where is she?"

"I don't know," Jerek admitted. "We didn't talk about that. Listen." The boy's face hardened, and Tel suddenly saw what he'd look like when he was older. If he ever got any older. "The griffins won't help us—they won't come at all until the Prophecy is fulfilled."

"You mean when we don't need them?" Tel gestured an apology. This wasn't Jerek's fault. "Sorry, my lord Luqs."

"Not as sorry as I am. I can judge from your reaction the kind of response I'm going to get from the others when I tell them." Jerek pushed his hands through his hair. If it got any longer, he'd have to braid it like a soldier. "There *is* something else we can try. I've arranged for you to go with Svann and the others, but—"

"It's Svann, isn't it? What's the Motherless dog done now?"

"Sit down and listen." Jerek rubbed his eyes. "Sorry. Can Ennick bring you some food, or something to drink?"

Shaking, Tel almost fell back into the chair Ennick had pushed forward for him. He put his hands down on his thighs and took a deep breath. The kid had enough to worry about without Tel yelling at him. He needed to take himself in hand. "No travel cake," he said.

"Ennick, some soup and a piece of crumble pie. That won't raise any eyebrows. Oh, and water." He turned back to Tel. "I'd ask for wine or beer, but I never have before, and that might make people wonder."

"You're the Luqs. What can they do?"

The boy's face stiffened. "Yes. I'm the Luqs when they want to have a meeting, or when they need something officially ordered. But when I ask for someone to go to Farama, they 'take it under advisement.' The rest of the time I'm just a kid, and they're busy protecting me."

Tel blinked. Of course, Jerek couldn't be more than, what? Fourteen? Normally, people weren't considered adult enough to make their own choices until they were seventeen—fifteen at the earliest, under special circumstances and after everyone could be sure they weren't Talented. You could enter the military at fifteen, for example, but you couldn't expect much advancement until you were older. You could get engaged, but not married.

"Sorry," he said finally. "How can I help?"

"I'm going to send you with Svann, but like I said, I really want you to get to Farama the Capital. Kerida said you're to meet her at the Ram and Boar. You're going to help her rescue the Princess Imperial."

"What's a Princess Imperial?"

Jerek's eyes narrowed. "Should I wait until you've had something to eat? You're not usually this slow."

Tel felt his ears grow hot. He rubbed his face. "No. Go on, please. I won't interrupt."

The boy watched him for what felt like a long time, and then his face relaxed as he told Tel about Bakura, and the Voice of the Emperor. Despite what he'd just said, he couldn't stop himself from interrupting Jerek with questions.

"How's this mask going to help us?"

"She believes the soldiers will obey her when she uses it. They're loyal to her brother first, not the Shekayrin."

"The Shekayrin can control people." Tel was grateful that Ennick arrived with the food. He needed all the distraction he could get.

"Not a lot of people, not all at once. They can be overwhelmed by numbers. Baku says that's how her people took Halia in the first place."

"Blades of grass."

"Exactly. If we get a sufficient number of people against them, we should be able to knock them out and take their jewels away."

Tel swallowed the spoonful of soup he had in his mouth. "I feel a 'but' coming on."

Jerek was silent for long enough for Tel to finish his soup and start in on the pie. The boy looked like someone deciding what part of the story he was going to keep back. Tel forced himself to keep quiet.

"She's afraid that this invasion isn't about her brother and his plans at all," Jerek finally said. "She thinks the Shekayrin—and this Pollik Kvar in particular—had another goal all along: to get themselves more jewels and take the Peninsula as their own territory. Griffins or no griffins, we still have to stop them. She can turn the army against them, but she must be free to do it. Right now, she's not even allowed access to any of the important officers. She says she can get out of the palace on her own, but she doesn't know anyone to help her after that, and neither do I."

"I've never been to Farama the Capital." Tel squeezed his eyes shut and shook his head. "Never mind, ignore that. Ker's a Talent and she's got a jewel. She could probably rescue the princess herself." *But she's asked for me to go to her.*

"Well, that's what I'm hoping," the boy said. "But I've got some information for you." He dug under his mattress and pulled out a few squares of dirty and much-folded paper. "I asked people who knew the capital well to tell me stories about it," he said, as he knelt on the carpet. "They think I'm curious because I'll live there one day, but I've made maps from what they told me." He glanced up. "Don't look, Ennick. You know how maps make you feel funny."

"Sure, Jerek."

Tel watched the boy spread out the pages, arranging them in order so that they presented one large picture. Jerek concentrated, his brows drawn down, his mouth in a straight line.

"You're sure rescuing this princess from the Halians is worth taking Kerida away from the Feelers and the Bears and putting her into that kind of danger? Is Bakura part of the Prophecy, or what?" Tel kept his tone level. Kerida thought that Jerek himself was the one the Prophecy spoke about, the one who would unite everyone, Talents, Feelers, UnGifted people, and—yes—even the Shekayrin.

Jerek stopped arranging the maps and looked up, licking his lips. "I've asked Larin, but you know what she's like. If she doesn't want to speak to you, you can't make her. But Larin doesn't tell me to stop Kerida from going. In fact, she gave me something for you to give her." He felt inside his tunic and finally pulled out a small bag, the leather so old it had begun to flake around the edges. Jerek emptied it out into his hand and, along with a lock of hair, a chess piece, and what looked like a dried nut, was a jewel. Unmistakably, a jewel. Jerek picked it out and handed it to Tel before hiding his other precious things away again.

"This is the one Luca found? The one that doesn't work?" Tel pressed his lips together, eyeing the jewel laying in the palm of his hand.

"Yes." Jerek sat back on his heels. "Larin said Kerida would know what to do with it." He drew down his brows, mouth twisted to one side. "Listen. I know that Baku can help us if we can get her away from the Shekayrin. Once—"

Tel wouldn't have noticed Jerek's hesitation if he hadn't been looking for it. Whatever he said next, it wasn't what he'd been about to say.

"They'll obey her, her brother's officers."

Tel nodded slowly. Did Jerek know how uncertain he looked? "I'll be expected to report to my Company Commander. They may already be wondering where I am."

"And I'll ask that you get sent with Svann and his party. It'll make sense because he'll look like he's coming back with approximately the same number of people he went with. That'll add weight to his story."

"I'm not arguing with you," Tel said. "But I just don't trust Svann, especially now that Ker's not here to Flash him."

"That's why Barid's going with you. He can check Svann as necessary."

Tel swallowed, and wished he felt as sure as his Luqs sounded.

Tel leaned his hips against a smooth outcropping of rock wall that seemed designed for just that, watching Svann out of the corner of his eye. Just a few paces away, the Shekayrin stared down at the jewel in his hand as if he expected it to talk to him.

"Maybe he does," Tel muttered. Wynn hovered at Svann's elbow, and Pella, along with a few other soldiers, was waiting nearby, but that didn't make Tel feel any better.

Barid came up on Tel's other side and found a perch of his own to lean against. Tel wasn't sure what to make of the Talent. Kerida was the only one he really knew, and she wasn't anything even close to ordinary. Though she *had* vouched for Barid. . . .

"Not looking forward to going back into the Peninsula, I

imagine," Tel said. He could have kicked himself. Why remind the man how much danger he faced?

"I'll be all right. I survived there for months; it can't be any harder now." Barid looked sideways at Tel. "After all, we're traveling with our own Shekayrin, aren't we?"

Tel examined the Talent closely. He was olive-skinned, like Kerida, but his hair and his eyes were much darker, close to black, and his nose broader. Though almost everyone had a nose broader than hers. Barid sat calmly under Tel's assessment, his eyes unflinching.

"You think that's an advantage?"

Teeth flashed white against Barid's beard. It was odd to see a Talent who wasn't clean-shaven. "You have a particular reason to dislike this mage?" Tel said nothing. Barid's eyes glanced right, to where Svann stood, still looking at his jewel, before returning to Tel. "When you watch him, you get a certain look on your face."

Tel felt his shoulders go back and tried to relax. "I didn't realize I was so obvious."

"Don't take offense. I don't think anyone but a Talent would have seen it, and as you may have noticed yourself, there aren't many of us." Barid shrugged one shoulder. "Which makes me wonder why I'm being sent with you, instead of staying here and helping Luca."

"You're being sent along to keep an eye on Svann."

"Well, no one's said that, not exactly. But what other reason could there be?" Another glance at Svann. "Luca Pa'narion says there's nothing to worry about, that he's examined him." Barid swiveled his eyes again, to leave no doubt who he was talking about.

"Kerida says the same." Tel felt his ears grow hot. This would be the first time he'd ever repeated anything that had been said only between the two of them. He had a feeling Kerida wouldn't be very happy about it if she found out.

"But you don't agree."

Tel shrugged. Barid switched his focus to his own crossed ankles, then looked across at Tel's feet. He frowned, mouth twisted to one side. "How tall *are* you?"

Tel laughed in spite of himself. "I'm not sure," he said, still smiling. "Last time anyone checked I hadn't stopped growing." It felt good to laugh with someone, even if the laughter died away quickly. Svann had looked up from his jewel, a puzzled look on his face as if he couldn't remember who they were or why they were there.

"The one who had me, the one they rescued me from when we were trying to use the Pass, he was like this one." Barid looked down at his feet again, his voice cool and gentle. "A nice enough person. Organized. Civil. Careful of his horses and of the people with him. I started to think he wasn't really that bad. That maybe the one I'd seen slaughter everyone I knew at Questin Hall was some kind of aberration. Lunacy isn't confined to the UnGifted."

"But," Tel prompted when it looked like Barid wasn't going on.

"But then we came across this woman who argued with him. She said that no matter what, her son had gone into the Halls of Law, so she knew perfectly well men could be Talents. That no one in their family was deluded. That she'd seen his Talent before he'd been examined. And that, furthermore, she was a good deal older than him and had a better understanding of the world, and he should listen to her."

Tel smiled. "Sounds like my grandmother. In fact, it sounds like everybody's grandmother. But I take it the Shekayrin didn't agree with her."

"With a perfectly calm face, slowly and gently, he touched her on the forehead with his soul stone, and she collapsed into the arms of the people with her. At first, I thought she slept, but once we had continued down the road, I heard the crying behind me, and I knew he'd killed her." Barid looked over at Tel, making sure he had his attention. "He didn't have to. It wouldn't have made any difference at all to leave her alive. You can't ever forget how dangerous they are." He shrugged. "You just can't."

Tel tilted his head back and shut his eyes. That summed up his own thoughts. He believed Kerida. He did. Svann was on their side. But for how long?

"Hey." Wynn gestured at them to join her. She still stood next to Svann, bouncing a little on the balls of her feet. She had her bright red hair braided into half a dozen smaller plaits and tied securely back. To wear it in a single braid would be to say to the world—and all the Halians in it—that she was a soldier. And women were no longer allowed to bear arms.

"Svann's got something he thinks is going to help you."

The Shekayrin looked up from the pack he'd rested on the ground at his feet. The sunflower tattooed around his left eye seemed to move in the flickering light. "Ah, Tel, good. I thought to wait until we arrived in Gaena, but Wynn Martan tells me I should give you this pass now, as we may be separated." Svann took what looked like a dispatch out of the pouch he wore at his waist. It was parchment, folded in thirds, with the ends folded to the middle. A wax seal had been impressed into the center, holding the folds solidly together. He offered the packet to Tel.

Tel reached for it, and then hesitated. When he saw the seal, he swallowed. It looked exactly as though Svann had used his jewel to impress the seal when the wax was soft.

"This declares you to be a courier for a Shekayrin, and no one can keep you from your errand. With it, you may use any road. If you are stopped, you merely show them this."

"And what errand am I on?"

"You will not be asked."

Tel pressed his lips together, nodding, but didn't take the pass.

"If you distrust me, Tel Cursar, please, have Barid Poniara Flash the pass." Svann spoke as if he wasn't worried, and as if the idea that Tel didn't trust him wasn't offensive. Tel hesitated and then waved Barid forward. He didn't care if they saw he was afraid; there were more important things at stake.

Barid took the package in both hands and closed his eyes. Tel knew from Kerida that it wasn't necessary, but many young Talents closed their eyes to help them concentrate. As they got older, more practiced, they weren't so easily distracted.

Barid opened his eyes. "It's what it's supposed to be. Exactly what he described."

"I'd love to have one myself, truth to tell." Wynn's eyes were huge in her face.

Svann took the pass back. "Here, Tel Cursar, place your thumb mark on the seal."

Barid says it's a pass. Tel held his breath as he touched his thumb to the seal. The wax felt warm. He took his thumb away and accepted the pass in his other hand.

"I'm not sure what my reception in Gaena will be." Svann spoke as though he was picking up the thread of a conversation. "So much depends on the reaction of the Rose Shekayrin with whom I served. Indeed, it may be best if you do not enter the town with us lest you be delayed."

"Gentlemen," Wynn interrupted. "It'll take a full day—and a bit—to get to the Simcot Exit. And while it's the closest one to Gaena, it's not *that* close." She turned to Tel. "Once you're changed, we can be on our way."

"What's wrong with my clothes," Tel said. "I put them on clean to speak to the Faro."

"We're with him"—Wynn pointed her thumb at Svann—"but you'll have fewer questions to answer when you're alone if you're wearing these." She gestured at one of the soldiers waiting behind Svann who came forward with a stack of folded clothing. Shirt, under and over tunics, trousers, all military in cut, they were neither the black of the Eagles, nor the purple of the Bears, but a dark gray Tel had never seen in any Wing of the Faraman Polity.

"You will find them a good fit, I believe," Svann said.

"The last soldiers we caught in the pass were wearing these," Barid said. "Before I was rescued, they told us that all the military in the Peninsula would be wearing this color in the next month or so."

Tel accepted the bundle from a grinning Wynn Martan. "Like I said, you'll be less likely to be stopped in the first place if you're in this uniform."

"And if you are stopped," Svann added. "You have your pass. You cannot be detained."

———

Ker had Weimerk drop her off in a farmer's field two hours before dawn. They were close enough to the road she and her parents had used to enter Farama the Capital when she was a child that she couldn't get lost. She stopped when she felt the smoother surface of the road under her feet.

<<Why do you stop?>>

It was actually a relief that Weimerk didn't already know. <<If I go that way,>> she pointed with her chin away from the capital. <<I'd be at home in four days.>>

<<Will you go there?>>

What would she find? Tonia hadn't heard any recent news. <<Later. When this is over.>>

Farama the Capital was made up of two sections: the inner, walled city that remained from Jurianol's day, when she had become the first Luqs and made the town her capital, and the secondary city which had sprung up outside of those original walls, as the population of the capital grew and expanded. The inner city still housed the Griffin Palace, and the principal buildings of the Polity, including the central Hall of Law, where the Inquisitors had their offices, and from where the network of Talents were administered and managed. Ker couldn't help wondering who occupied that building now. Or whether it still stood.

The entrances to the walled portion of Farama the Capital had always been gated, but Ker had never before seen one in use. In fact, if she'd thought about it at all, she would have guessed that the gates were ceremonial only. She saw now she would have been wrong. As she got closer, she could see the gates were in fine shape, well-maintained and strong. More than a touch ironic, that they'd been useless against the enemy within.

Ker had been putting off trying out her new Gift of invisibility. She'd felt comfortable enough when practicing with Weimerk, but now, alone, she didn't feel so confident. She couldn't leave it any longer, or she'd be at the gate before she knew it. If it wasn't going to work, now was the time to know. She slowed her pace slightly, and drifted off to the side of the road, out of the main foot traffic. *Paraste*. There it was, a beautiful moss-green color, a gray green, really, with maybe a hint of soft pink. She spun it thin, weaving and knotting it into a fine net just like Weimerk had told her, letting it fall over her like a lace bedcover. She remembered to check for her shadow. She grinned. Perfect.

Except for the small child—so small Ker couldn't tell if it was female or male—who stopped and stared straight at her. "Crap."

The child giggled. Ker let her invisibility go and squatted down to look at the child eye-to-eye. She put her index finger to her lips. The child's eyes grew wider, and she—definitely she—mimicked the gesture before running off. *Gifted*, Ker thought, eyeing the number of the child's colors. Indigo, or maybe black, the thread was too thin to be sure. Either a Time-seer, or a Far-thinker. If she lived to learn how.

Which means we have to get our country back.

When her heart slowed down to something that resembled normal, Ker built the moss-green net again. She waited, but apparently there weren't any other Gifted of any age in the crowd. She'd just have to hope that was also true of the gate guards—and that they weren't so bored they'd be easily distracted. By an unexpected shadow, for example.

Immediately ahead of her walked a farmer, his donkey cart heavily loaded with what had to be the last of the winter cabbages and squash. Ker shoved her hand into her pouch and wrapped her cold fingers around her jewel. She focused on one particular cabbage, perched shakily on the top of the heap. Concentrating, remembering the lessons Svann had given her, Ker pushed and lifted the vegetable, flinging it as far ahead in the line as she could manage. Immediately, voices were raised, turning quickly into cursing and accusations.

Ker's heart dropped as she glimpsed her own shadow. Using the jewel had weakened her invisibility, leaving her temporally exposed. *Nothing to see here*, she said to herself as she hastily respun her mossy-green net. She walked slowly but deliberately up the side of the column. *You don't see me.* She'd have to talk to Weimerk about this phenomenon later.

She should have known that the guards at the capital gates would react professionally, no matter how bored they might be. While two were wrapped up in dealing with the argument that had broken out in the line, a third stood back, hands on hips, eyes scanning back and forth, watching the crowd, not the argument. Ker breathed carefully, concentrated on keeping her pace even, on making as little noise as possible. On the completeness of the net she wrapped around herself. Her mouth dry, she was afraid to check if she could still see her shadow.

The officer's head swung toward her, and Ker held her breath. She kept walking, slow and steady, and his eyes passed right over her, as if he saw nothing. Hardly daring to resume breathing, Ker passed through the gates, and into Farama.

Her first impression was that the buildings were smaller than she remembered, and the cobbled streets dirtier. Ker had only been here as a child, when her mother had brought her and her older brother for the cycle of plays and musical performances that honored the Son in spring and fall. She was certain she could find her way to the Griffin Theater. From there, the Ram and Boar should be easy to find. If worse came to worst, she could ask. Surely everyone around that district would be used to people asking for directions.

As she remembered, half an hour of walking brought her to the three squares that made up the theater district. Around them were half a dozen playhouses, ranging from the imposing and grand Griffin Theater, with its enormous banner, to the modest stage known as the Luqs' Seat where one- and two-act plays were performed. Taverns and alehouses in the district often housed the players and were venues for singers and musicians.

Ker walked around the largest square, afraid to draw attention to herself by stopping, but no matter how casually she walked, she couldn't tell which of the streets leading out of the west side of the square was the one she wanted—if that even was the west side of the square. Tel was right after all; she could get lost in a corridor. At last she paused in front of a poster advertising an upcoming musical evening and triggered her Talent. *Paraste.*

This time when her aura appeared, it looked hazy, almost faded. So did everyone else's, she saw when she looked around her. Her pack felt suddenly heavier. She *was* Flashing, but it seemed that without touching the ground, she still couldn't tell which street she wanted.

Don't panic. Stay calm, breathe deep. You're tired, and you're hungry. This has happened before. Terestre. Sure, it had. Practically the first thing Candidates were taught at Questin Hall was that Flashing used up energy like any physical activity, so Talents had to stay rested, fed, and in good general health.

She'd ask at an alehouse or tavern, she thought. First, she could get something to eat, and by establishing herself as a customer, she'd be entitled to ask for information. The staff of an alehouse might be more willing to advise her, since they wouldn't have many, or any, rooms to let themselves. From the increase of walkers like herself, and the direction they were taking, the midday meal was just beginning to be served. Making up her mind quickly, Ker found an empty seat at a communal table in a small but well-attended tavern.

Ker sat between a large man wearing a blacksmith's apron, and a slim woman with a carefully painted face. Ker guessed she was older than she appeared, and probably an actor.

"Your pardon," Ker said, falling into the formality she thought the older woman would appreciate. She waited until the woman finished a mouthful of stew. "Could you tell me where the Ram and Boar is?"

The older woman swallowed and raised her brows. "You don't like the food here?" Her voice was almost as beautiful as her smile.

Ker found herself smiling back. An actor, definitely, and probably a singer as well. "I'm meeting someone there."

The woman nodded and broke a tiny piece of bread off her roll before handing the rest under the table. Ker hoped she had a dog.

"Yes, my dog is under the table." The woman's smile broadened. "Oh, my dear, you should have seen the look on your face. Like this." The woman's face changed so subtly Ker couldn't be sure what she'd done, but she was the image of someone worried, but afraid to ask anything.

"You must be a very good actor."

The woman shrugged up one shoulder. "Luckily, the arts have always been considered the property of the Son, so it's likely our festival can continue. Smile and nod, my dear, you never know who is watching. That's better. Now, what were you asking? The Ram and Boar? It's not too far off, in Threadneedle Alley, about halfway between here and the third-day market—your pardon, my dear, of course you don't know where that is. Turn left as you leave this place. . . ."

Ker listened, nodding, and then repeated the woman's instructions back to her.

"Very good, my dear. With your memory, and that magnificent nose, you'd make an excellent actor, if you should need to change professions. I don't think there's a noble role you couldn't play."

"Thank you, I'll keep it in mind." Ker finished eating as the two of them talked over plays she had seen and music she knew, though luckily the meal finished before Ker's scant experience became obvious. She rose, thanked the actor again, and was out on the street before she realized that she didn't know the woman's name. On the other hand, Ker hadn't given her name either.

The Ram and Boar looked exactly as she remembered it, even the man behind the serving bar looked familiar. This was the sort of place where a person could sit over her cup of kaff for an hour or two unbothered, so long as no one needed her table. All seats against the wall were taken, although one elderly man with wargame markers set up in front of him beckoned her into the seat across from him. Ker shook her head, smiling. She couldn't possibly focus enough to give the old man a good game. She bought a cup of kaff with milk, fragrant with cinnamon and steaming hot, and sat down at one of the smaller central tables. She pulled a deck of cards from the outer pocket of her pack and started laying out a one-handed game of Seasons. Like the wargame, the cards could be an excuse for her to sit undisturbed, while she thought about what to do next. How long would it take for Tel to get to her? Should she take a room? Did she even have enough money to pay for one?

She was just laying a Winter Inquisitor on a Summer Luqs when she caught movement out of the corner of her eye, gone before she could turn her head. Then, from behind, two hands came to rest on her shoulders.

"You don't know me," said a voice that sent shivers up her spine. A voice she hadn't heard for more than three years.

Jerek: My people are on their way. You should be ready to move any time now.

Baku placed her fingertips on her eyebrows and applied pressure to the ridge of bone. It was not a headache, but the general lassitude that Pollik Kvar had visited on her. Sitting in the walled garden helped, and here it was easier to Far-think to Jerek unobserved.

Jerek: Baku? Are you still there? There's something you're not telling me.

There are two things. Which one can I reveal? Would Jerek even want to help her if he knew she no longer had the mask? But she had to say something. Baku made her choice, and Jerek stayed silent for so long after Baku finished telling him what the Poppy Shekayrin had done to her that only the now-familiar feeling of space in her head told her he was still there.

Jerek: All the more reason for you to get away quickly, while he thinks it's not possible.

Baku: And if he is correct? It is not yet bad enough that I must ask him for relief, but—Baku had a sudden idea. **What of your griffin? Can** *he* **help me? Legends say they are all-powerful.**

Jerek: Kerida can. Another long pause. **At least, I think so.**

Baku: It is worth the risk. In any event, I would rather die free.

Jerek: I have a place for you to go once you've left the palace.

No. Jerek could not know that she had lost the mask. At least, not yet.

8

THE skin on Kerida's back shivered. She knew that voice. It wasn't possible, but she knew it. She gripped the edge of the table with both hands, afraid to look up. Afraid that it wouldn't be Ester after all. She'd given up trying to find news of the sister who'd been stationed with the Eagles in the Peninsula when the Halians came. After they'd killed all the Talents they could find, they started on all the military women who didn't surrender their arms fast enough.

Finally, Ker looked up, but only as far as the woman's shoulder. The server circled the table. She moved like Ester. The hand that reached for Ker's almost empty cup, nudging the cards aside so she could wipe the table off with a damp rag, had the same scar across the knuckles that Ker had seen a thousand times. Ker raised her eyes a little more. There was very little left in this woman of the Emerald Cohort Leader of Eagles Ker had last seen on the day Luca Pa'narion had discovered her Talent and taken her from that world forever. Ester's dark hair was long enough to braid, not cropped short to accommodate her helmet. She wore a loose, half-sleeved shirt, belted in by a large apron, instead of her black Eagles tunic. Ker would never have thought that her sister could look so ordinary. Or that she'd be working in an inn.

But the smile was the same, and the dark eyes. "Try not to look so poleaxed, youngster. It's a good thing no one's looking at us."

Ker coughed to clear the lump out of her throat. "Well, I knew there wasn't much in the way of advancement in the Eagles, but I didn't think it would come to this." The corner of Ester's mouth twitched. Promotion had always been a sore point in family arguments, ever since the younger of her two half-sisters had gone to the Eagles, who were limited to guarding the Peninsula, and the person of the Luqs. Nasts had always joined the Battle Wings, which saw more fighting, and therefore had more opportunities for ambitious recruits.

Ester's eyes clouded over, and the humor disappeared from her expression. "You'll be wanting a room, I take it?" She almost straightened. She almost stood like a military officer, but she remembered in time. In her eyes was the knowledge that, since the Halians came, she wasn't a military officer anymore and it was dangerous for her even to look like one.

Ker swallowed. If the Halians hadn't come, Ker would never have spoken to anyone in her family again. She'd stopped belonging to them the moment she'd entered a Hall of Law as a Talent. That she and Ester were here now was proof that the world had turned upside down. "If there's a cheap one available, yes." She gathered up her cards and shuffled them slowly. Her hands felt like she was wearing mittens. She'd planned to wait until closer to the evening meal to ask about a room. Her funds were limited, and she couldn't afford to pay for the use of a room she wouldn't need until tonight.

Ester looked sideways as though she were thinking. "If you don't mind sharing, you can bunk in the attic, third door on the left. I'll tell the boss," she added at Ker's nod. She watched her sister walk away, touching a shoulder here and there, greeting four laborers coming in the door by name.

The rest of the afternoon and early evening seemed to take days to go by. Finally, with supper over, and the night's drinking started, Ker was able to go upstairs without raising eyebrows at the hour. The little attic room was tucked into a warm corner, to one side of the kitchen chimney. There were only two beds, one made up with both sheets and blankets, the other bare, with the linens folded neatly at the foot of the bed. This was Ester's own room. Ker didn't even have to Flash it to know.

It couldn't have been very much later that Ker heard footsteps on the narrow stairs, coming toward the door. She got to her feet as the door opened, and she found herself in her sister's arms, ribs creaking at the force of her hug.

"Oh, Mother. Oh, Mother." Ester whispered against Ker's hair. "Oh, Kerryberry, you're alive." Ker blinked away tears. Her sister hadn't called her that since she was three years old. For an instant, she smelled the oil on Ester's leather harness, mixing with straw, and the tar they used to mark the sheep.

"We heard about Questin and thought we'd lost you."

"Lost *me*? What about you?" Ker was finally able to pull back, though she didn't let go completely. "No one could tell me anything about you, where you were, and—and they were killing female soldiers." Her voice broke as all the fear and anger and grief that she'd been pushing aside for months suddenly bubbled to the surface. She looked at Ester, really seeing her for the first time. Her hair had a dusting of white in it that made Ker think of their grandmother. Her face was thinner, and there were more lines around her eyes. She hadn't seen Ester at all for over two years, and for the two years before that, she'd only seen her in the black uniform of the Eagles.

"Ooof, put me down. You're worse than Tonia." Ker thumped back onto her feet as Ester let go of her.

"You've seen Tonia? Are the Battle Wings coming?"

"Mother and Son." Ker sank to the edge of the bed. She'd been so focused on finding Ester that everything else had flown right out of her head. "How much do you know?"

Ester sat on the other bed, so close their knees almost touched. "How much do I know? I know the Halians came, helped and supported by a network of spies and sympathizers. I know we fought them and lost—if you can call a total massacre a loss. If you can call our female officers and even plain soldiers killed without mercy a loss." Ester stopped, her lips pressed tight together. It must cost her every day, Ker thought, this pretense that she was just a servant in an inn. "If you can call the murder of the Luqs, to whom we pledged our lives to protect, a loss."

Hesitating, Ker put her hand on Ester's knee. It seemed presumptuous to offer sympathy, but impossible not to. "I was in Questin when we heard the news," she said.

"But you got away in time." Ester caught up her hands.

"I got away." Ker swallowed. This part was still hard. "Only me, and one other Candidate, though I didn't know about him until a few weeks ago. I've been with the Bear Wing ever since the Luqs was found."

Ester sighed, leaning back on her hands. "I'm not calling Dern Firoxi Luqs, not in private, and not in public if I can help it. I don't care how he's descended from Fokter the Fourth. No one who follows the enemy around like a dog is my Luqs. Ruarel was a selfish, arrogant woman, as I told her to her face, but she resisted the enemy, though it killed her."

"I don't mean Dern Firoxi. The Halians don't decide who becomes Luqs, the Wings do. And the Wings have acclaimed Firoxi's son, Jerek Brightwing."

"Brightwing?" Ester's eyebrows lifted. "And where is he?"

Ker looked down at her hands. "I'm not sure I can—"

"Kerida." Ester's tone made Ker sit up straight. "The Luqs of Farama is the Faro of Eagles, *my* Faro. I need to know where he is, and I need to know now." Ester had never been more completely a Cohort Leader.

"They're in the Serpents Teeth." Ker responded to the tone of authority. "I won't go into detail just now."

"And is Tonia there?"

Ker shook her head. "It's the Bear Wing. Last I saw Tonia was more than a month ago. She and the better part of her Panthers were in New Province, northeast of the Serpents Teeth."

"What's she waiting for?"

"News from Juristand. They've shifted the capital there until the Peninsula is free."

"Juristand." Her sister took the bridge of her nose in the tips of her fingers. "Don't tell me. We're to let them know when we've freed ourselves, and in the meantime they're too busy running the rest of the Polity to send us any help."

"I think that's the answer Tonia expects."

"Thank the Daughter our father's not here. He'd be saying he told us so."

Ker almost smiled. Their father, retired Faro of Panthers, had always spoken against splitting the administration of the Polity. "Without knowing what Juristand's answer is, I don't know what Tonia will do, but I'm hoping she joins the Bears in the Serpents Teeth."

"Most of two Battle Wings." Ester shook her head. "Even that may not be enough. Do you know about these mages—"

"I know all I need to." Ker tried to keep the bitterness out of her voice. "It's because of them the Halls of Law are destroyed, and all the Talents killed, even the youngest Candidates. And they're behind that network of spies and traitors you talked about. But we have weapons against them. Not many, but we have them."

"What weapons?"

Hitterol, the senior Mind-healer in the Mines and Tunnels, had once given Ker and Tel a block that prevented them from talking about the Feelers. She'd thought that block long gone, but the reluctance to speak now was still strong. "I've pledged not to speak of it," she said. Her sister nodded. Even senior officers knew that they wouldn't be told everything. "What about you?" Ker asked. "How did you come to be here?"

"We saw pretty early what was happening with our military women. Ordinary soldiers were given the chance to surrender, but not officers." Ester fell silent, her face frozen into stillness. "My people hid me among them," she said finally. "Just one of a Barrack." She gestured around her. "A few of us came here. The owner is an old friend, from when we used to come for the festivals. It used to be his father's place, and it's his now."

Which explained why the barman seemed familiar. "And you *work* here?"

"I *hide* here." Ester frowned and smoothed back her hair with her hands. "And other things I won't go into just now." She raised one eyebrow at Ker.

"I understand. There's things you can't tell me, as well."

Ester smiled. "How long can you stay? I could use a Talent's help."

———

"You know, I never expected to miss the Mines and Tunnels." Barid took the basket Wynn handed him and stood, ready to accompany her to the market. "I mean, sure I was nervous on the way here—especially after Tel Cursar left–but *here*? That was natural. Nothing here feels safe, no one."

"It's not that bad, is it?"

Barid waited until they were out in the sunshine to answer. "How you can go back and forth to the kitchens every day, talking and laughing—" He shook his head. "It's more than I can understand."

There'd been some argument between Svann and Granion Pvat, the Rose Shekayrin he'd left to administrate Gaena alone, but just as the Sunflower Shekayrin had predicted, Svann's status as a scholar saved him from more than a tight-lipped lecture from his colleague and the responsibility of some of the more disagreeable tasks.

"Still, I'm glad of the chance to get out of here, even if the market's just outside the door." He shivered. It was a lot colder out here than he expected. "*You're* not nervous, are you?"

"Nah, I'm city-born and bred, and this feels as normal to me as bells on Daughter's Day, truth to tell."

"I've been in cities, too, you know."

"I'm sure of it, but you won't see the streets and alleyways the way I do, the way someone who's lived in them would."

"Everything seems normal to me." Wynn's claiming more knowledge and experience rubbed him the wrong way. She was only a foot soldier, and he was a Talent. She needn't give herself airs.

"Like people are walking too fast, no one's strolling, even though it's a nice day, with the sun shining and warm enough to give us a promise of Rainmonth to come? Like it's midafternoon, everyone's had their dinners, so why aren't there more children on the streets, playing or running errands?"

"Is that all? I would have seen all that if you'd given me a chance."

"And would you have seen that we're being followed?"

"What? Where?" Barid felt every muscle freeze.

"When we stop at the poultry stall, while I'm buying the eggs, you look around, as if you're just bored, and you'll see a thin blond boy, slightly better dressed than the others around here."

Barid followed her to the stall and looked around as she'd told him. He saw the boy almost right away, and now that she'd mentioned it, he *was* cleaner and better dressed than the one or two other children he could see. The boy seemed preoccupied by the baskets of used shoes in front of him, but he glanced up once, as if he felt Barid's eyes on him. Looked Barid directly in the eye and held his hand up to his chest, thumb, index and middle finger extended, and tapped himself three times, before turning back to examining the shoes.

"He's signaled to us," he said to Wynn once they were out of earshot of the poultry man. "Like this." Barid laid his hand on his chest in imitation of what he'd seen.

Wynn nodded. "It's enough like one of the standard military signals that I think I know what he means." She stopped and turned around, moving her head back and forth as if she was looking for something. She laid the thumb and forefinger of her right hand against her cheek.

"What did you do that for?"

"Don't worry. He saw me."

"That's not what I'm worried about."

Wynn took his arm as they resumed their stroll. "He doesn't come to us openly, so that means he's got secrets. He signals for a meet, and that means he wants to tell us something. So now we'll follow him and find out what those secrets are."

"Are you insane?" Whispered through clenched teeth. She tugged on his arm, leading him forward.

"No, I'm a soldier, though there's many will say it's much the same thing, truth to tell."

She was smiling. Barid couldn't believe it. "We should go back. He's only trying to rob us."

Wynn pursed her lips and shook her head. "He doesn't have that look. No, it's something else."

"What do you know about it?"

"More than you, apparently. Look, Barid, there's a way to make sure, but I didn't think you'd want to try it. . . ."

Barid's shoulders crept up—that she could even *think* about him Flashing. He thrust his trembling hands under his armpits as though he were cold. "We're going back. We can't afford to take chances."

"We can't afford not to. Oh, all right, here. You take the basket and head back. I'm going to find out what the boy wants."

Barid hesitated, but his hand was already reaching for the basket's handle.

"Go on, what's the worst that can happen? They kill me? Every soldier takes that chance every day. It's different for you, of course. You're afraid. Go."

Barid jerked the basket out of her hand and stalked off. Stupid girl. Typical soldier's attitude, mistaking common sense for fear.

As Wynn had rather expected, the thin blond boy fell into step beside her as soon as she'd wandered back into the more crowded center of the market.

"You were with Jerek," he said out of the side of his mouth when they both stopped to examine some apples that had seen better days. "Jerek Firoxi. I saw you."

"He's Jerek Brightwing now," she answered in the same way, shaking her head at the stall owner and turning away, back into the open spaces between the vendors.

"He all right, then?"

"Who are you? Who do you run with?" The boy eyed her sideways, the fixed smile on his face was for passersby only. "Come on, who's your auntie? Or is it your uncle?"

"What do you know about it?" His eyes were wary now, his face stiffer.

"I ran with the Falcons, in Lausan, on the coast." Wynn bought a pastry, and she and the blond boy sat on a wall watching the market square to see if anyone was watching them. "I've had three, no, four aunties." Wynn handed the boy his half of the pastry. "And a couple of uncles."

"And that makes you my friend?"

"It's you came to me, remember? It's you who's asking me about Jerek. I thought you might as well know that I see what you are." She turned to him and smiled. "And I'm letting you see what I am. Or at least, what I was."

"How did you get away?"

"Joined the military."

Boy gave a grimace and looked away. "I've got my brother to think about. He needs me."

Wynn nodded. "I'm Wynn."

"Talian."

"How do you know Jerek?"

"We roped him in off the street, a couple of months ago, before winter. My auntie sold him back to his father. He was teaching me how to ride his pony. Is it true what they say about his father? He's the new Luqs?"

Wynn shrugged. "The Halians think so."

"So why isn't Jerek with him? He was quick enough to pay old Goreot what she asked for him."

Goreot must be Talian's auntie. "That was when he wanted to keep Brightwing Holding, and Jerek was the heir. Now Firoxi's got bigger fish on his line, and he doesn't want to share."

"So where's Jerek now?"

Wynn laughed and punched the boy lightly on the arm, as if he'd said something funny. Which, in a way, he had. "Why would I tell you?"

"I can help you. We saw you come in with the Shekayrin; we can help you get away."

"Out of the swamp into the quicksand, is that it?"

"We can get you to the mountains. We've helped others, lots of them."

Well, that certainly explained the trickle of soldiers who'd managed to find their way to the Mines. At least those coming from this area. "I've a job to do here," she said, without committing herself further.

"You'd rather stay with them?"

"What makes you so sure you know who 'they' are?"

Talian went pale and tensed, ready to run. "Rest easy." She put a hand, feather light, on his arm. "Don't run off yet. I just meant that things aren't always what they seem."

"How do I know I can trust you?"

That was the real question, wasn't it? How did anyone know anything anymore, now that there were no Talents to judge? But Talian came from the same kind of background as Wynn, a world on the fringes of the law, populated by criminals, who had no desire to call in the Talents to expose them and their enterprises.

"How did we ever know?" was what she said now. "It's not like people like us ever went to the Halls of Law." They shared a grin.

"What are you doing back here with him?" A tilt of the head toward the administrative building at the far side of the square.

Wynn thought for a moment. She knew Talian. She used to be Talian. She couldn't confide anything to him. He'd use it if it was profitable. Not because he was evil, but because that was the way of their world.

"You've waited so long, I know you're not going to tell me," he said. "But now I also know there's something to tell."

Well, she should have thought of that. She shrugged. "Not my story to tell," she said. "That's the problem."

He stood up and dusted crumbs off the front of his tunic. "If you need anything, come to Goreot's alehouse, Wainwright's Lane."

She smiled at him. "You'll help me for a price?"

He smiled back. "That's right."

———

Tel dismounted and wrapped the reins of his horse around his left hand. After all the checkpoints he'd passed through since leaving the others behind in Gaena, he knew the drill. Though there might be one mounted soldier as backup, guards at gates and checkpoints were usually on their feet. Not that there had been many gates. It seemed that most towns in the Peninsula no longer had them, except decorative ones that couldn't keep out so much as a child in a pony cart. That had been one of the reasons the Halians had found the Peninsula so easy to over-run and occupy—that and jeweled traitors in the right places.

Of course, even the people passing through checkpoints, let alone real city gates like these at Farama the Capital, were more often on foot than not, Just like the three people immediately in front of him. From the way they spoke to each other, it was clear they were family, and that one of them had been right when he'd said it was too early to gather enough wild asparagus to make it worthwhile to go foraging.

Once they were passed through, still arguing, Tel stepped into the shadow of the gate's arch and handed the guard on his left the horse's reins. To the man on the right—and it had always been men, every time he'd been stopped—Tel handed his sealed pass.

"Purposeforenteringthecity?" the man said without looking up. The fact that Tel and the guards were all wearing the same uniform never made any difference. Tel knew he wasn't required to answer. The pass answered all questions. He also knew that if he didn't say *something*, these guards would find a way to harass him. Oh, he could complain afterward, and the guards might be disciplined, but he'd still be delayed now.

Or rather, he could complain if he was on a real errand from a real Shekayrin.

Instead, Tel shrugged. "I'm to go to the palace," he said. "Someone there is supposed to check the seal and tell me which Shekayrin I'm to report to." They wouldn't ask why. He hoped.

Sure enough, the guard only wrinkled his nose and held the pass out to Tel. "Press your thumb to the seal," he said in a tone that let Tel know he wasn't in any way impressed.

Tel hesitated for only a second. He'd never been asked to do this at any of the previous checkpoints he'd been through, but again, he knew better than to ask the guard any questions. So, again, he shrugged and pressed his thumb to Svann's seal.

He almost pulled his hand away. The wax felt unnaturally

warm under his skin, as if freshly applied. When he lifted his thumb off the parchment, the image of it remained long enough for the guard to inspect it before it changed back to the imprint of Svann's jewel.

Tel waited patiently for the other man to decide he'd proven who was boss. As Tel suspected, after raking him with another skeptical glance, the guard tapped the pass on the palm of his hand.

"He can go." As if he actually had an option.

Tel scrambled as his pass was tossed at him from one side, and his reins from the other. "Noridinginthecitystableyourhorseassoonaspossible."

"Keep your nose clean," the first guard added. "Move along."

Tel could think of several sarcastic responses, but contented himself with moving along, vacating his spot for the next unlucky traveler. He didn't look back when he heard voices raised, though the skin on his neck crawled. In the normal state of affairs, a man like this one, half bully, wouldn't have been given an assignment that put him into direct contact with Polity citizens. But the normal state of affairs hadn't existed since the arrival of the Halians.

He knew roughly where he should head. Jerek had gathered enough information to give Tel at least an idea of which of the streets leading away from the gate would put him in the right direction for the Ram and Boar. He took the first turning that would put him out of view from the gate, and a young girl with pale hair and a rose-colored tunic fell into step with him.

"I've been looking for you," she said in a clear melodic voice. She probably earned money singing as well as her present business.

"Not interested just now, thanks all the same," he said, softening his words even further with a smile.

"You're too tall for me anyway, Tel Cursar, even if I didn't have other business with you." She smiled as she said it, but that had nothing to do with why Tel's heart skipped a beat. He slowed down a little, turning toward her, as if he was listening to her pitch.

"Do I know you?" he said, still smiling at her, keeping up the act. The girl put a hand on his arm, and her smile widened. Seemed she was thinking along the same lines. The gate guards were out of sight, and therefore wouldn't be wondering why he wasn't going straight to the palace, but there was no knowing who else might be watching.

"Not to say know me, exactly. But I'm to tell you it wasn't a bird's claw. You know what that means, I hope? Because the Daughter knows I don't." Still with the most enticing smile on her face.

Tel's heart lifted, and a wave of warmth flushed though his body. He saw the girl's eyes sparkle as his smile turned genuine. Of course, he knew what it meant. When he and Kerida had first encountered the Feelers of the Mines and Tunnels, they had asked her to prove herself by identifying a large claw they'd found down one of their shafts. It was far too big to be any bird's claw, of course, because it was a griffin's. One of Weimerk's, in fact, shed as he grew larger.

Only Kerida would have used that as an identification code. And as impossible as it might seem, that meant *she'd* sent this girl.

"So where do I go?" he said now.

"Where I'm going to take you, of course. Ah, if only you would look at me that way," she added, laughing. "She must mean a great deal to you. Right this way, if you please, sir. Right this way." She hooked her arm through his and looked up at him with the most coquettish smile he'd ever seen on a woman's face. He tried his best to smile down on her with the look of someone who accompanied her for the usual reasons. He wasn't at all surprised when her demeanor changed subtly as they turned off the street into a smaller laneway. Now she acted more like a girl out walking with her older brother. Her smile faded almost completely away, and she didn't sway at all when she walked.

He didn't know what to expect, so when she led him through a swinging door into a small courtyard, he hesitated before following her in. Now she took him by the hand and led him past a fenced-in coop for chickens, and what sounded like a dovecote, against the house wall. An older woman with the dark hair and skin of Ma'lakai gathered eggs. She didn't look up from her task as Tel and his guide passed her, though between them and the horse they made a fair amount of noise.

"Leave the horse here," his guide said. "He can't go the way we're going."

"What about my pack? Can it go 'the way we're going'?"

"Some other of my auntie's nieces or nephews will bring it along later," she said with a smile. Crooking her finger, she beckoned him to the right, where crates and boxes were loosely stacked. When she stepped up onto the lowest one, Tel realized they'd been placed to form a set of stairs.

"Duck down as much as you can," she said to him quietly. "You may be tall enough to be seen over the roofs." When they reached the top of the wall, they walked along it, passing by the roofs of two houses before she turned a corner and led him back in the direction they'd come along the street. Ingenious, he thought, people tended not to look up. They turned several more corners and walked at one point directly over someone's roof before the ache in his back and legs made him speak up.

"You realize I'll never walk upright again if it's much farther."

"See that blue-tiled roof? That's where we're going."

They were much closer to the center of town now, southwest of the gate he'd come in by. From here, he could just make out the complex of buildings that had to be the palace itself. They reached the blue roof, jumped down onto another, lower, roof, and Tel let himself down by his fingertips into a space far too small to be the stable yard for an inn, before dropping the last few feet to the ground. The tiny courtyard was crowded with ceramic pots containing what smelled like herbs, and still another chicken coop.

"Ahem." His guide still sat on the edge of the roof. If she started swinging her feet, he thought, she'd look like a child. She indicated an open doorway. "Through there, and it was nice to meet you." Without another word she turned, and in a moment she'd disappeared from view. Tel grinned, watching her go. That was the neatest way of disguising a trail that he'd ever seen. He turned back to the doorway and put his hand on his sword hilt.

"Well, my mother always said an open door is an invitation."

Ker walked around the room she shared with Ester and sat down on the edge of the bed. A moment later she was on her feet again, pacing the length of the attic room, eleven steps, turning and pacing back. Finally, she stood still, tugged Tel's plaque out from under her tunic, and held it in her right hand. Every time she Flashed it to find out how and where Tel was, she hesitated, torn between wanting to know, and not wanting to Flash that he'd been captured. Or worse. She drew in a deep breath. *Paraste.*

She ignored the auras nearest her and concentrated on Flashing. She let out the breath she was holding and felt the muscles in her neck and shoulders relax. Tel was safe. Tel was *here*. She shoved the plaque back under her shirt and stood up straight, pushing her hair out of the way with her hands and tugging her tunic straight. When she realized what she was doing, she laughed out loud. Tel wouldn't care what she looked like.

"Glad to hear there's reason for mirth." Tel stood in the doorway, ducking to get into the room without banging his head. Ker smiled, suddenly shy. He seemed so much taller than she expected him to be. Besides, he looked so strange dressed in the gray tunic she'd seen on other soldiers. He reached out for her, and she took her first real breath since she'd left him in the Panther's camp.

"I'd forgotten how tall you are," she said, coming forward with her hands outstretched. Tel caught them in his own and drew her into his arms. Suddenly, they were clinging to each tightly.

"I can't breathe."

She felt Tel's laughter burbling in his chest as he loosened his grip, but only enough to let him look into her eyes and tuck a lock of her hair behind her ear. His rough fingertips traced the arch of her cheekbone.

"Your sister—" Tel cleared his throat. "Your sister doesn't look much like you. Even allowing for the difference in age."

Ker's smile was so big she could feel it. "Her mother was my father's first wife. Killed along with most of her Cohort during the third Chadnian rebellion."

"Before you were born, obviously."

"How much more small talk do you think we'll need to feel comfortable with each other again?" Ker drew him with her to sit on the edge of the bed she'd been using, keeping hold of his hand, savoring the pressure of his arm against hers. Tel rocked against her and squeezed her hand.

"Tell me quickly, then. How much does your sister know— about us, for example?"

Ker whistled silently. "You mean *us*, as in—"

"As in Talent and soldier, yes."

"I haven't said anything other than that I was waiting for you. She might guess when she sees us holding hands."

"So, we don't hide it from her?"

Ker squeezed his hand a little tighter, afraid to let it go. The same questions still hung over them. How long would they be together? Would the presence of the Feelers change everything, or would they be expected to separate once Law was restored? "We don't hide it, no, but we'll wait for her to ask."

"And the others? The Feelers? Do we mention them?"

"That's not our secret. We can't risk telling anyone who hasn't been blocked by the Feelers themselves. If the Halians find out about them before we're ready, we could lose everything."

Tel tapped the back of her hand with a finger. "If she goes to the Mines, she'll find out for herself. In the meantime, we wait." He shrugged. "I know. It's the soldiers' lot. Put on your armor and wait for orders, march to the frontier, and wait for orders. Dig a hole and then wait some more. I hope this princess is worth it."

"Jerek thinks so. According to him, she could be a Feeler herself."

"That reminds me." Tel shifted until he could reach into the front of his tunic without completely losing contact with her. He pulled out a small leather pouch. Ker's eyebrows took on a life of their own when he emptied the bag out into her hand. A jewel. Inert, but a jewel.

"Remember this? Larin got it off Luca, and she gave it to Jerek to give to me," Tel said. "She said you'd know what to do with it."

"How did Larin get it? Never mind." It was almost impossible to keep track of what the little Time-seer was up to. There was a lot of speculation, especially among those who remembered the old Time-seer, Ara, as to whether Larin might have been more intelligible if her Gift had come at the usual age, instead of so early, or if she'd been able to finish her apprenticeship before the old lady's death.

Though there were many, Ker included, who weren't sure the woman was completely gone.

"Who knows?" Tel said, in an eerie echo to her thoughts.

Ker shook her head, turning the jewel over in her hand. "Well, I don't know what to do with it, that's for certain."

"Maybe you're *going* to know."

"The great thing about being in love with a Talent," Tel murmured into her ear, "is that you don't have to actually tell her how you feel. She already knows."

"Oh, you think so?"

A cough from the doorway ended their wrestling match before it could go much further. Ester came in and closed the door behind her. Tel got to his feet and came to attention in the only space high enough to allow it.

"Tel Cursar, Third Officer, Black Company, Emerald Cohort of Bears."

"Ester Nast, Emerald Cohort Leader of Eagles." Her smile was a twisted thing. "And currently working as a server and assistant bouncer here in the Ram and Boar." Her eyes flicked from Tel to Ker and back again. "What are you two planning for the future?" she asked. "Or are you just hoping no one will ever notice?"

Ker almost smiled at the look on Tel's face. It had always been difficult to hide things from her sister. "The Polity has changed, and even when we send the Halians running off to their ships, nothing is going to be the same," he said.

"Exactly, and one of the changes is that she—you," she corrected, turning to Ker. "You and the other Talents left will be needed more than ever."

Ker glanced at Tel and found him looking at her with eyebrows raised. He shrugged ever so slightly. Ester had once been Ker's Cohort leader, as well as her sister, and she wasn't comfortable denying her in either role. "There's more to it than that," she said finally.

"But you can't tell me what it is." Ester looked between

them, with narrowed eyes, her face suddenly hard, the face of a Cohort Leader, not someone's sister.

"It's not our secret to tell. Juria Sweetwater knows, if that sets your mind at ease."

"And I'm sure that makes her Bears feel much better. Does *my* Faro, the Luqs of Farama, know?" Ester's voice hardened to match her face.

"He does."

"Then it's for him to tell me, when I reach him."

***

Weimerk floated in a sea of colors, of light and of warmth, a small part of a much larger whole. At first, he had taken great delight in the joining. Sharing mind and spirit with all griffins was beyond all he had imagined. However, each time he joined, it took more effort, more energy, more focus.

He dropped out of the joining, feeling once again his own paws, his own wings, and his own stomach in need of food.

"This is not well done, young one." The old griffin Zeinin appeared to Weimerk's left. Zeinin was so old you could see marks of age. The way his right wing did not lie perfectly flat against his back and sides, the roughness of his feathers and fur, the crooked twist in his right rear paw. Even when joined, his mind felt faded and worn. "The joining gives strength and keeps us whole."

"If the joining gives strength, old one," Weimerk answered. "You yourself are not doing well to leave it." He knew what the old griffin would tell him. That he should forget about Kerida and his other friends.

Zeinin made a sound that was meant to be laughter. "When we left the Serpents Teeth, I was not so old as this, though even then I was eldest. Until the Prophecy is complete, I will always be the eldest."

Weimerk hung his head. He knew griffins were not only

hatched in the Serpents Teeth, but they returned there to die, their spirits joining the great auroras of the world, their bones returned to the rock. Since the griffins had sworn not to return to the mountain range until the Prophecy was complete, Zeinin could not die.

"I am sorry, Zeinin."

"You have done *me* nothing but good, young one. You are part of the Prophecy, one of the signs. This is the closest I have ever been to my death."

"I would have done more." Weimerk's tail lashed. "I would *do* more."

Zeinin shook his head. "You cannot live in two worlds, Weimerk. You have difficulty with the joining because you have two paws still in the world of humans. You must make a choice. Decide where all four paws will be."

"Deilih did not give me this choice."

The old griffin's chuckling sounded like a series of coughs. "Deilih is still young. Not so young as you, but young enough to see only one way. Young enough to feel she may make decisions for others." Zeinin flicked out his right wing, folded it again slowly. "Take careful thought. Consider what you gain, but consider also what you lose."

I N every story that Baku had ever read escapes were always made in the middle of the night. Jerek had disagreed.

"Think about it," he had said. "At night the halls will be empty of everyone except guards. If you're seen, you'll be stopped and questioned for certain. But during the day—"

"During the day I would simply be one of the many who are always in the halls and courtyards," Baku had finished, immediately understanding Jerek's point. "To be truthful, I find myself relieved." That there was something else she'd prefer to do in the daylight, she did not tell him. He would be sure to disagree strongly.

It was Jerek who had advised her to practice walking about in men's clothing, with her face uncovered, in the privacy of her own bedroom. It helped that men and women wore essentially the same clothing in Farama. Trousers or leggings, tunics long or short depending on purpose or formality, worn over shirts of cheaper or costlier fabrics, depending on the wearer's wealth. Boots or shoes, depending on the weather. A satchel, sometimes very decorative, to carry personal items, and a knife, sometimes very decorative.

"How can I get a knife?" she had asked.

"Better you don't have one," he had said. "Women aren't supposed to be armed, not even personal knives, not anymore. That's a question you don't want to be asked—in fact, you don't want to be questioned at all."

"If I am caught, I can say I am emulating the Emperor Cor Tyn Lao, who went about his people in disguise. In Halia, men expect women to have these romantic notions."

Practicing walking in trousers turned out to be a good idea. As did using the shoes Jerek had advised her to get. Her own shoes and boots were too easily recognized, much more so than she was herself, in fact, considering that her feet were all most people ever saw of her. She herself thought of how to obtain the shoes, asking her maids to find her something informal but sturdy to wear in her apartments and gardens, where comfort was of more importance than elegance. True, Narl Koven had raised eyebrows at this request, but several pairs of shoes had materialized, all with good thick soles.

Jerek had many good suggestions. Where to hide the clothes she meant to use, where to get them in the first place. Which pieces of her own clothing were suitable for her purpose.

"And try to take some food with you, at least one meal's worth."

"Surely I can buy food?" Baku was rather looking forward to trying the dishes whose wonderful odors she could sometimes smell wafting up to her from the market squares and the trays carried past her rooms.

"You have money?"

Baku had to let her embarrassed silence answer him. Of course, she had no money. What need would the Princess Imperial have for money? "I have jewelry," she had said.

"Bring it, but don't try to sell it yourself."

She pulled her tunic straight for the fourth time. She must go soon if she were not to lose her nerve completely. She had contrived to have both of her maids absent at the same time, but one or the other could return soon. Baku took a deep breath, nodded once, and picked up her satchel, putting her head and one arm through the strap, as Jerek had told her to do—though the satchel was larger than the one he had suggested. Before she could change her mind, she crossed her sitting room, using the long strides she had practiced. At the door she hesitated. The opening mechanism consisted of a lever instead of a knob to turn. Did one push it down, or move it upward? As she wavered, undecided, her hand over the lever, the door suddenly opened in her face and she stepped back, hands raised to defend herself, and a nearby nut dish leaped into her right hand. Shocked, Baku dropped the dish, which landed softly on the rug.

Narl Koven looked astonished for only a moment; she recovered quickly and shut the door behind her, leaning against it. She looked Baku up and down and gave a sharp nod.

"Don't be frightened," she said. "My path crossed with Kvena's, and when I realized you must be alone, I came back right away."

Baku drew herself up. "You cannot stop me."

"I don't want to; this is the best idea you've had since you got here. Have you somewhere to go? No, don't tell me where. Just say yes or no."

Baku nodded, speechless. Narl Koven was going to *help* her?

"Good. How were you planning to get past the guard outside the door?"

"None of them have seen my face." Baku shrugged. "I thought I could say I was a servant."

"And that would work, but they'd expect to see you coming out only if they'd seen you going in."

Baku's heart began to beat faster, and her breath came short. What an error she had almost made.

Narl looked around her, eyes narrowed, before finally pulling off the veil she'd thrown back on entering the room. "Here, why don't you be me?" She held up the veil. "It'll cover you to the knees, and from the knees down we look alike. See, even our shoes match."

Baku looked down at her feet and then at Narl's. Sure enough, they were both wearing a green half-boot with a low heel and bright silver buckles. She looked back up. "You knew? When you brought me the shoes, you knew?"

"I thought it was possible. I also know why you couldn't ask for help."

"What will happen to you?" She had not thought of that until this moment. Jerek would be ashamed of her.

"You think I'm going to wait around to find out? Don't worry about me."

"I do not know how to thank you."

"You're messing up Poppy-boy's plans, and that's thanks enough for me."

Baku smothered the bark of laughter that had slipped out at the other woman's disrespect. She touched Narl on the arm, wanting to hug her, but being uncertain how it would be received.

The look in the woman's eyes softened. "Go on. Get out. Don't look back. As soon as you're out of sight of the door guard, take the veil off." Narl took hold of the door handle. "Ready?"

Baku nodded. Narl opened the door in such a way that she remained hidden behind it, and Baku stepped out into the hall. The guard—she didn't dare look him in the face—straightened but didn't speak. She hurried past him, hoping she looked like Narl sent on an urgent errand. Once around the first corner, the veil was off and stuffed behind the nearest tapestry.

The one thing she could not have prepared for was how it felt to walk about in the free air uncovered. Her head felt lighter, and the air seemed to trace light fingers on her skin.

Of course, she'd often been without headdress, but never outside her rooms, never where the public might see her. And here she was without pins or combs or hair lacquer, just a braid down her back.

Now came the hard part, the part she had had no intention of telling Jerek. She did not know from where the knowledge had come, but she knew the location of the rooms belonging to the Poppy Shekayrin. Pollik Kvar used a suite on the same floor as Baku's own, though in the opposite section of the royal wing. According to what Dern Firoxi had told her during one of their numerous card games, at this time of day the Shekayrin should be in the council chambers, directing the Luqs in his rulings. She marched along firmly, "As though you have somewhere to be," was how Jerek had put it. She told herself it also kept her legs from trembling. She saw only one other person along the main hallway, a man dressed much as she was herself, who passed her by with lowered eyes. This gave her heart, and she was able to relax her shoulders.

She rounded the final corner and narrowly avoided walking straight into a thickset man wearing the gray tunic of a soldier.

"Whoa," he said, taking her by the arm and righting her. It took all of Baku's strength not to cringe away from him. She could not remember the last time she had been directly touched by a man, and she had never been touched by a stranger. Fortunately, the man released her at once.

"Steady, young lady," he said. "Where are you off to so quickly?"

Baku ducked her head down. "Message for the Shekayrin."

The soldier stepped back from her, and Baku risked a glance upward to his face. His lips were pressed into a thin line, and his eyes were narrowed. He looked Baku up and down, something no one had ever done to her, though she had seen it done to other women. Finally, he shrugged. "Message, eh? Well, you'd best get on with it. Third door on the right." He turned and walked away without another word.

He was angry, she thought, though not with her. He had not stopped her from proceeding, but he had wished to. She had her hand on the door handle before she wondered how she knew.

And how she knew that the rooms behind the door were empty.

Still, she pressed down on the handle slowly, letting the door swing open with its own weight. She hovered in the doorway. To shut the door behind her, or to leave it open? She could see advantages and disadvantages either way. Open. Three steps in Baku turned back and shut the door. The feeling of that open maw behind her was far worse than the fear of being shut in.

The sitting room itself glowed like an emerald, as sunlight shone through green window shades. Unlike her own rooms, Kvar's were furnished in Halian style, with open-backed stools, thick patterned carpets, and a scattering of large cushions. A hammered brass table held a delicate porcelain kaff set, inlaid with blue-and-green enamels. Her heart sank when she saw a row of five chests against the inner wall of the room. Would she have to search each one? Every minute she stayed in this room increased her risk of being caught. Flexing her fingers, she swallowed and stepped forward.

Once she reached the first chest, however, she found herself drawn farther into the room. She pushed aside a heavily embroidered tapestry and found what must be the door of the suite's bedroom. Nodding, she let herself in, this time leaving the door open behind her.

And there it was. Near the head of the bed stood a small table draped with a blue cloth embroidered with white poppies. And on the table, under the cloth, was an unmistakable shape. Baku blew on suddenly cold fingers and threw back the covering, exposing the small chest that held her mask. Now that her hands were once again upon it, she knew the box itself would not fit into her satchel. She would have to take only the mask. She pushed back the lid and opened the layers of silk wrappings with trembling hands.

There lay her brother's face. The Sky Emperor, Son of the Sun, Father of the Moon. The Lord of Horses, as Inurek Star had called him. She stroked the cheek of the mask, as though it were indeed her brother. It seemed to be smiling at her, the lips parted, about to speak. That must be a trick of the light, she thought. *The mask is not my brother; it is not speaking to me.* Yet, somehow, she had known that the mask was not in one of the chests in the sitting room. What did this mean? Even before she was netted, she had not known information of this kind.

Baku lifted out the mask with both hands. She wrapped it in the red silk of the innermost lining, tucking the rod into the last fold. With the flap on her satchel pulled back, Baku settled the mask in its new home, between two extra shirts and four chicken rolls wrapped in linen napkins.

She retraced her steps, turning at the door to make sure the room looked exactly as it had been when she entered it. Praying to the Mother that the soldier she had met before was not still in the corridor, she almost ran to the hallway that led to the public section of the palace. The relief of closing the Shekayrin's door behind her was so great Baku had to warn herself that the time to relax had not yet come. She could still be caught and returned to her rooms.

She had been through this part of the palace several times, either going to the audience room, or to the gardens of the larger interior courtyard, where the fruit trees were beginning to bud. The familiarity of the place almost made up for the strange feel of her clothing, and the way loose, unlacquered hair brushed against the skin of her face, and the way no one looked at her, and no one troubled to get out of her path. This last was almost her undoing. She stopped at the elbow of a man standing in front of a tapestry, apparently studying the stitching.

"May I help you?" he said. A Faraman citizen, his accent identical to that of Dern Firoxi.

She suddenly realized that she had stopped because she expected the man to get out of her way. "Your pardon, sir." She croaked as if she had a sore throat, hoping that would disguise her own accent. "I thought you were someone else." Ears burning, she stepped around him and headed toward the stairs at the far end of the corridor. She felt his eyes on her back as she went and hoped she imagined it.

She almost changed her mind when she reached the staircase. There were several people on it, moving up and down. She would not be able to hold the railing, as she had wanted to do. Her knees did not feel as if they would support her if she descended without that aid. Someone jostled her elbow and she jumped.

"Sorry," said a bright voice. "But you *are* standing right in the way." The words drifted back up to her as a boy a little shorter than she took the stairs downward. Before she could think about it anymore, Baku stepped down after him. If she fell, he would cushion her fall.

But she did not fall. She made it all the way down two flights of stairs, managing the broad landing without bumping anyone, or being bumped. When she reached the open, high-ceilinged entrance hall, she forced herself not to stop, but to head immediately across the flagstone floor inlaid with griffins to the wide opening of the front entrance. She was no more than a third of the way across when men in uniforms came in from the square outside, walking in a protective formation around a man she immediately recognized. The only man who could immediately recognize her. Dern Firoxi.

She lowered her eyes lest he should feel her gaze, but without moving her head. With luck no one would notice her at all. She was dressed as a commoner, a servant, someone who could have come in with a request or a message. Certainly, someone of no importance.

Jerek: Baku? Is something wrong? Are you all right?
Baku: It's your father. If he looks this way, he may see me.
Jerek: But—
Baku: I cannot talk now, I must keep all my wits about me.
Jerek: As soon as you can, then.

And he was gone.

Do not look this way, she willed, directing her thoughts to the slim dark man surrounded by guards and attendants. If she had any magic at all left that had not been netted, let it be this. Let her be invisible and unnoticed. The press of bodies around her eased slightly, and then moved completely away. For a moment she froze in place, sure that this movement meant she had been spotted, and the next sound she would hear would be the command of the Shekayrin. Instead, a large woman careened into her, almost knocking both of them down.

"Clumsy brat." The woman's voice was stiff and rough with the fear of her near fall. She thrust Baku away from her as if she were hot. "Country bumpkins should stay out of the way of civilized people. What are you staring at, girl?"

Baku bit the inside of her lip hard enough that she tasted blood. No one had spoken to her in this tone since she was a small child and her brother was far from the throne. She swallowed past a lump in her throat.

"Nothing, my lady," she whispered, just loud enough for the woman to hear. She gave one of the short bows, more than half a nod, that she had seen servants give. "Sorry, my lady." The woman snorted and turned away. Her heart hammering in her ears, Baku let her get several paces away before following the woman's stout back out the door.

The steps of the palace entrance were shallow and wide— wide enough that Baku required two paces for each step. She kept herself to a steady walk, though her pounding heart wanted her to run. She didn't hesitate at the bottom but set off straight across the rough flagstones of the square outside.

Straight across, Jerek had said, to the street marked by the statue of a soldier in crested helm and armor holding up an eagle on his left wrist. Or *her* wrist. The statue was too old, and too worn for anyone to be sure.

Narl Koven went through the clothes press she shared with Kvena and sorted out the clothing they would need, including a replacement veil for the one she'd given Bakura. She uncovered her small stash of money and distributed the coins into the pockets of the clothes she was wearing. Places where a body servant would normally keep a small sewing kit for hasty repairs, or a comb, or even, sometimes, a biscuit. She heard the door to the passage open and close, and an unfamiliar step cross the bare section of floor before the rugs began.

"Is anyone here? Attend me!" Dern Firoxi's voice.

What was the man doing here at this time of day? *Mother and Daughter, save me.* He'd visited the princess numerous times in the last few weeks, but only in the evening. She dropped the hooded tunic she had in her hands, thankful she'd already put away the noisier coins. She slid her hand under the lowest shelf of the clothes press, reaching all the way to the back. Her fingertips finally found the two narrow leather straps she'd tacked to the bottom of the shelf. From this improvised sling she withdrew a short knife with a plain flat hilt and a blade as long as her hand.

She shut the clothes press and turned to face the door, slipping the knife up her sleeve as the handle began to turn.

By the time Dern Firoxi stood in the doorway, Narl had composed her features, standing with her hands clasped in front of her, ready with a lie to tell him.

"Why did you not come when summoned?"

"Forgive me, my lord, I didn't hear you."

This seemed to satisfy him. "And where is the Princess Imperial?"

"The Poppy Shekayrin summoned her." There was more than one Poppy in the palace complex, but only one who didn't need to be named.

"You didn't attend her?"

"Kvena is with the princess," Narl said.

Feroxi nodded, but as though he hadn't really been listening to her. His eyes drifted around the room, coming to rest on the two packs on the bed behind her. Narl could have hidden the packs or grabbed the knife, she hadn't had time for both. Now it looked like she might have made the wrong choice.

"Going somewhere?" Narl had seen that smile before, and it led nowhere good.

"Discarded clothing, my lord, to be taken to the clothiers."

"The clothiers?" His eyebrows raised.

"Yes, my lord. They will salvage anything of value, and either reuse the material for other purposes or sell it."

He walked past her and stopped by the bed, hefting one of the packs in his hand. "And these discarded items are usually carried away in traveling packs?" He turned to face her, and this smile was one she'd never seen, and she liked it no better. "Do you know what the penalty is for stealing from the Luqs of Farama?"

Narl felt heat in her face. "I have served the Luqs of Farama since I turned fifteen," she said. "I think I know better than you."

His face stiffened, and he took a pace toward her. "*I* am the Luqs of Farama."

"Of course, my lord," she said in a tone that meant the exact opposite. At this point she had nothing to lose. As a thief, she was dead; as someone who'd lost the princess, she was dead. She might as well say what she wanted to say.

Firoxi's face stiffened, but before he could speak, they both heard the outer door open, and this time the footsteps Narl heard *were* familiar ones. *Kvena.* Firoxi started past her, heading for the sitting room. As soon as he got there and saw that Kvena was alone, he'd know that Narl had lied to him, and the search for the princess would begin. Was she even out of the palace yet?

Afterward, Narl felt that she'd hesitated forever, but Firoxi was only one pace closer to the door, when she moved. Feeling completely calm, she pulled the knife out of her sleeve, stepped lightly behind him, grabbed his throat in a strangle hold, and shoved the knife three times into his kidneys. He grunted, but no other sound escaped his mouth.

"You're no more the Luqs of Farama than I am," she whispered in his ear as his struggles weakened. "You're just a toy of the Poppy Shekayrin." When the struggling stopped, Narl lowered the body to the floor and used the small rug to pull, push, and shove it under the nearest bed. By the time Kvena appeared in the doorway, there was nothing to see.

"What are you doing? Where is the Princess Imperial? Those are my things! That's my pack!"

Narl looked the older woman in the face. This moment would tell her everything she needed to know. "Bakura has run away."

Kvena covered her mouth with one hand and sank to her knees. She did not, however, scream, faint, or cry.

"We will be blamed," she said finally, lowering her hand. "They will kill us."

"Then let's not wait around to be killed. Get up, come with me." As Kvena stood, Narl pushed a satchel of clothing into her unresisting arms and folded her veil back over her face. Good, the bulge of the satchel didn't really show.

"They will find us."

"They won't be looking for us; they'll be looking for *her*." Narl would have been more worried about Kvena, except for one thing: their entire conversation had taken place in Faraman. She beckoned the older woman into the sitting room and covered herself with her own veil.

How far could they get before someone raised the alarm? How far would they need to go until the Shekayrin couldn't track them? She never thought she'd say this, but thank Mother, Daughter, and Son, there were no Talents. If there had been, it wouldn't matter how far they went. A Talent would touch something that belonged to one of them and know right away where they were.

Jerek: Kerida?
Kerida: Here. Ker felt as though she'd been holding her breath until Jerek contacted her.
Jerek: She's out. All the way across the square and into Griffin Street.
Kerida: Are you sure you don't want us to meet her?
Jerek: Better you're not seen on the street together. We're not certain how far Kvar can see.
Kerida: Understood.

She didn't like it, but she understood. Poppy Shekayrin weren't best at Far-seeing, but it was just possible that Pollik Kvar could see the Princess—if he knew where to look. Ker grinned. A Talent would have been able to help him with that. Too bad he'd killed them all.

<<Thank you, Weimerk.>> The griffin didn't respond, but Ker could tell from the feeling of space and cold that the griffin was still with her. <<Weimerk? Thank you for connecting me to Jerek.>>

<<I am alone here, and I miss you, my dear one. I do not like these others.>>

Ker smiled at the sudden image of Weimerk lying with his eagle's head on outstretched paws. <<We're doing everything we can.>>

<<Faster would be preferable. I must go.>>

And, just like that, the connection was gone.

"What's taking her so long?" Tel murmured. "This isn't the only place we're needed."

Ker cleared her throat. It was hard to remember that the

griffin was safer than any of them. "I thought you would have learned patience by now." She laid down the seven of Summer and smiled at him. She remembered that in the military they were encouraged to develop the kind of patience that served guards on night watch and companies waiting for the call to arms. The kind of patience that had helped Tel, now changed into civilian clothes, grin at people from his post behind the counter when it was his turn to serve. Ester had put them to work, as the easiest way to explain their presence in the inn. Her friend Elisk Stellan, the innkeeper, had welcomed the help, seeing as how he didn't have to pay them more than their room and board.

"What if she gets caught? How will we know?" Tel's impatience was under control, but it was there in the way he flicked the next card down.

"The same way we know that she got out of the palace." Ker scrutinized the cards in front of her, making sure there was no seven. "Jerek would tell us."

Business slowed down enough after the midday meal to allow them to take a break from their duties. They'd fallen into the habit of playing Four Seasons. They were both good players, and normally the Seasons turned quickly, but today they'd been here all afternoon and Winter still hadn't passed from Ker to Tel.

And it wasn't going to pass in this hand either. Ker put down the four of Winter that she'd been holding in reserve, and Tel threw down his cards with a snort of disgust. Ker gathered them up, faced them all the same way, shuffled, and began to lay out the opening moves of another hand, two cards faceup, two facedown for each of them. Several moves later, Ker tapped her index finger on the tabletop, contemplating the Luqs of Spring, when Tel leaned forward to inspect the displayed cards and cleared his throat as a shadow drifted over them.

"Excuse me," a mildly accented voice said. "Would the proper move not be to place a Faro of Spring with the Luqs?"

"It would be," Ker said, looking up into a pair of storm gray eyes over broad cheekbones and a slightly flat nose. "But we're in the Winter round." Which was true oddly enough, since this was the code Jerek had suggested to help them identify the Princess Imperial. He could describe them to the girl, but Far-thinking hadn't given him much of an idea of what the Princess herself looked like.

Fortunately, Ker had her own way to be sure. *Paraste.*

Colors sprang into the air around them, but Flashing the girl's aura was like looking at the sun through a piece of smoked glass. Ker had expected more than the usual number of colors; after all, the girl could Far-think with Jerek, so there had to be at least some Feeler in her. But her colors were muted and pale, faded, as if echoing the exhaustion that was obvious, now that Ker thought to look for it. Something she needed to address, but not with the girl standing there, sticking out like a sore thumb. *Terestre.*

Tel tapped the tabletop with his index finger, his eyebrows raised. Ker nodded, eyes still focused on the cards. A shrug would have meant "no."

"Watch and learn, little one," Tel said in his most bored voice as his pushed out a small bench with his foot. "Watch and learn."

So, this is the Princess Imperial of Halia, Ker thought, as the girl shed her satchel and swung it gently onto the bench. Her thin hands with their polished nails lingered on it, as though she was having second thoughts about letting it go.

"You're safe with us," Ker murmured under her breath. The look on the girl's face wasn't exactly relief, and it wasn't exactly trust. It was more the look a soldier gives the medic when he was ready for the knife. An agreement to something necessary but not wanted. "Kaff? Almond biscuits?" Now *that* look was definitely one of relief. Careful to keep her face straight, Ker got to her feet. It was likely the girl had never carried her own dishes, let alone someone else's. Ester was serving behind the bar, and Ker gave her a nod as well as she placed her order. As staff, they didn't have to pay for the kaff, but the almond cookies weren't free to anyone. Ker balanced two cups on her left hand and wrist, picked up the third with her right hand, and carried them to the table while Ester counted cookies onto a plate.

Tel swept up the cards and started to shuffle them. Turning back for the cookies, Ker saw the girl's fingers trembling as she picked up one of the cups. Ker returned to the table as quickly as she could and set the plate down.

Kerida: Can you hear me?

All she got from the princess was a frowning glance. Ker sat down. It had been worth trying, but since she couldn't Far-think with Jerek directly, she hadn't really expected she could with the princess. She thought about asking Weimerk if he could connect them, but she resisted the temptation. Every time they communicated increased the chances that the griffin would be caught helping her.

"I'm Kerida, and this is Tel," Ker said quietly. She picked up her cup of kaff and raised it toward Tel before taking a sip. Jerek would have told her their names.

The princess swallowed and nodded. "I am Bakura. And I know how to play Seasons."

"We'll be the judge of that." Tel started to deal out the cards, this time for three players.

"I feel sorry for Kerida and Tel." Barid sat heavily on the bench seat in the center of the building's inner courtyard. Wynn looked around, frowning. Barid supposed it wasn't entirely comfortable for her to be back where she, and Tel, and Kerida had once been held prisoner. He smiled at her, patting the stone beside him.

"What they're doing is a lot more interesting than what we're doing." Wynn sat down, covering her knees with her cloak.

"That's not it," he told her. "Not it at all. 'Talents do not live in the world,' you know that, right? That's the rule, right?" She was pretty, Barid thought. Short, though.

And she took too many risks.

"Everyone knows the Law. What's your point?"

He blinked. What had he been saying? Oh, right. "You realize that they're working so hard to make things like before? And if things are like they were before, they can never be together again? Isn't that . . . what's the word?"

"Ironic?"

"That's it. Ironic."

"Barid, I think you've had a little too much to drink."

Not the first time Wynn had said something like this. "No, no, I'm fine. I only had a couple glasses of wine."

"You're thinking of the couple of glasses of brandy *after* the wine. I know, I was helping to serve. Honestly, Barid, you've got to be more careful."

"*I* should be more careful? *Me*? I don't go following people in the market." Barid burped. "I think we're not supposed to drink. Hey, I made a rhyme. Think. Drink. I'm thinking and drinking. I'm a thinker drinker." He laughed.

"Come on. Let's get you back to your room." He could hear the smile in the girl's voice as she stood up and took a grip on his forearm with one hand and his upper arm with the other. Barid slumped, letting himself go limp. He wasn't ready to go to bed.

"You shouldn't touch me, you know. I can Flash you too easily if you touch me. I'd know all your inner . . . innermost secrets."

"Shhh, not so loud." Now she was frightened. Barid blinked again and focused on her face.

"You don't have to be frightened, Wynn. I would never hurt you. Just because I'm not Kerida Griffin Girl"—he said her name in his best imitation of a Miner's accent—"doesn't mean I can't help. I can do things, too, you know. If anyone would let me."

"You'll hurt *yourself* if someone hears you, and that will hurt all of us."

"You're so nice to worry about me. You're a very nice girl. My sister was a nice girl."

"Barid, come on. Stand up. It's too cold for you to sit here." She tugged on his arm, but Barid just laughed.

"Not cold at all. Practically Seedmonth."

Wynn stepped back. She had her hands on her hips. Just like his sister, all right. Barid nodded.

"Fine, then. You sit here not being cold. I'll be right back."

Barid sighed and shut his eyes. She was always rushing off somewhere. Like that day in the market. "Wynn? That's funny. She was right here a minute ago."

"Who was right here?"

Barid jumped and slid off the bench and thumped onto the flagstones. That hurt. And now it was definitely cold. "Don't sneak up on me like that."

The voice got closer to him. "How drunk are you, boy? Where's your billet?"

"Not drunk at all, thank you very much. I mean, not at all drunk. Nothing to be afraid of. I'm perfectly safe. No one's going to find out, not from me. No sir."

"Why wouldn't you be safe, lad?"

Barid tapped the side of his nose and laid his index finger against his lips. "It's a secret." He nodded.

"I love secrets. Why don't you come with me and see if I can guess it?"

"You sure this is where you left him?"

Wynn Martan resisted the urge to look under all the benches, as if Barid was the family cat hiding under a bed. "He's the one who's drunk, not me. He was right here." She pointed at the stone seat. "And in no shape to walk himself away, either."

Pella Dursto drummed his fingers on the hilt of his short

sword. "It's not that I don't trust you, youngster, but I'd be a fool not to ask. If he didn't get out of here by himself, and again, I'm not doubting you, someone helped him."

"You think it's a problem?"

"I think it could be." Pella looked up at the windows of the top floor, the rooms that had been given to Svann when he'd come back. His old rooms had been taken over by the recently arrived Poppy Shekayrin. "I think we need to make sure that it won't be."

"Barid would never . . ." Wynn's words died away at the look Pella gave her.

"Never sober, granted. But drunk? He's been tight as a bowstring the whole week." The old soldier shook his head. "He's probably sleeping it off in his bunk, but we need to be sure."

Wynn took a deep breath in through her nose. She'd told Barid over and over that no harm had come from her talking to Talian that day, but he'd just gotten more and more nervous. Alcohol wasn't a cure for nerves; soldiers learned that early. "So what do we do?"

"You go to Svann and stay there until I come. I'll go see what I can find out."

Wynn nodded. Pella was right. Probably. She turned when she reached the doorway, half expecting to see Barid still sitting there. What she saw was the corner of Pella's cloak disappearing through the far door. Shaking her head, Wynn turned and ran down the corridor to the stairs leading to Svann's new rooms.

Barid gritted his teeth and immediately clenched his jaw as a red-hot poker was shoved behind his eyes. This pain was unbelievable. Why would anyone drink, ever, if this was what could happen? His father had been hung over once, and Barid had laughed at him. The clout across the bum his father had given him didn't seem so unfair now.

"Are you feeling better?"

Barid's head jolted up at the unexpected voice, and he broke out into a sweat, panting at the pain and the dizziness. He wasn't alone. And that wasn't Svann or Pella, let alone Wynn. He opened his eyes and closed them with a hiss. How could sunlight be so blinding? He shivered with more than pain. His eyes had been open long enough for him to glimpse a blue tunic. A Shekayrin. Not good. But which one? The Rose who'd been waiting here for Svann to show up? Or the Poppy who'd joined them three days ago? The mage bent down to look Barid in the eye, revealing his tattoo. The Poppy. Barid's stomach twisted, and he swallowed bile.

Thank the Mother he could use his block if the mage decided to examine him. They were like that, Poppies. Aggressive. Dangerous. Designed to prevent regular Talents from learning about the existence of Feelers, Barid had already used his block to save himself from the Rose Shekayrin who'd found him on the road after Questin Hall was destroyed. Creating the block was fairly simple. He only had to articulate his trigger word, Flash the Poppy Shekayrin while he was trying to examine him, and then let the mage see only what Barid wanted seen. He concentrated on forming his trigger word, only to have pain stab through his head, leaving him once again shaken.

Just how drunk had he been last night? And how long would this hangover last? He couldn't protect himself without his block. He tried to swallow, but his mouth was too dry. As if he'd spoken aloud, the mage held the cold edge of a metal cup against his lower lip. Barid wanted to gulp the water down, but that would move his head too much, so he sipped as slowly as his parched tongue would allow. He just had to keep his head. Don't give the mage any reason to jewel him.

"I'm Seklur Tvak. I've been interviewing all the staff here, on behalf of the Luqs of Farama, Dern Firoxi." He smiled. One of his front teeth slightly overlapped the other. "Last night you were a little the worse for drink, but you seem better now." The mage's voice was so soft and gentle it only felt like a hammer. If only he would stop talking. "Why don't we finish what we were talking about?"

What had they been talking about? The last thing Barid remembered was talking to Wynn and then . . . and then nothing, until just a moment ago.

"You were in service here as a clerk when the Rose and the Sunflower first came, correct?"

"Oh, no." Relief washed over him. "I mean, yes, I'm a clerk, but not here. Farther, uh, farther to the north." If this was the type of thing they'd been talking about, there was nothing to worry about.

"There, not so hard, was it? Thank you for correcting that for me. So, you came with Peklin Svann when he returned from the Serpents Teeth. I see. Then you'll be able to tell me what went on up there."

"But I don't know . . ."

The mage held up his hands palms out. "Now I know what you're thinking. You don't want to get anyone into trouble. But here, let me tell you what I already know. You just correct me, like you've done already. You'd be helping yourself at the same time."

That sounded reasonable. Barid took a chance and nodded his head—just once, as the poker stabbed him behind the eyes again.

"So." The Poppy smiled. "Svann went to the Serpents Teeth looking for soul stones. He didn't find any, but he did find other things." He smiled again and nodded. What was his name? "A whole network of tunnels, and people living in them. Poor misguided people causing problems for all of us, and themselves as well. Encouraging other fools to believe they can free themselves, when all they're really doing is getting each other killed."

Barid ventured another look, slitting his eyes against the sunlight. Why didn't someone close the shutters?

The Shekayrin had been leaning against a worktable, hands on the edge and ankles crossed. Now he approached Barid's chair. If it hadn't had arms, Barid thought he'd just slip to the stone floor. How could bones that felt too big for his body feel so much like jelly?

The Shekayrin brushed Barid's hair off his forehead, fingers cool against his hot skin. The gesture tilted Barid's head back until he looked the mage directly in the face. Then the grip tightened just enough that Barid could not move his head. "This explains why we've been having so much trouble around the approaches to the mountains, especially the pass. How many people are living in these mountains, do you think?"

Barid opened his mouth to answer. Tried to shake his head when no words would come out.

"Come now. We're not stupid, you know, and neither are you. You can see I already know. Your answers are only to let me check how deeply *you're* involved."

Panic threatened to shut his mouth permanently. How *could* the mage know so much? Was it Svann? It couldn't have been him, he was *never* that drunk. But he had to say something now. He couldn't let the mage suspect him enough to use the jewel. Not until he felt better, anyway. What had the Poppy asked? "I just met Svann there. I don't know anything."

"Well, *someone* knows. *Some* one of you is a spy. If it's not you, who is it?" The mage smoothed back his hair again and stepped away.

Barid's muscles froze him rigid.

"Is it the redhead? Perhaps she's a witch pretending to be a servant. Is she the one you're protecting?"

"No! Not Wynn." Pain throbbed through his head.

"Very well. And it's not you. So that only leaves one person." The mage nodded. "Svann is working with the enemy. I thought so."

"But I *don't* know. Really, I don't. That is, I can't be sure . . ." Barid's mouth dried, and this time no one offered him water.

If only his brain wasn't so fuzzy and so thick. *I haven't told them anything*, he thought. They already knew. Someone else must have told them. Svann probably gave himself away somehow. That had to be it.

The mage still looked at him, head tilted to one side, waiting for an answer. Barid knew he had to say something real, something definite. Otherwise, the mage would jewel him, and Barid couldn't afford that. He was too valuable; there were so few Talents. He had to stay alive.

"It must be Svann." That hoarse whisper couldn't be his own voice. But, after all, the Poppy was right about Svann.

"There now, don't worry so much. None of this is your fault. There's no harm in your discussing this with me."

Barid almost wept with relief. The mage was going to leave him alone. Only Svann would be in trouble, and Svann could handle himself.

"Come, let's find something cold for your forehead, and something soothing for your mouth and throat. Then I'll show you the map, and you can confirm the direction we need to follow."

"You were right to worry, Wynn. Barid's been in the Poppy Shekayrin's rooms all night." From the rumpled state of his clothing, Pella looked as though he'd been looking for Barid the same length of time.

"I was afraid of that, truth to tell." Wynn scrubbed at her face with her hands. She hoped she didn't look as bad as she felt. Only Svann, sitting behind his worktable, looked immaculate and tidy as usual, though paler, she thought.

"You must go." Svann turned toward them, determination in the look he gave her. "Now, before they come for me."

Wynn took a step closer to him. "Barid won't tell them anything. He's already been examined by a Shekayrin; he fooled that one, he'll fool this one."

Svann shook his head, gathering up the documents in front of him. Wynn's throat tightened. "We cannot be sure. He has not been examined by a Poppy Shekayrin. They are more . . . ruthless."

Wynn snorted, folding her arms. "Well, I don't see how going back to my own room with the rest of the servants is going to help anything."

Now he looked her in the eye. "I meant you must go back to the Mines and Tunnels. Before it is too late. Tel Cursar was right. We should never have come." He gestured at the documents. "What little intelligence I have been able to gather is not as useful as I had hoped."

Wynn dropped her arms and took a step closer. "I won't go—look, I know women in Halia don't bear arms and all that, but you know better now. I'm as much a soldier as Pella. Besides, we can't be jeweled, me *or* Pella. You've shielded us."

"That he cannot jewel you will in itself tell him that I see myself in opposition to him, that I felt the need to protect my servants from him."

Wynn blinked. He must be seriously upset. Not only hadn't he corrected her—as he always did—for using the word jewel as a verb, but he'd done it himself. "Then you come with us. Let's all go."

"The girl's being sensible, sir. You should listen," Pella said from his post by the door.

"We will draw unnecessary attention if we all leave at once. I am in no immediate danger. He may be a Poppy, but he is not so powerful that he can subdue me by himself, or even with the help of the Rose. The worst I face is confinement. You face much worse, Wynn Martan, as they can hurt you in ways they cannot hurt me. You know this. My shield protects the mind only. No, you must go, both of you. I will stay only long enough to cover your leaving and perhaps to free Barid, if it can be done. Then I or—hopefully—*we* will join you."

Wynn's stomach clenched. "Fine. We'll do it your way, leave separately and regroup once we're outside."

"Where?" Pella always dealt with practicalities.

"There's an alehouse in Wainwright Lane. We can meet there."

"Wait, before you go." Svann went into the inner room and came out with a purple leather pouch and a folded parchment packet, identical to the one he'd given to Tel. The papers on the table he folded up and placed in the pouch. "Here is what knowledge I have gleaned, and what money I have." He hefted the pouch and passed it to Wynn. "If I am not there in three days, you must use this"—he held up the pass—"and go."

"Just a minute." Wynn stepped back, holding her hands out. "We won't be going—"

"And if something should go wrong?" Svann interrupted. "If I cannot find you? This pass will keep you safe. You should carry it, Pella. You will be a soldier with a servant."

"We won't need it." Pella nodded at her as he shoved the pass into the front of his tunic. "We'll wait for you."

"No more than three days."

The cards slid out of Bakura's hands and cascaded across the tabletop. Ker laughed and gathered them up again, sliding them over to the girl's side of the table.

"Sorry," she whispered, laying her hands flat down on top of the cards. "Can we not go? Every time the door opens, I fear the worst." Tel reached over and took the cards into his own hands. They were steadier than the princess', but that's about all Ker could say.

"We need to finish our kaff and our biscuits before we can leave without making people wonder," she pointed out. "We should look like we've met by chance, and like we haven't a care in the world. Stop turning your head to look at the door. I can see it perfectly well from here."

In fact, Ker had started Flashing again, and her awareness of the street outside was even clearer than her sight. Net or no net, Bakura's aura showed the spikiness of distress and worry. Almost without thinking Ker reached out with her own colors, stroking the other girl's aura like she would stroke a cat. Like a cat, the aura smoothed and relaxed. Baku sat up a little straighter.

"We'll wait long enough that if anyone's followed you, they'll get impatient and come in," Tel added, shuffling the cards. "Once we know we're safe, we can move on."

"Whenever you are ready, then," the girl said, putting out her hand for the shuffled deck. "I believe the deal is mine."

They were still in the Summer round when Ker noticed Bakura handled each card as though it were heavy as a brick and set it down with an almost audible sigh. She'd had a long day, and a tiring one, but this much exhaustion after she'd been sitting down for the best part of an hour was worrying. They wouldn't be able to travel very quickly if the girl tired at every step.

"Are you ill?" she asked. Even if it was only her woman's time, that could exhaust a person.

"No, I do not believe so."

"May I Flash you?" Ker held out her hand for the princess to hold. She looked surprised she'd been asked.

"Yes, you may." Bakura placed her hand in Ker's as though she expected to be bitten. Her hands were soft. Obviously, the girl had never done any work at all.

"What can you see?" Tel asked the question the princess was probably afraid to ask.

"There's nothing *physically* wrong, but . . ." Ker hesitated, worried that she couldn't accurately describe what she saw. "She's been jeweled by two different mages." Ker didn't want to say the word "Shekayrin" aloud. "There's the original net, from a powerful Poppy Shekayrin, and a more recent misting.

The misting was intended to weaken you," she told Bakura. "It's quite clever, actually, because it sustains itself by drawing on your own energy."

"This must be what tires me so quickly." Bakura pressed her lips together and nodded. "Jerek said—we hoped—that you would be able to free me."

"So, what does the Council of Faros say?"

The lean graying woman sitting in front of her tossed back the cup of wine Tonia Nast had given her and wiped the corners of her mouth with her fingers. Carmad, her Laxtor, looked exhausted, but worse, she wore her bad news face. "You may want to eat first, Tonia."

"As bad as that."

Carmad shrugged. "A great many words, and not much to the purpose."

Tonia set aside the wine and handed her Laxtor a cup of the brandy she'd been warming over a candle. "But are they for the Brightwing boy, or not?"

"Yes, and no."

"Carmad, if you do not immediately tell me all, I will demote you."

Now came the grin. "Then I'll shorten it since I smell the stew coming. They're willing to consider the claims of Jerek Brightwing to be Luqs of Farama. As soon as he arrives in Juristand."

"Arrives in Juristand?" Tonia set the brandy down slowly. "If the boy goes to Juristand, the Council of Faros will shift the capital there, and the Peninsula will be lost. We'll have given everything south of the Serpents Teeth to the Halians." Tonia sat down, suddenly less than sure that her legs would hold her. "I told the Faro of Bears this could happen, back before we found the Brightwing Luqs. I thought I was exaggerating."

"There's another way to look at it," Carmad said. "There's more to this than where the Luqs of Farama sits. From what we've been told—and what we've seen for ourselves—the Halians are unlikely to stop at the Peninsula. It's not as though they are limited to movement on land. They can reach Juristand by sea, and sooner or later they will."

Tonia nodded, but she hadn't really heard anything. "And what about the Eagles and the Bears that have been captured or taken over by the enemy? Do we just abandon them, too? Many of us have family and friends in the Peninsula." *My father and my stepmother.* Her half-brother Fraxim, her grandmother. She didn't need to say this aloud; Carmad knew perfectly well that Tonia had family in the Peninsula. *And Ester? Does she live?*

She took a deep breath and refocused her attention on her Laxtor. "How do they suggest we get the Brightwing Luqs to Juristand?"

"You are requested to escort him yourself," Carmad said.

Tonia squeezed the bridge of her nose between her right thumb and index finger. "And the Bears?"

"They are to maintain their blockade of the Pass."

"I see." Tonia remembered what her sister Kerida had told her. The Bears, even with the help of their new allies, could not hold the Halians back indefinitely, unless the threat of the Shekayrin could be removed. Had Kerida found the griffins? Had *they* agreed to help?

"I thought there aren't enough Faros in Juristand to make such a decision."

"They are considering suspending that rule. And before you say it, yes, I know, there aren't enough Faros in Juristand to make that decision either."

Tonia nodded, her eyes closed.

"My Faro." Both the tone and the formality warned Tonia that something more was coming. Maybe something worse. She looked up and made a beckoning gesture with her hand.

"I didn't say the council would acclaim Jerek Brightwing," Carmad pointed out. "I said they'd consider him."

Tonia rubbed at her eyes. A moment ago, she'd been starving. Now she could barely stand the smell of her stew. "Oh, Daughter. Don't tell me they have someone else in mind."

"One of the other Faros has offered himself as a candidate, pointing out that a military hand is needed at present."

"I asked you not to tell me." Tonia pushed herself back as far as she could into her chair. "From the look that's on your face, there's still more. Who is it? Or do I really need to ask?"

Carmad nodded. "It's Rexun Pilari, all right."

Tonia pushed away her bowl of stew without looking at it. "Have I told you how my father had him transferred from the Panthers, back when I was just a Barrack Leader?"

"Many times. I'd be surprised if there are any senior officers anywhere who haven't heard the story."

"But they'd consider this yammerhead for Luqs?"

"You know that kind always finds friends—otherwise, how did he get to be Faro of Wolves?" Carmad shrugged. "There was another name proposed."

"I'm afraid to ask." Tonia sighed again and sat up straight. "All right, who?"

"You."

Tonia opened her mouth and closed it again.

"You'd make a good Luqs, Tonia. Everyone knows it—*you* know it." Carmad tapped the table with her index finger. "Even some who support Pilari said they'd back you instead if you wanted the throne."

Tonia fought against the sudden need to laugh. "You're right. I'd make a much better Luqs than Rexun Pilari. Maybe even a better Luqs than Jerek Brightwing."

"But?"

"But my father would never speak to me again. My grandmother would die of disgust and then come back from the Mother's Land to haunt me." This time Tonia did laugh, imagining the look on the old woman's face. She shook her head. "This is not what we do, we old Shield Families. We serve. We go out into the field and hold back the enemy and bleed and die and get cold. We sit in tents, not on thrones. Besides, if I agree and they put Jerek Brightwing aside, it will make the Bears renegades for having acclaimed him."

"What are you going to do, then?"

"What do you think?"

Carmad nodded. "I'll have the Cohort Leaders summoned."

"How will we contact them?" Carmad asked, once the Cohort Leaders had been informed of their Faro's decision. "Do we go to Oste Camp?"

"They're not at the camp," Tonia said. "The Bears are watching the Pass. We'll present ourselves there, and *they'll* contact *us*."

"My Faro, we can't enter the Pass, not without the Luqs' permission." Faros asked for permission to enter the Peninsula and left their Battle Wings behind. An old law meant to keep any Faro from usurping the throne.

"Teach an owl to hunt." Tonia frowned. "The law says that I can't cross the Teeth, not that I can't send an envoy. That old law might work in our favor this time. I can't be expected to fetch the boy out if I can't go in to get him."

Much later, the Faro of Panthers stopped kneading her Laxtor's shoulders and sighed. "What is it?"

"You didn't tell them. Are you planning to?"

When Tonia didn't answer right away, Carmad twisted around to peer up at her. "Come on," she said, shrugging on her shirt. "Your turn."

Tonia waited until the muscle in the top of her shoulders had begun to loosen under Carmad's oiled hands. "Did I ever tell you I saw the Daughter once?"

The hands stopped moving. "My Faro?"

Tonia tilted her head and skewed her eyes over. "I know what that tone means, Carmad, and I know what people think about the poor unfortunates who believe they've seen one of the gods."

Carmad resumed her massage, pushing her thumbs into the hollow above Tonia's collarbone. "No offense meant."

"Of course, there was." Tonia turned her head slowly from one side to the other. Carmad took a step back. "She was shorter than I expected," Tonia said, looking into the shadows at the far side of their bedroom. "Somehow you always think of the gods as being taller than ordinary people. She was beautiful, her hair all twisty, curly, like a black cloud, and her skin very dark, like some of her statues you see carved out of ebony."

"Darker than you, Tonia? Is it possible?"

Tonia twisted around until she could look Carmad in the eyes. "You know perfectly well we old Shield Families are only considered to have olive skin."

"And her eyes? What color were her eyes?" The teasing note had left Carmad's voice.

"Gray, of course."

"There *are* dark women with gray eyes," Carmad pointed out. "It's not that uncommon even among you old Shield Families. Your sister . . ."

Tonia nodded without speaking. "I know," she said finally. "But this woman turned to look at me, and her eyes were as deep as the ocean, and as wide as the sky." She looked at Carmad. "Not human eyes, not a normal person's eyes. And when she smiled at me, time stood still and the world around us stopped."

"A girl smiled at me like that once," Carmad said. "It was in a tavern west of Juristand, I forget the town, but I'll tell you, she could make time stop all right. She—" Tonia swung at her, but Carmad ducked. "Kidding!" she said, still smiling. But then her smile faded. "I believe you, you know, my Faro of Panthers.

You're very pragmatic, very practical. You don't see things that aren't there, so if you say you saw the Daughter, then I believe you." Carmad picked up the stone bottle of brandy she'd brought with them, hefted it to judge its contents, and poured exactly half into each of their cups. "What I'm not sure of," she continued, once they'd saluted the gods and each other, "is why you're telling me about these allies, and why you didn't tell the others."

"It's a little like what you just said," Tonia told her. "How would people react? But I know my sister, and I know what she'd likely lie about, and it isn't this."

"Well, it certainly isn't a useful lie, is it? If anything, it's more likely to make us think twice about having Jerek Brightwing as Luqs. Someone who's allied himself with Feelers? Whether people believe or not, that wouldn't be practical."

Tonia massaged the fine muscles around her eyes. "Of course, she's not my sister anymore. She's a Talent now."

Carmad grinned. "Our three didn't like that much, did they?"

"They don't like much ever, as far as I can make out." Momentarily distracted, they shared the look that everyone in the Wings occasionally had when thinking about the Talents that traveled with them. "But that means Kerida's doubly honest, doesn't it? Once as my sister, and once as a Talent."

"Who we won't be telling about this, am I right?"

"If the old stories are true, if Feelers actually exist—"

"Then the animosity between Feelers and Talents might also exist?"

Tonia looked at her coldly. "What have I told you about interrupting me?"

"Yes, my Faro." Carmad began bowing to her, hands crossed over her chest. "Sorry, my Faro, never again, my Faro." She looked at her from under her eyebrows, and Tonia snorted.

"All right. What do you think? Am I going to tell them?"

"I say no." Carmad drained her cup and frowned at the empty bottle.

"And what is my reasoning?"

"You won't tell the Cohort Leaders because the Diamond is sleeping with one of the Talents. No one's quite sure what a Talent can Flash about a person's knowledge and thoughts under such circumstances, but it's as well not to risk it." Tonia signaled her to continue. "And you'd like the Talents to find out only after they can't do anything about it."

"It's like you read my mind."

Svann: I fear we may have been uncovered. A Poppy Shekayrin has come, and Barid has been with him since last evening.

Kerida: What are you doing about it? Tel was saying something to her, and Ker held up one finger to silence him.

Svann: I have sent little Wynn Martan away, and Pella Dursto with her. Since we do not know what may come, we must act on the worst. My Far-seeing is not great, but I have been able to see that they have escaped through the kitchens and outbuildings.

Ker nodded. She, Jerek, and Wynn had escaped from the administrative compound in Gaena once before. Wynn had probably taken Pella the same way.

Kerida: Why aren't you with them?

Svann: If there is any way to recover Barid, I would wish to do so. But it made no sense for all of us to wait here. This way, if the worst happens, they—at least—will be able to return to you.

Kerida: Try not to let the worst happen.

Svann: As you wish.

She could feel him smiling. It didn't help her feel better. "I've got some bad news," she whispered to Tel.

Juria Sweetwater received word while she watched the training of a Barrack of Miners. These were some of what they called

UnGifted, those who were not Feelers themselves, but were daughters and mothers, sons and fathers. Unexpectedly, it was a Feeler who brought the news to her, a man named Palin, one of those who could see things at a distance or around corners. Juria supposed that Luca was busy elsewhere. Though it was a good thing, on the whole, that the Feelers felt comfortable in coming directly to her, without using a Guardian or one of the UnGifted as a spokesperson.

"There's a great many soldiers, if you please, my lady Faro, and they've stopped a good few spans from the Pass." The man shut his eyes. "They've unfurled a great banner, my lady, and it has a big cat on it, long and sinewy like, my lady Faro, if you take my meaning."

"It is just Faro, Palin Far-seer. You do not need to call me 'my lady' as well."

"Whatever you say, m— Faro."

"Thank you, Palin." Juria waited until the man had gone his way before signaling to the aide standing closest to her. "Ask the Laxtor to join me at his earliest convenience," she said.

He joined her a few minutes later, strolling as if there was no urgency. When he was close enough to speak privately, she told him. "The Panthers are at the Pass."

His brow furrowed. "Will the news they bring be good or bad, do you think?"

"To know that we would have to ask the little Time-seer, and we would probably get an answer we do not understand." She nodded at the soldier in charge of the training, a second officer from the Eagle Wing. "Well done," she called, and turned to leave the chamber.

Juria stopped so abruptly Surm almost walked into her back. "If the Panthers have come to join us, then Tonia Nast will require the Luqs' permission to enter the Pass, or the Mines for that matter. I can convey that permission."

"And if they haven't?"

"We will play those cards when they are dealt."

*   *   *

"Can you tell us why they're here, Larin?" Jerek's heart beat so rapidly he suspected that Juria Sweetwater, standing at ease in front of his chair, could hear it. There was no doubt at all, unfortunately, about Luca Pa'narion, standing to the other side.

This would be the first time that the amplified Council of Feelers had met for anything of consequence since Jerek had forced the Miners and the Springers to tolerate each other better. The new councillors had been provided with seats. Though one was only a cushion, the Far-thinker occupying it didn't seem to mind. Everyone looked to the little girl swinging her feet in the thronelike chair that was the seat of the Time-seer. Without stopping her feet, she wrinkled her brow and narrowed her eyes.

"I like cats," she said. "Panthers are just big cats, aren't they? Not as big as Weimerk, though, right?"

Jerek nodded. "That's right, not as big as Weimerk. I'm not sure anything's as big as Weimerk." He smiled at her, and Larin's lips spread wide in the biggest grin he'd ever seen from her. "Have you ever Seen these big cats in the Mines and Tunnels?"

She frowned in concentration, and her legs started swinging again. "Of course."

"Does it frighten you? Are you afraid when you have the vision?" Luca asked.

Now the child shrugged and smiled again.

"Encouraging, but not so very helpful," Ganni said. "Seeing as the child's afraid of nothing. What's the nearest exit to these big cats?"

Midon, the Far-seer on the council, spoke. "If what Palin told me was accurate, it's Rose Blossom Exit."

The exits, Jerek knew, were usually named after some characteristic of the exterior. This probably meant there were wild roses growing nearby.

"It is best if the Faro of Panthers comes to you, my Luqs." Juria never called him by his name in public, no matter how many times he asked her to. "But for that she needs your permission."

Jerek nodded. Juria herself, as a Battle Wing Faro, was here only because Jerek had given her his permission. And it was by her accepting it that she officially recognized him as Luqs. What changes were the Panthers bringing with them?

"In that case, tell her that she may come herself, but only her and no one else."

"A Faro would normally have a lesser officer accompany her, my Luqs."

Jerek shrugged. "Not this time, Faro of Bears. If she doesn't trust us, she can go away."

Juria took two Cohort Leaders and four guards with her. Surm would wait with the rest of the Wing, just in case. Rose Blossom may have been the closest exit, but it was not what Juria would have called close. It took the better part of an hour at double pace to reach the Panther Wing.

"Jerek Brightwing, Luqs of Farama, welcomes the Faro of Panthers and gives her his permission to enter the Serpents Teeth." Having delivered her official message, Juria could address Tonia Nast directly. "I did not think I would be seeing you so soon, Panther."

"Nor I you, Bear. I'll leave my Laxtor in charge in my absence and bring with me only my most senior Cohort Leader."

"That will not be possible, Faro Nast. The Luqs wishes to see you—and only you. No one else is to enter with you."

The Panther officers all began speaking at once, falling silent when Tonia Nast raised one hand. "I suppose it's either trust you or go away?" There seemed to be a smile crinkling the corner of her mouth.

"That is precisely how the Luqs put it himself." Juria

turned and with a gesture indicated that Tonia should walk beside her.

"I'm surprised you don't blindfold me," Tonia Nast said as they passed through the entrance.

"There's no need," Juria said. "If things don't go well, the Miners will simply close this entrance, and move the tunnels."

The Faro of Panthers stopped between one step and the next. "Wouldn't it be simpler to kill me?"

"Would it? I should think that would more likely bring all your Panthers down on us. We would waste our time avoiding them rather than fighting the Halians."

Tonia resumed walking. "Yes. Yes, I suppose it would."

10

"I THINK I can do it." Ker sorted through the cards in her hand, grouping the suits together. She had neither Summer nor Winter cards. "In the past I've worked with a Mind-healer. I enable them to see the mist and they brush it away." She picked up her kaff. Empty. Put it down again.

Once the deal came around to Baku, Ker triggered her Talent. Working on the girl's aura would be easier if her attention was focused elsewhere. Mind-healers always used their own silver color—though they didn't know it—so first Ker tried using her turquoise, flattened like a broom, to sweep away the red mist that hung over Baku's aura. The turquoise passed through the red mist with no effect. Ker drummed her fingers on the tabletop. She didn't have any silver in her aura, but she *did* have Feeler's Gifts. Through the jewel.

Ker tossed her three of Spring down on top of Tel's two of Winter, then watched him sweep up the trick. She gathered her red webbing around her, letting it change and shift through pattern after pattern. She felt she was on the right track, but what if using her jewel just strengthened whatever was trapping the girl? Ker had never used her jewel on anyone else, except that one time with Svann, and she'd hurt him. Ker frowned down at the cards in her hands and sighed.

Bakura's mist shifted and resettled. Ker sat up straighter and sighed again, stronger, more forcefully. The mist spread outward, thinning. Ker blew more deliberately. The mist brushed away and disappeared.

"Huh. Like steam from a cup of kaff," she said aloud.

"What?" Tel paused, holding a card halfway to the table. Baku sat up straighter, and she looked less pale.

Ker got to her feet, unable to sit still in the face of her success. "More kaff, anyone?"

She waited with one elbow on the bar, watching Ester serving mugs of kaff to four men seated at one of the round tables. Finished, her sister leaned her hip against the back of one man's chair as she spoke to him, her tray tucked under her arm. Two of the men—including the one whose chair Ester leaned against—had the now-familiar scruffy look of ex-soldiers who were out of work. *Eagles*, Ker thought. Two of Ester's own men, the ones who'd disguised and hidden her, and kept her safe.

Her own kaff arrived, but before Ker could pick it up, Tel joined her at the bar, signaling the man behind it to bring him one as well. He made no move to return to the table, where Baku was laying out the hand of Solitary Seasons called Green Jade. The princess looked better, less worn out, and Ker mentally gave herself a pat on the back. The first step in their escape was accomplished.

The barman set Tel's kaff down and moved a discreet distance away.

"She's looking better," Tel said. "You going to try the net?"

Ker took a sip of her kaff, grimaced at the heat, and shook

her head. "Let's get away first. I've never really done it before, and I don't want to try here and now."

"And speaking of escapes—" Tel picked up his own kaff and nodded at the barman. "Trying the gate at dusk when it's about to close feels like a mistake."

"I agree that normally we'd want to take advantage of the cover of a crowd, but there's nothing normal about this." Ker glanced sideways at Baku. "The invisibility trick is too risky." The Princess Imperial frowned at her cards, took a sip from her mug, and wrinkled her nose. She still wasn't used to the taste of kaff. When she saw Ker looking at her, she blushed and lowered her eyes again. The girl also wasn't used to people being able to see the expression on her face.

"It worked for you." Tel was nothing if not persistent. Ker regretted for what felt like the two hundredth time telling him how she'd magicked herself past the guards.

"It almost didn't, and I was only magicking myself. What if I can't do it for all three of us? I want to try something else, refocusing the guards' attention or—I don't know—putting them all to sleep. I won't be able to do that if there's a crowd of other people. Don't you think other people are bound to notice if the guards all suddenly fall asleep?"

Baku's head lifted, and she froze with a seven of Autumn raised in her hand. A small line appeared between her sculpted eyebrows. She put down the card as if she didn't know she was doing it. "Kerida, I think—"

Ester had also turned toward the door. The way she put her free hand on the shoulder of the man whose chair she'd been leaning on was unmistakably intended to keep him seated.

Tel looked between Ker and the princess, his eyebrows raised. Ker held out her hand, palm down. Her left hand had gone almost automatically to the pouch holding her jewel. *Paraste.* She muted the auras immediately around her, and sure enough, a mass of swirling colors shone through the inn's main door as if it wasn't there. Swirling colors including some red. *Just a jeweled soldier?* she asked herself. *Or a Shekayrin?* She nodded to Tel, caught Ester's eye, and tipped her chin at the door, holding up four fingers.

The door opened, and Ker started to relax, until the three gray-clad soldiers coming in were followed by a man wearing the blue tunic and black cloak of a Shekayrin. Not just a jeweled soldier then, but the jeweler himself.

Baku was still looking at her, eyes opened wide, and Ker shook her head minutely. *Stay where you are*, she thought, and Baku's shoulders lowered as if she'd heard her. The soldiers fanned out, one coming to the bar, one going to the back door, and the third edging through the tables until he could stand with his back to the fireplace. Their auras showed no signs of tampering. Ker set her mug of kaff on the bar top as quietly as she could. She ran her hand along the edge of the bar top, as if wiping off dust, reaching out to smooth down the intruders' auras at the same time. The three soldiers relaxed, but the Shekayrin showed no change at all.

Ker gritted her teeth. If it turned out she couldn't influence the mage the same way she did ordinary people, they were all in trouble. His aura *was* a bit dull, she thought, but not from anything she'd done. The red especially wasn't as bright and clear as Svann's. When the man's face turned in her direction, she saw a Rose around his left eye. What was a Rose doing here with soldiers? From what Svann had told her about the capabilities of the various schools, she would have expected a Poppy.

The room hadn't been all that noisy to begin with, but now the silence made Ker's ears hurt. No one spoke, but as the guards did nothing more than stand quietly, shoulders began to relax, and the flicking of a card and the click of dice meant that the gamers at least were returning to their play.

Baku kept her eyes down, laying out fresh cards. Her hands were steady, not a tremor showing.

The Rose Shekayrin walked all the way to the back of the room, his head sweeping to the right and left. He held up one finger to Ester, who approached him wiping her hands on the bar towel slung over her shoulder. He didn't wait to see whether she'd stopped, though she had. When he reached the end of the room, he turned and paced slowly back again, his finger still raised, as if he was telling the whole room to wait. He frowned in exactly the way someone does when he's wrong and doesn't want to admit it.

This time his path took him a little closer to their table. His eyes passed over the princess the same way they'd passed over everyone else. He didn't notice Baku's shoulders stiffen as he glanced at the cards in her hands and continued walking.

He stopped only three paces away, standing with his head tilted as if listening to something no one else could hear. He turned slowly and approached Baku's table again. Ker saw the girl's knuckles whiten as the mage came closer, and she finally pulled her hands back from the cards and put them in her lap under the table.

Ker stiffened, her own hands forming fists, as she came to the same realization that Baku had. The princess' face and hair had always been covered in public; it was only her hands that everyone had seen, and her hands were giving her away now.

The Rose Shekayrin slowed to a stop next to Baku's chair. Ker edged forward, drawing her aura together, ready to shield or strike as needed. The soldier at the fireplace moved forward, stopping only at the mage's signal.

"Well. Honored One." He joined his hands in front of him. "Come with me now, and we will pretend this little adventure did not occur. Your punishment would be minor."

"You mean *yours* would be." Obviously, she thought there was no point in denial, but Baku's voice hardly trembled. Unless you could see the way the girl's aura shivered in its net, Ker thought, you wouldn't notice.

The Shekayrin raised his jewel in his left hand, and a

blanket of red floated like a hovering hawk over the princess. More by instinct than design, Ker threw some of her own colors between the Shekayrin and his prey, dipping them into the red like a ladle into a pot and swirling it away. The look of startled affront on the mage's face as he felt his attack slipping was almost funny. Until he turned and raised his jewel toward Ker. He couldn't be sure what or who had interfered with his attack, but something, maybe the look on her face, or the way she stood, told him Ker had something to do with it.

She braced herself, but suddenly Ester was between them, sweeping Ker's feet out from under her. Ker went down, years of military training helping her to fall properly, without banging her head on the stone floor. It was then she saw that the bolt of red meant for her, invisible to everyone else, had struck Ester instead. On reaching her, the bolt transformed into a net that caught the colors of her aura like a hunter's net catches birds, and tightened, shrinking until it snuffed the aura out, and Ester slumped to the floor.

Without thought, though later she knew she'd cried out, Ker struggled to her feet, standing over her sister. Taking her cue from the other man, Ker flung out her hands, the gesture setting her aura free. She could only hope that being able to see the auras, and the webways of the jewels, would give her an advantage over the Rose. She'd defeated Svann once, and she could defeat this one.

But not in the same way, she realized, as she struggled with the red net that both held and supported the mage's aura. When she'd fought with Svann, she'd held his jewel herself. She'd torn Svann's net completely loose, like a gardener pulling up a plant. Svann had been given back his jewel, and like that plant, he managed to reroot his net, though it grew in a slightly different shape. Ker didn't want that; she wanted this mage to wither and die.

She snatched out her own jewel, and her own pattern, nimble and changing, fending off the Rose's next attack while she sent all her colors directly at his aura at once, directly for the core of red at its center. Her own jewel glowed brighter, the angles of her own facets slipping, changing, from one shape to another, until her web mimicked the Shekayrin's exactly. And then she saw it, the weak point. She took hold of the red web at the man's core, and concentrated.

Nothing. Ker wavered. The Rose Shekayrin moved toward her, his jewel directly in front of him like a shield, and Ker felt herself pushed physically, until the edge of the bar hit her in the back. But movement wasn't a Rose's strength. Baring her teeth and gripping her own jewel more tightly, Ker stepped forward over Ester. Abandoning caution, calculation, she closed all her colors on the man's inner web at once and smashed the strands apart like a child destroying a sandcastle. The red web shredded, disintegrating in her hands, and the man dropped, his hand falling open and his jewel rolling free onto the floor.

Ker dashed forward, afraid that someone else might pick it up. When she reached it, however, the jewel no longer shone with its interior glow of red. It had turned entirely black and looked like nothing more than a chunk of charcoal carved into a jewel shape. Ker squatted down on her heels and picked up the stone with the tips of her fingers. Like charcoal, it weighed nothing. On impulse she closed her fist around it, crumbling it in her hand.

"Kerida!"

Movement at the edge of her vision brought Ker's head up in time to see the guards advancing on her from their stations at doors and fireplace. With her own jewel still in her hand, she expanded her web outward, pushing the men back and pinning them to the walls, where they stood staring, blank-eyed. She rose to her feet, brushing off the dark residue of the jewel on her trousers. She had to brace her knees to stop from sitting down again. "Anyone who never wants to be questioned about this, now's the time to leave."

Later, she thought that it was a testimony to how well the place was run that everyone moved swiftly out the rear door.

"What did you do to him?" Tel crossed to her side, steadying her with a firm hand under her elbow.

"Never mind that. What did he do to Ester?" Ker knelt at her sister's side, breath caught in her throat. All she could think of was Sala of Dez, dead and empty at the hand of Svann, when he'd been their enemy. Ester had no aura, nothing, no colors at all. That meant . . . but no, there *was* a pulse, and her sister *was* breathing. Ker took a deep breath herself. "She's alive."

"Wait, do not rejoice so quickly." Baku knelt beside her. She lifted Ester's eyelids, one at a time, but they could only see the whites. She picked up her hand and let it drop, limp, back to her chest.

"What is it?" Tel said from over them.

Baku looked up, her face pale, her eyes bleak. "I have read of this. It is a training procedure, to train Shekayrin in the use of netting with the stone. At first, they are likely to destroy the target person, but they develop control eventually."

Of course they destroy. They can't see the Daughter-cursed net. They would have to do all their work with inner discipline and control.

Baku lifted her eyes once more to Ker's face. "This was meant for you, but this woman stepped between."

Ker answered the unspoken question. "My sister."

Baku's face froze, her eyes softening.

Ker tapped her fingers against her thigh. "Netting" was the mages' version of what the Halls of Law called "dampening," used as the ultimate punishment—or control—of Talents who could not conform to the Law. "What's happened to Ester?" she asked now. "Her aura is gone, not just netted like yours." Ker described to them what she had seen, the net closing on Ester's aura until it was snuffed out.

Baku frowned, her brows drawn down. "Your sister is not a mage. I would imagine that the Rose wanted to use the net to confine or control *your* magic, but in her case . . ." The princess stopped, shaking her head.

"There was no magic to confine." How was her voice so even? "It didn't stop closing in, because there was nothing there to stop it." Ker took hold of Baku's shoulder, turning her until they were face-to-face. "If the net had hit me, instead of her, I would have been . . . like you?"

"Left whole." Baku nodded. "Your Gifts confined, but otherwise yourself, I believe so. At least—" She shrugged. "When they spoke of netting, they had no idea they were speaking of something that could be perceived as a net by those who had the right Gift."

"Can we get her back? Remove the net?" If she could find it. Right now, Ker saw nothing at all in her sister. But to leave her like this was unthinkable. Ester was a soldier, and she'd rather be dead than this unseeing, unknowing lump of flesh.

Baku folded her hands at her waist. "It is what I hope for myself, but my knowledge is limited. I do not know whether it has ever been done," she admitted finally.

Ker thought of Svann and his scholarship. If anyone would know, it would be a Sunflower Shekayrin.

Kerida: Svann! Svann, are you there? Wake up.

But he shouldn't be asleep, not at this time of day. Ker tried again, but there was still no answer.

<<Weimerk?>> A feeling of space, cold, and wind rushed through her, but the griffin gave no other answer.

The light touch of Baku's fingertips on Ker's arm brought her back. The princess' dark eyes were full of determination. "Jerek said that if it could be done, you would be the one to do it, Kerida Nast."

Before Ker had a chance to respond, Tel cut in. "What about him?" He jerked his chin at where the Rose Shekayrin lay in a heap like a discarded rag doll. "Is he dead?"

"His aura is intact, except . . ." She squinted as if that would help her Flash more clearly. "The red's gone," she said. "Gone completely, not just hidden."

"Is that not the color you associate with our magic? The color that you have yourself, that enables you to use the soul stone?"

Jerek really told her everything. Ker nodded. Apparently, when she tore apart the central core of the man's webbing, she had torn his magic loose as well. She swallowed. She wasn't sorry; she'd meant to stop him, and she had. A part of her whispered in satisfaction, "Let's see how he manages *without* magic." But another part would have preferred to kill him outright. To strip a man of his magic and leave him alive? Her skin crawled.

Ker Flashed him again. "He came alone," she said. "With just these three men. They've been going door-to-door. He hoped to stay out of trouble by returning Baku to the palace before anyone else knew she was missing. Failing that, he could get the credit of finding her."

"That's all very well," Tel said. "But isn't he going to be missed?"

"I have a suggestion." The voice was so calm, so quiet, that all three of them turned toward it without any sense of shock. Elisk Stellan, Ester's friend and the owner of the inn, stood in the rear doorway. "You can leave this"—he indicated the Shekayrin—"to me. I know a man with hogs a few streets over." Ker's stomach heaved, and Baku turned pale. "It's not like someone could call the Halls of Law and have a Talent come to find out what really happened. But what about these soldiers?"

Ker glanced at Tel and found him looking back at her looking like he'd bitten into a lemon. She knew the military solution. "Let me try something first," she said. "If it works, I might be able to use it on the gate guards." Tel's mouth was pressed into a thin line, but he nodded.

This would just be a variation on the trick of making people not see her, she thought, of making them look away—though not quite so simple. Once, when she was still in the military, she'd watched one of the company surgeons use an old healer's trick to make a quartet of soldiers think they were asleep, and she'd made them do some very funny things. Ker thought that, with the help of their auras, she might be able to do something similar with this trio. She studied them carefully. They were already, for all intents and purposes, asleep on their feet. That would help.

"You can hear my voice," she said. "Nothing but my voice. You feel content. Relaxed. Nothing frightens or worries you." She paused and examined their auras critically. As far as she could see, they were as smooth and restful as any she'd seen when Errinn Mind-healer had worked on troubled people back in the Mines and Tunnels. "You will leave here and return to your barracks. You will not be worried. If you meet anyone, act normally, and say you were sent on patrol by the Rose Shekayrin. You don't know why," she added at a signal from Tel. "You don't know where the Rose Shekayrin is. The last you saw him was in the palace. You won't remember anything about this inn, you won't remember coming here at all. Walk out the door now," she said when they didn't move. "Go on."

The soldiers blinked at each other, frowning. Ker tensed, afraid her aura tweaking combined with the suggestions hadn't worked after all. From the corner of her eye, she saw Tel's hand move toward the knife he had at the back of his belt.

The shortest of the three men glanced at where Ester still lay on the floor but didn't react in any way. "All right, then," he said, in the tone of someone summing up. "If there's no trouble here, we'll be on our way."

Tel opened the door of the inn, and the three men walked out. Ker let out the breath she was holding.

"What of your sister?" Baku said.

"We'll have to remove the net." Ker wasn't going to think about "trying." She was going to do it. She knocked a knuckle gently on the top of the nearest table.

"Do you wish to try removing mine first?" Baku's voice, quiet and steady, couldn't disguise the trembling in her aura.

"I appreciate that," Ker said. And she did; it told her a great deal about the Princess Imperial that she would make an offer like this.

"Ker, we can't. Jerek—"

"Don't worry, I'm not going to. I know we can't take the chance." Ker looked down at her sister. "But I'm not leaving Ester like this."

Seklur Tvak: He spoke freely, but not as coherently as I would've liked. I was reluctant to use the soul stone. In his drunken condition, I thought I might lose the very information I wanted. I put together what I could, and the next morning I tricked him into revealing more. One thing seems clear: there are stones to be found in these Serpents Teeth.

Pollik Kvar: Well done. Very well done, indeed. With these weaker Poppies, it was often necessary to give extra praise. **Gather what strength you can and make for this Valley of Simcot. Secure Svann and take him with you.** Kvar could feel a headache beginning behind his eyes. The Poppy Shekayrin in Gaena made a good subordinate, but his power to communicate was poor. **And the boy likely has other information. There must be other openings, other tunnels. Bring him and continue to interrogate him on the road. Before you leave, relay these instructions to the others. Inform me which you cannot reach.** At least he wouldn't have to do *all* the work himself.

Seklur Tvak: Will there be enough of us? If these tunnels are numerous, perhaps impenetrable . . .

Pollik Kvar: Compose yourself. The chance to crush the resistance is too great to let pass. I will come myself and bring the men who can be spared from the capital. He would take all the Horsemen with him, he decided. Let them spend their lives finding a way into the mines. **Go. Communicate your progress at sundown.**

Kvar tapped his soul stone on the table in time to a dance tune playing in his head, and the sharp clicks, reminiscent of the tapping of the dancers' heels, were somehow satisfying. He played through the whole tune, with two refrains at the end, before stopping and enclosing the stone in his right hand. "Leave me." He didn't need to open his eyes to know that he was quickly alone. If there was one sound a Poppy learned early, it was the sound of footsteps heading away. He smiled for a moment before rubbing at his eyes. He rose and replaced the soul stone in the pocket created by the crest on his tunic.

Once, there had been enough stones for even those who became ill after only a few hours of use. But that was long ago, when the stones and the dust that stored them were plentiful. Now, such weaklings were weeded out long before they would even reach the status of a first-stage apprentice. Those who failed the first test of power rarely left the examination room alive. The Poppy had strongly supported such practices.

"And I will continue to do so," he said, tapping the stone in its pocket, "even should stones become plentiful again."

Plentiful stones to be found at the Serpents Teeth, once he moved the Horsemen there. Perhaps he should pay a visit to the Princess Imperial—perhaps this would be a good time to begin training her in how he wished her to use the Voice of the Emperor.

"I will bring her with me to the mountains," he said, though he would leave Dern Firoxi behind. The man had no military usefulness. "Whereas the girl's presence will make the Horsemen easier to control." Kvar smiled.

The young man standing outside the audience room door fell into step behind Kvar as the door swung shut behind him. He acknowledged no one as he walked through the halls on his way to his own rooms. Otherwise, they would never leave him alone, filling his days with petty inquiries, complaints about the work of their peers, and other such whining.

The door of his room opened in front of him at the flicking of his fingers, closing before his attendant could reach it. The man would station himself against the wall at the right-hand side of the door. His orders were to kill anyone trying to enter uninvited.

Humming, snapping his fingers to the same tune he had played in his head earlier, Kvar headed to his bedroom to fetch the mask from its casket. Another snap of the fingers raised the lid. He froze long enough for a bead of sweat to trickle down his back and for his fingers to cramp. He snatched his hands back, and the lid fell softly, without slamming, exactly the same as always. Exactly as though the mask were still within.

"Impossible." No one would have dared to enter his chambers. Not even Dern Firoxi, who at least in theory had the right to go anywhere he pleased in his own palace—not even he would have entered here without permission.

Kvar rubbed his palms together until the feeling in his hands was restored. He tore out the silk wrappings and padding that lined the box and threw them on the floor. It was only when he held the last piece in his hands that he realized one was missing. Here were the yellow, blue, and green. But not the red wrapping, the interior wrapping that enclosed the mask itself. Deliberately taken, then. Not a common thief, but someone who knew what they were taking.

Kvar stepped back from the empty casket and inhaled slowly. He needed to regain his calm. Only one person would have known to take the red silk cloth, imbued with dust, as well as the mask. In fact, only one person knew the mask was in his possession. Only one person.

He was several strides down the hall before his aide could even step away from the wall he'd been leaning against. Luckily for him, Kvar had more important people to discipline.

The guard outside the Princess Imperial's suite snapped to attention, fist over heart, before stepping aside. Kvar gestured and the right-hand door slammed back against the inner wall, cracking. Three strides into the sitting room Kvar halted. Empty. The windows were unshuttered, only the fine mesh blinds softening the sunlight that entered the room. There was plenty of light to see by, and there was no one here.

"Attend me," he called, but no one came. Even if the servants were in the bedchambers, his summons should draw them out. The rooms were so silent he could hear birds outside. The fluttering of wings, the senseless noises they made.

Unbelieving, Kvar strode to the bedroom door and flung it open. The bed was made, the room tidy. Not so much as a comb out of place or a pair of slippers awaiting the Imperial feet. He wrinkled his nose. There was a faint smell of almond oil.

Another faint smell drew him to the other room, obviously occupied by the two body servants. The edge of a carpet peeked out from under the closest bed. A crooked finger beckoned the rug out into the center of the floor and revealed the body of the Luqs of Farama.

Rage closed eyes and fists. *Where is she?*

As he rushed back to the entry, furniture and boxes, delicate little tables and glassware leaped out of his way, smashing against walls and floor. His attendant stood outside next to the guard, face impassive.

"Who has entered here? Who has left?"

The guard grew paler. "Since we came on duty, only the two servants have come out," he said. "The guard before me said the Luqs had gone in. He hasn't come out yet." The man ventured what he likely thought was a telling smile.

Kvar knocked him to his knees with a blow from his fist. In the last moment he refrained from exposing the death. One thing at a time. "The room is empty. Go to your commander.

Have the palace searched. Have the princess' women brought to me."

Peklin Svann frowned down at his meager collection of possessions. The black cloak and blue tunic that marked him as a Shekayrin. A pair of gloves with red embroidery on the edges. A book of short tales, for reading in the evenings. A square leather pouch he had hand-tooled himself before his magic came. Svann stood only in his shirt and leggings, his back to a brazier table, so he was not cold. Other Shekayrin owned more, but Sunflowers did not seem to accumulate much. Even their knowledge was not stored in books and scrolls, which could be easily lost or misplaced, but in their own memories. He picked up the pouch. He wished he had thought to give it to Wynn Martan. It could have lived on after him.

Weak though his magic might be in this area, Svann had been able to watch Wynn and Pella make it to the alehouse that was to serve as their meeting point—escaping through the kitchens and over the wall, as he had told Kerida. Endlessly resourceful, these people with no magic. Strange that he had never noticed that before. He had learned so many things since Weimerk the griffin had given him the gift of his friendship. For one, he had seen what friendship was.

He looked around the room, saw that everything was clean, the floor still damp. A page of blank paper lay to his right on the tabletop, next to a handful of aromatic cedar chips he had created with his knife from an old box. His preparations were complete. He had been hearing, and seeing, signs of the household waking up for some little time now. Soon the Poppy Shekayrin would come, and Svann was pleased that all was ready for him.

"You would not have left if I had told you," he said aloud, his thoughts drifting once again to Wynn Martan. "You would have thought that you could help by staying." He had told them the other Shekayrin were not strong enough to harm him. But with sufficient help, most Shekayrin could be overcome, even Poppies. They would be harder, since their strength was more physical, but it could be done.

Svann opened his hand, looking at the jewel lying on his palm. If they overcame him, and took his jewel, leaving him sweating, nauseated, shivering and writhing with pain that was no less agonizing because it was not real—then, then he might tell them anything, do anything, to get his jewel back. The noise at the door was almost a relief. Now the waiting would be over. He tucked the jewel into the front of his shirt.

The door swung, creaking on its hinges, and Seklur Tvak stood in the opening. Svann tossed the cedar chips into the brazier, to release their fragrance into the air.

"Svann," the Poppy said in his quiet voice. "I have heard some disturbing things. About how you have come under the sway of the witches, and the enemy they still delude."

Svann smiled. "Was that a question?" He picked up the piece of paper, his fingers nervously folding and unfolding, flattening, twisting, and rolling.

"I'm afraid there's no question, none at all. You see I have brought guards with me. Shall I let them loose, or will you surrender quietly and give over your soul stone for my safe-keeping?"

Svann placed his left hand over the spot where his jewel rested. His right hand poked the end of the thin paper tube he had created into the fire, withdrawing it when a feather of flame clung to the end. He studied the tiny flame for a moment before he let it fall, smiling toward the doorway, where neither Seklur Tvak nor his soldiers had seen they were standing at the edge of a floor dampened by oil they could not smell over the odor of cedar. The flaming paper ignited the lamp oil Svann had so carefully prepared.

"Come and take it from me," he said, as fire engulfed the

room. In his final moment, he was sure he heard the voice of the griffin.

———

Every muscle in Kerida's body twitched, and she shivered, hesitating between one stair and the next.

"What is it?" Tel carried Ester in his arms.

"Nothing, just felt shivery for a moment." Ker set her shoulders and continued up the stairs.

"Well, don't stop again. Your sister's no lightweight, you know."

Ker set her jewel down on the small table next to her bed and rubbed between her eyes. "Not getting through," she said.

"Something happened to Svann, do you think?" Tel sounded like he wasn't sure what he wanted the answer to be.

"I guess he could be asleep," she said. "I don't know enough about how this works." She drew in a deep breath. If she couldn't get any help from Svann, she'd have to do it herself.

They had carried Ester upstairs to the attic room Ker shared with her and laid her on her own bed. She breathed evenly, and she had a good color, but no matter what she tried, Ker couldn't see Ester's aura. She squeezed Tel's hand hard to keep from crying. Without much hope for success, Ker tried the griffin.

<<Weimerk?>>

<<What distresses you? Ah. Your sister.>>

Ker shivered. Weimerk's voice brought with it the space and the cold she expected, but also, this time, a feeling of calm and rest. Where was he? Did the other griffins know he was talking to her? She shook those questions out of her head.

<<Can you help me?>> she said, focusing on Ester so that Weimerk could see her, too.

<<It is foolish to net the UnGifted. It causes nothing but difficulties. Why do you not restore her?>>

Ker told herself to keep her temper. <<Because I can't find a net. There's nothing there at all, no net, no aura.>>

<<Does the Shekayrin live? No, I see he does not. What of his jewel? Ah, I see. How did you expect the web to live when the jewel that made it does not? Come. You must look at the problem with the other eye.>>

Look at it with the other eye? How was that helpful? What other eye? Ker gritted her teeth. She could almost see Weimerk with that self-satisfied look on his beaky face, blinking first one eye and then the other. One eye, and then the other. Weimerk's eyes were far enough apart that if he wanted to, he could easily look through them one at a time. The first time she'd met him, the first time she'd seen the auras, she had a glimpse of what it was like to look at two things at once.

By telling her this, he meant she should look at her problem another way. What was it Svann had told her once about the skewed logic of griffins? She'd tried to find Ester's aura, and she'd found nothing. And the net that was supposed to be containing her sister's aura? Not there either. So, what if she tried to put something where there was nothing? Weimerk had given her some of his own colors—why couldn't she do the same for Ester?

She was Kerida Griffin Girl. She *should* be able to do for her sister what Weimerk had done for her. A sense of warmth and pleasure swept through her, Weimerk's way of letting her know she'd come to the right answer.

<<I still don't know why you can't just tell me.>>

<<Then you would only learn to ask me questions. Not to reason for yourself.>>

"Kerida?" The tension in Tel's voice told her she'd been quiet for a long time.

"I'm all right," she said. "I have something else I can try."

This time she focused on her own aura, sorting through the colors until she isolated the three that were common to all people: yellow, blue, and green. They seemed to glow extra strongly, as if they somehow knew they were needed. She stroked the green with her hands, and strands clung to her skin, like wool being carded. She twitched several strands loose, and they automatically twisted around each other, forming a single, strong strand that looped itself around her wrist like a bracelet. She turned and pushed the green loop into the emptiness that was her sister Ester, holding her breath until she saw the color would remain there by itself. She repeated each step with the yellow and blue, until all three colors had been transferred to Ester.

At first, Ker thought she'd made a mistake, that nothing would happen after all. She tapped her right thigh with her fist.

"Wait," Tel said. "Give it a hundred count before you try something else."

She nodded, grateful for the calm in his voice. She had just reached the sixties when the three colors stirred, their movement sluggish but obvious. Slowly, they grew stronger, their glow brighter, until finally the familiar wavelike motion began.

Ker sat back on her heels and rested her hands on her thighs, waiting. Ester's breathing deepened, and Ker was certain that her sister's face had more expression.

"Ker." Tel's hand was once more on her shoulder. "Ker, we have to go."

"Not yet." She managed not to snarl at him. "Wait for her to wake up." She didn't want to nudge Ester awake. Working with Mind-healers had taught her that impatience could ruin a good cure.

"Ker, they're closing the gates. The city's on alert."

That did make her look up. "Closing the gates," she said.

"That's right." Elisk Stellan, Ester's friend, stood in the open staircase. "Curfew's early, and we're told the gates have been ordered closed. They must be after your girl here. For the Mother's sake, don't be caught here in my inn."

Ker straightened to her feet, her eyes still on her sister. "Ester—"

"She's in my care. There's nothing more you can do here but bring trouble on me and mine."

And after I've helped you and all. Ker knew what the man didn't say aloud. It would be a poor way to thank him for everything he'd done for Ester already, to say nothing of Tel and herself. "Don't worry," she said. "We'll be gone before they get this far." She leaned over and kissed Ester's forehead.

For the first time she noticed Baku waiting in the farthest corner of the attic room. The girl was as pale as her coloring would allow, her gray eyes round as an owl's, her arms crossed tightly in front of her, hands gripping the opposite elbows.

"It'll be all right," Ker said in her calmest tone. "We're leaving right now, and they won't catch us."

"What did you do?" the girl asked. "She wasn't there, and now she is." She blinked, and her dark brows drew down in a vee. "Now she is."

"She is, isn't she?" Ker looked from Baku to Ester and back again. "She really is."

Baku's nod was slight, the movement almost invisible.

"Ker." Tel stood near the top of the stairs. Their packs had been ready since Jerek had told them Baku was on her way. They had only to pick them up and walk out the door.

"Yes." Ker gathered up Baku with an arm around the girl's shoulders and headed her toward Tel. He picked up both his and Ker's packs and started down.

"Back door," she said, as they neared the bottom step.

"Teach your grandmother," Tel said.

Ker smiled for what felt like the first time in hours.

Baku had not been in the tavern long enough to know where the back door was, let alone where it led. She did not even realize the space behind the tavern was a courtyard. It was so small she thought it merely led somewhere else. There were ceramic pots containing plants that released odors reminiscent of cooking and the kitchen. Another smell lingered that she remembered from childhood, but she could not quite put a name to it.

Tel Cursar waved them toward a section of the wall that was bare of any plants. He made a small jump and hooked his fingers over the top of the wall, hauling himself up. Kerida handed him their packs, and then he lifted her up with a grip on her wrist. From the top of the wall, Ker reached for Baku's hand and lifted her up just as easily. From here, Baku could see they were on a blue-tiled roof. Tel Cursar spoke. "I'll lead, then Bakura, then Kerida."

Baku swallowed, but as it happened, she had less trouble keeping up than she had anticipated. Once or twice along the way she held her breath, where the top of the wall that was their path narrowed and great balance was needed, and again when they seemed to be walking directly over someone's roof. After turning several more corners, Baku stopped, holding her breath.

"Princess?" came a soft voice from behind her.

Baku shook her head and continued following Tel Cursar. This was not the time to say she had been stopped by the unfamiliar skyline and the realization that she would never see that of her own city again.

Tel stopped, beckoned her to his side, and pointed to a loose stack of crates and boxes. When he stepped down onto the highest one, Baku saw that they'd been set up to form a set of stairs. The unusual stairway led down into another courtyard, this one even smaller than the one they'd left behind at the inn. Small as it was, the yard held a coop for chickens, and a box-like structure full of what looked like pigeons.

"This is where I left my horse," he said. Kerida began to speak, but before she said a word, Tel raised his forefinger to his lips. "I know," he said. "Three people, one horse. It doesn't take a genius."

Still with his finger to his lips, Tel beckoned them toward a swinging door in the far wall of the courtyard. Apparently, the signal for "be quiet" was the same everywhere. Baku realized she was smiling and quickly settled her face.

The first room was clearly used for storage, though at this time of year most of the hanging sacks and stacked earthenware pots were empty. From here, they entered a room many times larger than the courtyard, though just as narrow, that was part sitting room, part bedroom, and part kitchen. An older woman with hair and skin several shades darker than Baku's own stood by an open fire, stirring a pot of something that smelled delicious before swinging it back over the flames. She didn't look up from her task as the three of them passed behind her, though they certainly made enough noise to attract her attention.

Perhaps she was deaf, or— Baku felt the hair on the back of her neck rising. Could this be part of Kerida's magic? Was this how they were to be smuggled past the guards at the gate? Another woman, younger than the first, though with the same coloring, lowered herself down a ladder Baku hadn't noticed, propped in a darkened corner. The younger woman froze, one hand on a rung, the other propping a basket against her hip. She held her position only for a second, the time it took for the three of them to take two paces, before resuming her climb down from the upper loft. The woman's back was stiff, and she turned her head away from them, even though she would normally have had to look their way as she stepped off the ladder.

They are deliberately not seeing us, Baku thought as she crept along behind Tel. It wasn't magic after all, just people not looking. She didn't know whether to be relieved or disappointed.

There were still people on the street when they reached it. Curfew had not yet begun. They moved at a casual stroll, as if they had somewhere to be, but were not in a hurry to get there. Watching a young woman carrying a small child, Baku stumbled on an uneven cobble and would have gone down if not for Kerida's hand under her elbow.

"Careful," she said, as if Baku needed to be told. Still, she managed to answer the other girl's look of concern with a smile. Kerida held Baku's elbow for a moment longer before nodding and gesturing toward where Tel looked back at them. Baku felt her head clearing, and her breath coming easier. She must be getting her second wind.

The number of people in the streets dwindled as they walked, and by the time they neared the gate, they were the only ones still out. What if the gates were already shut? Baku's heart began to pound, and she had to stop herself from catching hold of Tel's tunic from behind and tugging him back the way they'd come.

Not that Kerida would have let her do that.

Finally, there was nothing but air and pavement left between them and two guards talking to each other under the massive rolling doors. The gate *was* still open, but Baku could feel herself leaning away, though her feet continued to carry her forward. Tel made a signal, holding his left hand away from his body, and Kerida answered with a sound so low Baku was surprised Tel could hear it.

The gates themselves had been rolled free of the chocks that normally held them apart, leaving only a narrow opening. She could see massive bars waiting to be lifted into place. Baku glanced back to see what Kerida would make of this and saw the girl holding her right fist clenched against her chest, murmuring to herself, lips moving silently, her eyes closed.

Her eyes closed. Baku swallowed. She had seen much more intricate feats of magic in her brother's court, but Kerida walking through the square with her eyes closed, despite the uneven pavement, seemed so much more real than those elaborate entertainments.

As they drew closer, Baku's breathing grew faster, enough so that she had to remind herself to take longer, deeper breaths.

Ker had moved—still with her eyes closed—until she was walking with Tel on one side of her, and Baku on the other. She had lifted her fist to her mouth, as if she were speaking into it. She didn't walk faster as they got closer to the gate. In fact, she seemed to slow down. Baku wanted to scream at her to *get moving*! At any moment, the guard facing in their direction would shift his eyes from his partner's face and would be looking straight at them. In fact—

The guard appeared to be looking over his partner's right shoulder, but his eyes were closed, his mouth relaxed. He swayed slightly but was otherwise completely still. She could not see it, but Baku was sure the man's partner was in the same condition. They slept.

Baku was sure she did not take another breath until they were on the other side of the city wall.

"Can you close the door behind us?" Tel said to Kerida, a hint of laughter in his voice.

"Shut up."

By the time they were far enough away from the gate to think about stopping for what was left of the night, Ker's legs were shaking under her, and she left it up to Tel to look for shelter. She even considered using the lifting Gift the jewel gave her to move her own feet, but many Lifters couldn't move themselves, and this wasn't the time to experiment. She kept Flashing just enough to have an early warning if they came across anyone else near the road. Finally, Tel signaled to her.

"Olive trees." He used the soft tones of guards on watch at night. "Might be a tool shed."

It took Ker a minute to realize he meant for her to Flash for it. She was even more tired than she thought. She nodded and crouched down on her heels, placing her hands on the grassy verge of the road. It *was* an orchard, but not an empty one. A drift of pigs had been left loose to forage whatever the winter had left under the trees. Asleep this time of night, but they'd still have to be careful not to step on them.

"Sometime soon would be good."

As if his words conjured it up, Ker Flashed what she was looking for. "There *is* a shed," she said, straightening to her feet and dusting her hands off on her trousers. "It's quite a few spans that way," she added, pointing. "But the same distance from the road as it is from the holding's house. So long as we're careful around the pigs, we should be all right."

"Pigs?" Baku's aura was looking faded again. All the more reason for them to get off the road and rest, even if they couldn't risk a fire.

"It's not much farther now," Ker told the princess. "Walk where I walk. Don't worry about the pigs."

"**A**LL I'm saying is what have we got a pass for if we're not going to use it?" Wynn's feet were wet, which did nothing to sweeten her mood. The farmer's field was certainly flat enough for easy walking; there just wasn't any way to tell the wet patches from the dry. Spring rains were great for crops but not so wonderful for the feet. "Do you remember how long it took us to *get* to Gaena? *And* we had horses."

"Then it's an equally long time getting back, isn't it? And you're wrong on two counts. First, cross-country, as the griffin flies, is often faster than horses by road. We don't stop to feed them, or water them, or rest them. And the best thing to do with this pass"—Pella tapped the satchel hanging against his hip—"is avoid being asked for it." He looked up at the sky, squinted at a far-off cloud a little too dark for comfort, and grunted. "And don't think I don't know what you're thinking."

"Why? What am I thinking?"

"That Svann knows the way by road, so he won't find us if we don't stick to the roads. You're thinking we didn't wait long enough, that if we dawdle a bit now, he'll catch up. But only if he knows where to find us."

Wynn pressed her lips together. She hated to admit that was exactly what she'd been thinking. The hollow feeling in her chest grew. "He's dead, isn't he," she said aloud.

"I think so," Pella said after a silent moment. He spoke like a soldier, like someone who knew that death was always waiting. "We gave him the full three days, and then a bit; you know we did. He'd have come if he could; you know he would. He didn't come, and he didn't send word, and there's only one reason for that, isn't there?"

"Mother, Daughter, and Son welcome him into their company." Wynn hoped her voice was as steady as Pella's. He'd been a soldier much longer than she had, but she'd grown up on the streets. She was just as tough as him. Tougher.

"The Father, too. They believe that way, you know."

Wynn nodded. "What was the second count?"

"Huh?"

"You said I was wrong on two counts, what was the second?"

"I outrank you."

"You're not even an Eagle."

"I still outrank you."

Wynn walked along quietly for several paces. "I thought you were going to say that old Goreot was going to charge us triple if we stayed any longer."

"All right, you were wrong on three counts, then."

Jerek: You're free.
Baku: I am free of Pollik Kvar, yes, for which I am forever grateful. It is only that this freedom makes me feel the net all the more.

* * *

"I didn't think I would have to tell anyone, still less a Talent High Inquisitor, that Feelers are outlawed. To be dampened on discovery if they cooperate, executed if they don't. I may not be Inquisitor rank myself, but it doesn't take one to see where there has been a disregard of the Law."

Luca Pa'narion shut his eyes, and Setasan mentally squared her shoulders and prepared to fight.

"The law you refer to has been suspended at the request of the Luqs of Farama."

"The Luqs of Farama does not make the Law."

"I was about to say: 'and his council.'"

Luca's even tone only made her shake her head and pray to the Mother for patience. "His council—at least half of whom are Feelers themselves, and the other half military—no friends to Talents as I shouldn't have to remind you. And what *of* the Luqs? No one's disputing that he's of the blood, but he's a child, easily persuaded. The Faros listen to you—though the Mother knows why—and you could—"

"Setasan, this is not the time." His tone hadn't changed, but Luca's face had become a hard mask.

She took a breath . . . and closed her mouth on the words she'd been about to say. Six months ago, she would have said it was impossible for one Talent to use military force against another, but now she couldn't be sure. What she'd said was true. The Faros of Bears and Panthers both listened to Luca Pa'narion. If what he said to them about her was unfavorable. . . .

"Very well," she said finally. "We must speak of this again, but for now I will concede that it is not the time." She made the short bow exchanged between Talents and left the room.

When she reached the privacy of a neighboring tunnel, one of her two companions cleared his throat. "I thought we were going to withdraw our services?"

"Luca may be right." It made her lips pucker to say it. "But not in the way he believes. This may very well not be the time. At present, we need the outlaws to push the invaders out. We're of no use in battle, but these Feelers attend with the cohorts, right on the battlefield. Who knows? That might even thin their numbers for us. So, we let them help us win, and we deal with them later. One enemy at a time."

"I didn't come to eavesdrop." Cuarel handed him a cup from which Luca detected the welcome odor of hot kaff. "I heard you speaking to someone, I didn't know it was her." The Farthinker sat down beside him.

"You heard, then?"

"I suppose I didn't have to, really. She doesn't make any secret of what she thinks about us. Guess we got used to you, and the other Guardians, and Kerida Griffin Girl. We forget that most Talents will think like her."

"I don't know about most," Luca said. "But some, definitely. It's just that there are so few of us left. . . ."

"She's angry with you," Cuarel observed. "Seemed like she was about to bite you, couple of times, or at least wag her finger." She grinned.

Luca nodded. "Setasan wanted to be an Inquisitor. Long before my time, of course. But she's not Griffin Class. Her Talent isn't strong enough, and no amount of discipline or practice can make it stronger."

Cuarel looked at him sideways, with slitted eyes. "She gave in easily."

"She didn't give in. She's playing a long game." Luca rubbed his face with his hands. "I have to let her, though. One enemy at a time."

—————

"It's remarkable." Tel looked from one face to another.

Ker and Bakura shared an old wooden bench that had seen

better days, the mask lying between them on the rough wood, unwrapped and brilliantly white against its red covering.

"It is said to be white jade." The Princess Imperial traced her fingertip down the mask from eyebrow to chin.

"May I?" Ker's own fingers hovered over the edge of the mask closest to her.

The Princess Imperial licked her lips, looked up at Kerida and back down again, before giving an abrupt nod.

Ker laid the first two fingers of her left hand on the chin of the mask. "It's not jade; it's some kind of petrified bone. And it's warmer than I expected," she said. "It belongs to your brother, but I guess that's not news to you." She smiled, and the other girl relaxed, leaning back against the wall of the shed. "It's a part of him, isn't it? He shares it with you, the way he shares your blood and your love." Ker caught Bakura's eye. "Both are important, both needed for you to use the mask while he still lives."

"Can you see what he is doing?"

Ker, eyes closed, shook her head. "No, but he's relaxed, happy even. He's . . . he's not thinking about you, not just now anyway."

"Can you tell us anything else about the mask itself?" Tel said.

"They come from the far past of my people." Bakura stroked the mask with her finger again. "It is my brother's face."

"But it wasn't always." Ker could have answered Tel's question herself, but she sensed it might do the princess good to tell the tale herself.

"No. These are artifacts of the Horse People. Ours before we conquered Halia. There are four masks, one for each Horse Herd—that is what we call the Clans among our people," she broke off to say. "When the chief of a Clan died, any who would lead tried the mask. If the mask fit, if it took on the features of the candidate, that one became the new lord. Every five years the chiefs would come together to choose from among themselves the Lord of Horses, to lead them all into battle. Now, because our Lord of Horses sits on the Sky Throne, he holds all four masks, and it is his face we see on all of them."

"And that's how you know that the right person becomes Emperor?" Tel said.

"Yes." Bakura sat back again with a sigh. "And that is all."

"Not quite." Ker almost laughed at the look—half curiosity, half affront—on the younger girl's face. "You said there are four masks, but there are five."

"Impossible." The princess shook her head. "There have only ever been four."

"Except there are five."

"Five . . ."

"Think about it. Four people can be equally divided. How could they choose one of themselves to be lord over all? A fifth chief breaks the tie."

Bakura frowned, one brow up, one down. Ker had a flashing image of what she would look like as an old woman. If they all lived that long. Finally, the girl nodded. "Yes, I think it could be so. But then, where is the fifth mask?"

Ker shook her head. "All I can tell you is that this mask knows." Ker saw the look on the other's girl's face. "I'm sorry, I'm not saying it's aware. It's just, when you're Flashing, that's sort of what it feels like." Bakura nodded, but not as if she was really reassured.

"What about a demonstration?" Trust Tel to know the way to put the girl at ease and show her it was still the mask she'd had all along.

Bakura had her hand halfway to the handle of the mask before she hesitated. "I must warn you, it does not speak with my voice."

"Is it loud?"

The girl blinked. "No, not unless I speak loudly."

"Then go ahead."

The girl picked the mask up and with no further hesitation

fitted it to her face. Tel sat astride the bench behind Ker, and she leaned back against him, welcoming his solid warmth.

"Can you hear me? Does the magic work for you?"

Ker gasped, and Tel closed his arms around her. Even with the warning, the man's voice was astonishing.

"Just for a minute there, I thought I saw two of you, one sort of overlapping the other." Ker had only seen this phenomenon once before, with Larin Time-seer. Not every time the girl spoke, but often enough that Ker recognized it. "Can you see the future?" she asked now.

The mask looked down and up again. "Not now. Not since the netting. And not always clearly or well."

"Like Larin." Tel's voice rumbled against her back. "Not enough training. Wait— Time-seeing is a Feeler's gift, so it might eventually come back, net or no net."

Ker had a disturbing thought. "Do the Shekayrin see the future?"

"There has never been any mention of such a thing." Bakura lowered the mask, hands trembling. "Forgive me. I am suddenly very weak."

"Why is she still so tired?" Tel stood, as well as he could in the small shed. "I thought you removed the mist."

Baku packed the mask away, making a face like she was trying not to cry. She let the satchel rest in her lap and hugged it like a stuffed toy. Ker was certain the girl was unaware of her actions.

She tapped her fingers on one knee. "It's using the mask. Look," she added when Tel raised his eyebrows, "using a Gift is an exertion, just like fighting or marching. You can only do so much before you need sleep and food—"

"I have chicken rolls in my satchel," the girl said.

"Well, haul them out, Princess. They won't get any fresher hiding in there." Tel squatted down next to the princess and gestured to her to open her pack.

"No food, no sleep, and she's using her Gifts." Ker continued

as if there'd been no interruption. "No wonder she's exhausted."
Ker rubbed at her own face. Exhaustion was something she
knew about.

"Perhaps it is time for you to remove my net?" The girl looked
up without raising her head, half fearing the answer. A chicken
roll hung slack in her hand.

"Why not?" Tel's tone was full of reassurance. "She removed
mine." He rescued the roll and handed it to Ker.

Ker wasn't so sure. "You weren't netted, not like this. If you
had been, you'd have ended up like Ester." Who, with luck,
would be awake by now and angry with them for leaving her
behind. "Your net overlaid your aura and changed you, but it
wasn't . . . it didn't contain you in this way." Ker took a bite of
her roll and was pleased to see Bakura doing the same.

"Jerek believes you can remove it." A movement of muscle
in the side of Baku's jaw showed that she'd clenched her teeth.
She was prepared to be stubborn about this.

"I'd like to wait until we're back in the Mines and Tunnels."
Where she'd have the help of a Mind-healer. Ker thought about
contacting Weimerk, but she had an idea what he would say if
she didn't try everything she knew first.

"Please." Baku's voice was tight as a bowstring. "It cannot
be much longer. I . . ." She pressed her lips together and
blinked rapidly. "I would be more useful free. My visions
would return, I'm sure."

Tel grunted and swallowed the food in his mouth. "Would
Svann be any help?"

Ker knew what it must have cost Tel to make that
suggestion—he had to be desperate to be willing to ask Svann
for help.

"I can't reach him," she admitted. "I've tried over and over,
but I don't get anything."

"Do you think something's gone wrong? Or is he not answering you deliberately?" How quickly Tel returned to his
usual skeptical self.

"I don't know." Ker didn't want to voice her fears aloud. If "something" had happened to Svann, it had happened to Wynn Martan as well. "He's not very good at using the jewel to Far-think; he hasn't had a lot of practice."

"Then you'll just have to fix her yourself."

Ker pressed her lips tight. Just like that. As if her bones didn't feel like jelly, as if her eyelids weren't gritty with all the sleep she'd missed and all the magic she'd already done today. She took a deep breath in through her nose and let it out slowly. Baku would do this herself if she could. Mother knew Tel would do it for her if *he* could. She shoved what was left of her chicken roll into her mouth and wiped her palms off on her trousers.

"Let's have another look. Maybe I'll see something I didn't see before." *Paraste*. She was going to need all the help that her Talent and concentration could give her.

This time she focused on Baku's aura as if the net wasn't there. In addition to the three basic colors, the princess had the purple and the orange that were the colors of any Gifted person—no surprises. There was the black of a Far-thinker, and perhaps a streak of gold—that was unusual. Ker had it, but it had been a gift from Weimerk. There were still more colors, red among them, some wide ribbons but too faded to be sure of, some tiny threads like the ones she'd seen in Jerek. But there was one color Ker could see very plainly, as it was a color she had herself. Turquoise.

As well as everything else she might be, or might become, the Princess Imperial was Talented. Ker's own aura swirled around her in excitement. Baku had more colors than she did. More colors than Jerek. She was Feeler and Talent both, and if she could use a jewel, and take the griffin colors as well. . . .

"Faster would be good."

Ker only just stopped herself from giving Tel's aura the kind of shove that would have sent his body flying as well. But he wasn't wrong.

"She has a lot of colors, Tel. More than I've seen before in a human."

She turned her attention to the net holding Baku's aura, tracing each line, touching each joining with one of her own colors, until the net looked like a spider's web dusted with dew. This confirmed that Baku's net was far more intricate than the similar one that had touched Tel's aura. Since Tel wasn't a mage, or a Feeler, or a Talent, all that net had done to him was modify his thinking a little.

Though no one had thought it was "a little" at the time.

Now that she was looking more carefully, she could see that some of Baku's colors, certainly the black and the turquoise, were *outside* the net, which explained how she could Far-think, and how, like a Talent, she sometimes just knew things. As Ker refocused on the net itself, she wondered whether she could affect it the same way she'd done with Svann's. It had hurt him, but this one wasn't a part of Baku. Ker should be able to influence it without hurting the girl—or at least not much.

She reached into her pocket and pulled out her own jewel. Baku's eyes widened and her aura, even confined as it was, shivered.

"This will help," she told the girl. "With the jewel, I'll be able to use my own web, not just the colors of my aura."

"I am not afraid of you," Baku said. "But—" She indicated the jewel with a tilt of her chin. "Nothing good has ever come to me from one of those."

Ker thought for a moment. Around her neck, beneath layers of tunic, undertunic and shirt, was the small bag holding the blank jewel Larin had given to Tel. *No.* Ker let her hand drop. Too complicated. That had to be a last resort, she thought. Once everything else had failed.

Ker called up the patterns of her own jewel. The first one to spring up wasn't even the same basic shape as Baku's net. Breathing deeply, Ker let her patterns loose, watching them change until she finally had one that looked like a star-pointed spider's web. She floated her web over the other one and tugged it into a shape that matched Baku's more exactly. *Like making a bed*, she thought. Starting in the center, she began adjusting individual lines, twitching, moving, nudging, until she had an exact match. Or thought she had. When she mentally stepped back, and Flashed her creation, she saw that two tiny lines remained uncopied. Heart pounding, she filled them in.

"What is it? You are frightened."

"It's all right," Ker said, keeping her voice steady, though she *was* frightened. What might have happened if she hadn't noticed the flaws?

Ker closed her fists, and her net grew brighter until it obscured the other completely. She gripped the edge of her net and peeled it back and, as she'd hoped, the old net came away with the new, like a scab peeling off as a bandage unwrapped.

Just as she was starting to breathe more easily, the net slipped from Ker's control and snapped back to its original position around Baku's aura.

"Daughter curse you blind." Ker stuck her fingers in her mouth. They felt as if they'd been closed in a door. "All right, don't panic. I have another idea." Meticulously, Ker built her web back until it once more exactly duplicated the web holding Baku. This time she would try to change the pattern; *that* might make it easier to remove.

Again, the net snapped back into place, and this time the stinging in Ker's fingers didn't fade. She covered her eyes with the heels of her hands. "Mother, Daughter, and Son, help me!" She wasn't praying so much as cursing.

"I can't do it," she said finally. "It keeps slipping away. It's like trying to pull an eel out of the water with your bare hands." Ker kept her eyes closed. She didn't want to see the look of disappointment on Baku's face. Gradually, it seemed a vast space surrounded her, became part of her. As if Weimerk spoke to her, mind-to-mind. Ker lowered her hands.

"I'm an idiot," she said.

"No argument here," Tel growled.

"I'm doing the same thing I did with Ester, I'm trying to take something out. I should try putting something in."

"You said my aura is intact." Baku's eyes narrowed.

"What if I gave you more? What if your aura was too big for the net to contain?"

"I wish I could see what you're talking about," Tel said.

Ker sat back on her heels. "*You* can't, but I'll bet you that, with the right Gifts, Baku can." The princess' aura had at least black and turquoise outside the net. If she could see the auras, the girl might be able to free herself. Ker teased loose a thread of coppery metallic color, the first one Weimerk had ever given her, and wove it into a braid with the black and the turquoise, adding the moss green that would keep Baku from being overwhelmed by auras.

Baku inhaled sharply, gripping Ker's hands, but Ker could see that the new colors were blossoming, swirling inward and outward.

"Ker, there are people coming through the grove. *Kerida.*"

Ker split her attention and Flashed outward. "Eleven men," she told Tel. "Crap! And three of them Shekayrin."

She had the same Gifts the Shekayrin had—or she would have if she hadn't spent the last two days, and even the last few hours, using all the magic she had. Baku wasn't the only one who was worn out. And any one of the mages had more training in using their jewels than she had.

"Kerida." That was Baku's hand on her wrist.

She could waste this time, and what was left of her energy, keeping the enemy at bay for a few minutes, until her strength failed. Or she could help Bakura. The choice was obvious. Ker's job as the Second Sign, as Griffin Girl, was to do everything she could to complete the Prophecy. "See the child eyes of color and light. Holds the blood and the wings and the bone, child of the griffin." And that meant Baku. Ker was sure of it now. The girl had all the Gifts: Talent, Feeler and Shekayrin;

the blood, the wings, the bone. Or she would have. All Baku needed was a jewel of her own.

And Ker had one for her.

The blank jewel appeared in her hand, as if following her thoughts. If she was quick, she'd have time to tell Baku what to do.

"Ker, is this it? Is this what Larin meant?"

Without looking at him, Ker said. "I'm sorry, Tel. I love you."

"Never doubted it."

"Swallow this," she said to Baku. "Flash my aura," she added softly. "You know you can trust me. Swallow." The girl took the jewel into her mouth with a grimace, as if she had bitten into a sour apple. She swallowed. Ker waited. Nothing. The soldiers were surrounding the shed.

Baku licked her lips and opened her eyes. She reached out with her right hand and touched Ker's face with the tips of her fingers.

"You're so beautiful," she said. "All the colors."

Ker grinned. "You should see yourself." Maybe this was going to work. "You're part of it now, the blood and bone of the world. Reach for it." Baku's brows drew down into a vee, and she frowned. Suddenly her face relaxed.

"Now, do you see the patterns?" Baku nodded. "Are they changing, one after another?" The girl nodded again. "Keep them all, accept them all. Use them to match and remove your netting. Be careful to—crap!" The others were getting closer.

<<Weimerk! Weimerk, if you can hear me, help Bakura. She has a jewel—>>

The shed exploded away from them.

———

Weimerk awoke from meditation feeling uneasy. The skin between his wings itched, and no amount of movement or attention by beak or paws helped. Meditation was meant to create calm and harmony, not feed a sense of worry and anxiety.

<<Kerida.>> His girl was the most likely source of worry and anxiety. No response. Weimerk sat up, shaking his wings to straighten his feathers. <<Kerida?>> Still nothing. If she were asleep, or too busy to reply, he should still have had a sense of her. But he had nothing. Weimerk pulled himself erect, back straight, wings folded down, front paws neatly placed in front of him.

<<Jerek.>>

<<Baku?>> The boy was clearly deep in sleep.

<<I am Weimerk. You must learn to tell the difference between Far-thinking with humans and with griffins.>>

<<I would have known if you'd said more than my name.>>

Weimerk ignored this. He was not this boy's teacher. <<I cannot find Kerida.>>

This frightened the boy. He had squeezed his eyes shut, and his heart hammered in his chest. <<What's happened? Is she . . . ?>>

<<Dead? No. Were she dead, I would feel the absence. She is hidden from me.>>

<<I'll see if I can contact Baku.>>

<<My Kerida is with the Princess Imperial?>> Weimerk leaped to his feet <<Then I will find her.>> He stopped the connection. For a moment he considered telling someone, perhaps the elder Zeinin, but he shook his head. The old one had told him he must choose. The day for that choice had come. He launched himself into the air, headed out, and down, west to Farama.

Pollik Kvar felt for his jewel and lifted it to his eye.

"Good news, my lord." It was the Shekayrin in charge of tracking down the princess. "We have discovered them and taken them prisoner. One is a witch. She is netted and harmless. We have not yet executed her, but we are prepared to do so."

"Keep her alive." As with the boy in Gaena, there might be information to be had, now that she was netted and safe. "Does the princess have her mask with her?"

"Yes, my lord."

Kvar bent over the map again, putting his left index finger on the spot where the girl was, and his right index finger on the Valley of Simcot, where Seklur Tvak told him there was an entrance to the Serpents Teeth. He drew a mental line from the capital through the other two points. As he thought, no point in bringing the silly girl back to the capital.

"Keep her secure—keep all your prisoners secure until I come."

The great thing about clambering about on the sides of hills instead of taking the road like sensible people was that when soldiers came along that road, you had something handy by to hide behind.

"Though I'm getting a bit tired of hiding, truth to tell." Wynn Martan spoke so softly she was surprised when Pella grunted his agreement. They waited until the column of soldiers—nine Barracks, as far as Wynn could tell, nearly a full company—had passed them by, and the road had been clear for another half hour, before resuming their climb up the side of the hill. They hadn't gone more than a few paces when a voice murmured from behind a scraggly sumac bush.

"Is that you, Wynn Martan, or is it a tree on fire?"

"Well, it must be you, Midon Far-seer. Nobody else could think that was funny."

In a moment they were surrounded. Midon Far-seer, a Lifter Wynn didn't know, the Far-thinker from the Springs and Pools whose name she could never remember, four men who were clearly soldiers—though they were *all* armed—and one *un*armed person who must be a Talent. Kerida Nast was the only Talent Wynn knew who'd had any military training. The air of authority on the man coming up to her was unmistakable. She touched the part of her tunic where her military crest should be.

"Wynn Martan, Archer, Blue Company, Onyx Cohort of Eagles."

The man acknowledged her salute, grinning. "Kole Urlen, Barrack Leader, Blue Company, Diamond Cohort of Panthers."

"Panthers? That's good to hear." Wynn looked around, but Pella was hanging back, evidently having found an acquaintance among even this small a group. "Did you see us and come looking?" Wynn asked Midon.

"We were following those others." He pointed down the road with his chin. "Then I saw you hiding from them, so I told the Barrack Leader you must be all right."

"If you don't mind, Midon, I'll have to check them just the same." The man Wynn had taken for a Talent wove through the others and stopped in front of her. "Doyouconsenttoexamination," he rattled off.

"Yes." A cold touch to her throat and forehead, a brief feeling of heat, and the man had moved on to Pella.

"We didn't realize we were so close to the Mines." Wynn turned back to Kole Urlen.

"You're not. We've been following that company for the better part of three days. They were on their way to the Pass, or so we thought, when they turned around and set off this way."

"Why? What's over here?" Wynn looked in the direction the company of soldiers had gone.

"Nothing. Well, the Valley of Simcot's a day's march that way, if that narrow, rocky excuse for a ravine can even be called a valley. But nothing else."

"Valley of Simcot entrance is the closest one to Gaena." She nodded, turning to get Pella's attention.

"What do you know about this, Wynn Martan?" The Barrack Leader's voice had hardened.

Wynn waited to speak until Pella was at her side. "We have

reason to believe that someone has revealed the existence of that particular entrance."

Silence all around.

"Was it the mage?" Midon said.

"No. No, we don't think so." Wynn glanced at the Talent, who'd turned a little paler than the chilly air could account for.

Kole Urlen looked at Midon, who looked steadily back. They nodded simultaneously. Urlen pointed at one of the men standing by. "You, Lirik, go with the Far-thinker; if they've really gone to Simcot, report to base right away. We'll take these two back. When you're done, catch us up."

The Far-thinker hefted his pack. "I've let base know they're coming."

"Wouldn't have expected anything else."

Wilk Silvertrees blew on his hands and clapped them together. He reminded himself, not for the first time, that he should remember his gloves. Seedmonth it might be down among the grape vines and the almond groves, but here in the Serpents Teeth you wouldn't know it.

Sah Q'ua, Commander of Yellow Company, Jade Cohort of Bears, waited with him. Though the Ma'lakan must have felt the cold more than Silvertrees, he might have been standing in one of his deserts for all he showed of it.

"Best case," Sah Q'ua said, "is that we find out where all these people are going, now that they're not trying to cross through the pass. Worst case, they've found out that they can get their jewels in the Serpents Teeth, and they're planning an assault."

"You have always been a cheerful fellow, Sah."

"That's why you keep me around, Cohort Leader." The commander turned toward the south end of the clearing. "Here we are."

The first to show himself was Midon Far-seer. He sat on the

council, but he took his turn with the patrols just like everyone else. Midon headed straight to where Wilk and his Company Commander were standing, even though Wilk could have sworn no one could see them, barricaded as they were by rock and pine trees. Then again, the man *was* a Far-seer.

Midon nodded at them but waited for Kole Urlen to do the talking. When he arrived minutes later, with the rest of the Barrack behind him, Wilk counted and felt the familiar relief at seeing that all ten were there. Then he counted again, and saw there were two extra, one, as short as a soldier was allowed to be, with flaming red hair.

Wynn Martan. And Pella Dursto with her. What happened to Svann, and the Talented boy?

"Cohort Leader." Urlen touched his fist to Wilk, and then to his Company Commander.

"No doubt about it," he said. "We saw the two groups meet and were following them when we ran into Wynn Martan and Pella Dursto. They thought the enemy were headed for the Valley of Simcot. We sent these two"—he gestured at two of his barrack—"to follow, and sure enough, that's where they're going. Sir, if they're careful enough, and thorough enough, they'll find the entrance for certain."

"And we've no reason to believe they're not careful and thorough," Midon said.

"Were there any Shekayrin?" Wilk said.

"Not within my sight, Cohort Leader." Midon shrugged.

"There's bound to be, though, sir." Wynn Martan stepped forward, the man Dursto at her elbow like a bodyguard. "Otherwise, how would they know where to start looking?"

"You know something you're not telling, soldier?"

The young woman straightened to attention at being thus addressed. She stopped looking like a field worker and started looking like an archer belonging to the Eagle Wing.

"We've been betrayed, Cohort Leader—and before you ask, no, it wasn't Svann. In fact, we have every reason to suppose that he died covering our escape." The young woman's voice shook a little over the last few words. "I'm afraid it was someone else." Her eye flicked toward the Talent who stood to her left. Wilk nodded. Message received.

"Say no more. Save your breath to give your story to the Faros and the full council."

"It is very simple." It took all of Baku's will to keep her voice calm and measured.

"You don't think for a moment that I believe your ludicrous story of them kidnapping you?" Pollik Kvar was so angry he didn't seem to notice that she was sitting down.

"It does not matter what you believe." The more formally she spoke, the easier it was to remain calm. Why had no one ever told her this before? "It matters only what the people will believe. And they will believe what we tell them."

"Is it 'we' now, then?"

Baku slid her gaze over to the Poppy Shekayrin's face. Every part of her head was covered except her eyes. Without a veil to see through, they had to be left exposed. She was glad the mage could see her watching him.

"I have conditions."

"Which I'm sure I'll find amusing." There was no humor in his smile.

"You saw how your soldiers reacted to the mask." Luckily, no one could see how *she* reacted. She had not expected the mask to have an aura of its own. She knew now why Kerida had said there were five masks remaining out of an original eleven. That they were not made of jade, as everyone believed, but out of bone that time had turned into stone. She could Flash nothing more, or rather, she could, but she did not understand it.

"I'd like to know how you took it from my rooms. I should have interrogated your women before I had them executed."

A cold lump in her stomach suddenly blazed hot. He was lying; his aura practically *screamed* it. Her women were safe. If she knew how, she might even be able to Far-see where they were. At the moment, however, dealing with the Poppy Shekayrin demanded all her attention.

She made a brushing aside motion with her hand and lifted her chin. *Let him wonder why his lie did not frighten me.* "Nevertheless, the mask is in my possession, and it is known that I have it. And I can use it, which is evidently more than you can do." Anger flashed across his face. At least the scarves could hide her reactions. "Keep my companions alive, and I will use the mask as you direct—but only if they are kept alive."

"The woman is a witch."

"Even so."

"I can force the soldiers to obey me."

Baku shrugged. "Enough of them? All at once? Even if your magic *is* stronger than the magic of the Emperor's Voice, how many people can you influence before you cannot regenerate the soul stone? Before it will consume you to feed itself?" Baku's throat felt sore, as if somewhat swollen. She wished Kerida had been able to tell her how difficult it would be to get the jewel back after swallowing it. "These things have been known to happen."

"And how do you know of these 'things'?" The tightness in his voice made her smile.

"I am the Princess Imperial. I know many things."

"There is a supply of the stones in these mountains they call the Serpents Teeth," he pointed out.

"Something the average soldier does not care about," she pointed out in turn. "With my cooperation, you will reach the mountains more quickly, more easily, with the full support of my brother the Emperor's Horsemen."

His eyes narrowed as he weighed her words. That he was not happy, she could tell. She could also tell the moment when he decided to agree with her. In his way.

"Very well. Your companions will keep their lives. Of course, the witch remains netted."

Baku waved this away as if it was of no consequence. Perhaps it would be like her own experience, that some of Kerida's Gifts, unknown to the Mages, would be left free. "Return them to me," she said. "Since you have brought no servants, they will have to do."

"You are lucky they are not already dead." The Poppy Shekayrin left without waiting for her to respond.

Once alone, she sank onto the nearest seat, a stuffed leather hassock. She pulled the satchel containing the mask into her arms and held it tight to her, as though it were her doll, and she a child. She had put her soul stone into the satchel with the mask, carefully wrapped in a corner of the red silk. Now she took it out, folding it into one of her scarves which she wrapped back around her throat.

She concentrated, and all the colors of the rainbow shimmered and waved around her.

Bakura folded her hands, weaving the fingers together, to keep from forming fists. She was tiring. Now she knew why Kerida always seemed ready to sleep. As it was, it took all her concentration to Far-think with Jerek.

Baku: We went as far as we could on foot, but with Kerida so exhausted— Jerek, she was amazing. She killed a Shekayrin, and restored her sister, and—

Jerek: Where is she now? Is Kerida all right?

Baku: I'm afraid she has been netted, and they have taken her jewel from her. They are both in another section of the pavilion I am in. They are still alive, so there is still hope.

A sound nearby caused her to crack her eyelids open. It was astonishing how much harder it was to see with her head and face covered again. Of course, the tears that had sprung to her eyes did not help.

Jerek: How did they know where you were?

Baku: That I cannot know. Was there anyone else in the plan?

Jerek: Someone in contact with Shekayrin? Not that I know. But what about you? Baku could almost see Jerek shift in his chair as he asked the question. Was he alone? Did he have to hide what he was doing, as she did? Then the import of his question struck her.

Baku: I? You think that I might have betrayed the plan of my own escape?

Jerek: No, no. that's not what I meant at all. He sounded so flustered Baku hoped he was alone, or he would have given himself away. **I was asking how you were. Have they realized your net is gone?**

Baku: Why would anyone check? I had a moment when I thought he would simply take the mask from me again. But I saw that he could not.

Jerek: What? How?

Baku: I believe I Flashed it, if that is the correct term.

Jerek: What else can you do?

Baku: I am not sure—Jerek, I am afraid to attempt too much without Ker to guide me . . . having the jewel is thrilling, but now that I am freed of the net, the power I feel is frightening as well. And yet, I must help her, as she helped me. Again, there was a lengthy silence. This time, however, Baku could tell that Jerek was still Far-thinking with her.

Jerek: Don't do anything you don't need to do. We can't risk you. The mask won't work with the Shekayrin, will it?

Baku: That may be of no consequence. So long as he holds hostages, I must do as he asks. Until I am allowed to address the soldiers directly, I cannot know for certain if they will obey me as they would the Emperor. But, by the reaction of the Shekayrin, I believe it may be so— Hold! Someone comes.

She could Flash that a man stood outside the flap of canvas

that served her room as a door. Kerida would have been able to tell the man's name and history, but all Baku could do was recognize his aura as an UnGifted.

"If you please, Honored One, you are wanted. I am to escort you." She knew the voice. Inurek Star, the chief of her guard. At least he had not been made to pay for her escape. She would not ask after the guard at her door; she imagined she knew his fate.

Baku wished she could be sure that by escort Inurek Star did not mean guard. But that was only to be expected. Like the rest of the men, her guard chief had been given the kidnapping tale, and he would not want her to be taken again, lest all her guards lose their heads.

"I will come." She slung the satchel so that the mask hung once more at her side. "I must see why my friends have yet to be returned to me."

The first thing Ker noticed when she woke up was the headache. The second thing was that she was alone. She triggered her Talent automatically, looking for Tel's aura. Baku's would be larger, brighter, but Tel's she could Flash with very little effort. When she Flashed nothing more than the room she was in, she struggled to sit up, holding her head in both hands. Not a room. What her eyes saw as walls were nothing more than thick canvas painted over with tight, intricate mazelike patterns that pulled the eye if you looked at them too long. And she was lying on layers of rugs, with nothing but dirt under them.

A tent. She trailed her fingers against the nearest canvas wall. The tent was older than she was—or at least parts of it were. It had come from Halia in the Princess Imperial's baggage. A pavilion, really, more than an ordinary tent.

There. Tel, though she couldn't see his aura clearly. Muscles she hadn't known were tense suddenly relaxed. And Baku.

Both close. Ker sighed. Daughter, that headache was a killer. Ker gave up Flashing outside of her space, turning her awareness on herself.

And that was when she saw the unfamiliar net around her aura. *Don't panic.* She patted the spot where her jewel should have been and felt nothing. She examined every pocket twice, as if she'd get a different answer the second time. Panic caught her by the throat. "Breathe, breathe," she told herself. *Paraste*, she said, even though she was already Flashing. Her trigger word was so closely linked to a state of calm and quiet, that Ker began to feel better. "Deep breaths," she said, loosening her arms from around her knees.

"You can find it," she said, barely speaking out loud. "They can't hide it from you. They think they can, but they can't." She should be able Flash it the same way she could Flash Tel. It was as much a part of her now as he was. "It's only a net. I haven't been dampened." Matriarch, back in Questin Hall, had threatened Ker with that, when she was trying to sneak away, determined to return to her military life. Back before the Halians came and destroyed the Hall, and Matriarch and everyone else in it.

"Get hold of yourself." She imagined Matriarch's stern, contemptuous expression. Nothing the old bat would like better than to see her fall apart. "What are you, three? Your brain's still working, isn't it?" And so was her Talent—though now she knew why it felt limited. She was back to having to touch things to learn about them. But she could still see the auras. . . .

"All right." She began to shift through her colors, looking for the ones that would be the most help in dealing with her net. It didn't take very long for her to discover that she could only move one color at a time. It was like the children's game where you tried to race in mill sacks. You could either hop or take very short steps, but you couldn't run.

She released her breath in a silent whistle and shook herself. She had to make sure of one more thing. She concentrated on a nearby cushion and gave it a push. Nothing. She squared her shoulders and tried again. Still nothing. So now she was like Bakura. Her Talent and the Gifts Weimerk had given her were weak but still there. The Gifts that came from the jewel were gone. Maybe it wouldn't work for her, even if she got it back.

Well, she'd managed without a jewel before. She'd awakened a griffin and found a Luqs. She could do as much and more again. She'd get Tel, and Baku, and they'd all get out of here. If Baku hadn't been able to free herself from her own net, well, they'd take care of that as well.

"I'm Griffin Girl, for the Daughter's sake."

<<Weimerk?>>

Nothing. Ker's heart sped up, and her breath came short. "Don't panic," she said again. "Deep breaths." By the time she had her breathing back under control, Ker was thinking more clearly. The netting weakened her magic; she knew that already. Or maybe the griffin was distracted by something that had nothing to do with his Girl.

"Fine. No problem. I can do this." Ker sat up straight and rubbed at her forehead. When she saw how filthy her hands were, she wondered what her face looked like. She scrubbed her hands on her trousers. Not that *they* were all that clean. She settled herself with her legs crossed, her hands loosely open and resting on her knees.

She would get the net off herself, jewel or no jewel. She'd undone Shekayrin's work before she had a jewel. She'd freed Tel of the net that had made him her enemy, and she could free herself now. A little wedge of doubt cracked her confidence. She'd had help before. Weimerk and the other Feelers—Ganni, Hitterol, Cuarel, and Midon. Now she was alone. She squared her shoulders. She was stronger now. She'd learned so much, she'd *done* so much since saving Tel.

There'd never been anyone like her before, had there? She *was* Kerida Griffin Girl. She was part of the Prophecy, for the

Mother's sake, the Second Sign. She was the runner in the darkness, who spoke to griffins. Drumming her fingers on her knees, she tried to ignore the little voice telling her that her part might be over. That *she* didn't have to survive for the Prophecy to happen.

But Baku did. Baku was the child prophesied by the griffins. The one with all the Gifts. The one who would bring freedom and light, and the day of joining. And it was still Ker's job to help make that happen.

She needed to assess her situation. Find a new strategy.

The red in her aura that made it possible for her to use a jewel in the first place obviously wasn't strong enough without the jewel itself to free her of the net binding her. But she had other colors, the shimmering copper ribbon Weimerk had given her at their first meeting, and the moss green, the dusty rose color, the metallic flame.

In the capital, she'd used these colors to grab hold of the Shekayrin's inner web and tear it apart, destroying him in the process. But surely she'd damage herself if she tried that. She hadn't been able to get Baku's net off, even *with* her jewel. The net couldn't be lifted off from the outside. That's why she'd given Baku the jewel. Because Baku was on the inside.

"And so am I."

That was an idea . . . but would it work, without her own jewel?

"Only one way to find out." If she was right, it meant taking her free colors and inserting them into the net. The thought alone was enough to make her break out in a sweat. But she had to do *something. One step at a time,* she told herself. *Relax.* This was like Flashing. The information was always there, ready and even willing to be found. She just had to let it come to her. She rubbed her palms together, trying to warm her hands.

Ker triggered her Talent again and Flashed her aura, this time concentrating on the colors that were free. Her turquoise, a little faded. The griffin colors, subdued but still the brightest. She drew in the ribbons of color and set them to dancing, swirling and turning in on one another until they made a compact interwoven sphere. Ker smiled, reminded of the intricate glass balls people hung in their windows during the Festival of the Son. Her smile widened. This might be the answer.

She imagined herself a glass blower, blowing with great care into the colorful sphere, expanding it little by little. Unlike glass, her aura didn't become thinner or more fragile, it simply grew.

"It might work. Maybe." Ker would have been pleased, if she wasn't so afraid. She breathed deeply, letting the air out slowly. Now she reversed what she'd done, until her free colors became a tiny ball she could imagine sitting in the palm of her hand. Gritting her teeth, she moved the tiny ball of color closer to the net, floating it from spot to spot, looking for an opening large enough to slip the colors inside. Finally, she realized she was stalling, so she pushed her free colors through the very next wide space she found.

The free colors remained bright and healthy. That had to be a good sign. Once again, she began to blow. The ball of light shivered but didn't grow. Ker licked her lips and began again, calling especially to her griffin colors to extend themselves.

"Come on, come on. Grow, Mother take you. *Grow.*" Afterward, Ker thought that the Mother must have heard her, because finally the sphere of color grew larger, and still larger, until it filled the space within the net. This next part was the riskiest of all. What would happen when her colors touched the net?

Ker gathered her courage and continued mentally blowing into her aura. Slowly, her colors began to bulge the net outward. Ker shifted, her back itchy. She refocused. At first, the net just expanded along with her aura, but soon the red lines grew thinner and thinner, until the net was stretched so thin the red lines were no longer visible against the interwoven colors of her aura.

But it was still whole, still confining her. Struggling now, Ker continued to blow, until she felt she must be at her last breath. She imagined Tel grinning at her, shrugging his shoulder, the one that had been injured when she first met him. He waved her toward him, and she took a step forward.

Suddenly, she was free.

<<My Kerida! My own Girl. You are back. I shall come to you.>>

<<Weimerk, can I speak to Jerek?>>

"You are singularly calm for a man in your position."

For some reason Tel had expected this Shekayrin to be like Svann, but this Poppy was nothing like the Sunflower. Svann, for all his power, had a sense of humor, and what Tel now saw was a gentleness—something he never expected he'd think about the mage who had jeweled him into hating Kerida.

"Where was the Princess Imperial planning to go?" the mage asked.

"I don't think she was planning anything," Tel said as reasonably as he could. "It was all spontaneous if you ask me."

"I am asking you, and believe me, you will tell me." Pollik Kvar took his jewel out from his tunic pocket and held it flat on his palm, studying it almost as though he'd never seen one before. Tel felt the sweat break out on his forehead.

"Where did the girl get this? I have asked her, but I get no coherent answers."

Tel realized with a shock that the jewel in the mage's hand was not his own, but Kerida's. *Why can't she answer?* "The girl?"

"She is a witch. From whom did she obtain this jewel?"

Tel blinked. "I didn't know she had it." The Shekayrin wasn't a Talent, so he couldn't know whether Tel was lying, at least, not easily.

"Very well, a new question. You have been protected against me. Tell me by whom."

Tel was so tempted to reveal Svann's name he had to bite the inside of his cheek to keep from speaking. He told himself it wasn't Svann he was protecting, but Wynn, and Pella, and Barid.

"It is interesting that you will not speak, since logic alone should inform you that I already have the answer. It could only be the Sunflower Peklin Svann."

"So, since you already have all the answers, can I go?"

"There are other ways to persuade you to cooperate. The soul stone is not my only recourse."

"Fine, then. You want to know why I'm so calm? I'll tell you but listen carefully because I'm only going to say this once." Tel cleared his throat and cast back into his memory. *Come on, you've been hearing people recite this for months.*

"Let all the people of the land awake and listen, For the
　　day of joining comes. It comes near.
Watch horses of the sea come clothed in thunder.
　　Longships bring nets of blood and fire.
Blood of the earth. Which is the First Sign.
Hear the runner in the darkness, eyes of color and light.
　　Speaks to the wings of the sky. Speaks to griffins.
　　Which is the Second Sign.
See the bones of the earth touch blood and fire. Net the
　　souls of the living. Bones of the griffin. Which is the
　　Third Sign.
See the child eyes of color and light. Holds the blood and
　　the wings and the bone. Child of the griffin. Which is
　　the Fourth Sign.
The child rides the horses of the sea. Bears the blood
　　and wields the bones of the earth. Brings freedom
　　and light.
Freedom and light are near; the day of joining comes."

Tel folded his hands and smiled. "You see? It's not about me."

"What is this nonsense?"

"It's the Prophecy, you jackass. It means it doesn't matter what you do to me, or to Kerida, or to your princess for that matter. The Luqs Jerek Brightwing is the child of the Prophecy, and no matter what happens to us, the Prophecy will be fulfilled."

JURIA Sweetwater had not spoken with this Far-seer before, and she made an effort to look welcoming. The man's eyes wouldn't stop moving, as if he were looking for a way out of the room yet feared there was none.

"Can you tell us how many you saw?"

The man swallowed and straightened as far as he could. He had been injured, and without Kerida Griffin Girl here, healing had gone back to what it had been before someone who could look inside people came along.

"I don't have the numbers," he said finally, shooting a glance at her before looking away once more. He was a Springer, and it was possible that until now he had never seen any person other than the tribe he had grown up with.

"You did not see the enemy yourself?" Juria risked a glance at Tonia Nast. The Faro of Panthers had seated herself as far from where Juria sat with the Feeler as she could get. No point in intimidating the man to where he couldn't speak at all.

"No, I mean yes. I did see them." The Far-seer wrung his hands together. "I don't know the number. It's not ten." He held up his hands, fingers spread. "Not twenty." He glanced down at his feet. "Not a dozen. Dozens and dozens." He rotated his hands to indicate that there were many more dozens than he could count.

"I see." Juria felt like an idiot. The man couldn't count. "Thank you very much. You may go now."

The look of relieved gratitude on the man's face made Juria feel like a bully.

"What do you think it means," Tonia said, joining Juria at the main table.

"I think the man cannot count," Juria said, still staring at the curtained doorway the Feeler had used.

"That much was fairly clear, yes." Tonia poured herself a cup of water and sat back, nursing it in her hands as though it was a goblet of brandy. "Should we get a Talent to get an accurate number from him?"

"A good thought, though it will have to be a Talent he knows if he is not to be panicked entirely." Juria nodded at the runner just inside the doorway. The boy was gone before she returned her attention to the Faro of Panthers. "But to answer your real question, it appears there are other parties of the Halians Wilk Silvertrees told us about gathering near the Valley of Simcot— though not in it, as far as we can see." Frowning, Juria looked more closely at the map. "What I cannot see is why they would choose this area at all. There is no place large enough even for the troops that have already arrived."

"And they don't seem to care about the entrance there. They haven't even bothered to look for it."

At this moment the runner returned to the doorway and hovered instead of resuming his post against the wall.

"Your pardon, my Faro," he said, speaking directly to Juria. "But the Luqs wishes to speak to you privately in his rooms."

*   *   *

"When were you going to tell us that you could Far-think?"

Jerek wasn't fooled by Juria Sweetwater's impassive face. He knew frustrated anger when he saw it. He also knew resignation and fear, though there wasn't much of the latter in either of the Faros. They couldn't do anything to him, of course. They couldn't even discipline him, if it came to that. He was the Luqs of Farama, even though he might feel like a wayward schoolboy at the moment.

"When I decided it was the right time," he said aloud. He was gratified that his voice was calm and carried just a hint of reprimand—a tone he'd heard his father use many times, though Jerek managed to leave off his father's sneer.

"Of course, my lord." Juria bowed her head, but her lips were pressed tight.

"My lord Luqs," said the Faro of Panthers. "I thought only women could Far-think."

Jerek glanced up at Ennick standing to his left. He'd come to use him as an emotional gauge. Ennick reacted to the atmosphere of the room almost without being aware of it. Since the big man was relaxed, Jerek could be, too. He glanced at the doorway, where Wynn normally stood. He'd only seen her once since she'd returned with Pella, and now she'd gone to take her place among the archers, drilling for the upcoming battle. He'd have to ask for her to be assigned to him again.

"It's not just Far-thinking," he said now, looking first at the Panther and then the Bear. "I have all of the Feelers' Gifts. I didn't tell you because for a long time I wasn't sure, and then I didn't tell you because I wasn't sure how you'd react." Jerek paused, but neither woman spoke. "I'm very aware that you made me Luqs and that you can unmake me just as easily."

"Nothing easy about it," Tonia Nast said under her breath.

"So why are you telling us now?" The shadow of a smile

hovered over Juria Sweetwater's lips. "You could have kept it to yourself. We would never have known."

Jerek squared his shoulders. "It's more important we defeat the Halians than that I stay the Luqs," he said. He couldn't quite read the glance that passed between the two Faros, but—somehow—he felt better.

Tonia Nast snapped her fingers. "The Prophecy," she said, grinning. "When it says a child will unite the people, it must have meant that she—or he—would have Gifts. You're uniting not just the people of Farama, but all Gifted people."

Juria looked thoughtful. "You are the Prophesied One."

"Or it might be someone else." Jerek waited, but neither of the Faros spoke. "Or our child." Jerek wished his face hadn't grown so hot.

"Your *child*?" Tonia Nast never looked less like her sister Kerida.

"According to her marriage documents, the Princess Imperial is married to the Luqs of Farama." He looked from one to the other. "That's me."

"How do you know this?"

"I've been in contact with the Princess Imperial," he said. "She's able to Far-think as well."

Both women froze, though neither of their expressions changed.

"She's a Feeler?" Juria Sweetwater finally asked.

"I think she's more than a Feeler," Jerek said. "I think she's like Kerida; she has more than one Gift."

"And the Halians have not destroyed her?"

Patiently, Jerek walked them through the events, discussions, surmises that he, Kerida, and Baku had exchanged.

"The Griffin Girl knew about this?" Tonia's eyes were pressed closed. "Never mind, not important. When all this is over, we'll have to talk about how information gets shared in the new Polity."

"The point is that the Poppy Shekayrin, Pollik Kvar, is

bringing them here, to the Serpents Teeth." Jerek cleared his throat. What he wouldn't give for a cup of kaff. "Bakura because he thinks he can use her to control the army, and Ker and Tel to keep Baku happy. Also, he's calling every other Shekayrin, everyone who can get here quickly. Once they're here, they plan to locate our entrances as swiftly as possible and overwhelm us." He looked from one Faro to the other, but they were waiting for him to continue. "Now that they understand exactly what they're up against, they're coming in force. And I wouldn't be too sure that the Valley of Simcot won't hold them all. Enough Shekayrin working together can alter the landscape. If they want a large field to use as a firm base they can attack from, they'll just make one."

"This reworking can be done by Feelers, as well," Juria Sweetwater said. "They have been blocking entrances and moving tunnels around for years."

"There's a limit to how many people we can spare to block entrances," Tonia pointed out. "We can't pull *all* the Lifters out of their units, not with the Halians pouring into the area in these numbers."

"We could close what entrances we can while there is still time." Juria meant this as a statement, and it was taken that way.

"Ennick?" Jerek turned to the big man. "If I wanted to make sure no one could reach us here, where we all live, do you know where I would have to block the tunnels? And which tunnels to block?"

"Sure, Jerek, I know that. Tunnel seventeen where it meets tunnel four—"

"That's good, Ennick. I don't need you to tell me right now, I just wanted to know if you *could* tell me." He turned back to the Faros. "I think it means closing off tunnels, or whole sections of the mines, rather than each actual entrance. We'd lose a lot of area, and we'd be effectively letting them into the mines and tunnels."

"Where our people would have less trouble killing them."
Tonia was nodding her satisfaction.

Jerek stayed quiet for a moment. "We can't kill everyone,
not and fulfill the Prophecy."

"I find I'm caring less about that than I am the lives of my
people."

"Some of *them* are our people," he said finally. "At least half
of the soldiers we've seen used to be Eagles."

"Or Bears," Juria added. She shrugged her bearskin cloak
up closer to her face, as though she was suddenly cold.

Ker sat cross-legged facing Tel, with Baku between them on
the only chair in the room. It was clearly designed to be folded
for easy packing and transport, and at any other time Ker
would have liked to examine it. Tel looked paler than she'd ever
seen him, his skin less a contrast to his almost white hair. The
tan that came from days and weeks on the march was beginning to fade. She wondered what she looked like herself. At
least now she was clean.

"Don't Flash unless you have to," Tel told her. Pollik Kvar
had finally fulfilled his side of the agreement he'd made with
Baku and let them visit her. "Remember, they think you're still
netted."

Ker rolled her eyes. "There's a guard on each wall of this
room." The fact that they were in a tent made some things
easier and some harder. "They're close enough to hear us, if
they want to, so we should be careful."

"We will arrive tomorrow, they tell me." Baku's murmur
was so quiet Ker almost couldn't hear her. "Kvar has me practicing what he wishes me to say to the Horsemen and the other
soldiers."

Baku wasn't looking all that well either, Ker thought—
though, come to think of it, she'd never seen what the girl
looked like well-rested and happy. Her aura looked healthy

enough, but dark smudges under the girl's eyes suggested she hadn't been sleeping.

"I don't know what they think they're going to do with all these people in the Valley of Simcot," she said. "We've been there, and it's not large enough to hold even the soldiers with us, let alone any others."

"It's been a while since I studied the geography of the Peninsula," Tel said. "But I don't think there's any other valley nearby."

Baku frowned. "Are you certain? The Serpents Teeth is not that large a range of mountains, but . . ."

"No valley," Ker whispered. "Tel's right." She wasn't going to take offense at Baku's dismissal of the Serpents Teeth as less than imposing. Once she'd seen the mountains around Griffinhome, nothing else was ever going to impress her.

"There, you see?" Tel grimaced when Ker waved her hand at him. Those words had come out at normal volume. "No valley," he murmured.

"But there's a valley *now*," she said.

Baku sucked in her breath.

The girl *hadn't* been pale before, Ker thought, but she was now. "What is it?"

The princess probably wasn't aware that her head shook. "There is a desert," she said. "Very old. Before the horsemen came to Halia, it was already there. Legend says the Shekayrin had done it. That they simply removed the water from the land and left it dry. If they wish for a valley, a valley they shall have."

Now Tel was shaking his head. "What I can't understand, is how the Horsemen ever conquered Halia in the first place. Why didn't the Shekayrin defeat them?"

"Blades of grass," she said, and it took Ker a minute to remember where she'd heard that phrase before. That's what the Emperor's army was called. To show people how many of them there were.

"Still, you're saying that numbers alone could overcome the magic of people who could create a desert?"

"No." Ker cleared her throat. "I'll bet by the time the Horsemen came, there were fewer Shekayrin, and fewer jewels. That's why they're here. Remember what Svann told us. The numbers of Shekayrin dwindled as the supplies of the soul stone ran low."

"And the Halians of those days were not a warlike people," Baku added. "Their ruling classes were much given to philosophy, land management, and other such scholarly pursuits. Sunflower Shekayrin had great status then, and Poppies were considered merely useful."

"But there's enough of them here right now to make this valley?"

Ker nodded just as Baku said, "Yes."

"And when we get there? What's your role in all this?"

"Kvar will call upon me to use the Emperor's Voice. To rouse the troops. To take the mines." Baku pushed her veils back off her head. "They believe there are enough Shekayrin here now to counteract the Feelers."

"Are they right?"

"Jerek tells me no. He tells me that many of the entrances have been shut, and that the Shekayrin cannot be everywhere at once, whereas his people can be." She lifted her shoulders and let them drop again as if she'd only just learned how to shrug. "The problem, as I see it, is that neither side has accurate information about the other."

"There are seventeen of them," Ker said. "We'll have to tell Jerek."

Tel nodded his satisfaction. "We should be able to manage that number—" He frowned. "But counteracting one Shekayrin needs at least three Feelers. That's . . ."

"Fifty-one," Baku said immediately.

Tel whistled. "Close, very close. And not everyone has the same level of ability. What about you, Princess? Is there anything you can do?"

"If I am there, present at the right time, I believe so, but I must be present. However, I have been a mage for five days only, it may be that I know only enough to increase our danger."

Ker crossed her arms, not wanting to agree out loud. She thought back on the drills Svann had put her through. There was no one here to train the princess, and anything Baku tried on her own *could* be more hindrance than help.

"But I believe, with the mask, I can do something more to the purpose." There was excitement in the girl's voice.

"What did you have in mind?" Ker put her index finger to her lips as Baku was about to speak. "Someone's coming." She held the finger up until she was sure the person wasn't stopping at their tent. "Make it quick."

"If the Horsemen obey me—as even Peklin Kvar believes they will—instead of rousing them to fight your people in the mines, I will call upon them to turn on the Shekayrin." Lips parted, Baku looked back and forth between them.

"It's not much of a plan—" Tel began.

"Will it work?" Ker interrupted, willing at least to listen.

"Will they succeed against the mages? I cannot know. But we will at least create sufficient confusion that your people, strategically placed, can take advantage of it, and perhaps we will win."

Perhaps. There was a lot riding on that word. "Weimerk says he's coming."

"With respect," Tel said. "He's not here. If we wait for him, we may be too late."

Ker whistled through her teeth. There wasn't any point in asking Weimerk how long he'd be. Griffins didn't measure space or time the way people did. "All right, Baku, you tell Jerek—"

"No. I know nothing of military strategy. If we are to accomplish our goal, we must act quickly, and therefore it must be you who communicates the plan to him and coordinates the others. Once the plan is made, you may tell me what part I will play, and when."

Ker uncrossed her legs and rested her arms on her knees. Baku was right. They had to do this themselves. No griffins. Just Feelers, and Talents, and soldiers—and Baku. It would have to be enough.

"Too bad I don't have my jewel." Ker's aura shone bright and healthy, but her red ribbon wouldn't hold any pattern for long without her jewel.

Baku got a faraway look in her eye. "I think I can manage something."

<<Weimerk.>> He might not get to them quickly, but at least he could help Ker talk to Jerek.

Jerek: The Faros aren't going to like this. Jerek Brightwing signaled to Ennick and waited until the big man was by the door before continuing. People didn't *usually* walk in unannounced, but Jerek had learned to be cautious back in his father's house. Old habits were hard to break. **They think we've got an advantage in being in the mines, and they want to let the Halians come to us. They won't want to give up what they see as the stronger position.**

Kerida: But with our plan, they've got me and Baku as well. Otherwise, you'll be dealing with the Shekayrin by yourselves.

Jerek: Two thirds of the soldiers and all the Feelers to be sent outside? I'll try, but I can't promise anything.

Kerida: That's just it. Jerek. You have to promise. Otherwise, there's no plan at all, and we'll have to think of something else.

Jerek wondered if Ker could tell he was sighing. Ennick raised his eyebrows, his face beginning to cloud over, but it cleared when Jerek smiled at him.

Jerek: All right, give me the details.

Kerida: Do you have something to write with? Start at the Valley of Simcot. These are the changes you can expect. . . .

Ranks of soldiers at least eight-deep were lined up in the space facing the dais that held Pollik Kvar and two other Shekayrin Ker didn't know. She and Tel had been brought out first, even before the soldiers, when the sun had barely risen over the crags to the east, and their breath could still be seen in the cold air. Their hands and feet were bound, comfortably but securely. If she'd had her jewel, she'd have been able to loosen the bonds enough that they could run—if it wasn't for the Daisy Shekayrin standing behind them, quietly cursing the cold and his luck in assignments.

Baku mounted the dais from the far end, accompanied by six officers. Five of these were dressed in loose trousers tucked into boots, leather or sheepskin coats over high-necked shirts. Horsemen. Ker hoped that was a good omen. As the princess passed in front of Kvar, she stumbled and caught him by the sleeve. The mage looked as though he wanted to push her off but stopped when the officers nearest her reached out to help. Baku held them off with a graceful movement of her hand and resumed her walk to the center of the dais.

"Eleven mages," Ker said to Tel out of the corner of her mouth. "Counting Kvar."

From the look on his face, Tel was doing mental calculations. "And the others?"

"I'd say either too far away to get here in time or being distracted by Bears and Panthers."

"We won't get another chance to try this."

"Silence."

Ker winced at the blow to the back of her head, slumping as though she didn't have the strength to sit up straight. In fact, she'd managed five hours' sleep the night before, and felt more rested than she had in weeks. From here, Ker couldn't Flash if

Baku had been able to find her jewel. Though she had no idea what she could do about it even if the girl had been successful. She could move things when she had the jewel in hand, and she could move the jewel itself without having, well, the jewel itself, but she'd never tried it.

"The Talent's all very well, but it's a passive Gift," she murmured.

"Luca Pa'narion says that's why Talents turned on Feelers and mages in the first place, back before anyone remembers. Afraid because the other Gifts are so active."

Ker looked at Tel sideways. "Since when do you study with the High Inquisitor?"

He shrugged. "A man can't be on patrol all the time. And sometimes you're busy."

Movement on the dais silenced them. Ker lifted her eyes and focused on the small figure of the Princess Imperial. Baku lifted something white—the mask—to her face. Ker blinked and sat back so quickly that Tel put a warning finger on her knee. "Do you see it?" she asked him, though she knew he couldn't. "She flickers. She looks taller and dressed in green, and then she's her normal height wearing a rose-red gown."

"Do you know what it means?"

"I've seen it with Larin. Sometimes she looks old and bent, just for a second."

"Do you think Larin knows how this is going to turn out? Not that she'd tell us, or that we could understand the answer if she did."

Ker shushed him before the mage behind them could. Baku's image settled into the taller, green-dressed one, but Ker still Flashed two people standing where Baku stood. The girl was clearly unaware of it.

"Greetings, my people."

Even though she knew to expect a man's voice, the hairs rose on the back of her neck. She understood every word perfectly, though it wasn't speaking Faraman.

Every Halian in the crowd of soldiers fell silent and shushed the Faramans among them, who didn't know they were hearing the Voice of the Emperor. There was a ripple of movement as the soldiers all went down on one knee. The Shekayrin, she saw, stayed upright, except for one who began to kneel, only to be pulled up by the mage next to him. So, not everyone, even among the Shekayrin, was following wholeheartedly.

Baku was still speaking, or rather, her brother the Emperor was. The speech began with a lot of the usual business about what a good job they were doing, and how proud he was of them.

"I say that you have done well, but only in that you have done what was asked of you." From where she stood Ker could see that some of the officers in the first row had exchanged looks, without raising their bowed heads.

"A pity you could not do as *I* asked of you." A wave of sound passed over the mass of soldiers, almost too low to hear. "But you are not at fault. Rather, the Shekayrin have led you astray, and have caused you to disobey my wishes."

Two of the Halian officers in the front rank of soldiers rose to their feet and headed toward where Tel and Ker were seated.

"Kerida . . ."

"We're not their target. It's the Daisy Shekayrin behind us." Logical. He was the closest mage to them. Ker lowered her eyes and kept the smile from her face. It looked like their plan was working already—but the soldiers were stopped long before they reached her. It looked as though they were being held back by their own men, but Ker Flashed that the Daisy Shekayrin had done it. Moving wasn't a Daisy's strongest Gift, and Ker wondered how long he could keep it up.

Idiots, she thought. Didn't the mages realize that by turning their magic on their own soldiers, they gave weight to what Baku had said?

Movement drew her eye to the right. Pollik Kvar was striding from his position at the far end of the platform, reaching out for Baku as if he meant to grab her by the arm. While he was still a pace or two away, she turned her head toward him. And he stopped. Baku's timing made it look to those watching as though the power of the mask itself had stopped the mage. Ker knew that it was Baku. A ribbon of pink, a Lifter's color, flowed from the princess' aura and held the mage where he stood. Unfortunately, it was all Baku *could* do; she didn't have the knowledge or the skill to do more. *Hope she practices more than I ever did.* Ker had learned a lot from Svann and Weimerk, and some by trial and error, but she couldn't count the number of times she wished she'd practiced more when she had the chance.

Part of Baku's pink color snapped back to her, but the greater part still kept Kvar at bay.

The murmuring among the soldiers grew to a growl, as more and more of them got to their feet. Most—but not all—of these men wore the leather and rounded helms of the Halian Horsemen.

"We are Horsemen," the Voice of the Emperor said, "and we conquered in Halia as we conquer everywhere. Even the mages could not stop us. The mages would have you believe that we came here to Farama to bring new lands into the care of the Lord of Horses, to stamp out a nest of women rulers, but that is not a thing of horsemen. Before we came to Halia, our mothers and our sisters rode and fought together with their sons and brothers. It is true that in more recent times we have lived as the Halians do, with our women locked away, but I say to you again, this is no practice of ours. I know that away from the cities, and the offended eyes of Halians, horsemen live as we have always lived. Ah! I see that you believed the Sky Emperor did not know this, but I assure you, I am still the Lord of Horses. I did nothing to stop this practice, even though I knew it would be offensive to so many of what are now, also, my people."

This was all far removed from the script they'd agreed on.

Ker began tapping her fingers on her thigh. "Baku, what are you doing?"

"I tell you that my own sister, the Princess Imperial who stands before you now, was taught to ride, and to shoot, and walked about with her head uncovered, until she came to live at the Imperial Palace. That is how she is able to speak with my voice."

That wasn't *entirely* true, Ker Flashed.

"They also say that women could not have magic, when their own histories show that to be false." *How does Baku know that? Did Jerek tell her?* "They say that we horsemen cannot have magic, when the Voice of the Emperor proves that to be false.

"And so I tell you, that in destroying the women of power when you came to this land, you acted only upon the wishes of the Shekayrin, and not upon mine."

"She lies! This is a perversion of the Emperor's Voice. It is not the Emperor who speaks, but his bewitched sister. Rise up and destroy her!" Kvar had finally managed to free himself from Baku's pink ribbon.

"Rise up yourself!" The call came in both tongues, Halian and Faraman, though it appeared that some Faraman soldiers were trying to hush their fellows. The Halian calls soon changed, however as most began to shout "Challenge!"

Ker's stomach sank. This was completely off script.

The shout was taken up by more and more people, Halian and Faraman alike. Weapons were waving in the air, and dissenters among the ranks were silenced, some forcibly, by those near them. The roiling and twisting of auras was enough to make Ker dizzy. From the look on the Poppy Shekayrin's face, this wasn't the disaster for him that they'd hoped for. Even two of the mages standing on the edges of the waiting soldiers moved their position to where they could see Pollik Kvar more easily, as if they were expecting some type of signal.

Blades of grass. The Emperor's soldiers. There weren't so

very many of them right here and now, though; Kvar and his mages *were* outnumbered, but were they outnumbered enough?

"You have made many accusations against the Shekayrin. I say it is not the Voice of the Emperor speaking. I say that you lie. With the help of witches, you have warped the Voice to suit yourself. Our people have called for a challenge, and I agree. I challenge you to prove your case by open combat, your champion against mine."

"You think I fear a custom of the Horsemen? A custom of my own people? It is not so. I accept the challenge."

The roar from the crowd matched the roaring in Ker's head. This wasn't Baku. It couldn't be. This had to be the mask, the real voice of the real emperor. Now many of the soldiers began calling out their approval in still another language, which Ker Flashed was the language of the Horsemen themselves.

"Who do you think to use as your champion against me? The Sunflower Shekayrin Peklin Svann perhaps?" The tone when he said the word "sunflower" was enough to show what Kvar thought of that. "He is already dead. Who else do you think might serve you, traitorous woman?"

Ker's ears buzzed. She hadn't needed this confirmation, but it shook her just the same.

"I accept your challenge, and I say that you will not prevail against my champion. You cannot overcome her. You must prove, here and now, that your power is greater than hers."

Hers? Baku certainly wasn't ready for any such thing! This *must* be the work of the mask.

"I will choose as my champion Kerida Griffin Girl."

The crowd was roaring again—but it wasn't the crowd at all. The roaring was in Ker's head. Without her jewel, she had no chance to overcome a Shekayrin. Ker shivered. The Voice of the Emperor had found a way to destroy them all.

The smile on Kvar's face confirmed all her fears. "She is a witch, an abomination, cursed by the Father. I would not dirty my hands on her."

"You refuse?" The tone of satisfaction in the Emperor's voice gave Ker heart. "Then you lose by forfeit. That is the rule according to the form of justice you have chosen. None may follow you now."

"Very well." Kvar smiled, as if everything still went his way. "I will prove myself against your champion."

". . . 'against your champion.'" Jerek had his eyes shut tight, the better to concentrate on the information coming from Baku. This time there were images, something they'd never managed before. The vision was narrow, however, as though he looked through the eyeholes of a mask. "He's planning to cheat," he added. "They're all going to attack her at once. He thinks no one watching will know."

"Whose idea *was* this?" Tonia's tight voice showed her concern for her sister. "Ker will never be able to overcome them all. Will she?" Tonia directed the question at Jerek, and he shook his head. Not in answer but in impatience.

"This wasn't the plan." Jerek could hardly hear for the pounding of his own heart.

"Who knows what Griffin Girl can do?" Even Ganni's voice shook. The old Feeler was not nearly as confident as he tried to sound.

"We mobilize now. Tell the Cohort Leaders." That was Juria Sweetwater. Jerek didn't hear the reply.

Without warning, without even moving from his place on the platform, Pollik Kvar struck, a coil of red streaking out from his aura like the head of an asp. Ker ducked just fast enough for the red line to strike where her head would have been a second before. Kvar's eyes widened, and he bared his teeth, flipping his hand out to the side. At this signal, the Daisy behind Ker, along with the two mages standing near Kvar, also lashed out with spikes and spears of red, though none as fast as the first. She should have known he would cheat.

Ker braced herself, sure that one attack at least would reach her. Then Baku's aura flashed, her colors bright and strong, and the princess tossed a tiny point of light straight into the air over her head. Kvar's eyes turned toward it, and Ker knew it for something solid, visible to him and not just a piece of Baku's aura. His hand went to a pocket in his tunic, and his face hardened. Kvar held his hand out, a ribbon of red whipping forward to capture the object Baku had thrown.

"My jewel." The realization struck Ker like a splash of warm water. Baku had Lifted it from Kvar's pocket. Instinctively, Ker held up her hands, even though she didn't think she could catch her jewel from this angle—until it smacked into her palm with enough force that it almost knocked her down. Her own patterns jumped into life around her, swarming over and around her like puppies tumbling on the grass.

With this surge of new energy, her jewel tight in her fist, Ker broke their bonds with a gesture before jumping to her feet. No matter what happened, Tel would have a chance to get away. Not that he was likely to take it. Dying together wasn't as much comfort as the stories made out. Having the jewel gave her hope, but she'd need luck as well.

<<I am coming.>> Weimerk, his thoughts cold and tasting of clouds. The connection was gone before Ker could respond.

She straightened up and started casting out versions of her own inner patterns, matching and sapping the power from the bolts and waves of red the Shekayrin tossed at her like hunters spearing a bear. But that only held off the attack; if she concentrated on any one assault to destroy it, she exposed herself to the attack of the others. Defense was all she could manage, and defense alone wouldn't be enough. Eventually, they would wear her down. She Flashed the triumph that swept through Pollik Kvar as he realized that she wasn't attacking.

At that moment, a fresh burst of color swept through her,

leaving energy in its wake, and tasting entirely new and different.

<<It is not I.>> Weimerk didn't sound worried at all.

Baku. A net, larger than she had ever seen, soared from the princess's aura. It split into pieces and swarmed the nets and webs of the Shekayrin, all the Shekayrin, damping them down one after another until they hovered around their mages, perfectly still.

Kvar couldn't see the auras, but he could tell something had gone wrong. He pushed his way across the dais to Baku and seized her free arm. Baku struggled, but she couldn't fight him and maintain her hold on the other Shekayrin at the same time. Ker shot out her own ribbon of red, layered with Lifter's Pink, and wrapped it around Kvar's legs and arms. He pushed out at her, and while he couldn't shrug her off completely, neither could she tighten her grip. She was stronger, but he'd been using his jewel longer than Ker had been alive, and skill alone could be enough to overcome her greater strength. She could bash at him like a sledgehammer, while he could slip past her guard like the thin blade of a knife.

Trying to repeat what she'd done to the Rose Shekayrin in the capital, Ker focused on Pollik Kvar's internal net. Its red glowed like metal on a forge, and for the first time Ker felt real fear as Kvar turned his attention to her. A bolt of red, this one streaked with the other colors of his aura, shot back toward her. Bracing herself, Ker repeated the gesture that had swept the Rose's attack aside.

But a Rose is not a Poppy. And, in particular, not this Poppy. She managed to deflect the attack, but only just enough that the full force of the blow didn't strike her. She staggered, and she felt Tel's hands wrapping themselves around her arms just above the elbow, holding her steady. She wouldn't be able to make an assault on the core of Kvar's net. She couldn't even be sure she saw exactly where the weak point was—or maybe Kvar didn't have a weak point.

Seeing another blow coming, Ker spun her aura around herself, making sure the colors Weimerk had given her were woven through everywhere—strength and endurance, vision and invisibility. She kept spinning until her aura looked like the sphere she'd freed herself with. This would buy her time enough to think of something else. She felt the length of Tel's body against her back and leaned into him, letting the shield cover them both.

"Hold on," she heard him say, but she couldn't spare energy or attention to respond. Dimly, she Flashed that Kvar was still sending blows to her, and worse, there were other red webs coming to the mage's aid.

<<Hold fast, my Girl. I come.>>

A flare of colors to one side, bright and hot and dazzling, made Ker think that Weimerk had already arrived, but the newcomer wasn't a griffin. In drawing Kvar's attack on herself, Ker had given Baku time to gather her own strength.

"You idiot." She laughed out loud. Ker may have forgotten that she still had an ally, but Kvar had done much worse: he'd forgotten he still had an enemy.

Where Ker had seen herself as a sledgehammer, Baku was a mountain boulder, rolling downhill and gathering strength and momentum as she came. She smashed into Kvar from a direction he wasn't guarding, her aura knocking his colors aside like a game of bowls. Most of the colors in Baku's aura had double strands, even triple. With no fumbling, the princess gripped Kvar's net in a fist made up of every color Ker could think of and wrenched it free. It hung suspended for a moment, sheets and waves of red trying to reestablish itself, and then it was gone.

Pollik Kvar collapsed to the ground.

<<Baku?>> Ker hesitated, suddenly a little reluctant to draw the girl's attention to herself. She opened her eyes and saw that Baku was kneeling on the dais, one hand still on the mask, the other propping herself up. The two officers nearest her were

clearly trying to solve the dilemma of helping their princess to her feet without actually touching her.

<<Yes, of course it is I.>> **Or, if you prefer, I can Far-think you this way.** Baku evidently took pity on her officers, waving them off as she stood on her own.

<<Calm down, little one. Your thoughts are much too buzzy.>> Ker imagined Weimerk waving away a bee with one of his enormous paws.

Baku's laughter shook. <<That was a marvel. It did not come easily, but the knowledge appeared when I cried out for it. I greatly feared you would be overwhelmed by the Poppy.>>

<<You weren't the only one. What happened before? Was it the mask that made you accept the challenge?>>

<<I do not know. I felt as though it was indeed I who spoke, yet they were not the words I had intended to say.>>

For the first time in what felt like hours, though the position of the sun hadn't changed a bit, Ker looked around her, becoming suddenly aware of the noise of the crowd, and that she could still feel Tel's arms wrapped around her. The auras of the soldiers all sparkled in the light, all, she noticed, that same blue, green, and yellow, whether they were Faraman or Halian. With very few exceptions, the auras were upright, waving, and bright. When she refocused her attention on the physical world around her, she saw that all the Shekayrin were sitting down on the ground, eyes closed, some rocking. One with a bleeding nose. Farther away, at the limits of her Flashing, she could see more auras heading toward them from all sides. The Battle Wings.

<<Uh, Bakura.>>

"Kerida," Tel interrupted, his hands now on her shoulders. "The Poppy's still alive."

Ker looked where Tel pointed and saw Pollik Kvar lying rigid a few paces away from Baku on the dais.

<<Does he still have his jewel?>>

The Princess Imperial raised one hand, and a flash of black

streaked to her from the Poppy on the ground. <<It is dead.>> The coldness in Baku's tone chilled even Ker.

<<I could eat him.>> Ker gasped before she recognized Weimerk's mind.

<<You mean if you ever get here?>>

Almost as if they'd felt the passing of magic around them, the Halian troops were all once again on their knees, some of them with their hands over their heads. Only a few of the Faraman men were still standing, looking around them as if they didn't know where they were or how they'd gotten there. Ker saw with some shock that many of these men had red mists or even webs hanging over them.

Ker put her hand on top of Tel's. <<What about the other Shekayrin?>> she said, both in her head and aloud so Tel could hear her. *Please let her not want to kill them.*

<<I hoped you would have a suggestion. I cannot hold them in place forever, even if I wished to.>>

<<Mind your soldiers,>> Ker advised. <<The Battle Wings are almost here. The last thing we need is a battle.>>

Keeping hold of her jewel in her left hand, Baku picked up the mask and held it once more in front of her face. A wave of motion trickled through the assembled soldiers, as some of them rose to their feet.

"Rest easy, my people. My champion has prevailed, and the traitor Pollik Kvar has been defeated."

The same soldiers who had tried to reach the Daisy Shekayrin guarding Ker and Tel ran forward again, this time with wide smiles and drawn swords, obviously ready to execute him. Ker stepped forward, but Tel held her back.

"Don't interfere," he said.

"The Prophecy says everyone is going to be united," she reminded him.

"Maybe not *everyone.*"

Others in the crowd were also breaking ranks, though most of the soldiers stayed quiet, looking around with caution.

"Do not harm the mages," The Voice of the Emperor spoke quickly. "They are also my people. We will give them the opportunity, now that Pollik Kvar is defeated, to come to our side, should they wish it."

"What if they don't?" Tel called out exactly what many of the others were thinking.

"Then my champion and I will send them back to Halia." She raised her voice. "Bring them here to me." Baku indicated the ground in front of the dais with the hand that still held her jewel. "My champion will deal with them appropriately."

<<Lucky for you I've thought of something.>> Pulling their own auras into her hands, Ker quickly created a shield of colors, including the reds, punched it into a hemisphere, and set one down over each mage. They glowed like opals, restricting the Shekayrin's magic, but not netting or removing it.

<<Ah, I see what you are doing. You use their own magic against them. Good. You must teach me that technique. It is preferable to killing people. Come, join me on the dais.>>

The soldiers were once more on their feet pointing, picking up weapons, and re-forming their ranks. As Tel helped her climb onto the dais, Ker looked up to see the edges of the valley dark with people. The Battle Wings had arrived, and the valley was surrounded.

"Kerida! If the Wings come boiling over those rocks, we won't be able to stop these men from fighting. Can't Baku—"

Once more the princess lifted the mask to her face. "Be at peace, my people. These others are also my loyal followers, sent by the Luqs my husband to rescue me from the Shekayrin. Only their officers will come to attend me." The Halians stopped their preparations but remained alert and ready.

Baku: Jerek! Quickly, have your Far-thinkers stop your soldiers from entering the valley. We have prevailed, but this is not the time for these enemies to meet. Send me the Faros only, with their highest officers.

Jerek: I've told them. It's the Faro of Panthers with them. Tell Kerida.

"I could almost get that." Ker rubbed her forehead as if that would help. "He said something about the Faro of Panthers?"

"He wishes me to tell you the Faro comes, with her officers."

Ker started to giggle, suddenly shivering with chill. Her laughter died away as she saw some of the Halian soldiers nudging their fellows and pointing upward. When Ker lifted her eyes, she could just make out the golden shimmer that was Weimerk flying at speed. Almost immediately, he was hovering overhead, wings moving only slightly to hold him in place above them.

Without waiting to be told, the Halian soldiers broke ranks and scattered, leaving the griffin a clear spot where he could land.

<<You're late.>>

<<I am not. I am always here when I arrive, and never a moment later.>> Weimerk blinked his great eyes at her, and sat down, straightening his wing feathers with his beak. Had he grown bigger? Or was it just that she hadn't seen him for a while?

"What is it they're shouting?" Tel stroked the griffin on the foot, as though Weimerk was a cat.

"They are saying 'skyhorse.'" Weimerk shook his head and rattled his wings. "They should stop. Really, I am not a horse."

13

66 STOP looking at me like that." Ester Nast tied off her apron and smoothed it down with her hands.

"You sure you're up to working?" Elisk stood behind the bar, wiping out cups, checking their edges for chips and their glaze for cracks.

"I'm not up to lying in my bed any longer, that's certain." Ester came around the bar herself and began shelving the cups he approved where they would be handy for whoever had the bar shift that evening. "Why? Don't I look better?"

To her surprise, her friend took her question seriously, stopped what he was doing, and looked her over with a calculating eye. "You're a bit thinner," he said finally. "And there are some shadows under your eyes, but on the whole, you look younger."

"*Younger*?" That was the last thing Ester expected.

He turned back to the cups waiting to be checked over. "The gray in your hair's gone."

"What? I mean, I beg your pardon, Honored One?" Ker turned back to Baku. What should suddenly make her think of Ester?

"I said, they will find you a horse, Kerida." Baku lifted her arms. As the only woman available, and therefore the only person allowed to touch the Princess Imperial, Ker was helping Baku rearrange her clothing into something that would let her sit safely on a horse. Baku's veils had already been twisted into a headdress that was strangely similar to the helms worn by her Horsemen.

Before Ker could say anything, Baku's guard chief sent two of his men scurrying to the horse lines, arguing about which horse the champion should ride.

"Don't put them to the trouble," she objected. "We'll all be walking soon. No one can ride very far in these hills."

Baku smiled. "It is for the look of it. We are Horsemen. It is not fitting for my champion to begin a journey on foot."

Ker shrugged. That made a certain amount of sense. A moment later she saw Wynn Martan weaving her way through the surrounding soldiers, hair bright as ever, her grin splitting her face in half.

"Excuse me a moment, Honored One." Ker met Wynn a few paces away, and they grasped each other's wrists in a soldier's greeting. With so many strangers around them, it didn't feel comfortable to hug.

"How did you get here?"

"I was with the archers up on the ridge. When I saw how things were going, I came down for you." Wynn's grip was strong, and her grin never faded, but Ker saw shadows in her eyes.

"Svann would have loved this," Ker said, guessing at the cause of the other girl's sadness. "He'd be wanting to interview everyone and write a monograph or something."

Blinking, Wynn looked up as though she wanted to watch the eagle that hovered far above them on a wave of warm air. "It's not that, at least, it's not only that." Her eyes came back to Ker's face. "I found Barid."

"Barid?" Ker's stomach sank.

"You'd better come."

"One minute. Tel?" He was at her side immediately, but Ker waited, foot tapping, while he and Wynn greeted each other. "Stay with Bakura," Ker said finally. "Wynn has something to show me."

Without saying more, Ker followed Wynn back through the ranks of soldiers, to an area where wagons and carts of supplies had been drawn up in a loose square. They passed a few sullen faces, but most of the Halians looked at her with interest, if not approval. One or two backed away. Wynn drew her over to where several small, square wooden crates were stacked next to a handcart. Wynn indicated a dark corner with her chin, but at first Ker saw nothing. Then she made him out, tucked between a crate of provisions and a stack of sacks.

Barid sat with his back where crate and sacks met, his face pressed into his drawn-up knees, his arms tight around them. The bones on his neck stuck out plainly, and he looked scruffy, his hair uncombed, dirt in the creases of his hands.

"Barid." Wynn kept her voice low and sweet.

He flinched before lifting his head enough to expose one red-rimmed eye. When he saw who it was, he looked up, wiping his mouth on his kneecap. "Wynn? Wynn Martan?" He held an incredibly filthy finger to his mouth. "Shhh. They'll hear you."

Ker squatted down as close to him as she could get. "Who'll hear us?"

Barid lunged forward so quickly he had her forearm in his hands before she even saw him move. "Kerida? I didn't tell them. Honestly, I didn't tell them anything. They already knew.

They already knew everything. What could I do? There was no point in denial. No point."

His grip was painful enough to make Ker squirm. "It's all right, Barid."

"I couldn't let them kill me. I'm Griffin Class, it's important for me to be safe." It wasn't clear who Barid was talking to—his friends or himself.

"Stay here, Barid. You're safe now." Ker managed to free her hand without breaking any of his fingers. "The Shekayrin are defeated. I'll send someone to fetch you. One of the Feelers, all right?"

The smile he gave them chilled Ker's heart. There was nothing left of the Talent who had been her mentor in Questin Hall.

"What's wrong with him?" Wynn asked as they headed back toward the head of the procession.

Ker hadn't had to Flash Barid to know the answer. "Exactly what you think is wrong. He *is* the one who told them; he knows it, and it's killing him." Ker crossed her arms, hugging herself. "He must have decided to feed them bits of information, to keep himself alive, convincing himself each time that they were inconsequential. Fear is a terrible thing."

"Is there anything we can do?"

"Nothing *we* can do, no. But maybe a Mind-healer can help him." Ker pushed her hair back off her face. She'd lost the tie somewhere, and her braid had fallen apart. "Can you look after him for now?"

The other girl nodded. "We've a Lifter with us archers. He'll take care of things. Then I'll come to you." With a last touch to Ker's shoulder, Wynn disappeared into the crowd.

It took the rest of the day just to organize the marching order. The first issue was Bakura's escort. Six of her Halian officers and the Faro of Panthers were finally agreed on. The Halians—most of them Horsemen—looked at Tonia Nast out of the corners of their eyes, while Tonia smiled a tight smile that showed no teeth. Right now, the entire Halian group was so subdued from the magic they'd witnessed—the Voice of the Emperor, the attack and defeat of the Shekayrin, to say nothing of the griffin—that they would follow the Princess Imperial without question. She was theirs. She gave them rights and legitimacy.

"Just as my brother the Emperor intended," Baku said. Ker couldn't be sure if the princess spoke ironically.

The rest of the Battle Wing soldiers had formed into two groups, one the same size, more or less, as the Halian troop and marching with them, the other keeping themselves at a distance but near enough that they could watch the procession, just in case. With the remaining Shekayrin confined under the supervision of a team of Feelers, the only Gifted were with the Wings, but good soldiers always have a backup plan.

"You look worried." Ker rode just behind Baku's horse, with Tel on her left.

Tel shrugged. The shadows under his eyes looked like soot. "What do you think will happen with those Shekayrin?"

Ker leaned over and touched his knee. "I know you want them all gone—even dead—and I can't blame you. But you understand that can't happen, don't you? They're Gifted, just like us, just like the Feelers. We know what they want now, what they need. They don't have to be our enemies."

"Some will want to return." Baku turned around in her saddle; she'd overheard them. "I expect some of the Poppies will want to go back, they have more status in Halia than they will have here. But I have hopes the Daisies, the Roses, and the Sunflowers will decide to stay. Weimerk made an impressive entrance, and they will think on that."

The procession reached the mine entrance shortly after midday. It had rained earlier, but now the rocks were sparkling in the sun. The space around the entrance looked nothing like it had when Ker had last used the Valley of Simcot exit. The narrow ravine, with its sharp towers of rock and pockets of scrub pines and wild heather, had been transformed into a massive, shallow hemisphere, complete with rows of seats formed out of the rock.

"Makes a nice theater," Ker said, suddenly reminded of the actor she'd met in Farama the Capital.

"Messages will have to be sent all over the Peninsula." Ker heard her sister Tonia's voice from up ahead. "Other Halians, and those Faraman soldiers who've been jeweled and misted, aren't going to accept the new order as easily as the ones who've heard the Voice of the Emperor."

"Even those walking with us now might have a change of heart in a few days, when the wonder of it all has a chance to wear off," Baku said.

Which was one of the reasons they were all meeting *outside* the Mines and Tunnels.

The spot Jerek Brightwing waited for them wasn't even near the entrance, Ker saw with a nod of approval. The boy Luqs looked taller, and somewhat better dressed than the last time she'd seen him. His hair had grown long enough to tie back. The Faro of Bears stood to his right, Luca Pa'narion and Ganni Lifter to his left, and over his head the banners of Bears and Panthers moved in the breeze. Jerek held Larin's hand. Ennick was standing behind his left shoulder and started to wave frantically as soon as he caught sight of Ker and Wynn.

"Better wave back before his arm falls off," Wynn advised, doing the same herself.

Baku and her escort stopped a short distance from where Jerek stood. The boy came forward halfway to meet her. The Faro of Panthers stepped up to help Baku off her horse, waiting until the princess had straightened her clothes and adjusted her grip on the mask.

"Makes you wonder how they manage without female officials to help their ladies off horses, truth to tell." Wynn grinned and wiggled her eyebrows, making Ker stifle her laughter.

"Their ladies aren't allowed to ride, remember," Tel said.

"Right."

Tonia Nast took up a position on Baku's left, and the top Halian officer stood to her right. Ker moved forward until she was standing behind them, just as everyone had agreed. A junior officer held a long pole supporting a placard made of stiffened silk that proclaimed the presence of the Princess Imperial.

Baku's was the next move; all this had been carefully choreographed between her and Jerek, with a little input from the Halian officer, the two Faros, and Ganni Lifter. Still, the girl hesitated, her right hand tapping quickly against her thigh. Ker could imagine what was going through the princess' mind. For all that they had been Far-thinking for almost three months, Baku and Jerek had never actually seen each other.

Suddenly, Larin came racing over, ducking hands that reached out to grab her, and ran straight for Baku before anyone could stop her. She wrapped her arms around Baku's waist and hugged her so tightly the princess had to take a half step back to keep from falling over.

"I *told* them, I *told* them you were here. 'The child who rides the horses of the sea, who bears the blood and who wields the bones of the earth, who brings us freedom and light.'"

Ker shivered. Just for a minute, Larin had been speaking with the voice of the old Time-seer, Ara, and even now, the little girl's shadow was the wrong shape.

"That's you!" Larin bounced up and down. "And here you are. I told them!"

Before anyone could stop her, Larin had hold of Baku's hand and was dragging her across the space that separated them from the Faraman delegation. Tonia, the Halian officer, and Ker had to trot to catch up, arriving in front of Jerek at the same time.

"I thought you'd be taller," he said, smiling into Baku's eyes.

"Really? Because you are exactly as I pictured you."

The Halian officer cleared his throat. "I present the Honored Bakura Kar Luyn, Princess Imperial of Halia, sister to the Sky Emperor Guon Kar Lyn, Son of the Sun, Father of the Moon, and"—the officer's voice faltered, and he drew himself up even straighter—"Lord of Horses."

Juria Sweetwater stepped a pace closer. "I present Jerek Brightwing, Luqs of the Faraman Polity, Prince of Ma'lakai, Lord of Juristand, Faro of Eagles."

Ker suspected that the "Lord of Juristand" part had been added in to make Jerek's titles match the Emperor's, at least in length.

Baku cleared her throat and held out her free hand, palm up. "Husband," she said in a loud, carrying voice.

Jerek put his hand in hers. "Wife."

And that was it, as far as the Halians were concerned. Baku had been married to the Luqs of Farama the minute her brother had put his seal and thumbprint on the necessary documents. By accepting Jerek's hand instead of the other way around, she pacified the more traditional among the Horsemen who would recognize in that gesture that Baku's was the higher status.

<<I believe the appropriate human expression to use at this moment is "brace yourselves.">> Weimerk's unmistakable mental voice drew Ker's attention upward.

The sky darkened, and a wave of sound passed over all the waiting people. Luckily, the griffins didn't try to land in the newly created valley, perching on the craggy edges instead. More than half of the soldiers present kneeled, though Jerek and Baku kept firmly to their feet.

"Welcome, Child of the Prophecy." It was impossible to tell which griffin was speaking, but Ker thought she recognized Deilih's tone.

Baku pressed her lips together and moved to stand more clearly at Jerek's side, their clasped hands between them.

"We greet you," Baku said. "What is your business here?" Jerek added.

Clever, Ker thought. By finishing each other's sentences,

they demonstrated that they were of the same mind. That didn't make it less eerie, however, and it was going to take some time to get used to.

"Now that there is peace between the Gifted, we will return to our breeding grounds in the mountains you call the Serpents Teeth."

"You didn't help us when we needed you," Jerek said. "Why should we help you now?" Baku added.

"You succeeded by using the Gifts we gave you long ago."

Well, she's got us there. Ker caught Tel's eye and lifted an eyebrow. He lifted one shoulder and let it drop.

"You may lay your eggs here," Baku said, after a quiet moment. "And bury your dead as is your custom. But there is no need for you to be continuously present," Jerek added.

"Agreed." Every griffin in sight rose simultaneously and was gone.

"Well, that was abrupt," Jerek said.

"They don't really care about us," Tel said. "Even Weimerk didn't really care about the rest of us, only Kerida. He helped us because she wanted it, not because he wanted to."

Another shadow overhead, and a griffin landed on the field. Weimerk. A weight she hadn't been aware of lifted from Ker's heart. He hadn't gone with the others.

"Tel is correct. I do only what I 'want to,'" he said, digging his claws into the dirt.

Ker found Tel stretched out full-length on the grass, in the sunshine.

"This has been the longest three weeks of my life," Ker said as she sat cross-legged next to him and took his hand. "And they're still not finished. Where will the Feelers live now? Some of the Halians want to go home because they're not jeweled. How do we get them there? Though it seems most of the horsemen want to stay."

"We should create a Horse Wing," Tel suggested.

"It's not a bad idea, but I think they'll have to come to terms with the Eagle Wing first, since the Eagles will want to protect Jerek, and the Horsemen Baku." She looked at him. "It's been less than a year, but there were a lot of changes made that will have to be undone, just to turn Farama back into Farama. On top of that, they have to choose who's going as ambassador to Halia—though having seen the mask in action, I doubt there's much the emperor needs to be told."

"I guess their imperial selves will have to be getting back to Farama the Capital now, though they may not be Luqs of anything but the Peninsula. I'll bet those people in Juristand aren't going to give up their new power easily."

"They'll still have to send their Talents to us for training. There's no one left senior to Luca Pa'narion, and Talents will stand by Talents, not the Battle Wings." She could feel a headache starting. Errinn Mind-healer was going to have a lot to do.

"Even old pinch-face and her group?"

Ker grinned at this reference to the Panther Wing Talents. "They haven't been as vocal about things since the griffins came. I think Setasan's lost her following."

"Maybe *we* should go to Halia." Tel sounded wistful. "Be ambassadors or something."

"I don't think they're ready for female ambassadors."

Tel shook his head. "We should go somewhere, seriously, before someone does give us something to do."

Separates us, was what Tel was really saying. The whole "Talents do not live in the world" tradition wasn't changed yet . . . and might never be.

"Where *would* we go, then? And how would we sneak away?"

A snort made then both sit up.

"Come, have you not seen how I am grown?" Weimerk's voice came from above them. "I am large enough now to carry both of you."